GRIFFIN ©87

ALL FOR THE LOVE OF DADDY

A big, rich, contemporary novel...filled with all the love, pain, and suspense of modern family life ...filled with the great characters and wise insights readers have come to expect from

MARCIA ROSE

Also by Marcia Rose
Published by Ballantine Books:

ADMISSIONS

CHOICES

CONNECTIONS

SECOND CHANCES

SUMMER TIMES

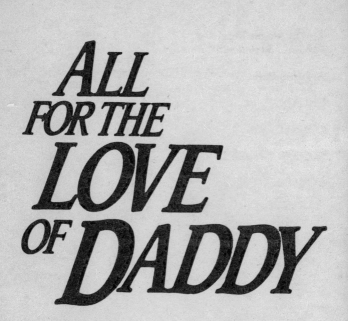

ALL
FOR THE
LOVE
OF DADDY

MARCIA ROSE

BALLANTINE BOOKS • NEW YORK

All rights reserved under International and Pan-American Copyright Conventions. Published in the United States by Ballantine Books, a division of Random House, Inc., New York, and simultaneously in Canada by Random House of Canada Limited, Toronto.

Library of Congress Catalog Card Number: 87-91486

ISBN 0-345-32991-0

Manufactured in the United States of America

First Edition: November 1987

All for
the love of
our daughters:
Sarah, Leila, Julia, Mara

CHAPTER ONE

Thanksgiving Day, November 28, 1985

Her mother's kitchen on Thanksgiving Day, Deena Berman thought, could be a stage set for a play about a well-to-do Jewish family getting ready to sit down to dinner in one of those high-ceilinged, sprawling old luxury apartments on Central Park West.

Yes, all the props were in place: bubbling pots on the stove; china bowls lining the counters, sterling silver platters at the ready. There was the round butcher-block table with its load of casseroles. There were the platters in the pantry, heaped with enough fresh fruit to feed a small country. There was the tea cart, every square inch covered with succulent desserts. There were the baskets of breads and rolls and biscuits. And, as seen through an oven door darkly, the obligatory enormous turkey, browning.

The scene was all set for the curtain to go up, and when it did, there they would all be: the women of the cast, all cooking, all busy, all intent. Easy, comfortable, intimate, funny, loving. The four Strauss girls, as Daddy liked to call them. In her head, Deena arranged the cast list, in order of appearance.

1

The mother, Sylvia Weinreb Strauss, aged sixty-nine. Next, the oldest sister, Elaine Strauss Barranger, forty-five. The youngest sister, Marilyn Strauss, M.D., thirty-six years old and, øh, my God, still single. And last but not least, of course, her very own self, Deena Strauss Berman, wife, mother, middle child. Age? Oh, hell, forty-three.

Of course, this wasn't a play; and it certainly wasn't a stage set. It was her childhood home, with her own family. And the kitchen smelled just as it always had smelled on Thanksgiving, ever since she could remember: a blend of butter, honey, oranges, sage, cloves, turkey, onions, apple pie, and pumpkin pie ... delicious. And familiar. That's what made it really wonderful. Deena stopped where she was, in the middle of the room, balancing the tray of delicate crystal, and took a deep and satisfied sniff. Everything was sweetly familiar, here in her mother's kitchen, on this day of the year. Sylvia did not believe in messing with a good thing; consequently, there was a place for everything and everything was in its place—and its place hadn't changed for forty-seven years. Deena could still find her way around this room in pitch darkness, get the box of Mallomars from the right hand side of the third shelf of the pantry, and make her way back into her old room—and never bump into a single thing.

"Watch your back!" Her sister Elaine laughed and edged past her. She was hefting a big platter of beautifully prepared raw vegetables. "Excuse me, I've been chosen to bring in the crudités." She gave the last word its French pronunciation.

"Crudités," Deena echoed. "Remember when they used to be just plain raw veggies?"

"Just before chicken soup became consommé." That was Marilyn, her younger sister, working busily on stuffing balls at the counter by the big wall ovens.

"After the glasses became goblets ..." Elaine chanted.

"And chocolate pudding turned into mousse ..."

"Oh, my God, remember?" Deena began to laugh. "The first time Sylvia announced we would be having mousse? The look on Marilyn's face ... remember? Sheer panic!"

"We've all heard this story five thousand times, Deena," Marilyn said.

"You couldn't see the look on your face ... it was hilarious! We all knew what you were picturing, we all could imagine right along with you . . . a platter with a big moose draped over it, antlers pointing at the ceiling."

"Well, you were America's sweetheart, as usual. Whispering in my ear, 'Don't worry, Mommy took the fur off!'"

Now Elaine began to laugh. "Oh, God, it *was* funny. But you were easy to get, Moo. Very literal-minded . . ."

"Unlike the rest of this family of stand-up comics and dramatic Sarah Heartburns. Oh, the pain of my childhood, you can't even imagine! Do you know, I was ashamed to bring my friends home, I was embarrassed by all of you."

"And still are?" Deena teased. When Marilyn turned and shot her a look, she quickly added: "Just kidding. Just that . . . well, it took you long enough to bring this guy home!"

"Nobody loves a wiseass, Deena," came the dry reply.

"Girls," their mother remonstrated. "Stop that! Marilyn is a doctor!"

"Oh, Sylvia! My daughter the doctor? Is that what you're pulling?"

"Never mind! Just stop picking on your little sister!"

Deena, bending to peer at her mother's profile as she worked busily on the fruit cocktail, stemming and pitting and cutting and chopping, was sure she caught sight of a secret smile twitching at the corners of her mother's mouth. Marilyn, meanwhile, cautiously gave her sisters the finger—behind their mother's back, of course. Sylvia Strauss was of the old school. It was possible that she would feel perfectly justified in sending them all to their rooms—rooms they had not inhabited for more than twenty years.

Still chuckling, Deena hefted the tray again, hipping open the swinging door into the dining room. As always on state occasions, the table was covered with Grandma Strauss's white damask cloth, set with Grandma Weinreb's sterling, and the entire room was redolent of furniture polish. Earline, Sylvia's weekly help, had done an extra-special job yesterday. When Deena came by with her contribution, the pumpkin pies, it was already past six o'clock and there was Earline, big and brown and corseted, polishing the brass doorknobs. "Earline!" Deena had protested. "The sky won't fall if every bit of this apartment doesn't shine and sparkle. Don't you have your own Thanksgiving to think about?" Earline had chortled and, finishing the doorknob, said, "I'm goin', I'm goin'. No hurry. My grands are doin' all the cookin' for us this year!" She crowed with delight. "That should be *some* dinner!" Deena could only agree; of Earline's seven grandchildren, four were working chefs. "Yes," Earline said, "We are a family of cookin' fools."

And the Strausses, Deena couldn't help thinking now as she carefully put down the tray of glasses, were a family of eatin' fools. There was going to be enough food today to feed them all four times over; there was always too much to eat and drink. If Sylvia had one fault, it was her tendency to excess. Even the china, her best, her favorite, was overly ornate. It didn't need gold fleur-de-lis *and* quadruple bands of gold overlying triple bands of maroon encircling a giant bouquet of wine-colored roses with gilded petals. But Sylvia knew only that it was English bone china and the most expensive pattern in Altman's and that it had plenty of decoration. Actually, Deena had adored this china when she was little and had longed to have it for her own when she grew up. Now, of course, she couldn't imagine why. It was overdone, she thought, but ultimately lovable. Just like a lot of her mother's stuff. And furthermore, should she ever arrive here on a major holiday and discover different china on the table, all tasteful and restrained, she would feel cheated. The table, in this dining room, was *supposed* to look heavy, laden, rich: in other words, exactly the way it looked . . . yes, even including the gilt cornucopia centerpiece from Czechoslovakia filled and overflowing with fresh fruits and dried fruits and unshelled nuts.

Yes, other things in this world could change: and, in fact, everything did, sometimes in ways Deena didn't particularly like. In ways, in fact, she didn't even want to think about, especially on Thanksgiving Day. Let everything else change, but not her mother's house! She eyed the table again. The water goblets were now in place and yes, they looked wonderful. All that was left for her to do was the wineglasses.

As she went back through the swinging door, she caught sight of her dim, wavery reflection in one of the glass-fronted pantry doors. It caught her by surprise. She looked good, by

God. Her new shorter haircut was flattering, fluffing around her face as it did, and now you could see the diamond studs Daddy had given her on her fortieth birthday. Luckily, she had the Weinreb high cheekbones; she only wished she had the Weinreb big round blue eyes; but no, she got hazel. Oh, hell, it was enough to be sexy, right? She laughed at herself. Sexy! Nobody was ever going to call her that, not anymore. Well, she wasn't. She was forty-three-year-old Deena Strauss Berman, mother of four, housewife, part-time guidance counselor at the Clayton School, and recently, sometime college student.

Before reaching for the wineglasses, she gave herself one more look. She was doing a lot of that lately: checking herself out. As if she might have changed noticeably within the last couple of minutes. She'd have to stop. Besides, what did she think she was looking for? She gazed at the somewhat distorted image in the glass. Attractive. She'd give herself attractive. Not bad for an old babe. No sagging under the chin, no dark circles under the eyes, no tiny wrinkles. Come to think of it, she actually looked younger than Marilyn, even though she was seven years older. Marilyn looked awful, she thought, all raw and creased and timeworn like those pictures of mountain women. But maybe that was unfair. Marilyn was a natural blond; she used no makeup, and she didn't bother about being stylish. She didn't bother about the way she looked, period. Today, for instance, she was wearing pants and a man's sweater. For Thanksgiving dinner! And her pale curly hair was just piled up and loosely held with a pair of wooden chopsticks. Why didn't she care? Why did she make herself almost defiantly plain? It certainly wasn't the way she had been brought up. Hell, no . . . even the thought made Deena laugh a little. Hadn't *she* been brought up by the same exacting standards? A lady didn't laugh too loudly; a lady didn't put her elbows on the table; a lady didn't let a boy touch her in the wrong places (and there were no right places); and a lady always, always, always was careful about what Sylvia called Very Good Grooming.

It was a shame about Marilyn. She might be a doctor, but she didn't look very happy and fulfilled. Of course, she was smaller, thinner, and paler than the rest of them. When she was a little girl, it had made her seem golden . . . a blonde in the midst of all these dark-haired, vividly colored, big-boned women! Back then everyone said Marilyn was going to be a real beauty. What they secretly meant was that Marilyn was going to look like a shiksa, a gentile, a WASP. Well, she did, but not in any wonderful way. She just looked worn down.

And then Deena had to smile at her own hyperbole. First of all, Marilyn didn't look *that* bad. And if you were going to go in for overstatement, you might as well save it for the most overstated of all of them, Elaine. Elaine Barranger, the tallest —nearly five feet nine—the best-looking, with her wonderful cheekbones and her aquiline nose, her big blue eyes, her thick black shiny hair with a dramatic white streak along one side. And the biggest of all. Elaine was, to put it nicely, statuesque —forty pounds overstatuesque was the way she liked to put it. It didn't seem to make a difference, men still tended to follow her down the street. Not that it mattered to Elaine; she was all business. Elaine looked the most like Sylvia, but Sylvia was on a much smaller scale and didn't give off those same vibrations of superpower, personality, and pizzazz.

And me? Deena thought. What do I give off? Practically nothing. Yup, she was a typical middle child in every way: middling slim, middling smart, middling satisfied, not so gorgeous as Elaine, not so plain as Marilyn . . . dammit, even her hair was not as curly as Marilyn's, not as glossy as Sylvia's, not as black as Elaine's.

But enough of this. It was getting to be annoying, this habit of woolgathering at all odd hours of the day or night. The other night, at three A.M., she had awakened and found herself thinking about her children when they were babies and was suddenly flooded with enormous anger at Michael, who had been largely absent through those difficult years. God, she was tired, she was tired of her life. Tired of taking care of four kids who were now old enough to take care of themselves . . . not to mention a husband so busy with his law practice and his Nazi-hunting meetings that she hardly saw him anymore.

She shook herself, impatient with her own fussiness, and began to collect the wine goblets from the cupboard. It soothed her just to handle them, they were such an integral part of her childhood memories of special occasions. She remembered vividly the year she was finally trusted to have a real wineglass by her plate instead of her blue Shirley Temple mug. Now that she thought of it, where was that mug, was it still in the little cabinet next to the refrigerator? Probably. Sylvia was not one for throwing *anything* away.

Oh, hell, she thought, what is all this meandering down memory lane! Quickly she loaded the tray and, quickly set out the wineglasses and marched herself back into the kitchen. And just in time, because Sylvia was calling: "Deena! It's three oh nine!"

"I'm here, Syl, you don't have to yell."

"Well, it's time . . . past time." Deena knew what that meant; the work schedule for the day was neatly printed and posted on the wall next to the stove. Her green beans almondine were on the list for three o'clock. She laughed to herself. That Sylvia! The Schedule Queen of the Upper West Side and probably the known universe. As she went to get the bundle of beans, both her sisters had stopped what they were doing and were looking at their wristwatches, loudly counting off the seconds.

"Three-*ten*, Sylvia," Elaine said. "Ten minutes late. Shall we send Deena to bed without any dinner?"

And Marilyn, "At least the punishment would fit the crime."

They all laughed. Mildly, her back stolidly turned to them, Sylvia said, "You want to know the big problem around here? Everyone's too busy talking back to their mother to do their job." Then she laughed. "I don't think that's good English."

Deena looked at her mother's straight back, smoothly encased in pink cashmere from Saks, her capable hands continuing with whatever they were doing. Bless her, she always did her job, and did it on time. It could be a royal pain, particularly when she was pushing *you* to meet her schedule. It might be Daddy who told all the funny stories and created most of the laughter and pinched the cheeks, and handed out the silver dollars. Daddy might be the star of the show—and he was, he was—but he'd never be able to do it without Sylvia hustling everyone into place. Deena found her mother's skill at this sort of thing a wonderment. Where the hell did she find the energy? And, right in the middle of all her tight, perfectionistic timetables, she was very likely to make a lighthearted little crack. It suddenly struck Deena that her mother actually *enjoyed* all this work and all this organizing and all this hustle and bustle . . . yes, the very things that drove her daughters crazy.

Impulsively, she went to the sink and put her hands on Sylvia's shoulders. "Tootsie," she said, "I want to go on record as saying you are a genuine wonder." She leaned forward to give her a kiss, but Sylvia said, "That's nice darling. Later. The beans, the beans."

There was no use protesting. The beans were slated to be done by 3:30 and that was that. Which meant she had exactly eleven minutes and thirty seconds to do them. How nice, she thought, somebody had already put out the serving dish for her. But when she reached over, it had something in it, something strange and new, something that looked suspiciously like tofu and black Chinese mushrooms.

"Whose casserole is this?"

"Which one?"

"The one that looks a lot like tofu and mushrooms."

"It *is* tofu and mushrooms," Marilyn answered. "And it's mine. What's that look, Deena? Don't worry; I've taken the fur off."

They were still laughing when the door swung open and immediately the large airy kitchen seemed crowded. Jack Strauss had arrived, letting the door bang against the wall, charging in, a whirlwind of energy, already in the middle of a sentence. Deena loved her father's voice, which was deep and just a bit gravelly from all the years he'd smoked big black cigars. And she loved his booming laugh, his extravagant gestures. Had he ever in his life sidled into a room? Slipped into a room? Even just plain *walked* into a room? Probably not. The dramatic way was the Jack Strauss way.

". . . And here they are, right where I thought I would find them, in the kitchen . . . eight of the most beautiful legs in New York City!"

"Eight of the tiredest legs," Marilyn countered. "And anyway, Daddy, our *legs* are not the issue."

"My little feminist!" Jack boomed. "I'm sorry I noticed you all have gorgeous legs. So do me something! I'm a leg man, always have been. That's how I picked your mother. There she was..."

"We've heard it, we've heard it," his wife said. "The Staten Island ferry. The wind. My skirt. My legs. Enough, Jack!" But she was laughing and her cheeks were pink with pleasure. How nice, Deena thought, to be affected like that by your husband after so many years.

"And anyway," Jack was going on, some of his words piling over his wife's, "don't tell me *tired* legs, Marilyn. You, the skier, the hiker, the mountaineer! How many Alps did you climb last summer? Twelve?"

"Two. And it's not a joke, Daddy."

"Joke! Joke? Who's joking? Do you see me laughing? Look, look at me, like a judge, like a rabbi, like a professor, serious..."

They all, obediently, almost automatically, turned to look at him. Deena smiled. At seventy, he looked years younger. Well, he took good care of himself, watched his weight, worked out twice a week at the gym, went under the sunlamp, walked to work. And he looked terrific; no paunch, no flabbiness, built like a block, thick-chested with heavy muscular legs and a big head with a lot of pure white hair only recently beginning to recede slightly from the broad forehead. His hair was his great vanity; he still took himself downtown every two weeks to Sal for his haircuts.

Gazing at her father today, his hair gleaming against the omnipresent tan, resplendent in gray cord pants and a deep red cashmere sweater, Deena thought, not for the first time, how lucky her mother was. They were both still full of pep, still traveled, still joked around, probably still made love. Most of his friends were already like little old men, bent and fussy and ready to give up. How lucky they all were, the Strauss girls!

"What do you want, Jack? Come on, we have work to do."

"First, a kiss from the prettiest girls in the room."

"Oh, Daddy..." This was an old, old routine. He went to each of his daughters, holding his cheek at the ready, and got smooched by each of them, as noisily as they could manage.

"Best for last," he said—this, too, was in the script—and bent to his wife, planting a solid kiss on her neck.

"Oh, Jack!" She wriggled away from him. "Not while I'm

cutting! Now go, if you don't have anything better on your mind."

"I have something better on my mind. Food. It smells fantastic in here. . . ." While he spoke, he prowled the kitchen, peering into pots, opening the oven door, sticking his finger into the bowl of cranberry sauce and licking it off with relish. "My God, what do you call *this*?" Deena didn't have to look to know that her father had just discovered Marilyn's contribution to the feast.

"What do you call *what*, Daddy?" Butter wouldn't have melted in Marilyn's mouth.

"This . . . *stuff* here, this black and white stuff . . . Whatever it is, I hope to hell you're not planning to put it on the table with the *food*!"

They all began to laugh, all, Deena noted, except Marilyn, who flushed deeply and said, "For those of us who aren't totally provincial in our tastes, it is considered quite a delicacy."

"Oh, Marilyn," Deena said as her father drew his brows together; if she didn't defuse this very quickly, he very well might get hurt and there would go their lovely family event! "That was funny; it was only a joke. Wasn't it, Daddy? Of course it was only a joke. Come on, Moo, have you lost your sense of humor up there in Vermont?"

Sure enough, Daddy brightened right up, and gave Marilyn a quick hug around the shoulders. "Come on, baby, lighten up. It's Thanksgiving, let's give thanks that the Strausses all have quick wit and tough hides!"

Marilyn muttered something or other; apparently it was enough, because he took a bottle of seltzer from the fridge and headed for the door. "Sylvia. It's the fourth quarter."

"So go watch."

"Watch! You think I enjoy it? Football! Soccer is a sport! Even basketball . . . But football! Biff, bam, hit 'em, sock 'em, knock 'em down, kill 'em! That's not a sport!"

Marilyn said, "So why do you bother watching?"

"Why do you think? Your mother makes me. She's made me watch the football since Elaine was two, so I'd stay out of her way."

"What a lie!" Sylvia said, laughing. "Beat it, would you?

You know you watch because it's what men do on Thanksgiving."

He shrugged and said, "So. Dinner. In about twenty minutes?"

"Whenever you say, Jack."

"Good." And he was gone.

"Why whenever *he* says?" Marilyn demanded tightly as soon as his footsteps had receded down the hallway.

"He's the head of the family," Sylvia said. She looked startled. "You know that."

"Well, it would make a lot more sense if the ones doing all the work got to say when dinner is served."

"Marilyn, darling, that's unworthy of you. For thirty years I've been making Thanksgiving dinner, and for thirty years he's been coming in here at the middle of the fourth quarter to announce that he's hungry and to complain about football, and for thirty years I've been telling him whenever you say, and for thirty years, Marilyn darling, I've always served dinner when it's ready and when *I'm* ready. And that, my darling daughter, is what you young people call A Working Marriage, excuse me, Relationship."

The hidden message, of course, was You Aren't Married, Marilyn Darling, So You Don't Know How It's Done. Deena wanted to laugh aloud at the subtle way Sylvia always managed to score; but neither Sylvia nor Marilyn would find it funny. Come to think of it, Elaine was right about Marilyn. Their baby sister was pretty literal-minded. You had to be very careful how you joked with her. And look how she was always on Daddy's case. They all knew Sylvia just indulged him; it didn't mean a thing. Why not just laugh it off, the way the rest of them did?

It was hard to understand Marilyn sometimes. Well, she was seven years younger than Deena. By the time Marilyn had got to her teens, both her older sisters were married and long gone. She'd had all of Daddy's attention, something Deena had longed and longed for when *she* was growing up. She'd been like an only child. You'd think she'd be the closest to Daddy; but instead she always found fault with him. He was mischievous and could be a bit of a tease, but come on, was there a man in the world as good-natured, as generous as Jack Strauss?

And, hey, Marilyn's taste in men was not so perfect. The three Deena had met were not exactly what she would call winners. And that included her current amour, or whatever they called it in Vermont: John LaSalle, tall, bearded, pony-tailed, and laconic-was-putting-it-mildly. He was at this moment drinking her father's best twelve-year-old Scotch in the den, watching the game with the rest of the men on her father's rear-projection fifty-inch TV, brand new last week, and probably adding nothing to the conversation except an occasional grunt or monosyllabic comment. He was very nice to look at; in fact, Deena and Elaine had given each other their special look of total understanding this morning when they both first met him. What in the world, they wondered, had they seen in each other: the dark smoldering rather sexy outdoor type and their brilliant, pale, rather neuter sister? "Can you imagine them in bed?" Elaine had giggled. Deena didn't say so, of course, but she often had that same thought about Elaine and her husband, Howard, Howard being a small, neatly built man and Elaine being . . . well, she certainly outweighed him by more than twenty pounds. But it wasn't really any of her business, particularly since, let's face it, she wasn't doing so well in that department herself these days.

"I could have told you," Sylvia was saying, "that your father wouldn't go for anything different like tofu and mushrooms, not for Thanksgiving."

"My father doesn't have to eat it," Marilyn said, tight-lipped. "But he could learn to keep his mouth shut."

"Marilyn!"

"Well, he could, Sylvia, and you know it. What he said to me was extremely rude."

"But funny," Deena could not resist adding.

"That's the trouble with all of you," Marilyn snapped. "You think if it's funny, it's fine."

"Your father," Sylvia said patiently, "loves his family traditions. Look, you think I wouldn't like to try something new on the menu, a different stuffing maybe?"

"Would you *dare*?" Elaine laughed. "That's Grandma Strauss's recipe!"

Sylvia rolled her eyes, making all of them laugh. "You think I don't know that? I had to wait for years before she'd give me her secret ingredient. You have no idea . . ."

"Oh, yes, we do, Syl. We hear it every single Thanksgiving."

"Say, what *was* it, Syl?" Deena asked.

"What was what?"

"The secret ingredient."

"You think I'm going to tell you?" Sylvia's little smile was so smug and self-satisfied that it made all three sisters shriek.

"Very funny, very funny. But it wasn't funny at the time. You have no idea—"

The three of them, together finished, "—how difficult that woman was!" and they all broke down again.

"Let me tell you something. That woman was more than difficult. That woman was a pain in the ass!"

"Sylvia!" Deena could see in her sisters' stunned faces a reflection of her own stupefaction. Their mother, who never had been known to utter even a mild expletive, a woman who thought "you jerk" was cursing?

"I never heard you use a word like that before!" Deena exclaimed.

Mild as milk, Sylvia said, "I never used a word like *ass* before. But, since I'm in Group—"

"In *what*!"

"Not now, not now . . ." A quick glance at the wristwatch. "The candied sweets have to come out."

"Sylvia! You can't just leave us hanging like that."

"Since I'm in Group, I *can* leave you hanging like that! That's a joke, and the candied sweets really have to come out this minute. Deena, I hate it when you give me your wounded-deer look."

That's a rotten thing to say! she thought. First of all, I don't *have* a wounded-deer look; secondly, I don't have it on my face because I don't *feel* wounded; and third, you shouldn't say you hate anything about your own child. But she didn't say it aloud; she never had. Instead, she took in a deep breath and pretended to need something in the dining room.

What she needed in the dining room was simple: to be alone. She stood by the table, staring at nothing, blinking rapidly, fighting off the threatening tears. Dammit, she was *not* going to cry. She'd been leaking tears altogether too often these past few weeks. Dammit, what was wrong with her? She must not cry; if Sylvia came in here and caught her crying, she'd be sure to give her a talk about her "monthly" and how she always had been supersensitive. And anyway, why should she cry? Because Sylvia said something a bit insensitive? So what else, as the man said, was new? Sylvia's "frankness" was famous within their family circle. She ought to be used to it.

Hadn't it happened the last time she and Sylvia spent some time alone together? Sure it had. They met at Altman's to have lunch in the Charleston Gardens and so that Deena could help her pick out a dress for an upcoming wedding. Shopping was not Deena's favorite thing, but what the hell, she thought, she hadn't seen Sylvia for two weeks and she happened to like the restaurant even though Sylvia called it The Creamed Chicken Room.

She was all set to have a wonderful just-us-two-ladies-to-gether tête-à-tête when she ran up to her mother, her heart filled with warmth and joy. Sylvia had given her a quick hug, the once-over, and then said: "Taupe is not your color, Deena darling."

Honestly! But she had laughed it off, as usual. "You sure know how to make a lady feel old and tired, Sylvia darling, you know what I mean?"

"Oh, listen, the sweater is *gorgeous*, and you look wonderful. But it needs a touch of color, that's all." And before Deena knew what was happening, she'd been steered to Scarfs on the main floor and found herself the owner of a turquoise silk number signed by somebody or other. That was Sylvia!

Yes, that was Sylvia, all right. Deena often told people, "When my mother takes my face between her two little hands and says, 'Let me look at you, darling,' I'm never sure whether she simply wants her fill of her beloved daughter's face . . . or whether she's checking for flaws." So it was plain dumb to be fussing at this late date, fighting off incipient tears over some dumb remark.

She went over to the big windows overlooking Central Park, slipping behind the heavy crewel draperies, wrapping

herself in them like a big warm blanket, and leaned her forehead against the cool glass. This had been her refuge in childhood, the place she came to when she needed solace and
solitude: this particular window looking out on this particular
vista of endless treetops curving off into misty skyline way on
the other side of the park. How far away the East Side had
seemed when she was a child! When she was a child, though,
she believed that Central Park was—as her daddy often told
her—her yard. "See that? I had that made for you and your
sister," he'd say with a laugh. "I told them, 'No buildings! My
little girls need a lot of room to run and play.'" And he'd
laugh again, squeezing her or throwing her into the air.

Suddenly the memory came into her head, complete down to
every tiny detail: the pearly gray dawn—how many years ago?
she must have been no more than three years old—forty years
ago, when Daddy had come tiptoeing into their room, the big
sunny room she and Elaine shared, finger to lips, eyes sparkling
with his pleasure to bring them in here. She could almost smell
the furniture polish, all lemony, and the pungent fragrance of
eucalyptus leaves, stuffed into a huge vase in the corner. . . .
Lord, that vase had broken long since—she should know, she
had broken it, riding her new three-speed bike through the
house.

He had lifted her up, that Thanksgiving morning, to look out
of the window and, not knowing what to expect, she had nearly
lost her breath. Mickey Mouse! Gigantic, colorful, bouncing
around in the dim early-morning light, big as life. No, bigger!
Right in front of her dining room window, looking right at her.
"Mickey Mouse!" she had squealed. "Daddy! Look! Mickey
Mouse!" She remembered the prickly feel of the bristles on his
jaw, his early-morning unshaven jaw.

"That's right, sweetie-*piele*. Daddy ordered Mickey Mouse
just for you."

Years later, when she recalled this with Elaine, her sister was
insulted. "No, he didn't! He said he'd ordered it for me!" And
then they had both just laughed and laughed until the tears came.

"Deena?" It was Michael at the doorway. "Is that you,
hiding?"

She unwound herself from the drapery so that he could see
her; but she wasn't about to move. "I always loved looking

out over the park from here," she said. "Come look, Michael, it's already getting dark on the East Side but there's still sunshine here."

His voice was dry. "That's because it's clouding up."

Now she looked directly at him. "I know that . . . never mind. It looks kind of lonely down there without the balloons, doesn't it? My sisters and I just love that stupid parade. None of us would miss it for the world . . . I guess because Daddy had us convinced he'd ordered it especially for us."

Michael gave a little laugh.

"Why shouldn't I have believed him? He never lied to me!"

"Just what is *that* supposed to mean?"

"Nothing. It's not supposed to mean anything."

Deena studied her husband briefly, feeling very distant. Handsome Michael, still handsome at fifty, with his long legs and broad shoulders, the square-jawed face with its even features. The thick curly hair, carefully barbered, was salt and pepper; the first time she'd seen him, it had been perfectly black. But back then the deep creases either side of his mouth had been dimples, dimples that suddenly appeared whenever he smiled.

Now she tried a smile but he would not smile back. Why in hell couldn't he just smile at her? Surely, on Thanksgiving, with her family—and being with her family was something he always loved—surely today he could manage one little ghost of a smile.

"It would be a nice change, Deena, if you didn't pick fights with me over nothing."

Deena sighed. "Let's make up, Michael, okay?"

"I don't see that I have anything to make up for."

"Oh, Michael!"

"Deena, do me a favor and stop dramatizing."

"Michael, do me a favor and stop telling me I'm dramatizing every time I try to talk with you." He waved off her words and she felt her chest constrict as tears formed suddenly in her eyes.

Michael looked at her coldly. "Tears again? I don't know what you think they're going to do to me, but frankly, I'd rather watch football."

"That's why we're in trouble." To her horror, the tears began to run down her cheeks.

"It would be wonderful if we could get through one day, Deena, just one day without a scene."

"Michael, don't do this to me . . . to us."

"We'll talk later."

"You always say that. But somehow, we never do. You're never there!"

"Deena, for God's sake. This isn't the time. It's Thanksgiving."

"I don't need you to tell me how to behave," she choked out. But she was, quite literally, talking to the wall. He had marched out, leaving her feeling like a fool.

That's what came of marrying at nineteen—and an older man of twenty-six, to boot. You began your relationship in the position of beloved but slightly dopey acolyte . . . and there wasn't a man in this world, Deena figured, who would allow a woman in that wonderfully subservient posture to escape from it. Here she was, twenty-four years and four children later, still struggling, still trying to convince him—and herself, too, a lot of the time—that she was grown-up, that she might possibly even be right every once in a while.

As Deena straightened her shoulders, taking in a calming deep breath—Sylvia's answer to every one of life's difficulties—there was a sudden burst of noisy laughter and chatter from the foyer. The kids had arrived . . . finally. It saddened her, it really did, that they disdained the Macy's parade as being too childish. It wasn't too childish for her, no, nor for her father. You'd think they'd love it forever; it had always been part of their childhood, too.

She let out the deep breath. It hadn't really calmed her down. Oh hell, it was Thanksgiving, they were all together, and the kids were here. And now she heard the rumble of male voices, so the football game had been abandoned. It must be time.

Just then she heard Sylvia's voice calling down the hallway. "Hello, my darlings! Hello, hello, you're just in time for a little bite. Don't take me seriously, Noel!"

There was general hilarity at this and cries of "Go for it,

Noel!" Calling the Thanksgiving feast "a little bite to eat" was one of Sylvia's more timeworn little jokes—one that she bravely continued using each year. Bravely, because seventeen years ago, the year Noel Barranger had turned five and discovered his own peculiar sense of humor, he had taken that little bite right on his grandmother's ear. Deena would never forget *that* moment—none of them would—because Sylvia had dropped the boy, yelling "Ow! You devil!" and Noel, suddenly and unceremoniously dumped on the floor, had begun to laugh like a lunatic.

Now Sylvia laughed and shouted, "Never you mind, one of these days I'm gonna pay Noel back for that one! So just watch it!"

"You do that, Granny," Noel laughed, "and I'll have to drop *you* on the floor."

And then there were the sounds of loud kisses and the usual kibbitzing. Lucky kids . . . they were used to having a funny grandmother. Lucky all of them, that no matter what else was happening in their lives, they had each other, they had their closeness, their laughter, their family.

Michael Berman lifted the video camera to his eye and squinted into the viewfinder with satisfaction. There, nicely framed, was his father-in-law, the archetypical paterfamilias, just pushing his chair back a bit from the table, the remains of his meal—a lone drumstick so gnawed, the bone looked polished—on the plate in front of him. He was patting his muscular belly and grinning with pleasure; and if that scene didn't say "Thanksgiving," nothing did. Almost automatically, Michael started the film moving.

"Oy," Jack moaned. "If you knew how I'd like to belch right now . . . !"

"Don't you dare, Jack," Sylvia said quickly; but her mild remonstration was covered by shouts and squeals from the four grandchildren egging him on.

"Go for it, Papa!" "Give us a good loud one!" "Don't listen to Granny, you have to make room for dessert!"

Jack smiled, loving the noisy response. Kids and their antics didn't bother him, never had. In fact, he thrived on the tumult and excitement.

Now Jack gestured for silence, shaking his head. "Not at your grandmother's beautiful Thanksgiving table . . . no, no, no arguments, my girls have worked long and hard to give us this feast. We're not going to do anything that might spoil even one precious moment."

"Hear, hear!" Michael said. He put the camera down and lifted his wineglass. "To many more of these precious moments." He glanced sideways, trying to catch Deena's eye. What was wrong with her, anyway? She'd always been so ebullient, so good-natured, so *up*. Now, all of a sudden, she had become a creature of moods, up and down, up and down, and she was spoiling more and more of life's good moments. God knew there were few enough of those at best, and they were certainly precious.

He could recall every high point in his own life. The day he graduated from Harvard Law at the top of his class was one. He had looked at his mother and his father, realizing that finally he had done it; he had fulfilled their hopes and their dreams, he had made it all come true for them. Each one of his parents was the end of the line. Having lost everything and everyone to Hitler's madness, they had conceived him as a memorial to the sixty-seven Bermans and Feigenbaums who had perished in the death camps. And that had been his family group, when he was growing up in the Bronx—his mother, his father, and sixty-seven ghosts.

No wonder he had fallen in love with Deena almost at first sight. No ghosts clung to her! No ghost stood a chance of survival in the vital, noisy Strauss household with its jokes and music and laughter.

Their wedding had been the quintessential Strauss family gathering. *There* was a memory worth holding on to, worth savoring! The crowded candlelit synagogue, heaped with yellow and white flowers, filled with family . . . *filled with family*, that had been the wonder of it. Even cutting off the guest list at second cousins once removed, there were two hundred and fifty smiling faces watching as he and his beautiful young bride slid the weighty gold rings onto each others' fingers. And she had been lovely back then, with her proud breasts and long slim legs, her hair hanging halfway down her back, so thick and heavy, she could never keep it pinned up. Back then her eyes had been filled with love and admiration when she looked up at him.

Now? Now he never knew what he was going to get from her. Some days, she was giving and caring, like the old Deena, the girl he had chosen. But often, like today, she looked at him as if she didn't know him.

But what nonsense! Romance didn't last forever and they had been married almost twenty-five years, good years, most of them, so no use grieving over it. What was really important was what had come of the marriage: his children. Four children and each birth had been an occasion for joy and gratitude. Each time he had gazed down at another new redfaced healthy squalling infant, he had been filled with the sanctity of what they had accomplished. Nathan, Judith, Zoe, Saul: their names were the roll call of his immortality, his future, his reason for living. Four miracles, each one defying the Nazi horror. To create a family, to maintain and sustain it: that was why man had been put on Earth. He believed that with all his heart and soul.

Michael took a big gulp of his wine and brought his thoughts back to the present. Sylvia was wheeling in the tea cart, loaded with desserts, to the accompaniment of loud applause from her grandchildren. It was time to start filming again.

"Good Lord!" Marilyn protested. "Four kinds of pie... Black Forest cake... *and* cherry cobbler... *and* chocolate mousse? Sylvia, have mercy! That's called instant cardiac arrest!"

"If that's called cardiac arrest, Marilyn," Jack announced, throwing his arms out as if to embrace the entire cart of sweets, "then I say it's a helluva way to go!"

"That's not funny, Daddy."

"Not nearly as funny as that concoction you brought."

Marilyn flushed deeply, and for a moment there was an awful, awkward silence. And then Noel, ever the charmer, said, "Hey, Papa, Moo is the one person at this table who can leap over mountains in a single bound. She must be eating *something* right!"

Marilyn relaxed visibly and then, to everyone's surprise—the man hadn't uttered more than a dozen words all day—

Marilyn's friend John cleared his throat and said, "Marilyn is the living proof of her beliefs. She sees patients long hours, sleeps maybe four hours a night, and, most important, can still ski any man into the ground."

Deena laughed. "Marilyn always had more energy than an entire small town."

Not a hint of a smile on the gaunt face. "She still does . . . but not on *this* kind of a diet . . ." Raking with his eyes not only the dessert cart but the heaped fruits and nuts, the teapots and coffeepots, the dishes of candy and glazed ginger.

At this, Noel burst out laughing. "Spoken like a true liberated health freak, John," he said, and finally John gave a ghost of a smile and muttered an apology in the direction of Sylvia's chair.

"Yeah, but I'd rather have Granny around to cook when I go skiing!" That was Zoe, whose small size belied the prodigious amounts of food she regularly put away.

"Oh, Lord," Elaine cried, "I can see it all now: Sylvia's Ski Resort. The pot roast! The sterling silver! The scatter rugs!"

"Oh, yes, and by the door, a box filled with hats and mittens," Deena put in, laughing. "And a nice Jewish mother on guard to make sure you're dressed warmly enough!"

"And, and, and," Zoe put in excitedly, "another Jewish mom at the top of the lift, who looks you over and tells you when it's time you got inside, you look frozen."

Now they were all howling, Deena gasping out, "The expert trail is Call your Mother . . ."

"The novice trail is called Guilt Trip," Saul added.

"Oh, very funny," Sylvia said, firmly slicing her pies into eight equal wedges. "You have a very funny family, Jack . . . yes, I blame *you* . . ." She was smiling, of course; she loved all the high spirits. "But, on to more important matters, may I have a show of hands for pecan pie, please?"

"Oh, hell!" Marilyn, turning to John, said, "Dammit, we *can't* pass up Sylvia's pecan pie!" Again, everyone erupted into peals of laughter. That was the saving grace of this family, Michael thought. They always saw the funny side. Even Marilyn was capable of being lighthearted on occasion. He wished Deena would lighten up again—not just today, and not just for a minute or two, but back to the way she used to be.

Look at her now. Two minutes ago she'd had her head thrown back, absolutely unselfconscious, laughing and making jokes. Now she was back to glum, picking at the pie on her plate, and avoiding his eyes. Moody, just like a goddamn kid. He wondered why he hadn't thought of that before, because that's exactly what Deena's erratic behavior reminded him of: their own teenaged children.

Deena felt her husband's eyes on her, all right, but she was damned if she would look at him. She was having a wonderful fantasy about her film-writing professor, and Michael wasn't invited.

Tuesday night, just as she was putting the finishing touches on the pies, the phone rang and it was Luke. The class was going to go see a film the day after Thanksgiving . . . he knew it was a bad time for a lot of people, but it was an *important* film, and it had been made by a friend, so . . .

She said yes; in fact, she said yes before she even thought about whether it was possible. Her film-writing class was her declaration of independence, and if the professor was an appealing, sensitive, bearded male person who seemed to be ever so slightly and ever so lightly flirting with her, well, there could be worse fates than spending two hours in a darkened theater next to him. Because in her fantasy, they were, of course, sitting side by side and, in her fantasy, his hand reached for hers and then . . .

She couldn't continue, not with Michael staring at her like that, appraising her. Her husband was in the habit of making judgments about everyone and she was number one on the list. There were no gray areas in Michael's world; there was right and wrong; there was black and white, good and evil, love and hate. All very admirable, perhaps, on an ethical basis; but very goddamn difficult to live with.

She wondered lately whether he had always been so rigid, so humorless. He couldn't have been; she wouldn't have put up with it. He hadn't been, of course he hadn't. At the law school picnics he'd always done the three-legged race with her, he'd played tug-of-war in the mud, he'd laughed and joked and drunk a lot of beer, just like the rest of them.

And surely, if he'd been a grim young man, Daddy would have had something to say about it. Daddy had always had

ALL FOR THE LOVE OF DADDY   23

something to say about every young man who came calling.
"A little short, isn't he?" or "Not from the great brains, what
do you think?" or "That suit!" or "That Brooklyn accent!" or
"That haircut!" Always with a lot of laughter, of course; but
you got the idea: you'd better not get serious with *this* one, not
if you wanted to remain Daddy's girl. But Daddy hadn't had a
bad word for Michael. On the contrary. He'd said, "Well,
that's the best thing *you've* brought around in a long time,
Deena darling. Especially after the last two undernourished
pishers. And a brilliant student, too."

She had basked in the warmth and the light of Daddy's
endorsement . . . so different from his disdain for Howard, for
most of the young men who came around. And, of course, she
was terribly attracted to Michael. He was so good-looking, so
smart, so mature, so serious about life. She couldn't believe
her luck that this *man* actually wanted her, a kid of eighteen.
By the age of nineteen she was married and by the age of
twenty, a mother. And so, just like in all the stories, they lived
happily ever after.

Until recently. Mad as hell was where it stood today,
Thanksgiving Day; but Daddy would never forgive her if she
let her personal problems interfere with his favorite family
day.

Even as she had the thought, Jack cleared his throat and
stood, wineglass held aloft, waiting for them all to notice him
and to quiet down.

Daddy grinned and said, "Thank you. And now that I have
everyone's attention—that means you, too, Zoe darling—let
me say that I'm about to give all my girls some very good
news. And, unless I miss my guess, the fellas who were lucky
enough to land them aren't going to be so miserable, either."

At Deena's side, Michael picked up the video camera and
began again to take pictures. Jack's smile broadened. It must
be *really* good, Deena thought. "My dearest ones . . . Cut it
out, kids . . . I'm serious now," he began, and his eyes filled a
little. "My wonderful, wonderful family. I've . . . ah . . .
I'm . . ." He drew in a deep breath and blew it out. "I've been
made an offer I'd be an idiot to refuse. Thirty million dollars.
So . . . I'm going to accept. I'm selling the business, I'm retiring, I'm going to make all my girls rich! *Very* rich!"

As he spoke, they had all automatically lifted their wine-glasses for the toast. But with the last word, instead of every-one sipping and smiling, there was a sudden buzz. Elaine felt stunned. Daddy: retired? Not working? She couldn't picture it. She had never, in her whole life, thought of him without also thinking of the business. He *was* the business. When she recalled her childhood, the image of his elaborate, carpeted office was as vivid as the image of her mother bustling around the kitchen. Or her own blue and white room, for that matter. Daddy's office: it had been the most exciting wonderful mys-terious important place in the world when she was a child. It was her best treat, to be dressed up and taken downtown on Saturday to visit Daddy's office.

No, no, it was unthinkable that he should sell. He'd built the business from Grandpa Weinreb's little carpentry shop. From one room on the Lower East Side to a multi-million-dollar construction company that got regular write-ups in the real estate section of *The New York Times* . . . he'd done it all himself. He'd been one of the first to realize the potential of inexpensive tract housing after World War II . . . one of the first to see what could be done with the Upper West Side. And, ten years ago, as soon as it could be legally done, he'd begun converting industrial buildings in Manhattan into luxury residential cooperatives. Each time, there had been people to tell him he was crazy. But Jack Strauss always managed to put himself into all the right places at all the right times and he'd moved quickly from success to success. And now, to give it all up, just like that? How could he? For a million million dollars, how could he think of walking away from it?

"What do you think you're going to do with yourself?" Deena said. "Stand in Bloomingdale's, holding Sylvia's coat? Follow her around the supermarket, pushing the cart? You'll hate it!"

"That's right, Daddy!" Marilyn cried. "What are you *think-ing* of? You always said they'd have to carry you out feetfirst! You haven't changed! Retirement? It'll kill you!"

"Bite your tongue!" Sylvia said quickly, before the Evil Eye could hear what had been said and make it come true. Elaine would have found it amusing if she weren't so damned pissed. And there *he* stood, so pleased with himself, beaming happily, looking around expectantly, waiting for their excited approval and gratitude. It would never occur to him that someone might be hurt by what he did. What he did was automatically okay. Dammit.

"Dammit!" she said aloud. "I'm sorry, but, dammit, it's just not fair!"

In the moment of utter silence there was a thump as Michael quickly stopped his interminable moviemaking and put the camera down. In a flash Elaine knew exactly why: because there was to be no record of any unpleasantness.

Then, "Elaine!" Sylvia protested; but Jack motioned her to silence.

"*Bubeleh*, Lainie, what is this? What is the problem? Didn't you hear what I said? Eighteen million dollars, divided by four . . . *you* figure it out!"

"I have plenty of money! I'm not talking about *money*, dammit! I'm talking about a business . . . a *family business*, I *thought*." She felt Howard's hand on her back, knew it to be a message for her to calm down. She shrugged away from him. She didn't *want* to calm down.

"Sweetie pie!" Jack spread his hands, his face a picture of amicable reasonableness. "What *is* it? You don't want me to retire? Hey, don't worry, it doesn't mean I'm old. It only means I've decided to have a little fun. Before they carry me out of here feetfirst in a plain pine box. *Bubeleh*, don't take it to heart."

He was unbelievable, that man. To deliberately misunderstand her that way: it was so Daddy-like, so frustrating, so maddening! She shook her head emphatically. "Dammit, you know that's not what I'm talking about. I want you to have fun; I'm delighted you're retiring before you have a heart attack or something. What I'm talking about, as I'm sure you know, is the *business*, Daddy. Why the hell are you selling it to strangers when it belongs in the family?"

Vaguely, she heard her mother's murmured remonstrances; they mattered not at all. "Elaine, Elaine," Jack said with his best condescending smile, "there's nobody in this family who can run that business. Or even *wants* to."

The bastard! She pushed herself to her feet with such force

that her chair tipped over and fell with a crash. She felt hot and dizzy. And she was shaking, trembling so violently that she had to cling to the edge of the dining table to hold herself still.

"*I* can! And I *want* to! As you damn well know!"

"Elaine! Stop it!" Again, her mother and again Daddy gave the sign that she should stay out of it. He gave a theatrical sigh and reached deliberately for the wine decanter to refill his glass.

"Elaine, listen. You're a terrific manager, I'd be the first to say so. But . . . construction? Real estate? In this city? It's a dirty business. Not for a woman—." He paused, filled his glass, twinkled at her. "Leona Helmsley notwithstanding." And he couldn't help glancing around the table, inviting his audience to respond. But nobody was laughing this time.

"I can't believe," Elaine said, her voice quivering in spite of her best efforts, "that you're still talking that male chauvinist garbage. You can't leave the business to us because we're only *girls. Only* girls."

"Now, now, Lainie. Enough of this nonsense. I've been very patient, but enough already! You know how I love my girls; they're my national treasure, you know that." He smiled at her.

"Forget that! Just talk to me like a grown-up for a change!" For a second she half-expected him to reach over and give her an annoyed shake, like he used to when she was little and got on his nerves. "Sweet Somethings grossed nine million last year, so you can stop treating me like a little girl. I want that business and I deserve to run it. I deserve at least a chance to show I *can*."

"No more!" he said, and his voice had changed, had hardened. "No more. You've hurt me deeply with your attitude and I'm ending this conversation right now."

"That's right, *you* end it. You don't care about anyone else, you never have!"

Even at her age, even at forty-five, she felt a momentary panic, that she had been too harsh. Had she gone too far this time? Behind her, she heard Howard's murmur: "Elaine. Enough."

"I'm going to forget you said that, Elaine. It never happened. So. I'm calling for a toast. Who'll give it?" She almost had to laugh out loud as Deena and Howard and Michael all jumped to their feet at once. And the scene was over. Except, not for her.

CHAPTER TWO

Thanksgiving Night, November 28, 1985

"Jack, Jack," Sylvia soothed. "Let me say it again: We brought up your daughters to be aggressive and strong and smart, am I right?"

"You're wrong, you're dead wrong. Maybe *you* brought them up that way . . . I didn't."

"Oh, really? Who was it took Elaine to the office, age five or maybe six, nearly every Saturday? Huh, Jack? Huh? And let her see what it was all about? *Who?*"

"She played with the carbon paper, for God's sake, Sylvia! She drew little pictures . . ."

Sylvia began to laugh.

"What's so funny now?"

"Jack, Jack, have you really forgotten?" She sighed, moving to the big dressing table to remove the ornate diamond earrings that had been her gift from him on their fiftieth anniversary last year and were far too heavy for her. They hurt her ears, in fact. But you couldn't tell him.

She eyed him in the mirror. He sat on the edge of his bed, taking off his socks and shoes, flinging them across the room in the general direction of his closet. Jack had always flung his clothes from him; and watching him now, she felt a momentary nostalgia for a time when he had thrown his clothes halfway across the room because he was so eager for her. So many years, so many changes, so many disappointments. But thank God they both still had their health and all their children and all their grandchildren, too.

He was still scowling. If she knew her Jack—and she did —first she had to make him laugh and *then* she could make him listen.

"Jack, you really don't remember that Elaine always drew letterheads." He shrugged, not meeting her eyes in the glass: his way of letting her know he was still mad. "Some little pictures she did: *Elaine's Business Company, Inc., Elaine, President*. You really don't remember? You showed them to everybody—for months! One you kept in your wallet until it crumbled from old age. 'A chip off the old block,' you said. 'She's so much like me, too bad she wasn't a boy.' You still insist you don't know from it?"

He looked up from under his brows and a tiny little smile quivered at the corners of his mouth. "All right, all right, yes."

"Yes what?"

"I remember." It was muttered.

"And now, suddenly, you're surprised?"

"I thought it was *cute*, Sylvia. Just little-girl stuff."

"But Jack. All these years, she's been in business, an equal partner with Howard, you know that. You know they've done very well. So what *is* this?"

Heavily, he got to his feet, began to undress slowly, letting the cashmere sweater drop to the carpet. Sylvia sighed inwardly; more than fifty years, and still confronted with the same nightly choice: Do I pick it up now and show myself to be the servant around here, or do I wait until the morning to do it, when I can no longer stand the sight of it?

"That's the *shmatte* business. Come on, Sylvia. Fancy lingerie, sexy nightgowns, maribou slippers, strapless bras! That's right for a woman. It's a different story in construction. You should know that! And, goddammit, so should Elaine! You know what kind of slime I have to deal with every goddamn day? You know how those union guys can turn the screws on you? It's disgusting. And take it from me, it's no place for a woman. My God, the language alone—!"

Sylvia paused in the act of folding her clothes and began to laugh again. Then she stopped herself. "Oh, come on, you think in ladies' lingerie everyone's a gent? You think it's so different just because she's dealing in lace and sheer nylon and maribou and high-heeled slippers? Elaine's had plenty of slime to deal with, believe me. You don't meet many classy people in the garment district." Now she allowed herself a giggle. "And, Jack, she's had a few propositions."

"All right, all right. I get your point. But still. She should have waited. She shouldn't have shamed me in front of the entire family—in front of the children . . ."

"When was she supposed to say something? Next week, when it's all over?"

"Even tonight, Syl. But in the other room, at least. You know, if she hadn't jumped on me that way, and in public, I might have given a different answer. I wouldn't have felt so attacked."

Sylvia thought that over for a moment while she peeled off her girdle and put on her nightgown. In fact, he probably would have reacted exactly the same way. Jack Strauss did not take kindly to anything he perceived as criticism. But what was the real objective here? Was it to make Jack see how stubborn he really was? Or was it to get her daughter the chance she deserved? No contest! She'd just have to do whatever was necessary to defuse him. And she knew how. She'd had years of practice, hadn't she?

"Jack, you're absolutely right, you're absolutely right. One hundred percent right." She peered at him; had she overdone it? But no. He had turned, at first surprised and then pleased and then supremely self-satisfied. Of course he was right; wasn't he Jack Strauss and didn't that make him automatically right?

Sometimes she hated herself for these little games. But when it came to her daughters . . .

"You mean that, Sylvia?"

"Of course I mean it. It was very thoughtless of Elaine." At least she wouldn't tell him any lies. "She should know better. She should have picked a better moment. It wasn't polite, at the very least. But Jack . . ."

"Here it comes! The pitch!" But now, his supremacy restored, he was smiling. "'But Jack,' *what?*"

"But Jack, imagine how she feels. You know how she admires you . . ."

"Yeah, yeah . . ."

"How she's modeled herself on you . . ."

"Keep going. You're doing fine."

"How she's always hoped you'd take her into the business with you . . ."

"Sylvia, listen. When she was majoring in business administration in college, I told her to forget it. I told her to pick something clean, something nice, something a woman could do and still take care of her family. A teacher. A social worker. All right, all right, if she loved business so much, she could go for CPA."

"Jack. She *is* a CPA."

"All right, all right," He was in his pale blue pajamas, turning down the covers on his bed, yawning. Their conversation was over . . . or so he thought. But *she* wasn't quite finished, not yet. He got into bed with his glasses and a book.

"Not all right. That's the whole point. All these years she must have hoped that after she proved herself, after she made such a big success, you'd show yourself to be the rational, reasonable man she knows you are . . . and you'd give her a chance. Jack. A *chance*. Not a promise, not a contract. A chance, that's all. One little chance." She was watching him carefully in the mirror as she pretended to be busy brushing her hair.

Now he put down the book and took off the glasses and now, at last, he allowed his eyes to meet hers as she got into her own bed. "You're getting me where I live, Sylvia! You're getting there, Sylvia! One or two more compliments and you'll have me, Sylvia!" They smiled at each other.

That's what kept her with him: the comfort of it and the occasional shared moment of complete understanding, like this one.

"One chance, Jack. That's all she's asking. I figure, if you let her look around the place and hear her ideas, maybe see what she can do, then, in all fairness, you could say no. Or," she added after a moment, "you might even say yes, you know."

"You think so?" The smile was replaced by a thoughtful look. "Well, maybe. Nah, don't turn out the light yet. I want to read for a while."

"Elaine, Elaine," Howard soothed. She was pacing back and forth, back and forth in their bedroom, the filmy ecru negligee billowing out behind her. She had taken her hair, her beautiful long black shiny hair, out of the pins, out of the braid, and it flowed out behind her, thick and wavy and gorgeous, the way he loved it. It was all he could do to concentrate on the problem at hand. Which was to calm her down and get her back on the track.

"Damn him!" she gritted out. "All those promises! All those years of waiting! Proving myself, over and over again! And still not good enough!"

"Elaine, please sweetheart, don't cry. Come here and let me make you feel better."

"Howard, I love you, but right now, dammit, I *want* to cry. I feel cheated, dammit, I feel cheated and betrayed! How could he do this to me, after all the times he said soon, soon, he'd take care of me, make sure I got my fair share. . . ."

"Sweetheart, that's what he thinks he's doing. Giving you your fair share of the business."

"I don't want it this way, in *cash*, and he knows it. He's always known it. How could he make such a total fool of me in front of everybody? The whole family knows how he's been leading me on all these years. Why the hell did he think I worked so hard for my CPA?"

"Darling. Please." He felt a bit helpless. What could he say, after all? It was true. Jack had teased her with his "somedays" and his "one of these times" and with his "when the time is right." Business was Elaine's life. And she was brilliant at it. Look what she had done with his little underwear store on the Lower East Side: turned it into Sweet Somethings and they had just been written up in *Business Week*. And that was the point: they'd made it. She was getting itchy to get her hands on something else . . . he'd felt it for the past year. She kept talking about buying another business, about expanding from just sexy lingerie to maybe evening gowns or accessories or swimwear. Every time she heard about a possibility, her eyes would light up and she'd be on fire with ideas. Tonight, Howard knew, had been devastating to Elaine; it was the end of the dream, the myth, of getting a piece of the action from her father. The *real* action.

"Elaine. Sit down, at least, and let me rub your back. Let me rub your back and relax you. You can't even talk about it now, you're steaming."

"Damn right!"

"I'll talk to him. You know he's reasonable . . . about most things."

"Not about me. He still thinks of me as only a girl. *Only* . . ."

"He's a man of his time, Elaine. That's how they all felt. Don't worry. I'll talk to him, we'll have a drink or two, we'll have the biggest steak at Peter Luger's, and he'll mellow out, as Noel would say. Somehow, I'll mellow him out."

"Well," Elaine said, stopping her crazed back-and-forth striding and looking directly at him, "if anyone can mellow Daddy out, I guess it's you. Although, really, sweetie, this is my battle. No, no, you shouldn't have to torture yourself with a fabulous steak at Peter Luger's, with those thick fries, with the apple strudel and whipped cream . . . no, no, I can't let you do it, I can't let you sacrifice yourself." Now they were both laughing.

"You know what I love about you, Elaine?"

"Sure, tiger. My intelligence, my acumen, my sense of humor, my wit, my charm . . ."

"And your modesty," he finished. They grinned at each other.

"Oh, Howard, baby, honestly . . ."

He held out his arms. "I know, sweetie, it ain't easy, dealing with an old MCP like your beloved daddy. Remember, I've had my magical moments with him myself. It only took me three months to convince him I wasn't a fag."

"Oh, do I have news for you. He never believed it until I

finally screamed at him that we were sleeping together and *had* been for a year!"

Howard gaped at her for a moment. "After twenty-two years you tell me?"

"Are you mad at me, baby?" She stood there, all five feet nine of her, looking timidly at him.

"Well . . . not exactly *mad* . . ."

"Can't I make it up to you?" So saying, she dropped the pale peignoir to the floor and stood there, eyeing him, licking her lips, her nostrils flaring a little bit. She was wearing an ecru satin teddy, beautifully cut, with a laced front that exposed about one-third of her creamy, full breasts. As he watched her, she let one of the straps slip ever so slightly off her shoulder and began to croon, "Before I take off model eight-hundred-seventy-four Z in ecru with the toffee trim, also available in black slash black, red slash black, or white slash pink, sizes four through forty-four, just let me show you a little more . . ." She walked closer, swaying slightly, and her eyes had taken on the familiar glazed look that signaled desire. She was beginning to smile that small familiar catlike smile . .

"Let's take our time tonight. Noel's out late, and we can sleep late tomorrow . . . so slowly, just unlace the top lace, tiger."

Smiling, he followed instructions and soon they were undressing each other with slow, caressing hands. Together they sank onto the bed, his lips avid on one erect dark nipple, one hand moving down over her soft round belly, the fingers creeping into the tangle of curly hair. They were now both groaning with their pleasure.

Elaine stretched one arm out to turn out the light, but Howard lifted his head. "No, no, not yet. I want to look at you."

"Marilyn! Marilyn! Take it easy. I have to get back, sure, but not in one hour. Slow down!"

As soon as he spoke, Marilyn glanced at the speedometer, surprised to see the needle edging toward eighty. She eased off on the gas a bit, congratulating herself for not snapping at him. She was not only driving too fast, she was gripping the steering wheel so hard that her fingers were cramped. "Sorry," she said. "I guess I'm in a hurry to get away from them. Always a scene! Always a drama!"

She couldn't see him in the darkness—there were no lights on the thruway—but she knew her words were bound to upset him. John was a big one for Family with a capital F. His own family was a large tribe: brothers and sisters, aunts, uncles, and endless cousins who mixed and mingled and fought and feuded and loved and lauded each other—everything with equal emphasis, it seemed to her.

John was unfailingly loyal; well, he was able to be unfailingly loyal because he never looked beneath the surface of *any* behavior. The time she'd pointed out to him that his brother Pete bullied him, he had laughed at her. "That's just his way," he said. "Doesn't mean anything." John's explanation for any of the infinite variety of relationships was essentially the same. People were who they were and things went the way they went and you just accepted all of it ... particularly if it involved your family.

"You make too much of it," he said now.

"That's unfair!" she retorted. "I wanted to sink under the table and disappear ten different times. But the topper was Daddy and his big surprise! Honestly! It's just like him to spring something important like that on everyone at a family dinner, where nobody dares argue ... !"

"Whoa," John said in a particular tone of voice she called careful and which set her teeth on edge. "Hold on a minute. What's this about Daddy all the time? From where *I* was sitting, it was your sister Elaine who started the whole thing!"

"Stop right where you are," Marilyn said through her teeth. "Don't you dare bad-mouth Elaine. I'd kill for Elaine!"

Now he laughed. It was unusual for him to laugh, and the sound was startling. "Jesus, Marilyn, I didn't think you had any feelings that strong."

Tightly: "She was ready to send me through medical school."

"That's very nice. But ..." He was perplexed. "But I thought you told me—"

"Yes, yes, *he* paid my way. But she talked him into it."

There were several moments of silence. Then John said:

"All right, so she backed you up when you wanted to go to med school. She still started it this afternoon."

"Dammit, John, you don't understand at *all*!"

"Maybe not! But I don't get it. You tell me all about your horrible old man, how you could never talk to him, how he never cared what you wanted from life. And then . . . and then I meet him! Jesus, Marilyn! I meet a good-looking dude in top shape, outgoing as hell, a real personality, a guy who's always hugging and kissing and making jokes."

"So?"

"You're doing it again. Speeding. So, all I'm trying to say is, maybe *you're* the one who doesn't understand. Don't take me wrong, Marilyn, I'm not saying none of it happened. But your father sure ain't what you led me to expect. Here's our exit."

"I *know* where we are, John, for God's sake. Give me *some* credit."

"Hey! Take it easy. All I said was—"

"Well, you don't know him!"

"Hell, I spent all day with the man!"

She wished she could make him understand about Daddy. About all of them. What he saw was a family of friendly, outgoing people. "Even the kids come up with one-liners," he'd said, laughing a little. He *admired* her family, Marilyn had realized with a shock. He thought they were warm and wonderful. Good Lord, he thought they were like *his* family; he'd said so this morning. What she saw as intrusive and invasive and smothering, he saw as genuine, as loving. "What you see is what you get," he told her. "Everything's right up front." That's what *he* thought. But that was exactly what she didn't want to talk about.

Turning off at Exit 24, she said in a calmer voice, "Look. The first thing you have to know about my father is that he wanted boys. He didn't get any. So he was mad. So, being my father, he got even."

"Looks to me like he loves his daughters."

"Oh, for Christ's sake, John! It was made very clear to me that I was supposed to be a boy, that I was a disappointment —just because I was born female!"

His big hand covered hers for a moment. "Not to me. And, if you ask me, not to him, either. You hear the way he brags about you, how proud he is of you, tells his friend on the phone he has to go because his daughter the doctor has just come in all the way from Vermont! Come on, kiddo, give the guy a break!"

She was very glad to have the business of pulling up, lowering the window, paying the toll, raising the window, getting back into traffic, looking for the northway entrance. It was maddening, the way he dismissed every problem. He had to be the only adult living in the twentieth century untouched by the notion that human behavior had underlying motivations.

On the other hand, it was probably one of the reasons she depended on him. After spending all day, nearly every day, as a family physician, dealing with all the twisted motives and meanings and behaviors and interactions of her patients . . . trying to separate the psyche from the soma, the real from the imagined, the dangerous from the merely quirky, it was a relief to come home to John and deal with straightforward solid reality.

Home to John. It was still new to her, that idea, even after almost a year. She had been very leery of the whole idea, very leery. But it had worked out. And that surprised her, too. If she thought about it, her relationship with John was just one surprise after another. And if people wondered—and she knew they did—how a medical doctor could find happiness with a taciturn, undereducated ski resort manager and general handyman, well, it was none of their business, but she and John had hit it off from the moment they met. And they were still hitting it off. From the moment he moved in, he fit right in—even to picking the big old wing chair by the fireplace as his own. That was fine with her; the big old wine-colored sofa was her special place and most evenings found her stretched out on it, reading. She loved her house; it was a big old Victorian complete down to the last piece of gingerbread on the front porch eaves and it had plenty of room for living and her practice. Her office was totally separate. But it was right there; if she was needed in the middle of the night, she could be there in half a minute. John loved the house, too. Bit by bit he had fixed everything, starting with the old clanking plumbing.

In fact, she had really decided he was the man for her the day he had come by with a twisted ankle and the kitchen water pipes had burst while he was in the examining room and, pain and all, he very calmly, very expertly, very quickly limped about, repairing the damage. She had just stared at him in wonderment, at how swiftly and efficiently he dealt with it, and all with good humor. She had gone weak with gratitude and admiration.

She hadn't really stopped being grateful or admiring. But she had to face it: human behavior didn't interest or intrigue him. Whereas she had every reason to know that what people did to one another was at the root of just about every evil. If the day ever came when she told him everything that had happened in her family, he'd probably say it wasn't any of his business. Going beneath the surface just made him uneasy. He was at his best with straightforward things that could be solved by action. And she admired that about him! She loved it! He could fix anything, could and did, with great composure and confidence. But never in this world would he be able to understand the way she felt about her father.

"Give the guy a break?" she echoed. "Why the hell should I?"

He laughed again. "Well, for one thing, he sent you through medical school. How's that for a reason?"

"Dammit, John, only because he was talked into it."

Quietly, John said, "You're raising your voice, Marilyn. Tell me something: Did you ever walk up to him and say, 'Hey, Dad, I want to go to medical school, how about it?'"

"Of course not! He'd have said no. No question. I know exactly what he would have said. 'Marilyn, Marilyn . . .' No, excuse me, he'd have called me Moo Moo, just to put it on record that I was still a child as far as he was concerned. 'Moo Moo, sweetie-*piele*, what's this talk of medical school? Medical school, that's not for a girl! Tell you what: you want a doctor, you marry one!'" She stopped, triumphant, a bit out of breath. Her imitation of Jack, she knew, was very good.

Next to her, John drew in a breath. "The fact is, you live hundreds of miles from your family and they shouldn't have the power to get you this riled. You've made yourself your own life, with your own rules—and done a damn good job of it, too. The town thinks very highly of its lady doctor. You're awfully good, not just the medical part, but all the rest, too, calming people down and getting them to look at the *real* problem and sending them back home with a little hope . . ."

She knew what he meant. On the job, she was totally sure of herself, endlessly supportive, and full of energy. He was right; it was embarrassing that she should go home for a brief visit and find herself angry and bitter all over again, and hear herself bitching and moaning about things that had happened long long ago, in a different life.

"Anyway," he finished his thought, "I think you're terrific, kid." There was a pause, a long, weighted pause that she recognized; and then, ever so casually, he added, "Why don't we get married?"

It was perhaps the dozenth time he'd asked her and she was going to have to say no again. She hated this. She wished he would stop bringing it up. "Because," she answered, "it's more fun living in sin!" and he said it was good to hear her laugh again and they began to talk about his new snowmaking machines and the weather and the problems he was having with one of the oversexed instructors who went after every pretty female skier . . . and pretty soon her heart stopped racing and everything was back to normal again.

CHAPTER THREE

Saturday, November 30, 1985

At 9:03 in the morning, Deena was on line in D'Agostino's and, for a change, not hating it. Her mind was a million miles away . . . no, scratch that, a mile and a half away in Soho, in the Film Forum, sitting next to Luke Moorehead with his big warm hand holding hers. Which is exactly what had happened last night. Lovely.

She had just begun to unload her cart, when a voice from somewhere at waist level piped, "Excuse me. Please may I go ahead of you?"

She looked down at a slim little boy with a mop of dark hair and an earnest expression who reminded her of her first-born, Nat, years and years ago, of course, and it made her smile. There was a skateboard tucked under one arm, a huge bag of dry dog food hugged to his chest with the other.

"Sure, go ahead."

"My dog is sick and he needs to eat. He's a golden re-triever."

"That's one of my favorite dogs," Deena said.

His face brightened. "Oh, do you know Ranger?"

She was enchanted. "Should I? Is he famous in Brooklyn Heights?"

"Well, the little boy said, "he stands five foot seven. On his behind legs."

"And I stand five foot seven on *my* behind legs, too."

He laughed, that delicious little boy, looking up first to make sure she had meant it to be funny. And he was still grinning after he'd paid for the dog food and was skateboarding out the automatic door.

She paid for her groceries, feeling better and better about life. What a wonderful story this was going to make. It would be perfect in the new scene she was writing for class. Trying to write. Even Michael would have to enjoy the tale of Ranger the Famous Dog of Brooklyn Heights who stood five foot seven on his behind legs.

And he did. When she got into the house, he was waiting for her, miracle of miracles. He even took the groceries and said, "I'll help you put them away. I want you to come with me to buy a new coffee maker..."

"Michael, we have a perfectly good coffee maker."

"I mean an espresso machine. I saw one in the window of Leaf and Bean... it looks just like the machines they always had in the Village coffeehouse when you and I were first dating. Just looking at it, I could taste that wonderful strong coffee... Well, why not make it at home."

She wasn't particularly interested in espresso coffee, nor in tagging along with Michael while he acquired a new gadget. He was more than likely to discuss every single attribute and failing, to ask a million questions, and to ultimately try the patience of the salesman as well as hers. She did not like shopping with him. However, it would be mean to turn him down. He hated to shop alone. And he was obviously trying, in his own way, to make up... and far be it from her to step on his good mood—a rarity, these days. Anyway, a little boredom on Montague Street might be fitting punishment for a little flirtation with her teacher.

So, out they went, arm in arm. She enjoyed recounting her little saga of Ranger the Famous Dog, and Michael chuckled at it. In the shop, though, it was pretty much as she had imagined: she, standing first on one leg and then on the other, while Michael examined dozens of different coffee machines and asked penetrating questions about pressure gauges and exactly how many ounces comprised "a cup" and other less-than-fascinating details. Luckily, at these times, her active participation was not required and she could drift and dream, coming to life only to say the obligatory "Whatever you want, Michael, is fine with me."

This time, of course, the drifting and dreaming took her right back to last night and to Luke Moorehead. Luke Moorehead...tall and lean and blond and bearded. And young. Very young: twenty-seven years old, to her forty-three. Last night she had kept repeating those two numbers to herself. Last night, even as she offered him a lift home, she was telling herself the following story: she was *not* repeat *not* going to make a fool of herself with this very young man who, let's face it, was just being nice and friendly and wasn't really coming on to her.

She thought she was going to just drop him off, but he didn't want to be just dropped. When she pulled up on West Fourteenth Street in front of his loft building, he made no move to get out of the car and instead, started a conversation *about* the car. He liked her car. Hell, everyone liked her car. It was the favored car of the year. Which was, of course, why Michael had bought it for her.

"I didn't *want* it," she found herself telling Luke. "I really liked my old car just fine. In fact, I had just broken it in. So it looked a little shabby...*I* loved it. I even had a name for it. But it was not considered 'appropriate' for the wife of Michael Berman, Esq. And so, he 'surprised' me for my birthday." To her amazement, she found her eyes filling once again. "He had traded in my lovely old Volvo—*without asking me*! And he expected me to be delighted!"

"Oh, Jesus, that's terrible," Luke said, and patted her shoulder. Deena had to blink very hard against the tears that threatened to spill over. She certainly didn't want to start boo-hooing and spoil everything. It had been so nice, having a man actually *listening* to her, his eyes on her the whole time, one arm casually flung across the back of her seat. Oh God, casually! She was so painfully aware of that arm, his hand ...of *him*. She had to stop this.

"I know," Luke went on, "how painful it can be when someone gives you the present *they* want and not the one *you* want. When I was eleven, I desperately wanted a puppy for my birthday, and my old man more or less agreed that I could have one. I made all kinds of promises: I'd feed him, I'd take care of him. I even had a name for him. . . ." And here he gave her a little nudge and they smiled at each other.

"I'm not going to like the ending, am I?" Deena said.

"*I* didn't. What I found on the morning of my birthday was a bike." He paused and breathed out noisily. "Jesus. A bike. And when I bawled, my old man said, 'Better a bike rusting in the rain than a puppy starving to death because of your carelessness.' I never forgave him for that, never."

"Oh, Luke, how awful for you!"

They had looked at each other in the dim light cast by a nearby streetlamp. "You're a lovely lady, Deena," he said in a low tone, and there was a jolt in her chest as she waited, half in dread, half in anticipation, for . . . what? She didn't want to know the answer.

But when he stirred himself and said, "It's late, I'd better be going," she knew instantly *that* wasn't what she'd been waiting for.

"We've been here an hour," he went on, "and your husband will be worried."

"Michael? Worried? *If* he's even home yet, which he probably isn't." Oh my God, did that sound like an invitation? It wasn't. Was it?

Luke yawned and stretched in his seat. "I have three hours of editing ahead of me," he said. He turned to smile at her. "It's been wonderful, talking to you like this. I mean it." He leaned over and gave her the lightest of kisses on her mouth. It felt exactly like an electric shock. And then the door was open and he was gone, in a rush of bitter cold air, and all that was left was a glimpse of his face as he bent down outside for one moment, giving her a jaunty little salute.

She drove on home then, lecturing herself on reality, motherhood, apple pie, and the foolishness of middle-aged women allowed out on the loose in New York. In the dark. At the movies.

"Deena! I'm talking to you!"

Deena blinked and came abruptly out of her reverie, into the store with her husband. "Sorry."

"Well? What do you think?" She hesitated. She hadn't heard a single word. He gave her a look and went on. "Copper, do you think? Or stainless steel?"

"Oh, stainless steel, by all means." Did she sound enthusiastic enough? Apparently yes, because he smiled and said to the salesman, "You heard what the lady said. Stainless steel."

He was so happy with his new toy. He even put his arm around her shoulder as they strolled and gave her a squeeze. At the corner of Henry and Montague, waiting for the light to change, the woman next to her, struggling with her dog, said in a clear voice. "Will you stop that, Ranger?"

Ranger! Without even thinking about it, Deena turned and said, "Hi, Ranger. Are you feeling better?" She told the startled woman about her encounter this morning, ending by saying, "He's a darling boy. Your son, isn't he? I don't have the wrong Ranger, do I? I don't usually talk to strange dogs."

The woman began to laugh. "You've got the right Ranger, and thank you, yes, he is feeling better. And thank you, yes, Todd is my son and he usually is darling. Wait till I tell him I bumped into you and you asked after Ranger. He'll love it!"

They grinned at each other, two strangers linked together for a moment by sheer delight. Deena turned to Michael. But Michael was no longer next to her. She turned every which way; where in the world could he have gone? And then she saw him across the street in front of the bookstore.

She crossed to him and the minute she was near enough to hear him, he said, "What the hell was *that* all about?"

She decided to keep it light. "You remember, Michael. I told you on the way over. The little boy and his famous tall dog?" She smiled at him but got no response.

"How could you be sure it was the right dog?" He turned and started walking home.

"How many golden retrievers named Ranger hang out on Montague Street?"

"Deena," he said, stopping to turn to look at her, "it's no longer cute to clown around with strangers on the street. You're too old for that. It's . . . it's ridiculous. I had to walk away."

"Why? Why did you have to walk away, Michael? I'd really like to know?"

"It was embarrassing."

"Not to me. And not to Todd's mother. So why did it embarrass you?"

"Because . . . oh never mind, Deena, you're *always* embarrassing me."

"Oh, really? Well, you embarrass me, too. You needn't look so shocked and dismayed and perplexed, either, Michael. How about the night I invited my screenwriting class to come use our VCR?"

"What about it? I didn't say or do anything to embarrass you."

"No, of course not! All you did was stand there in the doorway, looking like a cranky old man, giving everyone your best lord-of-the-manor glare."

He made a face. "You always exaggerate. I didn't glare. I was surprised to find this bunch of strangers in my home, eating my food, drinking my liquor, and lounging all over my furniture. Surprised and, yes, I admit it, a bit uncomfortable. But . . . glare?"

"You glared, Michael and then you walked away without a word."

"What did you want me to say?"

"Hello everyone might have been nice."

He shrugged. "I was tired. I had been looking forward to a quiet hour or two with my wife. . . ."

"Bullshit!"

"Deena!"

"I'm sorry, Michael, but it's been a very long time since you've spent even a quiet minute or two with your wife. Don't expect me to believe that fairy tale!"

"Believe what you like, I did nothing to embarrass your . . . ah . . . classmates, nothing at all."

"You didn't have to *say* anything, Michael. You made it very clear that they were not welcome. Suddenly they all stopped smiling and laughing and suddenly nobody had anything to say to one another and suddenly everybody was gone. It was horribly embarrassing!"

"I can't be held accountable for their assumptions, Deena. Or for yours. At least *I* know when to keep my mouth shut."

She could feel the flush creeping up her face. "Meaning?"

"Meaning *you* never know *when* to stop."

"That's unfair . . . and it's not even true."

"You're not as funny as you like to think you are, Deena."

"Dammit, Michael, you knew what I was like when you married me." He motioned to her to lower her voice; she was damned if she would. Let anyone who passed by hear what she had to say; to hell with it. "Well, you did. I remember very well, Daddy saying to you, 'Michael, you're getting my clown. You'll be giving her straight lines for the rest of your life.' And do you remember what you answered?"

"What?"

"You said, 'I hope to give her everything her heart desires, sir.' You don't remember that?"

"No, I don't"

"Well, you said it. And now, let me tell you something." With every word, her anger expanded in her chest. She felt a choking sensation. "Here's what my heart desires, Michael. My heart desires that you leave me the hell alone."

Softly, reasonably, calmly, he said, "You're crazy, Deena." Suddenly, she could not stand being anywhere near him. She marched away, red splotches dancing in front of her eyes, heading blindly for home. If he dared to tell her once more how crazy she was, she would deck him. Pow, right in the kisser. She kept walking as fast as she could, fighting for breath, fighting for control, thinking, Fuck you, Michael, fuck you, fuck you, fuck you.

CHAPTER FOUR

Wednesday, December 11, 1985

As Deena rounded the corner of Forty-ninth and Madison, ducking her head against the chill wind that had sprung up overnight, she saw Noel and Zoe, half a block away and moving as fast as they could, bent almost double to escape the air's icy sting. She thought of calling to them, but even as she opened her mouth, they jumped into a cab and were gone. It *was* them, wasn't it? Of course it was; she couldn't mistake her own daughter, particularly since, this winter, Zoe was enamored of a marine sergeant's dress overcoat which she wore with a yard-long bright red muffler. No, you couldn't miss her, not in the light of day. But what in the world were they doing here? Hadn't Zoe said she was going up to Scarsdale today to visit a school friend?

It *was* nice, that two cousins were still friends after all these years. They'd always had a special closeness dating from the moment when Noel, at the ripe old age of two, had seen baby Zoe, no more than ten days old, and announced, "That *my* baby!" They had all laughed; how cute, how adorable!

47

Then Howard made the mistake of being reasonable. "Now, Noel, you know she's really Aunt Deena's baby."

And Little Noel's face had turned bright red with baby rage and he had stamped his feet, insisting, "Mine, mine, *mine!*" As it turned out, he'd been almost right. In a way, Zoe *was* his baby . . . she'd been under his special protection from that day to this and, as far as Deena knew, they confided in each other about everything.

Just a couple of days ago, Elaine had said, "I've never heard of cousins that close."

"Oh, Elaine, of course you have. Remember me and Cookie?"

"Oh, yeah, for a year or so. But we were both *girls*. Who ever heard of a boy and girl telling each other all their innermost thoughts?"

"I think they're both lucky, Elaine."

"Did I say I didn't approve? Did you hear me say I didn't like it?" And then Elaine had laughed at herself, adding, "Okay, okay, so I've worried a little bit from time to time that they might want to get married. Remember Aunt Helen and Uncle Lou?" And Deena had to laugh with her. Because Aunt Helen and Uncle Lou on Sylvia's side had been first cousins who married and the lone issue of their loins was Filthy Norman, their least favorite cousin, none too clever, and besides, he had *six toes*. Never mind scientific facts. Six toes was the *least* that could befall you if your parents were first cousins.

Personally, Deena didn't worry about Zoe and Noel becoming romantically involved. They were more like brother and sister. And that was no surprise. Noel was an only child and, without brother or sister of his own, he picked Zoe as substitute. Elaine didn't seem to realize how much he'd needed the warmth and security of a family; she'd gone to work barely a year after his birth and almost immediately had begun to build what would become Sweet Somethings, Lingerie for Every Woman sized 4 to 44. God, for the next five years Noel had eaten dinner five nights out of seven at Deena and Michael's, when Deena and Elaine were still living in the same building on West Ninety-fourth Street, before Michael had bought the house in Brooklyn Heights.

And there was the Rockefeller Cafe, at the end of the avenue of gilded angels with their golden trumpets. It was hokey but wonderful, Rockefeller Center in the Christmas season. And Elaine was already sitting, waiting for her, at a table by the window.

"Bah, humbug!" Deena greeted her. "How are you and how's the Christmas season at Sweet you-knows."

"The Christmas season at Sweet you-knows, my dear Deena, was last July. We're into bathing suits right now." Elaine laughed and added, "And don't try to fool me with your bah-humbugs. You've always been a sucker for Christmas."

"No, I haven't, not since I was eleven and I went on that hunger strike to force Sylvia to let us have a tree."

Elaine laughed and poured her sister a glass of wine. "Do I remember that! Sylvia just shrugged and said she was planning to put you on a diet anyway. Ha! You never needed a diet in your life! It was her way of saying, 'No way, baby.'"

"Hey, I still want one!"

"What Deena wants, Elaine will provide. Look outside, sweetie." They both glanced out the window, where the gigantic spruce, decorated with its huge multicolored balls and oversized twinkling lights, dominated Rockefeller Center. It dwarfed everything: the skaters on the rink, the crowds gathered at the railing over them, the avenue of gilded angels, the flags of all nations snapping about in the wind, even the outsized golden Prometheus who stretched his arms out above the scene.

"Elaine, what can I say? You're too good to me." They raised their glasses, smiling at each other, and drank. "But I still say bah humbug, and anyway, I'm Jewish, so what's in it for me?"

"Don't bad-mouth Christmas to a lady who sells sexy underwear." She eyed Deena speculatively. "Speaking of which, I don't know what model number you're wearing today, but you look terrific, you know that? Sexy, in fact."

Deena flushed a little. "Why so surprised?"

"Sexy's never been your style, Deena. And, frankly, you haven't been looking so hot lately, kind of down, kind of . . .

wan. And all of a sudden, here you are, *radiant* . . . yes, you are, so don't give me that look!"

"Well, I don't feel any different and I don't think I look any different and nothing in my life is different," Deena lied.

"Oh, come on, Deena! Half the time lately you've been in ga-ga land!"

Deena began to laugh. "Ga-ga land? Did I hear you correctly?"

Elaine fought it but finally gave in and allowed herself to laugh, too. "Seriously, Deena, you're lost in yourself an awful lot these past couple of months. Even Sylvia has noticed. You know Syl: she called me and said, 'Elaine, I want you to talk to your sister.' And then, of course, *I* had to say, 'About what, Sylvia?' And then *she* had to sigh and say, 'If I have to spell it out for you, okay then, I'll spell it out for you. Deena is not herself, that's all I can tell you, and I'm sure you know exactly what I'm talking about.'"

Now they were both laughing too hard to talk or to drink. It was funny, but it wasn't, Deena thought. Sylvia invariably used that gambit when one of her daughters had some kind of problem with which she would rather not deal directly—and that meant Something Big with a cap S and a cap B. She could talk to you about any *little* thing—and often did, as they all knew. She could tell you your makeup was all wrong . . . that you were looking too tired . . . that you didn't treat your father right . . . any of those things. But not anything emotional, certainly not anything remotely psychological in nature. No, anything *that* intimate got the you've-got-to-talk-to-your-sister treatment.

As soon as she was able, Deena said, "You can tell Sylvia I'm just fine."

Elaine eyed her a moment, then blurted out: "Is Michael having an affair?"

"Is Howard?"

"I'm sorry. I'm not doing this right. It's just that you have a kind of glitter and I thought maybe you were nervous about Michael . . . or something."

It occurred to Deena that Elaine was finding this very difficult. "Look. Elaine. I look good because I went out and bought myself a whole new bunch of makeup. My life is like anyone else's . . . there are ups and there are downs. And, if Sylvia really wants to know what's bothering me, you wouldn't want to tell her because it's Saul." Under the table-cloth, where her sister couldn't see, her fingers were crossed.

"What's with Saul?"

"Oh God—! I don't even know how to feel about him!" She pictured him, her baby, seventeen years old, tall, gangly, awkward, skinny, good-looking, oversexed, brilliant, irritating, exhausting, and of all the damn things, a redhead. She sighed; she found herself constantly sighing when she thought about him. "At home he buries himself in his room with the computer and pretends he can't hear me when I talk to him. At school he's like a wildman, doesn't bother to come to class regularly, spends a lot of time hanging out—I see him all the time, Elaine, whenever I'm out of my office there, and he's never in class, he's always in the hall or on the stairway or outside, making a nuisance of himself. And you know Michael: his notion of dealing with Saul is to make demands. Saul must do this and he must do that. But when the shit hits the fan, he's nowhere to be found."

"Sounds like your typical teenager."

"And your typical father? Never mind. That's what I thought. About Saul, I mean. But . . . well, he took one of those standardized tests at school in math. You know how good he is at math. Well, he got them all wrong. Every one!"

"Impossible!"

"That's what the headmaster said, too. He called Saul in and asked what it was all about. According to him, Saul just stood there and smirked. 'You're the best math student in this entire school, Saul,' he told him. 'There must be *some* explanation for this.' Oh hell, to make a long story short, Saul had finished the test very early. They wouldn't let him leave the room and he got bored so he moved all his answers over, one column to the left . . ."

"Why, in God's name?"

"Exactly. It was so self-destructive." She sighed again. "Well, Saul has been seeing Dick Seltzer, a kiddy shrink in the neighborhood. And now Dick wants to talk, to Michael and me. And Michael won't."

"What do you mean, Michael won't."

"Don't get me started, Elaine. Michael won't go. He says no way. He says he's not talking to any psychiatrist, not about *anything*. Period."

"Not even for his son."

"The way Michael sees it, Saul is brighter than the headmaster, he's too bright for his own good, and if I, his mother, would stop fooling around with my silly writing class quote unquote and paid more attention to his behavior, he'd straighten right out."

"Maybe he *does* need extra attention, Deena."

She tried very hard to keep her voice even. "This I'm hearing . . . from a woman who always said that her son raised himself?"

"Noel never gave me a moment's trouble."

Because I took care of him so often, Deena thought but did not say. *Me*, he gave a few moments of trouble. "I do hope," she said sweetly, "that you're not telling me I'm a lousy mother."

"Dammit, Deena, of course not! I didn't mean you. I meant that righteous bastard, his father."

"Now, wait, Elaine, before you bad-mouth Michael, it's not that simple." And, dammit, that's what she was *always* telling herself when Michael got to her. "It's not that simple, people are not statistics, they're not fictional characters with just one set of attitudes." And nice women did not hate their husbands, not even for a moment. She knew Michael had hang-ups when she married him. She had listened to his tales of childhood: of his grim, sad parents who could never forget their suffering. And who could never let *him* forget it, either. She knew it wasn't going to be easy, living with him. But she had been nineteen; at nineteen, you don't know what the hell you're talking about when you say it's not going to be easy.

And there was their waiter once more, hovering. But this time, Elaine said, "Oh, good. I'm starving." She laughed. "As usual."

"Me, too," Deena said.

Oh, sure, Elaine thought. You, too. She knew what Deena was going to do: order the diet special and pick at it. But it shouldn't make her feel bad, she scolded herself, not at this

late date; and besides, she liked her body and so did Howard,
and fuck the whole anorectic world! But still . . . It must be all
those years of Sylvia's subtle and not-so-subtle hints. "Maybe
you don't really want that other piece of pie, Elaine." Or
"Even too many apples put on the pounds." But she always
prepared elaborate meals and she always served everyone and
you always had to clean your plate even if dinner was something you hated. At least you had to clean your plate if you
wanted dessert, and Elaine Strauss always had wanted her
dessert. So why hadn't her mother kept all those heavy desserts off the table?

Oh, shit. What was the sense of going over and over the
same garbage? She was a big girl and always had been, in
spite of the endless dieting. Except, of course, for her wedding day. For that occasion Sylvia had arranged treatments
with a world-famous diet doctor. Treatments! Six months of
taking the crosstown bus twice a week to get weighed and shot
up with a magical potion! The object: she should fit into her
size ten wedding gown. Had it worked? Yes, it had worked.
You only needed to flip through the fifty-page, padded,
leather-bound, white and gold Our Wedding album, to behold
a beautiful slender young woman nobody had seen before or
since.

Of course, it had all come back, all forty-six pounds.
Within six months she was the old Elaine . . . and, as subtly as
she could manage, she was hiding her body from Howard—
getting undressed in the bathroom, walking around in nightgowns, turning out the lights before they screwed. Then, one
night, he grabbed her as she walked by him. He was sitting,
buck naked, on the edge of the bed; she was swathed in several yards of pale blue nylon replete with ruffles and lace.
"Elaine, we've got to talk."

She laughed, feeling a little self-conscious. "Sure, honey,
what about?"

"You've become . . . you're hiding from me and I've got to
know why. Have I done something? Said something to hurt
you? Please, you've got to tell me because it's making me
crazy."

When she broke down and told him she was afraid the sight
of her body would turn him off since she'd gained all the

weight, he looked at her with stupefaction. Then, he pulled her down next to him and held her close, kissing her neck, her ears, her throat, her shoulder, her chin, her nose, her hair, her hands, telling her over and over again how much he loved her. "Don't ever say such a thing to me again, ever," he told her. "I love you, Elaine. I love *you*, the person, not you the size ten or you the size fourteen or whatever. I don't care." She had begun to cry then, and when he tipped her face up and kissed her tears away, he smiled at her. "And anyway, how could you even think it? *Now* you're back to me and where you were when I fell in love with you. Which reminds me . . . since I never got to see all of you back then because your father might walk in any minute, how about it now?" And he, very slowly, undressed her, kissing every part of her body as he uncovered it, and then, very slowly, they made love and she cried again. What a man! She'd really picked the right one.

So to hell with dieting. If she was going to pay for this lunch—and she was—she was damn well going to enjoy it. Deena was having her usual broiled fish with a Tab. Let her. Elaine smiled up at the waiter and said, "Fettuccini Alfredo. Oh . . . and bring us each another glass of wine, stop that, Deena, I'm about to propose a toast and I'm damned if I'm going to do it on Tab with lemon."

Elaine eyed her sister across the table. It got tiresome, sometimes, trying to guess where Deena stood. First, she complains about Michael—and with good reason—and then, the minute I agree with her, she turns around and begins *defending* him. She wished Deena would either fish or cut bait. But of course she wasn't going to. So, Michael was a bit uptight; so, *Deena* was a bit uptight herself! So, he took himself too seriously and was something of a dictator, something of a male chauvinist! Let Deena come with her big sister and spend a little time in the business world . . . she'd soon see what slime was walking around out there calling itself a man! Next to some of the guys Elaine dealt with every goddamn day, Michael Berman looked pretty goddamn good.

And anyway, who in this world was perfect? Even perfect Howard had his flaws. Their marriage hadn't gone along without its bumps. When Noel was a year old, they nearly got separated when she said she was going back to work. Howard wanted her to be a full-time mother. She wanted to do something more interesting with her life than sit home and schlepp the kid to the playground. "Howard, darling, my brain is *already* turning to Jell-O . . . have a heart!" In the end he said okay, but only if she'd come into the business with him. And look how well it had worked out. He wasn't afraid of competition from her and when she had wanted to change the business, he was willing to listen and willing to change from retail to mail order. And now they were one of the largest.

The trick was not to cave in but to fight it through when there was a problem. The real trick, of course, was to know what you wanted. Deena had always been a little too quick to bend, in her opinion, too easily swayed. If Deena could figure out what it was she wanted in this world, she could probably have it. She had a lot of freedom in her marriage. Michael wasn't there half the time. So okay, that could be a pain in the ass; but it could also be a good thing for her. She had the time, the money, and the smarts to do whatever! Who else, in this day and age, could loaf around, playing at a part-time job, going back to school like a kid, narding around, still trying to find herself—*find herself*, at the age of forty-three! Come on! She was damned lucky! But instead of making the most of it all, she *kvetched*.

As for herself, she had a business to run, an important vendor coming at three. And when Sid Levine said three sharp, that's exactly what he meant. She had to be there. Howard always closed the deal and did the final numbers, but Sid liked her around, liked thinking he could sneak a look down the front of her dress every once in a while. And every once in a while, she let him. What the hell!

Luckily, here came the waiter with their wine. "Good," Elaine said, lifting her glass. "I want to toast you, Deena."

"Me?"

"This is the Twenty-third Annual Howard Barranger Celebratory Luncheon . . ."

"Is it really? Already?" They were both smiling . . . beaming, really. It had been Christmastime, twenty-three years ago, when Deena had interceded with Daddy. He had been adamantly against Howard, whom he disparagingly referred to as "that weak-voiced male," or, more usually, "that *faygeleh*."

"Huzzah," Deena said. "I'll drink to that. And to Howard. To Howard and Elaine and twenty-three more years."

They sipped, they smiled at each other. "To you, Deena. Thank you." And now Elaine took a deep breath. "I need you again."

"Tell me. If it's in my power, you know I'll do it. What is it?"

"I'm not comfortable with Daddy's sudden turnaround. It's not like him."

"Sure it is. You know what happened. Sylvia talked him into giving you at least a chance."

"Of course it was Sylvia. No, it's the *way* he's doing it. Suddenly, he's all affability, all welcoming. Come in, let's make a deal, I can look through the books. Linda will be glad to help me, check with Lawrence about any figures I don't understand, go look at the building, put it all in writing, whatever I want to say, however I need to do it . . ."

"That's bad? That sounds good."

"I don't trust it. You know Daddy as well as I do. He really deeply believes in the inferiority of women—"

"Elaine! Shame on you! He always encouraged us!"

Elaine waved her down. "Encouraged! Just as long as you did what he wanted you to do! Remember my CPA?"

"That! That was years ago. You've proved yourself to him over and over again."

"Deena. Try to listen to me, okay? First of all, he's opening up his arms too wide. That's not businesslike; that's a daddy indulging his little girl. And that's what I smell about the whole thing. Like, he's not taking it seriously. He's inviting me into . . . I don't know, it feels like an empty room he's inviting me into. I'll get there and guess what? No party."

"I hope I don't hear you accusing Daddy of lying to you."

"Would I accuse your beloved Daddy of lying? No, no, don't look at me like that. Let's call it . . . withholding, okay? My feeling is that he doesn't *really* mean it. That this isn't *really* a business deal. That he hopes I come up with zilch. I wouldn't even be very surprised if I wasn't given the real stuff to look at."

"Elaine! Now you *are* saying he's lying."

"Not really. Half-truthing, maybe. I don't know . . . I'm not accusing, I'm telling you, sister to sister, how I'm feeling. Look, Deena, I'm very serious about this. Sweet Somethings just about runs itself nowadays. I've been looking around for another business; diversity or die, right? I had no idea he was even thinking of selling Strauss Construction . . . Jesus, he always promised me the chance, dangled it in front of me. You know me, how I always loved buildings, how he used to take me around with him and have me guess how much a building was worth—"

"You were usually right, if I recall."

"That's right. Twelve years old and I could eyeball any building in midtown and tell you its worth in dollars per square foot! Dammit, Deena, I'm a helluva businesswoman! And he still thinks of me as the twelve-year-old who did this party trick that made all his friends *kvell*! 'Well, I see you've got your boy, Jack!' That's what they used to say—the idiots!"

"Oh, Elaine, they meant it as a compliment."

"But, Deena, it's *not* a compliment . . ." She could see by the look on Deena's face—the look that said as plainly as words, Subject Closed—that this was not the time to pursue Jack Strauss's male chauvinism. Daddy could do no wrong as far as Deena was concerned.

"Elaine, Elaine, go argue with the wall," Deena said, and it made them both laugh.

"I need you to go with me."

"Go with you? Where?"

"To the office."

"You don't need me, Elaine. I don't understand business, you know that."

"I want you there. Please. If you're there, he won't . . . do a number on me. If you're there, he'll be more relaxed and more reasonable. Oh, yes, he will. And what's more, *I* won't lose my temper." That should get her!

"Elaine, come on! I don't really make all that much difference! You're just flattering me. I'm flattered, I'm flattered; but you don't really need me. He knows damn well how brainy you are!"

"Oh, really? You think so? I've never been able to do enough to satisfy him, never! My CPA is the Jack Strauss Memorial Certification. Remember? When I was in college, begging him to let me come into the business with him? He told me if I was really serious about business, I'd go for my CPA. So I went for it. And I *still* wasn't good enough—not for *this* business. Oh no, that's for the men, not for mere women! What did I need? A sex-change operation?"

"Elaine!" Deena was a bit chagrined, but also amused. "Everyone's staring."

"Let them stare! *Will* you? Go with me?"

"Sure, sure. How could I say no to this dramatic marathon appeal? I'll go with you. Name the time. Oh. But not this afternoon."

"Why?" Elaine teased. "You got a heavy date?" She was only kidding, so the sudden flush that stained Deena's cheeks took her totally by surprise; she tucked away her observation for a time when she could think about it. "Okay," she went on quickly. "Not today. But tomorrow. Four o'clock okay?"

"Swell. Whenever you say. But you're wrong about Daddy. You'll see."

"I only hope I'll see . . . or, even better, that I'll *like* what I see."

CHAPTER FIVE

Thursday, December 12, 1985

The private elevator made its way slowly up to the penthouse floor, so Elaine had time to check herself out in the mirrored walls. Good. She looked confident, well-put-together, and businesslike. Oh, Christ, yes, above all businesslike. Because she knew him; he was more than likely to greet them with open arms, tell them how lovely they were looking, and call them his "best girls," and there would go any hope of getting down to real business! So . . . dressing for success was required, and she had done it quite well, she thought: the suit was black and tailored, but the blouse was pink and flowered —so he wouldn't laugh and *accuse* her of dressing for success. And the silver fox was as subtle reminder that she was, after all, his firstborn; it had been a gift to her on her forty-fifth. She licked her lips to bring up the shine and gave herself a satisfied smile.

"Don't worry, you look wonderful," Deena said.

"Who's worried?" But she had to laugh when Deena gave her a Look. They both knew with whom they were dealing.

"Just don't let him get to you, Lainie."

Elaine stifled a sigh. No use trying to explain to Daddy's favorite little girl how he always found fault with his eldest. If it wasn't something about her personally—"Forget to get your hair trimmed? No? Then what's that mess in the back, you call that a style? Shag is a good word for it"—it could be a comment about her business—which he loved to refer to as the *gotke* business: "Saw that ad in the Sunday *Times*. That model looks like a streetwalker." It could be anything: and it was always said lightly, it was always accompanied by a laugh. But it was always something. Always.

Once or twice she'd tried to make her sister understand, and Deena's answer had been, "But, Elaine, he only does it because he knows he'll get a rise out of you. Any time he tried it on me, I just laughed, so he stopped." Oh, sure. The fact was, he'd never given Deena the needle, really. But there was no way to make her believe it. Deena was his favorite child, and that's all there was to that.

She glanced at her sister's reflection. Deena looked younger, somehow, with an inner glow, like a woman in love. Probably that's what was bothering their mother, considering how many times Deena had hinted that she and Michael were having serious problems. Hell, you only had to be with them on Thanksgiving to feel the chill between them. But it couldn't be another man! That wasn't Deena's style at all. She was the original good girl, the one who followed all the rules. Look how she had wasted her intelligence and her talent all these years because the world said that a good mother stays home with her children, and she just automatically went along.

So she finally had signed up for a night class this year. Big deal. About time Deena got herself out of the house. Now let her quit that pretend job over at that self-indulgent private school and start herself on a real career. In fact—Elaine congratulated herself for this brainstorm—why not involve herself in the family business? If, of course, Daddy ever really let them in. Hell, Deena would do interiors; she had a creative bent. Didn't matter *what* she ended up doing! Let her deal with reality instead of fantasy. *Playwriting!* Honestly! Of all the goddamn notions! Let her put her enthusiasm into Strauss

Construction, let her work with her sister and find out the thrill of having something to show for all your effort.

"You don't have to tell me to stay cool," she answered finally. "I've already told myself about three hundred times. 'Don't lose your temper. Don't let him get to you. Watch your language.'" They both laughed because, of course, that was exactly what Deena had been longing to say but didn't quite dare. Of course, there was something Deena didn't know, something that Daddy had damned well better have an answer for, or there were going to be *plenty* of fireworks. "That's what you're here for, Deena," she added. "To be a calming influence." Deena made a deprecating face. "Oh, yes, you know you're good at that."

And then the door slid open and there they were, in the middle of the African jungle. Or so it seemed. Deena immediately had a wiseass comment: "I guess if Daddy's Tarzan and you're Jane, that leaves the role of Cheetah to me, doesn't it?"

"*I* like it," Elaine said. In fact, she loved it. She loved the way Daddy used his office as a showcase for the company. She did it, too. The showroom of Sweet Somethings was awash in pink velvet, lace curtains, bronze sconces, and all the accoutrements of a lady's boudoir, including thick pink wall-to-wall carpeting and—her very favorite touch—a mirrored ceiling. That ceiling had sold more lingerie than her top salesman. The buyers just loved it, thought it was a wonderful joke. And they didn't mind the fact that if you glanced up when the models were parading, you got a little extra cleavage.

Of course, there was nothing like that here. But this reception area had class. Daddy changed the decor completely about every four years, and this was only six months old. The last go-round, everything had been wood paneling, polished brass and black leather—kind of British-barrister's-office. Deena, naturally, had dubbed it Macho Man Meets Charles Dickens. This time, the walls were bronzed mirror, the floor was quarry tile, with a fountain set in the middle, and there were a dozen or more mirrored planters, each one holding a fully grown tree, all of them flourishing in the filtered light from the skylight plus up-lights cleverly hidden in the shrubbery. The thing Elaine loved the best about all this glitz was the fact that everything was reflected and re-reflected, again and again and again, on into infinity—not only the trees and the white bird cages filled with flowers, but the receptionist herself, the only unchanging item in the reception area, the stalwart and faithful Miss Madeleine Harvey, age unknown, with her carefully done faintly blue hair and her neat knits in various pastels. And here she was today, sitting bolt upright behind the enormous glass-topped desk with its white telephone console, dressed in powder blue, doubled and redoubled, front and rear, ad infinitum.

"Hello, hello, hello, hello," Deena greeted Miss Harvey and all her reflections.

Miss Harvey giggled and said, "Oh, Deena, you are the one. And Elaine, too! To what do we owe the honor?" She eyed them with fond indulgence. "We don't often see both of you at once." Her carefully cultivated British speech held the faintest whisper of Flatbush, Elaine thought. But she couldn't put her finger on exactly what it was that gave it away. She and Deena exchanged their Look; they had often conjectured on the possible reasons for Miss Harvey having decided at one point that she should pretend to be English, when her face and her mannerisms and everything about her fairly shouted "Brooklyn, USA."

"I'm sorry to say your father isn't here right now," Miss Harvey went on. "A meeting in Long Island City."

"A meeting? You're kidding!" The man was unbelievable: setting a definite date and time with her, even double-checking with her at her office no less, and then not *being* here! She felt all her resolutions melting away in a blaze of anger. "A *meeting*? He had an appointment with *me!*"

"Elaine, Elaine," Deena was patting her on the arm, just the way she used to when they were little. "Hold it down. It must have come up at the last minute . . ."

Elaine shrugged off her sister's placating hand. "I don't care. He could have called me. He *should* have called . . ."

"As a matter of fact," Miss Harvey began, "it was—"

"I don't care! He's got a fucking telephone, doesn't he?"

"Elaine!" Both voices spoke as one, but holding the exact same note of ladylike horror. Deena now steered her away, out of earshot.

"It's absolutely typical of him, Deena, absolutely typical! If it's only me, then he can just take off without saying a word! But I'm not dropping in today—this was to be a business meeting, which, by the way, Deena darling, concerns every last member of this family, not just me, and he has a helluva nerve, bringing me all the way crosstown—that goddamn traffic!—just to stand me up . . . !"

"Elaine, please wait a minute . . ."

"You think I'd take this from a buyer, or a vendor? Or *anybody* I do business with? Not Mr. Neiman or Mr. Marcus, or Mr. Lord and Taylor . . . nobody is big enough to do this to me!"

"Elaine, it was a last-minute thing. He couldn't help it, I'm sure."

"Goddamn it, Deena, I'm a busy woman. I have a catalog to get out, I have models to deal with, I have buyers, vendors, the auditors are due next month, there's a UPS strike threatened. Don't ask!"

"I know how hard you work, Elaine, but he didn't do it on purpose, I'm sure he didn't."

What the hell did Deena know about it? "You think I can take time off whenever I feel like it?" she demanded. "Like *you*?"

Deena's lips tightened ever so slightly. "Don't start in on me, Elaine. Please. Okay? Just don't start." Was Elaine making a crack about yesterday? No, she couldn't know that Deena's important appointment consisted of pacing her kitchen until Luke Morehead telephoned.

"This time, you don't know what you're talking about, Deena."

"I understand why this makes you angry, but there's sure to be a reasonable explanation. You're jumping to all kinds of conclusions before you give Daddy a chance to explain. I can't see that he's done anything so terrible. And if he has, *then* you have the right to be angry."

"Oh, really? I have your permission?" Now she was really burned. Furthermore, she was a little tired of having to deal with this thing all by herself. Dammit, she didn't care *what* Howard thought was the politic thing to do, the nice way to handle it . . . it was just too much! "Listen, Deena," she said, lowering her voice a little, "I have news for you. Remember how we each had fifteen percent of the business? You and me and Marilyn and Sylvia?"

"Of course. But wait a minute. What do you mean, *had*?"

"You catch on fast. Remember last week when I called you about it and asked if you'd back me up with your shares? Well, I called Marilyn, too. And then, I went to see Sylvia . . ."

"And? What are you trying to tell me?"

"Sylvia said well darling she'd be happy to help but unfortunately she no longer holds fifteen percent." Elaine paused, waiting for the words to sink in.

It took only a couple of seconds, and then a frown appeared on Deena's brow. "What happened to it?"

Elaine lowered her voice to a near-whisper. "She wouldn't tell me, would you believe? Got all mysterious and would only say that Daddy asked and she gave him half."

"Why, do you suppose?"

"I'll tell you what *I* suppose. At some point, he needed cash fast, so he took Syl's shares and sold them."

"He needed money so badly? But . . . *why*, for God's sake?"

"Good question. I was hoping he'd have a good answer for me today. And you see, all of a sudden he's very busy, very far away, and very unavailable. What a coincidence. It's the kind of *coincidence* that could make a girl lose her temper."

"Oh, Elaine! He may be difficult, he may be temperamental. But, come on, when has he ever been *sneaky*? I'm sure there's an explanation."

"There damn well better be." Then Deena suddenly put her finger to her lips, and a moment later Elaine heard the cheery plastic tone of Lawrence McElroy's best executive voice from right behind her shoulder.

"Well, well, look who's here, spitting nails! Don't look so surprised, Elaine, I saw you from my office and you had the same look on your face as the year you lost the sack race to me. I hope I'm not in for a bloody nose this time!" He laughed, putting an arm around her shoulder and squeezing. The fat bitch! he thought. He'd love to know what they were doing, nosing around here. The Strauss princesses had never shown much interest in what Daddy did to keep them in their overpriced clothes and exclusive private schools and their big fat allowances. They wanted something, he'd give you hundred-to-one odds they were here to get something out of Uncle Jack.

Jack, Lawrence reminded himself, not for the first time. Forget *Uncle* Jack. Old habits died hard. He'd been Uncle Jack for years, as far back as Lawrence could remember.

But once he started working here, Jack told him to cool it. "Makes the other men think we're related," he'd said. "I mean, it sounds like you're trying to *make* them think we're related . . . oh, shit," and he'd laughed like hell, "just call me Jack like all the rest of them, okay, Lawrence?" And he'd put his arm around Lawrence's shoulder and gave it a squeeze. A helluva guy, Jack Strauss.

So what were they after, these two? Why couldn't they leave the old man alone? They were out of his house, they were both married, with children of their own. And loaded, the both of them. What did they want? He knew the look on Fatso's face; she was up to no goddamn good. Gimme, gimme, he'd seen it a thousand times. She had a helluva nerve, wearing the fancy fur coat Jack had given her, to ask him for more. It was just like DiSanto said at the job meeting yesterday, "What do women want? I'll tell you what they want in one word. *More.*" They'd all laughed at that one; all of them were married, or had been. Except him.

While all these thoughts flew through his head, he had moved to Deena, Deena the beautiful, to give her a hug, and she leaned into him for just a second and then backed off as usual. Deena the cocktease. She could turn it on and off like it was coming out of a faucet. Jesus Christ, what a crush he'd had on her. He'd been a horny teenager, thirteen maybe, and she was what? Eighteen? Nineteen? Anyway, she was already married. But that didn't matter; she could have had seven husbands, it wouldn't have mattered. She got to him and she knew it and she played it for all it was worth, like leaning up against him all the time. Oh, she made believe it was accidental, but he knew . . . She liked giving him a hard-on, it amused her.

Hell, wasn't that the way they had always treated him, all of them, the mother and those sisters? Always having their little "in" jokes that no one else could get. When he was small, he was too naive to realize; later on, when he wised up, it just made him fucking mad, it made him hate them.

His mother was always telling him that Uncle Jack was just like family, Uncle Jack took care of them, she said, Uncle Jack was good and wonderful and Uncle Jack was kind to them, didn't they always get invited to all the Strauss social functions and family celebrations? Every birthday party, all the weddings and bas mitzvahs. Lawrence should be grateful, she said.

He remembered getting dressed for Marilyn's Sweet Sixteen, at Tavern-on-the-Green, whistling, brushing his hair, fourteen years old and feeling like hot shit. He'd dance with all the girls, get a feel here and there, maybe even get one of them outside with him in the dark under the trees. He knew he was good-looking. His mother didn't have to keep telling him; he could see it in the eyes of all the girls he met. Not to mention how many girls called him on the phone.

He'd never forget that birthday party, never as long as he lived. At first, Marilyn kind of said hello over her shoulder and took his carefully chosen gift and handed it, unopened, to her mother. And she didn't introduce him to anyone and when Mrs. Strauss took him around, the girls all looked at him as if he were a bug on the wall. He supposed later it was because he was in his good blue suit with a white shirt and a rep tie and a haircut for Christ's sake; whereas they were all super-casual in their tie-dyes, headbands, and hair, hair, hair. Of course, he must have looked straight out of St. Anthony's Catholic High School . . . which he was. It was so humiliating, so fucking humiliating once he realized how out of place and out of step he was. Why the hell had they invited him? They always invited him. But why? To show off how rich and powerful they were? To show him how small and insignificant and unimportant he was? He'd never forget it, never. He remembered looking up at the decorations, the huge *16* made out of glittering cardboard and the five million balloons and streamers, and thinking what a crock it all was. They could keep their fucking invitations! He just wished he had the money they'd spent on the fucking balloons!

Okay, if that's how they were going to be, he'd at least get his money's worth. He hung around the big table and ate all the best stuff, the roast beef, the turkey, and lots of those fancy cakes, the little ones. He thought of taking a few, wrapped in a napkin, to give Mom, but Jesus, if anyone saw him!

And then damned if Marilyn, the little Golden Girl herself, didn't come up to him and ask him to dance. He nearly dropped his teeth! The band was playing a Beatles tune, a slow one, and when he put his arms around her, very carefully, damned if she didn't just snuggle right up to him! Pressed her tits right into him. He almost died! What should he do? Back away and act like a little gentleman, or give her what she wanted? She was hot, all right, rubbing up against him as they danced. Oh, boy! His cock came right up. Could he push it up against her? Yes, he could; she didn't move away, not even a little.

So it really wasn't a surprise when she suggested that they go outside for a breath of air. Breath of air, my foot! She stepped right into his arms and began kissing him like he couldn't believe. Frenching him! Whoop*ee*! just like he'd always dreamed of! And he did it back to her and she *liked* it. He'd tried it before, with a girl at the St. Agnes dance, and she'd slapped his face. But not *this* girl. She moaned and held him tighter and then she reached down for his hand and *put it right on her tit*. He got so excited, he didn't hear a thing—shit, he didn't know where the hell he *was*, hardly—until a hand clamped down on his shoulder, yanked him away, and a voice bellowed, "What in hell is *this*?" Oh, Christ! Uncle Jack . . . and with a look on his face that could kill!

"You," Uncle Jack said to Marilyn, "you get back in there where you belong, with your guests." She disappeared very quickly and then he turned to Lawrence.

"As for you . . . I'm very disappointed in you, Lawrence. A real man restrains those feelings when he's with a nice girl."

"But Uncle Jack, it was her. She asked me to d—"

Uh-oh. Now he'd done it! Uncle Jack's face turned almost purple and for a minute Lawrence thought he was going to get belted for sure. "You damned ingrate! If you don't have more respect for me than *that*, then I don't want to have anything to do with you!" His voice was low and icy. Lawrence had never seen Uncle Jack like this and it scared him. "You'd better get some lessons in decency, young man, and loyalty, or you'll never get anywhere in this world."

His words filled Lawrence with a mixture of shame and resentment. He could feel himself blushing like a goddamn girl, and worse than that, he could feel tears forming. Tears! He prayed to the Virgin, he'd promise anything if only he didn't cry in front of Uncle Jack.

Later, he couldn't even remember what else Jack said to him. It was plenty: something about trust, something about his poor mother, all the usual shit. Christ, he made Lawrence feel like a fucking criminal! And it wasn't even his fault!

He left right after that, without going back inside, without saying good-bye to anybody. He rode around in the subway for a while, fuming, furious, so that he could get home late enough to satisfy his mother.

He walked through Stuyvesant Town in the dark, hating it, hating the big blocks of apartment buildings, all alike, with too many people all crammed together; hating the goddamn neighborhood, way over here on Avenue C, in the gut end of Manhattan, not like Central Park West; hating his too-tight squeaking shoes and the sweat under his arms and hating his mother for waiting up for him, all eager and full of hope, waiting to hear how much fun he had had with the rich kids. Shit!

Sure enough, there she was in her quilted robe, curled up on the couch, sipping from a cup of tea, smiling at him. He was going to lie to her, he really was. But the minute he saw her, so expectant, so goddamn dumb, he exploded. "Don't ever ask me to go to another goddamn Strauss shit party again!"

"Lawrence!"

"Goddamnit, Mother, don't ask me, don't ever make me do it again. Don't you realize how they think of us? Don't you see it? They feel sorry for us, Mother. We're the poor slobs who live in a low-class neighborhood!" And, in spite of her head-shaking, her frowns of denial, he persisted. "Oh, yes. Marilyn didn't want me there, her friends wouldn't look at me or talk to me or dance with me. I was dressed all wrong, the only one who was nice to me was Mrs. Strauss, and do you know where I've been since ten-fifteen? On the subway, going back and forth on the A train for three and a half hours!"

"My poor baby!" She started to get up from the sofa but he waved her down.

"Just stop, that's all. All these years you've been saying they're like family. They're *not*. They don't want us."

"Lawrence, please. They mean to be kind."

"Well, they're not. They're—"

And then he had to stop because he couldn't think of the word to describe the look of amusement on Elaine's face or the stuck-up way Deena had said, "No thank you, not right now, I'm tired" when he asked her to dance or the way those two friends of Marilyn's, the two blond girls had looked at him and giggled.

"They're not," he finished weakly. "And I'm not going again."

"Your Uncle Jack will feel so badly . . ."

Why did she have to bring *him* into it? Christ! Just the thought of Uncle Jack made his face feel hot. How would he ever face him again? What would Uncle Jack say about this to his mother? Oh, God, what a screwup! Jesus, he wished he could go back in time; he wouldn't even *go* to that goddamn Sweet Sixteen!

Miserable, he blurted out, "I don't give a damn how Uncle Jack feels!"

Too late to take it back; she had begun to cry, the way she did, without making a sound, just letting the tears flow out of her eyes, biting her lips and clenching her hands together in her lap.

He fled to his room, sitting on the edge of his bed, staring at the collection of college pennants Uncle Jack had brought him for his wall, thinking, Damn them, damn them, damn them! All those years he'd gone to all those parties believing he was welcome. And all that time it had been a lie, they had been pretending, laughing at him and his mother.

Oh, he shouldn't have said that, about not giving a damn about Uncle Jack; he knew it would make his mother feel bad. Uncle Jack was what she called a Very Special Friend. He was her boss first and foremost, but he was more than just her employer.

"When your daddy died in the war," she had explained over and over, "I had nobody and Uncle Jack helped us out. He found me this apartment when apartments were impossible to find; he paid for everything when you were born. And now he comes to visit you all the time because he believes every boy should have a man in his life." But he knew it was more than that. Uncle Jack *was* wonderful to him, played with him and listened to him and brought him presents. But it didn't take a genius to figure out that, after a while, Uncle Jack came around as much to see Lawrence's pretty blond mother as to toss a softball around with her little boy.

Agh, but that was a long long time ago. A lot of water had gone under the bridge since Marilyn's Sweet Sixteen. He'd seen her about a year ago and it made him laugh. Their darling Golden Girl had grown up into a bull dyke, wearing lumberjack shirts, for Christ's sake, and army boots! So she was a doctor, big deal! He'd rather die than go to her if *he* got sick. Which he never did.

"Well, Deena, you're looking super." He meant it. She was wearing tight pants and high-heeled boots, very sexy. She always did have gorgeous legs, and even as a teenager she dressed to show them off—them and her tight little butt. Whenever he thought of Deena, that's how he pictured her, in skintight pants. Today she had on a suede jacket, zipped open so the whole world could see it was lined with fur. She would! That was Deena Strauss, all right, excuse him, Deena Berman: to put the expensive fur on the inside and then, oh so casually, let everyone know it was there. She wasn't fooling him; he'd known her for years, more years than she probably wanted to admit. How old was she now . . . forty-two? Forty-three? She didn't look it, whatever it was. He wondered if she had had a face-lift . . . and then he wondered how much that jacket cost . . . must have set her husband back a couple of thou, anyway. "That's a great jacket," he said.

She gave him one of her best smiles. "Why, thank you, Lawrence. My husband gave it to me for my birthday."

For once she actually looked and sounded friendly. Lawrence felt warmed and expansive and he grinned at her and said, "You must be awfully good to deserve that!" Oh, shit, the look on her face! Low-class Lawerence had gone and

said the wrong thing! Oh, Christ, did he remember that look
from when he was a kid! What made her think she was so
fucking special? He joked like that with all kinds of women—
and he knew plenty of women—and none of them took it that
way.

She gave him one of those forced smiles she was so good
at and said, "I've always been very good to everyone I care
about." He guessed that told *him*, all right! He never knew
what the hell he was supposed to do with the Strauss girls; it
was a no-win situation.

What a turkey, Deena thought, he was never ever going to
grow up and act like an adult human being. He had always
managed somehow to say exactly the wrong thing to her, yet
here he was, Daddy's vice-president and, by all accounts, a
very good one. Daddy said he was the best outside man they'd
ever had. "He's got that Irish charm, that Irish gift of gab.
Lawrence can talk to anyone, and he's smart, too." Well,
maybe so, Deena thought, but you couldn't prove it by her.
When he was a little boy, she had found him whiny and obse-
quious, always talking too much or trying too hard and making an ass out of himself. And he wasn't much different now.

"Never mind all this social chitchat," Elaine said in a tight
voice. "Have *you* any idea where Daddy went? I need to call
him."

"You can't call him. He's in a *very* important meeting."

"He *had* a very important meeting . . . with *me*."

"Well, this is *really* important, Elaine."

"And what's that supposed to mean?"

"Six million dollars worth of importance."

Lawrence twinkled at Elaine and Deena thought, He looks
just like a Ken doll and he thinks just like one, too. There was
no denying that Lawrence McElroy was a handsome man, if
you liked them blocky, square-jawed, and black Irish. She
didn't, at least not *this* one. But she knew she was in the
minority. Daddy constantly commented on how the ladies fell
all over Lawrence. Apparently, they didn't know him, because
if they did, they would realize that he was Lawrence the Toy
Boy, all surface charm and no substance. Look at him now,
with his yuppie outfit—navy blue suit, light blue shirt with
white collar, rep tie, everything absolutely what was In this

very moment—striking his best Young Man on the Fast Track pose. Daddy kept saying how competent he was; how highly he was thought of. She just couldn't believe it. Well, maybe he was better with men. Right now he was not doing well at all with her sister, try though he might. His twinkles and smiles were not having the desired effect on Elaine, who had worked herself up to blast-off condition.

"And what am *I*? Worthless? The man made a business appointment and I came all the way crosstown to be here on time and if he couldn't be here, he owes me a telephone call at the very least Goddamnit!"

By the time she finished, she was yelling; and Deena put a warning hand on her shoulder. The whole office didn't have to know about this. She wished to hell Elaine would calm down. She wished to hell she hadn't allowed her sister to talk her into coming today.

As evenly as she could, she said, "Elaine, this isn't going to help anything," preparing herself for an onslaught. "Let's go downstairs and have a cup of coffee and discuss it." For a moment she thought it was going to work, but then stupid Lawrence had to open his stupid mouth.

"Good idea. Elaine always did have a real short fuse."

It took Elaine about six tenths of a second to turn scarlet, to thrust out her jaw, and to snarl, "Oh really? And I've heard you have a real short cock, little man!"

Deena turned instantly to Miss Harvey, who had her head carefully ducked away from them. But anyone could see the look of shocked consternation refected in one of the ubiquitous mirrors.

"Go fuck yourself!" Lawrence gritted. "You ball-breaking, castrating bitch!"

"Lawrence!" Deena found herself shouting; and she was by no means the only one. Linda McElroy, Lawrence's mother, Daddy's long-time secretary, had appeared noiselessly in the doorway leading to Daddy's suite. Once again Deena marveled at Linda's impeccable neatness. She had never—not even at one of the office picnics, where everyone was running around jumping and leaping, competing their hearts out in all kinds of races—had one hair out of place.

She looked like an aging Miss Rheingold—and, in fact,

she had actually been a Miss Subways, years ago. No, Deena took it back, she really looked like an aging Barbie doll, still curvaceous, still beautifully made up, still pretty. She must be close to sixty, Deena thought, but she certainly didn't look it—not at first glance, anyway. And still not the least expression on her beautifully modeled face to even hint at what she might be thinking or feeling.

Her voice was mild. "Lawrence, I'm sure you'll excuse us." And she gestured to the two sisters with her lovely manicured long-fingered hands. "Dee Dee? Lainie? Would you come with me now?"

How her voice changed, Deena marveled, without it being terribly blatant. The nonjudgmental, distant tone with which she had addressed Lawrence was suddenly suffused with warmth and welcome. "It's *so* good to see you girls."

Still hoping to make some sort of peace out of the situation, Deena laughed lightly and said, "Let me tell you, Linda, you're the only person in the entire universe I'll allow to call me a girl." And Elaine added, "Not to mention 'Lainie' or 'Dee Dee.' Honestly, Linda, can't you forget you ever heard those names?" She was smiling.

Linda laughed. "I'm sorry. It's all those years of seeing the two of you at the company picnics, so adorable, dressed like twins . . . your mother insisted on that, you know! Lainie in blue or green and Dee Dee in red or lavender . . . dancing around, begging me to make pigtails . . ."

A sudden complete memory flashed into Deena's head. "With flowers in them . . . remember, Elaine? Oh, Linda, I'd forgotten about the pigtails with daisies woven into them. Oh, God, I *loved* them!"

By this time they had made their way down the mirrored hallway with the thick gray carpeting to Linda's large airy office right next to Daddy's. Linda preceded them, walking with dainty steps that Deena found an irritant. Dammit, the woman never relaxed. Every single gesture, even the littlest one, was carefully posed and carefully performed. Just like Lawrence, it occurred to Deena. Well, big surprise! They were both so studied! God, if she had to work all day with either of them, she'd go right out of her mind. They were unreal. And yet, Daddy thought the world of both of them, doted on them.

It didn't seem to fit. Daddy was so exuberant, so uninhibited, so *natural*! It just didn't make sense.

Linda sat down carefully behind her big shiny Louis XIV desk—her entire office was antique reproductions, a sudden contrast to the high-tech glitter of the rest of the place—and graciously gestured them to the velvet-upholstered love seat facing her.

Why was she suddenly so damned aware of all this? It was bothersome. For many years she hadn't really looked at Linda —or Lawrence either, for that matter. They were just kind of *there*, four times a year at office functions, twice a year at Sylvia's giant cocktail parties, blending into the woodwork, just part of the background. She hadn't really bothered her head with Linda since the year she turned eleven.

Before then, Linda had been the effusive, warm, beautiful blond lady who magically appeared every once in a while from the recesses of that magical place called Daddy's office, in order to play with Deena and Elaine, to read them stories, to make pigtails, to twirl them around, to play endless games of London Bridge, Candyland, and, later on, Monopoly. And then, that year, suddenly, Deena had seen that the warmth, the hugs and kisses, the little cries of delight, were false. Something calculating and cold in those wide gray eyes had rung a warning bell in her brain. For the first time she had seen how when Linda swooped down on them to give them perfumed embraces, her attention was really directed elsewhere, to Daddy. And eleven-year-old Deena had known then, suddenly and certainly, that the whole thing was a big act, meant for an audience of one. Linda didn't really like Deena and Elaine, not even baby Marilyn, whom the whole world adored. She didn't care about them at all, Deena had realized, except that they were Daddy's girls. She was buttering up the boss!

"Now then," Linda said with her best smile. "What seems to be the trouble? Maybe I can help."

"Can you make Daddy appear?" Elaine demanded.

"Nobody, Elaine dear, can *make* your father do *anything*." A little laugh, just to show she was making her little joke.

"He had an appointment with me."

Linda glanced down at her giant desk calendar. "I don't have it here."

"That doesn't mean," Elaine said in a tone Deena recognized as an early-warning signal, "it doesn't exist." She pulled out her blue calfskin date book and opened it for Linda to see. No more scenes, Elaine, Deena begged silently.

"Elaine, I'm not doubting your word. I'm merely telling you *I* had no idea . . . if I had known, I surely would have called you when this Long Island City thing came up so suddenly."

"Well, maybe it doesn't matter," Elaine said in a mollified tone. "I just need to have a look at some of the files. Daddy asked me to give him some ideas about the project on Ninth Avenue."

"Oh, dear, I wish I could help you, Elaine. But I can't. I'm sorry."

"You don't have to do anything. I'll just go quiet as a mouse into the office for an hour or so and find what I need."

The look of genteel horror on Linda McElroy's face was a mime's delight. "Oh, no! You can't do that!" Deena wanted to laugh but knew she mustn't.

Elaine's voice took on an ominous edge. "Why the hell not?"

"Because, Lainie dear, the first thing your father ever told me when I came to work here was nobody goes into his office without his express permission."

"My dear Linda, of course he didn't mean me."

"Oh, Lainie, I wouldn't let your mother herself in there without his say-so."

Elaine got up from the love seat and dragged in a deep breath. Looking up at her sister, Deena thought how imposing, how formidable, how almost frightening Elaine in full force could be. It wasn't just her size, nor her blazing good looks nor her ramrod-straight bearing. It was the power of self-confidence; it almost seemed to emanate from her in visible rays, like the drawings in a comic book. Linda seemed to shrink a bit, but she was not ready to give even an inch—not to mention the key to Jack Strauss's private office.

"Look, Linda, it's none of your business, but there are good and sufficient reasons why I have to get in there." In answer to Linda's stubborn shakes of the head, she forged on. "We're missing some shares, the ones Daddy gave the women in his family. I have to find out what happened to them, see? That's all it is . . . nothing to do with any of the business he's doing now . . . it's those shares that concern me."

Linda continued to shake her head and at the same time she couldn't prevent a smirky little smile from curling her mouth.

The words came straight from Deena's mind to her lips: "*You* have those shares. My mother's shares."

"I have shares. But they're mine, please understand *that*."

Elaine interrupted. "Wait a minute, Linda. We're all capable of adding it up . . . and if you have any shares at all, they are the ones my father took back from my mother."

Stubbornly: "I don't know where he took them from. He gave them to *me*."

Deena persisted, puzzled. "But . . . why would he do that?" By this time she had gotten up to stand by Elaine's side, and with that, Elaine put a sisterly hand on her shoulder.

"I know why," Elaine said in a strangled voice. "You . . . and Daddy!"

Deena turned to stare at her sister. They looked at each other in silent and dawning comprehension. Then she looked over at Linda. Oh, God, no, Deena thought, feeling sick to her stomach.

Linda had come to her feet, her hands splayed on the polished desk, her face paper-white, her posture rigid. "What a disgusting thing to suggest!"

Elaine gave a nasty laugh. "Yes, it is!" she agreed. "But true, nonetheless. Isn't it?"

"Think what you think."

But Deena didn't like anything that was whirling through her brain. She couldn't seem to take her eyes off Linda; she felt mesmerized by the sapphire earrings twinkling in her ears, earrings Deena suddenly knew with certainty had been a gift from her father. Then she felt Elaine's arm around her shoulders, felt Elaine turning her around, heard Elaine say, "Come on, Deena, let's go."

CHAPTER SIX

Thursday,
July 27, 1950

New York that summer of 1950 had been stifling; and today you could hardly breathe. The sidewalk was so hot, it was burning her feet right through her new patent leather pumps. So Linda Collins hurried as she made her way toward Union Square. But the most important reason for her rush was she had something really special to tell Frances Corwin, her very best friend who worked in a big insurance office over on Twentieth Street. Most days, they had lunch together; in fine weather, Union Square Park was their favorite spot. It was always green and cool and inviting, no matter how high the humidity got. And in New York City, as Linda was learning, the humidity often got unbearable.

And there was Fran, sitting on their usual bench under a big tree, fanning herself with a newspaper, waving hello. When Linda got close enough, Frannie called out, "Love your hat!" Linda smiled broadly; she loved it herself. It was a white straw sailor hat with a broad brim and a bright navy blue ribbon that hung down her back. Her dress today was also nautical: blue piqué with a big white sailor collar. Linda smiled at her friend. "Thanks. Love yours, too." And they giggled; their hats were identical; they had bought them together just yesterday at Klein's. Two-fifty, on sale.

"But you're so dressed *up* today," Frannie added as Linda carefully arranged herself on the bench, first putting down a newspaper to sit on. "What's the occasion?" Her big brown eyes sparkled with anticipation. They told each other *everything*, so Frannie knew what was going on with Linda and her handsome boss. "I just know something's happened. Tell all, Linda!"

Frannie was still living in a tiny room at the Webster Apartments for Working Women. Linda had started out at the Webster—in fact, that was where she and Frannie had met, in line at the basement cafeteria—but Linda had known from the first that if she wanted to find a rich, sophisticated man, she'd just better move onward and upward, and just as soon as possible.

Frannie's mother, up in Schenectady, though, was horrified at the idea of her daughter living on her own. She wouldn't *hear* of it, not even as Linda's roommate. Frannie really believed her mother would have a heart attack if she went against her. And so there she still was, stuck where you could only bring your date into one of the Beau Parlors. These were like stage sets, all fixed up to look like a living room but totally open to the view of anyone and everyone who walked by. Naturally, she didn't date much. What kind of man would be interested in a girl who lived in an old-maid place like that?

So Frannie lived vicariously a lot through Linda's love life. She got just as excited over Linda's various suitors as Linda did . . . sometimes, even more so. It was great fun to tell her stuff; she wanted to hear every single detail. Nothing ever bored her. So, Linda had a little fun taking her sandwich and fruit very slowly out of the paper bag and then unwrapping the wax paper very slowly, making Frannie wait. Truthfully, she could hardly stand it herself, waiting to tell.

"He asked me out for dinner," she announced, sitting back to enjoy Frannie's squeals of excitement. "I mean, a real date."

"Well, he *should*. I mean, all those times you worked late and ate sandwiches up in the office . . . you even broke dates for him, Linda! Maybe he's just being nice?" One of the irritating things about Fran's interest in Linda's life was that sometimes she set up objections and arguments instead of being enthusiastic and encouraging. And then Linda would have to justify her position.

"No, it's not that at all. He put his hand over mine and, Frannie, I swear, I could feel the electricity. *Oooh.* I just know he feels the same way I do. He *must.*"

Frannie said, "Men always like you, Linda. You're so pretty! And now you're a celebrity, too. I don't know why you even bother with him, he's so old. Well, I'm sorry, but he *is.* And after all, you're a Miss Subways; your phone's been ringing right off the hook." Modestly, Linda lowered her eyes. "Well, then. A little crush on your boss is okay—I know I've got one on *mine*—but after all, Mr. Strauss *is* married."

"Not happily."

"They all say that!"

Linda held her tongue. She could say, "What do *you* know about what all men say?" but she wouldn't. She knew where Frannie got her ideas about men: *True Confessions.*

"Didn't he pack them all off to the mountains for the whole summer?" she said. "You don't think that was *really* because of the heat wave, do you? Ever since she left, Frannie, he's been . . . different." She took a small bite out of her sandwich to hide the smile she couldn't stop, blotting her lips with a tissue. "We're going to a really nice restaurant—where we can get better acquainted, he said. Frannie, I think I'm going to have a very important decision to make. Lordy, it kept me up half the night." She paused; it was important that Frannie realize how serious her next words were going to be. "Do I want to be responsible for breaking up a marriage?"

"Oh, Linda, you wouldn't! Aren't there two children already . . . and her pregnant? Isn't she having the new baby soon?"

"In the fall," Linda said shortly. "But the decision isn't all in *my* hands, you know."

"Oh, Linda! Do you think he really would?"

"You should see the way he's been looking at me. He's falling, Frannie, and falling *hard.*" They both giggled nervously. "I've known the way he feels for months. You remember, I told you how he brushes up against me or holds my hand a little too long and tells me how sweet and pretty I am and how good I smell. What do you call *that*? And you remember how he put up the Miss Subways poster, right in his private office where everyone could see it, the minute it came out. He ordered two dozen from the Transit Authority and he's been handing them out! Frannie, he brags about me! Tells everybody he has the best-looking secretary in New York City! What do you call *that*?"

She sat back, a bit breathless, and fanned herself again. Frannie, momentarily silenced by this impressive list of love signs, finally said cautiously: "You know what everyone always says, Linda: 'They never leave their wives.'"

"Frances Corwin, shame on you! Who's talking about him leaving his wife? We haven't even had dinner yet!" And then Linda smiled. "But I know when a man's got it bad and this man has got it bad, *real* bad."

It was the perfect place for a romantic dinner: dim, candle-lit, even air-conditioned. The carpeting underfoot was soft and thick, the waiters were all wearing tuxes, and she was very glad she had put on a really good dress. Jack asked for a banquette so they could sit right next to each other. And then he got as close as he could, so their knees were touching, and threw his arms across the back, his fingers resting lightly on her bare arm. It gave her the shivers and it made her feel shy all of a sudden. She slid a glance at him from under her lashes.

He was so handsome! She'd always thought so, right from the first. She liked stocky men with big chests and deep voices and thick wavy dark hair. She loved the smell of his shaving lotion in the morning and the blue shadow that appeared on his jaw every afternoon.

She bet he had a lot of hair on his chest . . . oh, just the thought of him that way made her blush! He must have noticed it because he moved away from her a little. Underneath his gruff, tough business manner, he was a true gentleman. Oh, she knew what they'd say about him back home. They'd say well, he might be rich and successful, but he was a Jew. Well, yes, he was; but *some* people were able to outgrow small-town attitudes and prejudices; and anyway, everyone knew Jewish men made the best husbands.

He lifted his martini, and she raised her cocktail, and he said, "Together at last!" It was so thrilling. She took a little sip. Then he linked their arms and offered her his glass, turning it so that she would put her lips where his had been. She took a tiny sip, making a face. "This is much too strong for me!"

Jack laughed. "It's a man's drink, that's why."

Smiling into his dark eyes, she held her glass up to his lips; but he shook his head. "Anything that comes pink, no thanks!" Why did he say that? It made her feel like a fool. But then he laughed and said, "I was only kidding, don't look like that, okay?" He bent his head and lightly kissed her fingers. Oh, God! So romantic!

He ordered dinner for both of them without asking her what she wanted. "Let me choose for you," he said, and the way he looked at her when he said it made her feel faint. Jack Strauss was so very definite, so very strong, so very sure of himself. She loved being with him and having him take care of everything. That's how it was supposed to be. Most of her dates didn't know *anything* about how to treat her. The local movie, supper at a cheap Italian restaurant, a boat ride up to Bear Mountain . . . was any of that stuff supposed to impress her?

This was more like it: dinner at The Embers, one of New York's best nightclubs, and George Shearing would be playing later on. She looked around to gather details she could relay to Frannie tomorrow, the big grand piano, the mirrored walls, the beautiful clothes the women were wearing. And the jewels! And she was here, Linda Collins from Norfolk, Virginia, sitting right in the middle of The Embers waiting for her steak dinner, medium rare, sipping on a cocktail, sitting next to a rich older man who was crazy about her. This was the life!

Over dessert he cleared his throat and said, very seriously, "Linda, we have to talk. About us." And she nearly stopped breathing. It was happening, it was really happening.

"What about us?" A shy look, up from under her lashes. And sure enough, it got to him; he reached over and grasped her hand.

"Linda, you must know how I've been fighting this . . . you're blushing again, I love how it makes you look. You're so beautiful, Linda, so pink and white and delicate. Whenever I look at you, I want—"

Oh, he couldn't stop now! "Yes?"

"I want to take you in my arms and kiss you until you faint. Sometimes—" He moved close again and grabbed her other hand, too. "Sometimes, I get crazy from wanting to hold you. Why, Linda, you're trembling. Have I frightened you? Listen. If I'm out of line, just say the word and it never happened, I never said a single thing. And I promise you, it'll never happen again, Linda?"

His eyes pleaded with her, his mouth was so close to hers. She felt dizzy with it all. She would never forget this moment, never as long as she lived.

"Oh, Jack," she burst out. "Please don't talk like that. I've been waiting for this for so long! I've been fighting it, too! But I'm so crazy about you, I can't fight it anymore!"

"Oh, Linda! Oh, baby! Oh, you doll!" He caught in a rasping breath and then, right there at the table, bent his head and put his lips on hers. He was kissing her and it was so impulsive and romantic. It was obvious he just couldn't help himself. And she couldn't help kissing him back.

And then he pulled away, breathing hard. "We'd better get out of here."

She was a little nervous about letting him into her apartment. What if he took it for an invitation to go all the way? But if she sent him home, maybe he'd never ask her out again.

She should have known better. He was a gentleman, never even touched her until after she'd gotten them both a lemonade from the fridge and they were sitting side by side on the sofa. She didn't want him to misunderstand. She might not be a virgin, but she had been *engaged* to Edgar. She was no easy woman even though she'd been jilted by a man who didn't deserve her in the first place, and was now forced to make her own way and live by herself in New York City. She'd not given herself to anyone else and she'd been propositioned—plenty!

She was so glad she'd straightened up this morning; the

room looked real pretty. You'd never guess this was her bed-room, too, not by looking. The daybed came from the Salva-tion Army store down the block; she'd recovered it herself in a pretty pink chintz and shined up the brass. In a secondhand shop on Second Avenue she found the oak table with the carved pedestal and then, in a magazine, she saw the cutest idea: you took four different chairs and painted them all with gold paint. She'd made the curtains herself, too. And, this morning, she'd put a pink silk scarf over the lamp on the end table—it was something Fran had seen in the *Woman's Home Companion*—and it made the light soft and romantic. Jack looked around and said, "What a pretty feminine little place. Just like the lady who lives here." And he reached over and took her hand. And didn't let it go.

There was low music coming from the radio, and after a minute or two Jack pulled her up with him and said, "May I have this dance?" She nearly melted away with tenderness. He was the most wonderful, sophisticated man she'd ever met in her life, and she didn't *care* that he was married. She didn't care what happened; she could never give him up.

They didn't really dance, just held on to each other and swayed and then he began to kiss her neck right under the ear and when she sighed, he moved his lips to the pulse in her throat and then down to the swell of her breasts just above the neckline. She couldn't help moaning a little and his grip tight-ened on her. The next thing she knew, they were kissing deeply, rapturously, his arms wrapped tightly around her, hers around his neck.

They kissed and kissed, murmuring sweet words to each other, and then suddenly he pushed himself away from her. In a gruff voice, he said, "I'd better leave before—"

"I know, I know."

"Linda, this is crazy. I like you much too much."

"Oh, Jack!" And then they were kissing again. And again and again. When his hand reached down the front of her dress and she felt his fingers on her nipple, she shuddered with excitement and this time *she* pulled away.

"We shouldn't be doing this! You're a married man!"

"That has nothing to do with us! I'm crazy about you, Linda, you're everything I ever dreamed of!"

"Am I, Jack? Am I really?"

"The first minute I saw you, I took one look and I said to myself, Jack Strauss, there's your dream girl come to life. You're so feminine, so soft and sweet and giving . . . and that Southern drawl, oh! When you talk, it's like music." He reached out for her, pulling her close, and bent his head to kiss her again, but she shook her head and took two tiny steps backward, away from him, putting her hand gently on his chest.

"No, Jack, it's time for you to leave now. I may be a woman, but I can be tempted. I may as well warn you right now, Jack Strauss, I am a woman of strong passion."

"Oh, Linda! Don't send me away, please! I'm a lonely man and I need you!"

"Oh, Jack, you must go, you really must." Oh, the woebegone look on his face, it was wonderful. "For now," she added.

"Then . . . you'll see me again?"

"Whenever you want, *Mr. Strauss*."

He buried his lips in her neck, nibbling softly at her skin and growling in his throat. "No more Mr. Strauss! Never again. Promise."

"Oh, Jack! Of course I promise."

"Tomorrow night. Dinner. And then, how about a carriage ride around Central Park in the moonlight . . . and then . . . *home*."

"Yes, Jack," she said, her heart full to bursting. "Oh, yes." She could hardly wait for tomorrow. She had so much to tell Fran!

CHAPTER SEVEN

Saturday, December 9, 1950

It had been just after lunch. The good smell of Sylvia's mushroom barley soup lingered in the air, even out in the hallway, where Jack was rummaging in the closet for his heavy coat. Deena clung to his legs, putting her hands in his pockets looking for Life Savers; he absentmindedly tousled her curly hair, dragging her along as he moved. Neither he nor the child seemed to mind.

Sylvia appeared from the kitchen, wiping her hands on her flowered apron. The most casual observer would have known immediately that this woman was the mother of this little girl. They both had the same oval face, the same large brilliant eyes, the same thick curling dark hair. They looked so much alike, it was startling.

"Remember, it's Hanukkah, Jack."

"After two pairs of ice skates and two new dolls with their magic skin and their trunks of clothes not to mention two real pearl necklaces, how could I forget Hanukkah? Deena, darling, don't do that now. Daddy's got to get going."

"Just come home before dark, okay? So we can light the

menorah. Don't get lost at the office like you've been doing
lately."

Jack gave his wife a sharp look, but her face was as bland
as butter, smiling a little, her eyes wide and clear. He patted
her shoulder. "I hear you, I hear you. Deena, *bubeleh*, don't
step on Daddy's feet."

The little girl said, "But I want to walk with you, Daddy."
Without waiting for further permission, she put her feet on top
of his and grabbed him around the waist.

"Deena," her mother protested. "Did you hear what Daddy
just told you? You're seven years old, too big to walk on
Daddy's feet!"

"It's all right, Sylvia." He marched up the hallway with the
little girl clinging to him, laughing loudly. At the end of the
hall he paused to turn around and almost collided with Elaine,
coming out of her room at a run. "Lainie! How many times
have I told you, watch where you're going! You've gotten so
clumsy all of a sudden. Maybe you should go back to dance
lessons and take off some of that extra weight."

Elaine, all dressed up in a new plaid skirt and Mary Janes,
stopped dead and looked down at herself with dismay. From
the other end of the hall her mother said, "Jack, you know
that's baby fat. Elaine is a growing girl." Elaine at nine was
the first girl in her class to need a bra and the first girl in her
class to have a boyfriend. Her face was stunning although
surprisingly delicate in contrast to the rather tubby body.

Now, her fists on her hips in an obvious imitation of an
adult, she demanded, "Yes, Daddy, I'm a growing girl! And
anyway, what the hell is going on here? We're due at the
office!"

"Watch your tongue, young lady, before I wash out your
mouth with soap. What kind of language is that, to use to your
father?"

Elaine pouted while Sylvia burst into laughter. "Jack, Jack,
where do you think she learned it?"

"Not from me! I never talk like that!"

She laughed harder. "Oh, no! Not you!"

"What's so funny? I don't."

"Daddy, that's what you say all the time!" Elaine insisted.

"Enough from you, smart mouth!" Elaine scowled like a

thundercloud and ran into her room, slamming the door loudly.

Her arms still wrapped firmly around him, Deena chanted, "Daddy says, What the hell is going on here and Daddy says, No good bastard when we're in the car . . ."

He looked down at her. "You, too? I need another woman giving me a hard time? Off my feet, you monkey!"

"But, Daddy, I want another ride!"

"A bike is to ride, not a poor tired old daddy!" But he was grinning broadly. "Go!" He gave her a little spank on her round behind, watching her fondly as she ran off.

"You see?" he said to Sylvia. "You heard? She listens to the big one using that language, and right away she's copying."

"Excuse me, but Deena was quoting you, Jack, not her sister."

"Same thing."

She opened her mouth, a little frown between her eyes, when there came a loud crash and then an even louder wail from the living room. Both of them raced in, to find Deena half under her shiny new bicycle, the remains of a Chinese patterned vase lying in shards all around her.

"Deena!" Sylvia scolded as she ran to her daughter, picking up pieces of the debris. "How many times do I have to tell you, no bike-riding in the house! Now look what happened! You broke my best vase and you could have hurt yourself."

"*Shah, shah* Sylvia. Don't make a federal case, all right? It's only a vase; I'll buy you another vase; hell, I'll buy you half a dozen . . . don't cry, *bubeleh*, you weren't hurt, that's the important thing!"

"Half a dozen antique vases you'll buy me?"

"Some antique. Your grandmother paid two rubles to some peddler." He turned ostentatiously to the little girl, lifting her up, and stage-whispered: "I never liked that vase anyway. You did me a favor."

"Jack! What kind of thing is that to tell a child?"

"What's more important, your child or a piece of junk? Deena, go get your sister. Tell her I'm leaving for the office, with or without her, so she can stop sulking. Shake a leg!"

As soon as Deena was gone, Sylvia turned to him, hands

on hips. "I'd like to know, Jack, I'd really like to know just what you think you're doing."

"What? Doing what?"

"How do you justify being so rough on Elaine and then turning right around and letting Deena get away with murder? She wraps you around her little finger, and if you think the big one doesn't see it—"

"I know, I know," Jack said, shaking his head. "But Elaine just gets to me lately, gets on my nerves. She's so loud, she's so bossy, she's such a wisemouth, can't wait for anything, so sure she's right all the time, and she eats like it's going out of style—what are you laughing at *now*?"

Sylvia walked over, putting her hands on his muscular arms and smiled up at him. "You mean, she's so definite, so aggressive, so clever, so dynamic, so self-assured, and loves all of life, including food . . . right, *bubeleh*?" And waited for him to catch on—which he did, of course, after a few seconds. "Like someone else we all know?" she added.

"I hear you, I hear you. Yeah, yeah, maybe it's true, she's too much like me. Deena, now"—and he gave her a little pinch on her cheek—"Deena reminds me of you. That must be why I find her so delicious."

"Give me a break, Jack! Don't try your soft soap on *me*."

"Sylvia, shame on you!" He threw his head back and laughed. "Don't I have three daughters as living proof how delicious I find you?" And he roared at his own joke.

"Oh, you!" She was blushing a little. Then she added, "But since we're on the subject, how about coming home a little earlier from the office from now on, so you maybe won't be so tired at night?"

He gave her a wink and a light kiss on the cheek. "Whatever your heart desires, Sylvia darling. Ah, here's the big girl now! You still mad at Daddy, Lainie? A little? Never mind, I'll buy you an ice cream and you'll forgive me!" He laughed heartily.

"A double dip?"

"A triple dip." He gave Sylvia a what-did-I-tell-you look.

Now the wail of a baby was heard from down the hall. Sylvia immediately turned, saying, "Marilyn's awake. Wait, I'll get her," and left the room. Jack continued to talk with

Elaine, walked her into the hall, helped her into her hooded coat, made sure she had mittens. When, a moment later, Sylvia appeared, holding a wide-eyed golden-haired baby in her arms, they were gone.

"Oh, I thought Daddy and Lainie were going to wait, but they went to work. Let's you and me go find Dee Dee."

Out on the sidewalk, Jack said to Elaine, "Hold it a minute, Sweetie-*piele* . . ."

"You just remembered to make an important phone call, right, Daddy?"

He turned to stare at her. "How old are you, Lainie? Nine, huh? I keep forgetting how smart you are," he remarked, patting her on the head.

When he went into the phone booth, he carefully closed the door, smiling at her as he dialed.

When the phone at the other end was picked up, he spoke quietly and quickly. "Linda? Listen, sweetheart. I had to take Elaine today. Well, because apparently I promised her last week, and Sylvia reminded me. So I had to. Don't be that way. Linda. Linda, please don't. Of course I do. Of course I want to. Listen, listen. I'll have a nice present for you. Yes, a real one. One night next week . . . Thursday . . . okay, okay. Please stop, Linda. You don't want to do that. Okay, okay, Monday. Yes, Monday. That's a promise. A real one."

At her desk in the office, Linda put the phone back on the cradle, blinking back tears. It was the second Saturday in a row they hadn't made love on the couch in his office. Maybe he was getting tired of her. But she mustn't think that way. Of course he wasn't. Didn't he just promise to come to her apartment on Monday? And then, his usual visit on Tuesday. Two nights in a row! Bliss! Unless . . . Unless that meant he'd skip Tuesday now! Oh, damn! She hated this, just hated it! When was he going to finally tell his wife about them and they could stop this sneaking around and she could finally relax and stop worrying all the time about losing him? Oh, she couldn't stand it if she lost him!

She mustn't think that way. It didn't do any good to think that way. She had to get out of here, get her mind onto something else. She dialed a familiar number and sighed with relief when the phone was picked up on the other end.

"Frannie? Well, he's done it again! Second Saturday in a row!"

"I've told you a thousand times, Linda . . ."

"I *know* what you've told me a thousand times but I can't help it. I just love him so much!"

"He's married, Linda."

"Dammit, I *know* he's married. Married and with three little girls! And *how* I know it! That's why I can't see him this afternoon; he's bringing Elaine to the office. Well, I'm not going to hang around here all afternoon, pretending to work, while that brat messes around with the mimeograph and bothers me every ten seconds!"

"So. Does that mean you'll go to Macy's with me after all?"

"Yes, Frannie. And how about that movie you wanted to see?"

There was an awkward pause and then Fran said, "As a matter of fact, don't faint, but I have a date tonight. With Ed. The cop we met that day, remember? In the park?"

"You'd go out with *him*?"

"Why not? He's nice, he's sweet, and he really likes me."

Linda tightened her lips. "He's skinny and uneducated and do you know what cops make a week? Nothing!"

"I like him and I don't find him skinny *or* uneducated, Linda. And at least he's not married!"

Linda banged the receiver down without another word. Dammit. Fran just kept harping and harping on the same old tune. She wished to hell she'd quit it. It was so disappointing when your best friend got jealous and turned on you. And then the tears came, and she couldn't seem to stop them.

CHAPTER EIGHT

Friday, December 13, 1985

Eleven A.M. and classes were breaking—as anyone within a radius of three blocks could easily hear. Deena, who had been peacefully checking the attendance list for the middle school, braced herself for the onslaught. Any second now, ten grubby little boys would burst into her office, English homework in ten grubby little hands, ten mouths going all at once. Sometimes it made her shake her head in disbelief, what was she required to do here at the Clayton School as middle school coordinator. Check homework! She had thought that particular chore was well behind her when her kids became quote mature unquote. And yet, here she was, supposedly a professional but still playing Mommy.

Sure enough, here they came, louder, sweatier, and messier than memory, crowding around her desk, clamoring for her attention, hands darting out with papers that might or might not be last night's fourth-grade book report assignment. "Hold the phone, you guys!" she said in a loud voice. "I can't see anything with all of you jumping around and waving papers in my face. I know the hand is quicker than the eye. Let's just make sure you've really done your assignments."

She was glancing over the seventh or eighth of the papers dealing with *Huckleberry Finn,* when she caught sight of Stacey Baldwin lurking in the hallway. Smiling, she motioned the girl to come in. Stacey had problems. If all had gone well, Stacey's problems would soon be taken care of. "All right, guys, company dis-*missed*!"

"Well, Stacey. Let me guess. You're here to tell me about the meeting you and your parents had with the head of the middle school."

Stacey, tiny, blond, sweet-natured, smiled shyly.

"So? What happened? You want to tell me? Because"— Deena reached out a hand to the little girl—"I want to hear about it."

Stacey put her hand into Deena's. "We had the meeting," she said. "And we're going to do the three things."

"Three?" Deena was puzzled. When she had discussed Stacey with Ron Herbert, the head of the middle school, they had agreed that she needed *two* things: vision training, and psychotherapy to help convince her she *wasn't* stupid.

"Well, one, I'm going to vision training and, two, I'm going to have someone to talk to. And, three, I told my mom and dad they should stay home more."

How about that! Talk about the mouths of babes! Deena grinned. "Well, good for you, Stacey! I'm sure it's going to work out just fine."

She sat smiling at her desk, very damned pleased with herself, and very damned pleased with little Stacey, too. Who'd have thought that this quiet little kid had the guts to stand up to her high-powered lawyer parents?

When Bob Harter walked in with his lunch in a plastic container, she greeted him by saying, "Well, Stacey Baldwin gave her parents hell." He smiled, listening to the story with interest; he was Stacey's homeroom teacher and it had been Bob who first brought her to Deena's attention.

While they were sipping at their tepid coffee, Bob gestured to her bulletin board. "Time to change that, don't you think?"

"What?" And then she saw what he meant. The November

Film Forum calendar. She felt flustered. "Oh. That. Oh . . . yes, I'll take care of it."

She carefully didn't object when he unpinned it from the corkboard and tossed it into the wastebasket, saying, "It's nearly January . . . it *will* be January when we get back from vacation. And a new year." He laughed, saying, "Deena, Deena, Deena! You can't stop time this way. If you're worried about the passing of time, get a face-lift!"

She laughed, too, but she eyed the calendar, lying on top of the rest of the trash in the basket, thinking, Later. Later, as soon as he's out of here, I'll get it. Because, of course, the reason it had stayed on her bulletin board was because it was a souvenir of the night she and Luke had sat together in the darkened theater, the night he kissed her. She certainly couldn't confide any of this to Bob. Was it her imagination, or was he regarding her rather speculatively now, peering at her over his glasses, stroking his full curly beard? In any case, his look rendered her totally nervous and she found herself babbling to him about her bulletin board.

"I guess boys never had them," she said, "but it was *de rigueur* for a teenage girl when *I* was a teenage girl . . . and for God's sake, Bob, don't ask me when *that* was because I don't think I want to tell you. One's bulletin board was the map of one's life. We tacked up pictures of our family and our pets, souvenirs of all the important social events, pictures of movie stars we had crushes on, our corsage from a dance if we were old enough and lucky enough to have one, and on *my* bulletin board anyway, a matchbook from the Copacabana, which I would rather have died than admit was given to me by my cousin Jay and not picked up while on a mysterious 'date' about which I was pledged to secrecy."

Bob laughed and she hoped she had diverted him. Because, in truth, besides pictures of her children, and important phone numbers, everything on her bulletin board was a souvenir of Luke. Merely *thinking* about Luke in front of Bob Harter, who was Saul's history teacher, a straight arrow, a thoroughly married man, and a trustee of his church, she felt a bit breathless with her audacity. To cover her inner confusion, she added: "Copa matchbook aside, this bulletin board bears an amazing resemblance to the one that was in my room at home . . . except for one thing."

"What's that?"

"I always had a picture of Jacques D'Amboise."

"The ballet dancer?"

"The famous ballet dancer. But back then I only knew that he was Daniel in *Seven Brides for Seven Brothers*. Oh, God, was I in love! He looked out of the screen and our eyes met and it was fate!" Even she had to laugh at that. "I had pictures of Jacques D'Amboise all over my room . . . in frames, Bob, in the fanciest fake gold frames I could find at Woolworth's! They *stayed* on my walls. Oh, I was always a faithful girl—" And here in her recitation, she paused for a second, feeling a tiny twinge. "Absolutely faithful," she repeated stubbornly, as if someone had argued with her. "Not until the day I came home at the end of my freshman year at college did I see how silly it was, at the advanced age of eighteen, to have pictures of a ballet dancer on my wall, instead of real-life boys. So I took them down. I was torn, I really was. It was supremely difficult for me to end that particular relationship; but I had to admit it was time.

"And that night, at the dinner table, my sister Elaine, always Miss Mouth, rang her spoon against her water glass and said she had an announcement to make.

"'Deena has taken down all her pictures of . . . are you ready for this, can you take it? . . . Deena has taken down all her pictures of Jacques!'

"And my family, being my family, gave me the business, you wouldn't believe it if I repeated it, you really wouldn't. Beginning with my mother pretending to faint and continuing with my father asking me very seriously if we'd had a fight, and ending with him, just as solemnly, telling me he was secretly glad because after all, Jacques wasn't Jewish."

It made an amusing little tale and Bob Harter was amused and, in fact, so was she. Even after Bob left for his 1:40 class, it was still making her smile.

And then the mail came in, a largish bundle dropped on her desk. She loved mail, and she slipped off the rubber band expectantly. In December there were likely to be three or four Christmas cards from other guidance counselors, reading experts, sometimes even from a school family grateful for her help with a confused teenager. There might be an invitation to a party at one of the other private schools in the neighborhood, or maybe to Celia's first grade class, where she would be seated on the floor and treated to warm lemonade and lumpy red-and-green-sprinkled star-shaped "cookies." Last year, they had forgotten the sugar.

And there, in the middle of tracts against hunger and notices of conferences and advertisements for textbooks, smiling up at her, was a picture, a glossy black and white picture, of the young Jacques D'Amboise. Her heart gave a great jolt; it was as if she had conjured it up out of her memory and she kept staring at it, unable, literally, to believe her eyes. And then it occurred to her that she might turn it over, and when she did so, it was a postcard with a message scrawled on it. The first thing she read was the signature—a big sprawling "L"—and then she found it impossible to read the message above it. It wasn't intimate words of love, it wasn't even very personal, just a note to say he'd happened across this in a postcard store and thought it would give her a kick.

She had to close her eye and lean back, calming herself. So a picture of Jacques D'Amboise had arrived right after she'd been talking about it! So what? It wasn't magical, not at all. A week ago she'd read a monologue in class, an assignment; it was called "My First Real Love Was a Movie," and it was all about how she'd seen *Seven Brides for Seven Brothers* fourteen times, about how she still, all these years later, searched Section Two of the Sunday *Times*, in case one of the scratched old prints was still showing somewhere—"scratched is better than not at all," she had written—and about how she'd finally ordered a cassette for her VCR only to have the store run out of them. As comedy, it rated perhaps four on a scale of ten; but apparently, Luke had listened and, Luke-like, had acted on it.

And of course, that was why she spent so much time thinking about him: because he was so unlike any other man she had ever known. Yeah, sure, Deena, your extensive experience with the male of the species: Daddy; a few uncles; three cousins, including Filthy Norman; a few fumbling dates in her early teens; her sons; and, of course, Michael. Not one sensitive, tuned-in, caring, intellectual companion among them. You couldn't count Daddy; he loved her to pieces and he knew her better than anyone in the world. But there were things you could never tell your father. By the age of ten, if you were a smart little girl, you came to realize that Daddy didn't *like* it when you were unhappy, so you just never let him know. That didn't go for the good news, of course not! There was no one better than Jack Strauss when you'd had a triumph! He would crow and chortle and grin and heap you with presents and praise.

When she first met Michael, she thought she was far too sophisticated to need presents and praise; in fact, all that noisy carrying-on was beginning to embarrass her. The first night she talked with Michael, his cool distance seemed a sign of maturity and superiority. But as the years went by and they settled into their life together, she found it more and more offputting and alienating. And now, lately, as she began to write more scenes taken directly from her childhood memories, she realized how much she missed the warmth and security her father had always given her. Yes, even the decibel level.

Funny. The same warmth and concern in Luke Morehead had initially aroused her suspicion: Was it all an act? Why should he care?

Of course, on the other hand, that's what he was there for, to pay attention to his students, to take them seriously. He was the same with all of them.

On the other hand, did he send picture postcards of a personal nature to all of them? She doubted it.

And on the other hand, what if Luke was just a tease, a man who considered his evening class a meat market where he could pick and choose the most succulent cuts at his leisure?

But on the *other* hand—and if that added up to four hands, or even five, so what?—Luke had kissed her and that kiss, if nothing else, had been sincere.

Not only that, but let's face it, Luke Morehead was the first man in twenty-five years who really listened to her, who really heard what she was saying, who cared and responded to her as a person. Not as daughter, sister, wife, mother, none of those titles, but as a singular woman called Deena. She had come to trust and appreciate his attitude and, even more, to hunger for it.

"Mom!"

She jumped, literally jumped, in her chair.

"Oh, hi, baby," she said, hoping her voice did not sound as guilty as she felt. He made a disgusted face—at the "baby," no doubt—so she figured it didn't.

"Aren't you gonna ask me what trouble I'm in *this* time?"

"What trouble are you in *this* time, Saul darling?"

Now he grinned, delighted with his own cleverness. "Financial trouble. That's all, really truly, honest to God, I really mean it. No dean, no headmaster, no lunch money."

He was in a good mood today for a change. Well, it was a welcome change. She eyed her baby, her nearly six foot baby, with his barely-there beard and wearing a sweater at least two sizes too small for him. She could think, just offhand, of seven things she'd like to tell him to fix about himself. But that was *not* a good idea with your typical teenager, as she had learned the first three times around.

"And so you come to Señora Peso," she said, leaning over to get her handbag from the bottom of the desk.

"I come to Madame Franc . . . Lady Pound . . . Signorina Lira . . . Frau Deutschmark . . . whoever."

She couldn't help laughing. And that felt so good for a change. He'd been so terribly surly lately. She often felt helpless with him because she never knew what she was going to have to deal with. Every day was different but mostly it was bad news. Why did everything have to go wrong at the same time? Not bad enough, this business with Daddy; not bad enough, her problems with Michael. No, Saul had to pick the very same season to do his adolescent rebellion, too!

She watched him leave the office and sighed deeply. Lately, every time anyone asked about him, she felt an anxious twinge when she lied, "Oh, he's fine, you know teenage boys." Oh, she had to talk very fast when the subject of Saul came up these days, to hide her guilt about him. She didn't know him, not really. Alone of all her children, he was an unknown quantity. Oh, she could list his traits, describe his physical appearance, she could make it sound as if she knew exactly who he was. But she didn't; when she talked to him, she was always puzzled, and a little fearful. How could she give him guidance, she who took money for giving it to everyone else's kids?

Again, she sighed. Motherhood was a helluva way to make a buck! No matter how difficult, writing had to be easier! In any case, she certainly enjoyed it a helluva lot more. When you wrote scenes, you could make everyone say what you wanted them to say. You could change what they said, any time you wanted to. You could make everything come out absolutely perfect. For a change. She leaned over, retrieving the Film Forum calendar from the top of her trash, and tucked it into her top drawer, smiling. Only three more days and it would be Monday and she would be going to class. That's what it was for, this feeling of expectation: the writing class, the new feeling of accomplishment, the companionship of other people who wanted to write, the intellectual challenge.

What a terrible liar she was.

CHAPTER NINE

Monday, December 16, 1985

Winter in New York: it deserved a song of its own. Frosty, still, the lowering sky reflecting back a hazed mix of all the neon colors and glittering lights of the city, every streetlamp haloed as a thick curtain of soft muffling clean snow fell straight down. Like a child would draw it, Deena thought, walking very slowly toward Washington Square arch, letting her head fall back, enjoying the tiny *splops* as the large snow-flakes fell onto her skin and instantly melted.

Beautiful, she thought. The city at its best, quieted, slowed down, and blanketed in white. How would she describe it? And then she laughed at herself. She wasn't sauntering along in what promised to be the blizzard of '85 in order to drink in the winter wonderland of Washington Square Park at night, not at all. She wasn't slowing her steps in order to do an exercise in description. She was stalling, that's what she was doing, in case Luke Morehead should be coming along behind her. *In case!* Even that thought was phony baloney. She was *hoping* he had followed her from class. Foolish hope. Well, when a middle-aged woman allowed herself to get caught up

in a . . . flirtation? Yes, flirtation with a man of twenty-seven
. . . twenty-seven! One of her own sons was twenty-three, for
God's sake!

So why was she dragging her footsteps this way? It must be
the wine. Luke had brought a couple of bottles into class, to
celebrate the winter break. No class for over a month didn't
sound like cause for celebration to *her,* but what the hell.
She'd had three glasses anyway. Three glasses of Soave had
left her feeling a bit giddy and totally irresponsible. It was a
nice feeling, but the snow was already starting to pile up in the
streets and the few cars venturing out now were slipping and
sliding sideways. Giddy and irresponsible were not recom-
mended when one was about to drive home, which she was.
Wasn't she? Of course she was. But she probably ought to
walk around for a while, just to make sure she was completely
sober.

It was a lovely feeling, being a little high, out in a snowstorm at night in Greenwich Village. It made her feel young, a
daredevil girl, ready for anything. Luke hadn't given her any
encouragement. In fact, tonight he had very carefully stayed
away from her, treating her with the same casual camaraderie
as he did everyone else in the class. Not one sign or signal,
not even a wink or a lingering look—and after she'd made
herself late for class, fussing with first one outfit and then
another, wanting to strike just the right note of casual sexi-
ness! She had finally settled on turquoise pants, that fit *just*
right, and a matching silk sweater. Quite smashing, she had
thought, eyeing herself in the mirror; and then she had spent
five more minutes choosing exactly the right earrings: Should
it be the big silver drops with the turquoise stones, or the big
round pastel mother-of-pearl disks Elaine had brought her
back from a business trip to Paris?

What idiocy, like something from a trashy romantic novel.
Would Luke "look at her and suddenly realize the fires that
secretly burned within him?" And would she "meet his eyes
across the room and feel the flames of desire sear her breast?"
What utter nonsense! The answer to both of the above was a
resounding not on your life, toots!

She really should know better at her age. But she had been
so sure that he would make an opportunity to speak with her

privately—or at least semi-privately—that she had saved up one or two clever little anecdotes to make him smile.

Now the snow was falling so heavily, you could hardly see a foot in front of you. Her car was parked right down this block and really, she ought to get right in it and take herself home before the snow got too deep. Would Michael worry if she were hours late getting home? He had a meeting tonight, and it was highly likely he was still there, totally engrossed in the search for Otto Schwartz or the latest communiqué from South America or whatever. At any rate, it was for sure that not even a fragment of a momentary thought about his wife would cross his mind.

When the hand came down on her shoulder, she was so deep in her thoughts that she jumped—heart speeding up—and whirled around. It was Luke, whose big broad smile faltered when he saw the look on her face. "Sorry! Sorry! That was stupid of me, Deena, I should have said something." He was slightly out of breath and his curly hair was thickly powdered with snow. "I wasn't even sure it was you when I spotted you from up the block. I ran all the way," he finished. "Where'd you disappear to so fast? One minute you were there, I turned to say good-bye to Joe and Laurie, and when I turned back . . . *gone*!"

No doubt about it, he made her feel breathless. There really was something happening between them, all the more enthralling because it was unspoken.

"And now that I've found you," Luke said, "let me walk you to your car . . . why are you laughing?"

"Because . . ." Giggles overtook her, and so she just pointed.

"Oh. We're standing next to it, right? Okay. Come around the block with me and I'll walk you to your car."

"I'd love to, Luke. But I can't. If I don't start for home now, I'm afraid I won't get there at all."

He looked at her thoughtfully. Then, in a very low voice, he said, "And would that be so terrible? I'm sorry, I had no right to say that."

"It's okay. I—being snowbound would be lovely, in fact."

"Deena. Do you really mean that?" He took off his glasses

to peer into her face, and she was overcome with the desire to put her palm flat against his cheek tenderly.

In her best plain voice, she said, "I really mean it. But this really is a major snowstorm and I really have a family at home and . . . responsibilities."

"But I hate to say good night."

Impishly, Deena said, "Oh, you don't have to. You can help me dig out." She grinned up at him and was rewarded with one of his eye-crinkling smiles.

Bowing, he said, "My pleasure, ma'am."

She let him shovel around the back tires while she scraped the windows clean, not that they stayed that way, not at all. It seemed as if the snow was falling faster than she could clear it away. It was thick and wet. In a way, she was glad, since the job could be dragged out. She loved knowing he was there, even though they weren't having a real conversation.

Finally, he straightened up and said with regret, "I'm finished." It was such an exact echo of her own feelings that she laughed aloud in delight.

"How come I'm so funny? Just for that . . ." He stooped down and, grabbing handfuls of the fluffy snow, began to fling them at her. In a minute they were throwing hastily made snowballs at each other, laughing and moving closer and closer.

Deena put her hands up in surrender. "No more, no more. Look, the front windshield is already totally covered again. I really have to go, Luke." I don't want to, she thought, but I shouldn't tell you.

Without another word he reached over and pulled her into an embrace, tipping her head back with one finger under her chin. "Deena, Deena, Deena," he murmured. "Don't look at me like that or I'll have to kiss you. On second thought, maybe I'll have to kiss you anyway."

Deena pulled back in alarm. "Not yet! I mean . . . no . . . I mean . . ."

"I know what you mean. Yes, I really do." He let go of her, still smiling, and said, "Look, Ma, no hands."

In answer she reached up, as she had imagined before, laying her hand against his face and brought him close enough so that, standing on her tiptoes, she could kiss him. His lips were cool and firm and, after a moment responsive. He stepped close to her again and once again wrapped her in his arms, and her lips parted as she pressed into him. She loved that clutch of excitement in her chest, the heat climbing in her loins. They clung to each other, open mouth to open mouth, body pressed to body, kissing hungrily.

He lifted his head finally, and murmured, "Come home with me, Deena."

She pulled back from him, terrified at the strength of her own responses. "I can't! I can't! Don't ask me why, I just can't!"

"Say 'this time.'"

She looked up at him, his bearded face secret and shadowed in the lamplight, snowflakes clinging to his beard and eyebrows. "This time," she said softly, and she was moved when he gave an almost imperceptible sigh of relief.

"Will you make a definite date with me, Deena?"

"Luke, I want to see you. But I'd be a nervous wreck, afraid we'd be seen. I'd be jumping at every footstep and looking over my shoulder all the time. I promise you, it would be awful."

"We don't have to go *out*. Listen to me, you could come to my place. It's really very nice. I'll cook dinner for you; hey, I'm a great cook, didn't I ever tell you that? I'd love to cook for you. Will you? Yes? Good, when? Tomorrow? No? Then the next day."

Deena had to laugh at him. "Tomorrow, Luke, is Friday. It's the weekend." And when he frowned a little and looked blank, she gently added: "My kids are home on vacation and, well, weekends are . . ." How to say it without scaring him away? Without reminding both of them that she had a husband? "Weekends are family time."

"Of course, I'm a dummy! But . . . well, the thing is, I'm going away for all of next week."

"Well, then . . ." She hoped her disappointment didn't show. And then she hoped she didn't sound too uninterested, either. Oh, hell, she didn't know how to do this!

"Damnation! For two cents I'd cancel the whole damn thing, but it's not two cents, it's two thousand dollars in my pocket. So . . . a week from Monday, okay?"

Deena swallowed. Now or never, she told herself. And then her voice refused to leave her throat and she nodded. He leaned down to give her a brief kiss, murmuring against her mouth, "Good night, Deena, sweet dreams. I know what *mine* will be, until that Monday. . ."

Luke walked all the way home; it wasn't really that far and with the snow swirling around his head and only the occasional lone car sloughing through the white-choked streets, it was strangely peaceful. He took the long block from Fifth to Sixth Avenue with easy strides, not hurrying, not really caring that his shoes were getting soaked. He was a happy man. The mating dance was in its last stage. She was coming for dinner in a week and they both knew, he was sure of it, they *both* were aware of what that meant. He wanted her and she wanted him and the waiting, the anticipation, the growing desire, were leading to that fabulous, longed-for conclusion. The lovely Mrs. Berman would be in his bed in one week's time, in his bed and in his arms and in his very fond, not to say, passionate embrace. He could hardly wait, except that, of course, the waiting was what gave it that special flavor.

He had noticed her right away, at the first class meeting. Very striking-looking, a bit older than his usual student, more than a bit better dressed, and quite a bit more affluent or he was losing his ability to size them up on the hoof. But what had really brought his gaze back to her again and again was the tension in her body. She sat very straight in the chair, fixed her eyes on him without blinking, folded her arms tightly across her chest, and never moved the whole time.

He had her figured for an uptight, frustrated, bored and boring society matron, who thought a course in playwrighting would let her "express herself." Was he wrong! The second class, she'd given up the tweed suit and high heels for a sweater and skirt and bright-colored tights; he remembered that very clearly because suddenly she looked like a kid. And when she read her first assignment—a memory piece in one scene about family life—it had been so damn good, he couldn't believe it. It was well paced, it kept the class's attention and, dammit, it was *funny*! Oh, not slapstick or a laugh-a-minute, but witty.

And then he had to talk to her, to see if she was really like that and she was. Of course, since then she'd done several scenes of family life—they all took place around the kitchen table—and they were always full of humor. And love, too. Here was a woman, happy with her life, for Christ's sake, and with of all the goddamn things, a happy childhood.

She'd done a scene about a child's hunger strike over a Christmas tree that was not bad at all, and one about leaving for camp the first time, and the first one, the one about the birth of a new baby in the family. He'd thought he'd enjoy meeting them, to see how much of it was true and how much a fantasy. Now he didn't want to, now that he was getting to know her, now that he wanted her.

He'd been attracted to her all along, but he was never going to do anything about it. Too old, too rich, too married. In fact, he had started romancing a bubbly little blonde from his afternoon class. Gillian Everts, age twenty-three, single, outgoing, and enchanted by her "professor." Altogether much more suitable a choice for a man who was serially monogamous, essentially a one-woman man but not yet ready to settle down for the long haul and so forth and so on. But, Christ, had Gillian turned into a pain in the ass! It started with cute little messages left on his answering machine—cute, yes, but four times a day? And then she escalated to popping in from time to time, waiting for him by the downstairs door, buying tickets for this, that, and the other. She'd even had him ballooned for his birthday, delivered by a scantily clad young woman. Hell, he would have enjoyed it all, maybe, if it hadn't been so soon in their relationship. But it must have cost her fifty bucks and she hardly knew him!

The night, just three weeks after he'd first asked her out, when he came home to find Gillian in his kitchen, preparing dinner, had been the clincher. "What are you doing here?" he'd demanded, a clammy feeling of desperation clamping his chest. "How did you get in?" He longed to push her out the door. Of all the goddamn nerve! She just giggled and said, "I convinced your super that the lasagna would spoil if it didn't get started right away."

He *had* kicked them *all* out then: Gillian, her fur coat, and her lasagna, and everything else he could spot that might be hers. So he'd lose her as a student; he didn't care; in fact, he hoped she'd never turn up again in class. And she hadn't. And he discovered that he didn't mind the end of their romance, either; in fact, it was a relief, just to be left alone, for Christ's sake.

When he told his buddies about Gillian, they all gave him the business. "You kicked her out, you asshole? She would have taken care of you but good!" They couldn't get over it, that he had objected to a good-looking broad who was crazy about him and was ready to do anything to make him happy. They thought he was nuts. But he had discovered something about himself. He didn't *want* to be taken care of. He supposed he had always known it, but he'd never put it into so many words. Luke Morehead wanted his space, wanted his privacy, and wanted his life his way at his speed and in his own good time. He didn't want any goddamn woman who imagined she was in love with him to think she had the right to intrude into his life, goddammit! Jesus Christ, why else was he twenty-seven and still happily single?

Deena seemed to understand that. She was very private herself. That was one of the things that had come to enchant him about her, she revealed herself in very little bits, in very small doses. Not only in her writing, but talking, too. Take her husband, for instance. She'd never talked about him at all; in fact, he'd had to go back and look at her registration card to see whether she was divorced or married or what, and then the damn thing said *Ms*. Deena Berman! So he'd had to ask her and the only way he could figure how to do that was to have a show of hands in class and pretend he wanted to discuss a scene someone had written about an argument between husband and wife. Her hand shot right up and then he'd wondered why she didn't write about *him*. Her husband. She didn't; all her scenes were set in the late 1940s, the early 50s, all about her childhood. It had surprised him that she had four kids. Somehow, he had figured that any woman who wanted four children would find them absorbing. But when he asked her why she didn't draw from her life, her kids, she gave him a look and then laughed and said, "Write about four teenagers?

All I want is to *forget*!" It wasn't an answer, of course, not to his real question; and now that he was alone on a snow-covered sidewalk at 9:00 of a winter evening, it occurred to him that she almost never gave an answer to any personal question; she made a joke instead.

Well, now the laugh was going to be on her because now he knew her well enough, had seen and felt enough of her responses to know that Mrs. (or Ms., if she insistead) Berman was a lady on the verge, a luscious ripe plum ready to fall from the tree, a real woman whose tightass husband didn't deserve her, didn't appreciate her, and probably didn't pay enough attention to her, not even in bed. No, scratch that, *especially* not in bed. Oh, it was going to be good! Her lips, her soft cushiony mouth, had been trembling under his, just before, and the heat rose from her body to warm his face. As they kissed, he had felt and heard the sharp little intake of excited breath and then her arms had gone more tightly around his neck and her mouth had opened and... Okay, Luke, he told himself, that's enough of that. You've got almost two weeks to wait.

He slogged along through the deepening drifts. It was getting more and more difficult by the minute. So much for the romance of a blizzard! It was getting windier and colder and he could no longer feel most of his toes. He hoped it was better to drive in than it was walking. Dummy, he thought, exasperated, he should have asked her to call him when she got home. He couldn't very well call her, not at this hour, and not with that husband! Shit!

His block was deserted and now gusts of wind were whipping up swirls of powdery white and dumping them across the street. His own building was already drifted in and he had to scrape himself a path with his boot to get to the front door.

He unlocked the door and took the steps, two at a time, unzipping his parka as he went. Christ, it was good to be home. It was warm and it was quiet, no traffic noises tonight to disturb him while he worked. Good. He'd get in a good productive two, three hours, then grab something from the fridge. He let himself into the loft, automatically checking the answering machine. It was blinking. Maybe Klaus had called; or the people from the coast—he'd better think of exactly what he wanted before he called them back. And as he moved to the stove and put the fire on under the coffeepot, the phone rang and he ran for it. In a minute he was totally engrossed in a discussion of a forthcoming job. When the coffee boiled over, he never noticed.

It was a harrowing trip home. At least, it would have been if she had been her normal self. As it was, she was in a glow of erotic anticipation so that she was almost to Canal Street before she was awake enough to become nervous. Broadway, being heavily trafficked, no matter what the hour or weather, had two clear lanes melted into the snow, and when she turned on Canal, it was more or less the same. So the streets weren't so bad, but there was practically no visibility. The streetlamps and the twin red lights of cars in front of her were blurred by sheets of whirling snow and she had no sense of where she was in relation to the rest of the road. She got herself behind a large truck, telling herself that truck drivers were good drivers even though she wasn't sure that was true, and followed slavishly, inching along at twenty miles an hour, praying that he was heading for the Manhattan Bridge. Once she was on the bridge, she was nearly home. Once she was on the bridge, she was okay. She kept repeating that to herself, like a magical incantation.

All the while, in the back of her head, sat Luke Morehead; but she resisted looking at him. She was not going to allow herself that pleasure, not until she had all the time she needed to play back everything that had happened tonight, like a wonderful movie, in her head. She was going to save it until she could savor it.

So she concentrated on her driving, concentrated on those two blurred twin red beacons in front of her. And even after they were safely on the Manhattan Bridge, she and her truck, she only let herself think about other things. Michael . . . no, that was no good. Not tonight, not Michael, with his tight-lipped disapproval and his way of giving her his back all the time lately. God, she was beginning to hate the sight of his back, the muscles in his shoulders, the thick neck with its carefully barbered salt and pepper hair, the little brown mole between his shoulder blades, the thin line of black hair that outlined his spine—all the features she used to trace with her finger or her tongue, loving, loving all of it, loving all of *him*. What was the use of remembering any of that? It had been so long since they'd made love. It had been longer than that since she had felt loving toward him. No, it was not pleasant these days to think about her husband.

At last she was home. Carefully she eased the car through the soft, unplowed drifts, driving very slowly. Thank God the parking garage was only a few feet from the corner.

Walking home to Monroe Place was a great deal more enjoyable than driving. Safer, too. Deena scuffed through the untouched snow, loving the look of it, loving the deep quiet of the neighborhood. How Daddy had objected when she and Michael bought the house, you'd have thought they were moving to the ends of the earth instead of just half an hour's drive away. Of course, when they were still on the West Side, he'd been in the habit of dropping in every evening before he went to his own apartment. Now, thinking about that, she found herself feeling guilty. Could it have been then, when she moved away and took his grandchildren with her, that he began to carry on with Linda? It was so hard to believe! It was impossible that her handsome, lively, intelligent daddy would carry on with his empty-headed *secretary*! It was such a cliché! It wasn't true; it couldn't be. Linda had just made the whole thing up: a fantasy to fill her empty life.

But when she suggested that, Elaine had just snorted with derision. "Oh, come *on*, Deena, that's not only naive, it's a little bit dumb. I, for one, feel that Daddy ought to tell us *his* side of it." And when Deena said she didn't think she could do that to Daddy, Elaine said, "Will you grow up, Deena? We shouldn't '*do that*' to him? Think what he did to Sylvia!"

Well, they were never going to argue about it, never. Elaine had called her every single day since then, pushing her to make a date to talk to him about it. Until finally, this morning, she'd said, "Okay, Deena, it's now or never."

And Deena had found the courage to yell, "Well, it's *never*!" And she had hung up, *hung up* . . . on Elaine! She had sat there, on the edge of her bed, her hand pressed to her chest, where her heart was going a mile a minute. But her feeling of guilt was quickly overshadowed by an even greater surge of relief. Dammit, this time she was not going to do what Elaine wanted. If it *was* true, she didn't want to talk about it. She didn't even want to *know* about it.

Her sidewalk was neatly shoveled, only lightly dusted with snow, which meant it had been very recently done. And a much more thorough job than Saul's usual. Well, well, apparently wonders never did cease. Maybe that last warning from the headmaster had gotten through to him somehow. She climbed the steps and let herself in, smiling a little, recalling Luke's mouth, insistent upon hers.

She took off her coat, lost in a reverie, standing in the front hallway. Luke was an adorable man, and for the first time in ages her blood was aboil, her senses were quickened. And she was going to do it, she was really going to do it. She could hardly believe her own audacity, her own daring, her own desperation.

Michael's voice speaking her name was so unexpected, so unwelcome, that she felt attacked.

"Michael! What are you doing home?"

"If I didn't know better, I'd think you didn't *like* my being home early."

He was smiling, she realized, *smiling*. How many weeks since she'd seen a smile on his face? She smiled back, hesitantly, wondering what was going on. There was an air about him tonight; he was somehow different.

Even as she thought it, he came over to her, put his arms around her, and gave her a long, open-mouthed kiss. For a moment she was so surprised, she could only stand there, unresponsive, thinking how different he tasted and felt. He couldn't know! Oh, of course he didn't know; and she kissed him back. When he lifted his head from hers, he said, "If you could see the look on your face!"

"What look, Michael?"

"That sweet look of surprise you always get after we kiss."

What sweet look of surprise? Deena thought. She did the proper female thing: she lowered her eyes and made a soft sound.

"And I," Michael went on, "have something for you that will *really* surprise you."

"Oh, really? What?" This was so unlike him. For him to be kissing her and talking surprises to her in his best romantic tone was such a radical change, she could not even *imagine* what he had in his head.

He was waving two pieces of paper under her nose. "For us! A week on a windjammer!"

"A week on a what?"

"A sailing ship, a real one, Deena, a tall ship. In the Caribbean."

What? "But . . . why? I mean, what's the occasion?"

"Deena, I realize I've been very involved with work lately and perhaps haven't had enough time for you." She could not look him in the eye. "When one of the junior partners said he had these two tickets he couldn't use, and offered them at the meeting, it suddenly struck me: This would make an ideal getaway, just what every wife and mother needs to fight off empty-nest syndrome."

So that was going to be the party line: Empty-nest syndrome, my ass! she thought.

Without lifting her head, she said, "So you took them off his hands."

"You've been saying you'd like to go where it's warm instead of skiing every winter. And so . . ." He stepped back in, his arms going around her again. "You'll have a lot of shopping to do, very fast."

Her heart sank. "*Fast*, Michael? Why fast? When exactly are we going?" Even before he spoke, she knew. "Next weekend. We'll spend until Monday at the best hotel as a prelude. And then we'll board the ship Monday night and go for six days on the high seas." He looked so pleased with himself.

Deena forced a smile onto her lips. She felt sick to her stomach with disappointment. And, as he murmured, "It'll be a second honeymoon for us, Deena," her lovely dream of

Luke, the one she'd been hoarding all the way home, faded, dissolved, and completely disappeared. Out of sight, out of mind, out of the question.

If your husband made an attempt to fix up your marriage, it didn't matter how bad things had been, how feeble the attempt; not even that it was too late, and that, frankly, she wasn't interested. None of that mattered. She had to go.

CHAPTER TEN

Tuesday, December 17, 1985

Linda buzzed the inner office, her heart thumping in her chest. With the first sound of Cleary's raspy voice, she'd become agitated but she mustn't let Jack know. "Mr. Cleary on line one," she caroled, trying to sound her usual cheerful self. And then, her lips pressed tightly together, sat back in her chair to listen. Yes, listen in on Jack's private conversation with George Cleary of Cleary Concrete. He hadn't asked her to and that meant he didn't want her to, but she was damned if she was going to let that stand in her way.

The nerve of him, planning to sell the company without telling her! Without a word, not to her, not to Lawrence, for pete's sake, and he kept *saying* that Lawrence was his number one man, his good right arm. She knew what that meant: That meant he was planning to cut them out. *Cut them out!* He might just as well cut out her heart! She, who had been his confidential secretary not to mention his one true love for years and years, the woman who had given up everything for his sake, who had been willing to do anything he wanted, who

113

gave him everything that mattered to him. Dammit, it just wasn't fair! He had no right to do this to her and Lawrence!

And then she told herself to calm down. She told herself it was more important right now to hear what they were saying.

Cleary was saying, "But I thought it was settled, Jack."

What? Linda's heart sped up again. What had she missed?

Jack laughed a little. "It ain't over til it's over, George, you know that! Something came up out of the blue."

"Come on, Jack, none of your out-of-the-blues, if you don't mind. Let's have the truth of it! What's up?"

"I swear to you, Cleary, we have an option on a building, absolutely gorgeous if it goes through. A prewar mortgage, an old lady . . . don't ask. It was at a standstill for a long time, I thought it was dead. And all of a sudden there's some action. All of a sudden they want to cut a deal. Well, what can I do? Hell, George, what would *you* do?"

"Put you on the back burner, same as you're doin' to me."

"We've had our eye on it for three years, we made an offer almost a year ago, and we've been breathing down their necks ever since. I talked to the guy yesterday—I was all set to tell him never mind—and suddenly there's movement. You know how it is."

"Yeah, yeah." There was a loud sigh from Cleary's end. "So what now?"

"Lemme see . . . I'm looking at my calendar . . . not that week, and then it's New Year's. How about I get back to you about the middle of January? I'll have my girl call your girl and they can set up a nice lunch. How's '21' sound . . . ?"

At this point, Linda cut off the sound of their voices. She didn't have to hear any more and God forbid he should catch her. She'd die, just die! He had no idea how much she knew of what went on in Strauss Construction, things she wasn't supposed to know. And she wasn't about to tell him. A girl alone had to take care of herself; she'd learned that a long time ago. She had no real hold on him. And here was the proof. Very important things were happening; and yet, the two people in the business closest to him were being totally left out! Every time she thought about it, it made her blood boil!

The door to his office banged open and out he charged. He was such a bull, her Jack! As forceful and masculine today, at the age of seventy, as the day she'd first met him. And, she thought as he leaned over her desk, hands braced on the edge, still handsome.

"Linda," he said, "I ask myself a hundred times a day, what would I do without you?" His talk with Cleary had gone his way, and he was feeling high-spirited as he always did when things went his way. He could still turn her right around just with a smile, and as he smiled at her now, her anger drained away.

Anyway, it was true. He wouldn't know *what* to do without her, and if he thought about it for even one minute, he'd realize that. And she'd make sure he had reason to think about it.

Sweetly, she smiled back at him and put her hand over his. "Jack," she said in a low voice, "you haven't been over for dinner for a couple of weeks and I've been missing you. I mean, really *missing* you."

He leaned a bit closer and she thought she saw that old spark in his eyes flaring up. "Put me down for day after tomorrow. Thursday."

She felt herself blushing, she just couldn't help it, even after all these years. But don't think she didn't write it down; she certainly did because if he "forgot," she'd have it right there on his very own calendar to show him.

"I'm on my way," Jack said, "to the club. Lunch with Harry. If Lawrence comes in, have him—"

And then a voice from the doorway said, "Lawrence *is* in." There he was, her handsome son, her darling boy, looking so alive and excited. It must be good news!

"Well, Jack," Lawrence said, clearing his throat, "I have some good news for you."

"You got it! You got Salisbury to sell! By God, you did, didn't you!" He rushed over to Lawrence, who was grinning ear to ear, and gave him a big bear hug. "At last! At last! We've got our whole parcel and now we can really start to make plans!" He backed off, beaming, and added: "Goddammit, and you did it!"

"Aw, come on, I didn't do the whole thing. I just sewed it up. You did the preliminaries all those years. And anyway, it was all your idea in the first place, going to the Queens side of the river."

"Hell, it doesn't take a genius to figure out that all the East Side has got to look at is Queens! But if you're in Queens, you get that beautiful view of Manhattan. Anyway, it's one thing to have the idea and it ain't bad to get seven guys to sell you their tenements cheap. But it's something else again to get the lone holdout to sell. That's what I call the tough stuff."

"Well, thanks, Jack, but I still say—"

"I don't want to hear any more. You'll find out in your pay envelope who *I* think deserves the credit! No, no, don't thank me." He laughed heartily. "Not until you see how much!"

He left a few minutes later, and Linda signaled her son with a tilt of her head to hang back so they could talk. The McElroys had a whole lexicon of eye signals and gestures they used to give each other silent messages. It had become so ingrained in both of them, they didn't even think about it.

"Yeah?" Lawrence said as soon as Jack had disappeared into the elevator. "What's up?"

"Lawrence, you've got to learn to act more self-confident."

"Don't start with that again, please, Ma. I know what I'm doing."

"Listen to me. I know my Jack Strauss. He only respects strength. You've got to act strong with him; otherwise, he'll just walk over you on his way out the door."

"Ma, for Christ's sake, I'm not the office boy. I've been here a long time and I already have his respect. You heard him."

"I also heard you, and you sounded like a boot-licker."

Lawrence narrowed his eyes and regarded her. "Okay, let's have it. What's *really* bugging you? And don't tell me my personality because I know my mom and something new has come up, hasn't it?"

"Cleary called before. Jack is stalling him and I can't figure out why."

"I'm not surprised. He never really did want to sell the business. Cleary made it sound too good to pass up, that's all. And Jack likes to play Mr. Wheel-and-Deal, you know that. Now he's had second thoughts. Because, when you get right down to it, Jack loves every goddamn one of the buildings he's worked on, *loves* them. You should hear him! 'My build-ings are my immortality!' Stuff like that. He brags about them all the time, loves to take out-of-towners around in the car and show them off."

Linda stubbornly shook her head and Lawrence leaned over the desk, bracing himself on his hands and peering di-rectly at her. "Don't shake your head; it's not bull. I kinda get that feeling myself. Whenever I go by the South Street project, I get a little thrill, you know? I mean, it's exciting to think you're part of a great city . . . that you took something that was just an idea and made it happen. It's *exciting*. If I owned this company, I wouldn't want to sell it so fast, not even for a big price."

Linda muttered, "By all rights it should be yours."

Lawrence laughed. "You know what you've got, Ma? You've got delusions of grandeur. You think because you've been sitting in this office forever that you're a part owner."

"Okay, but the fact remains that he's still considering sell-ing to Cleary, and there still hasn't been one syllable to either me or you."

"But you just now said he's stalling. So he's probably not going to sell. He probably just waited, to make sure he knew what he wanted to do. Why should he tell us before he's sure?"

"I'm worried. I'm worried that he'll suddenly decide that it's yes and he'll sell and we'll be left high and dry."

"Not to worry, Ma. You have those shares; they'll be worth a lot. As for me, well, Cleary would be a fool to try to run this outfit without me. And he knows it."

"What if Jack asks for those shares back?"

Lawrence drew back, surprised. "What are you talking about? They're yours. They're in your name. He can't ask you to give them back. Legally, he doesn't have a leg to stand on."

Linda got up from her chair, frowning, pursing her lips. "Don't talk about legalities to me, Lawrence. We're talking about a personal relationship here. If he demands them, I'll just *have* to hand them over!"

Lawrence looked at his wristwatch. "You know what I think? I think you're way ahead of yourself. He isn't selling,

he isn't asking you for your shares. Why don't you wait until
it happens before you start worrying?"

"Lawrence, I've given my whole *life* to this business . . . to
Jack Strauss! You don't know the half of it."

This was plainly an old familiar refrain to Lawrence. His
eyes went blank, although he kept the smile. "Come on, Ma,"
he said. "None of that now. I have a lunch date and I'm already late."

"Lawrence, I'm *really* concerned—for both of us. Jack is
seventy; he could take it into his head to do anything at this
point! And you know, the girls have been up here, sniffing
around. They must know *something*."

He came over to her, putting an arm around her shoulder
and planting a kiss on the top of her head. "Let me handle
this, okay? I've already started to provide for the future."

"Lawrence, you aren't—"

"Shhh. I never said anything; you never heard nothing.
Isn't that our family motto? Just remember: I'll always take
care of you."

Linda relaxed a little into his embrace. "Oh, Lawrence,"
she said. "You've always been a perfect son."

The West Side Club dated from the thirties, a fact made
obvious by its furnishings, which reflected what was considered suitable for males at that time: heavy, dark, with a quantity of leather and tapestry and wood paneling.

Jack Strauss and his closest friend, Harry Ginsberg, were
seated in the mahogany-paneled dining room at their usual
table in the far corner. The remains of lunch had been pushed
away and they were both puffing leisurely on their panatellas,
chairs moved back, legs stretched out into the aisle.

"Women!" Jack was saying. The two friends grinned at
each other. How many conversations had they had together
over the years, where one or the other of them threw up his
hands and said "women" in just that tone of voice: five
hundred? A thousand? It had been plenty, they both knew that.
"Women!" he repeated. "Nothing but complications!"

Harry, a tall, heavyset man, completely bald but with a
thick white mustache, laughed. "What now?" he asked.

"Agh, I had to cool the deal with Cleary. 'Elaine must have

her chance,' Sylvia says. And what if she actually does a good job? I'm going to have to do *something* for her. In the meantime, I can't put her off much longer. What a headache! Bring a woman in and right away, complications!"

Harry raised one eyebrow. "Come on, Jack, don't blame it on Elaine. We both know better. She's just a convenient excuse."

Jack puffed thoughtfully for a minute or two. Then he looked Harry straight in the eye and said, "You're the only one I'd admit this to, but you're right. When you're right, you're right, Harry, and you happen to be right! I got carried away Thanksgiving, I admit it. I looked around the table at all my loves ones and I said, what can I do for them that no one else in this world can do and, well, you know what happened."

"I know. You think I'm blind. I don't see how indecisive you are since then? That's not the Jack Strauss I've known for over forty years!"

Jack nodded. "It was an impulse and then, once I said it, I felt obligated to go through with it. I don't know. On the one hand, let's face it, I'm not as young as I used to be; but on the other hand, I'm not finished yet!"

Harry lifted his coffee cup in salute. "You're telling *me*? Don't you still beat me at handball?"

"Here's how I feel about it," Jack said, leaning forward, elbows on the table, very earnest, very intent. "I've given my whole life to that business. And it's paid off. Now I should sell it?" He shook his head. "It'd be like selling . . . I don't know . . . your kid! Women have babies . . . men have businesses." Pleased with the sound of that sentiment, he repeated it.

"So why not hand it down to your children?"

"I should hand it to a bunch of women who will just piss it away?"

"Hold on, Jack. I happen to know Elaine and she's one helluva smart cookie. No reason Elaine couldn't run that business and run it damn well!" And then he grinned and said, "Ah-ha!"

"What . . . ah-ha?"

"Ah-ha! I'll tell you. You're bothered because you don't

want to share the power with Elaine. That's what it's all about!"

"Agh!" Jack waved the thought away. "You know as well as I do that there can be only one boss. And don't talk equal partners to me, Harry! And if I let Elaine in, forget fifty—fifty! That girl is a regular takeover type, just like her mother."

Harry shook his head, relighting his cigar with extra care. "Seems to me," he said cautiously, "that Sylvia never tried to take over anything. Seems to me, she's been one hundred percent behind you in everything. Made a nice home for you, raised three beautiful daughters, one of them a doctor. Seems to me, if Elaine takes after anybody, it's her old man!" He looked at Jack from over his glasses.

"You don't know Sylvia as well as you think, Harry. By you she was always a wonderful woman. You didn't have to live with her. Don't get me wrong, I love that woman, but she always had a mouth on her! When she was younger, I never got a moment's peace and quiet, let me tell you. 'Come home early.' 'Come home earlier.' 'Why do you have to spend so much time at the club? You have a stripteaser there?' 'They threw out the first ball at Yankee Stadium today. Now I won't see my husband again until the leaves fall.' But why am I telling *you*, Harry? You heard it all from me back then."

"Yeah, yeah, I remember when you started up with the shiksa. Sylvia was such a doll, I never could understand the big attraction."

"The shiksa," Jack repeated, his tone softening. "Listen, there was good and sufficient reason, believe me. I felt like I was in jail, I felt . . . trapped. Two little girls and another baby on the way. It was my whole future laid out in front of me, so I couldn't escape. I don't know how to explain it, I felt suffocated. And there she was—Linda, little Linda Collins, Miss Subways, blond, soft, pretty as a picture, sweet-natured and that Southern accent! Smart, too, let me tell you, but not smart-mouthed. Did what I told her, loved doing it, hell, she adored me! Agh! She was there for the taking; I'd have been a fool to turn that down! And let's not forget, Sylvia wouldn't let me near her when she was pregnant and I was going crazy. Hell, Linda probably kept my marriage going."

"So you always liked to say," Harry commented dryly.

"Well, it was true! And she was terrific in bed, too! Still is, in fact." He gave a self-conscious grin.

"At this late date? You trying to tell me you two still—"

"Well . . . every once in a while. You know, sometimes I get the urge . . . thank God!" They both laughed. "Well, I've got to get back. I promised Elaine I'd make a definite date with her. And now that I've told Cleary it's no go for the time being, I guess this is the time. Dammit, though, I shouldn't be so good to her, not after the way she talked to me Thanksgiving—and in front of everybody!"

"Better a daughter who talks too much," Harry intoned, "than a daughter who won't talk to you at all." Jack acknowledged this with a nod. "You remember, Jack, those five years when my Mimi wouldn't talk to me. It was hell. I want to tell you, I'd have *loved* to have her at Thanksgiving dinner, even giving me the business! But she wouldn't have a thing to do with me. And why, I ask you, why? I still don't know!"

"What's to know? Stan Weiss's oldest girl, he says, he still can't have a decent conversation with her . . . and it's twenty-six years! It gave *him* an ulcer."

They gave each other a look of complete understanding. Life would be a lot simpler if it weren't for women.

CHAPTER ELEVEN

Thursday, December 19, 1985

Suddenly the showroom came alive with a soft pink glow and the models began their stately, stylized procession, while hidden speakers played muted music. Nothing too intrusive. Eva came out first, wearing a draped Grecian-style gown in Sweet Somethings' signature color, a peachy pink called Sweetheart Rose. Next was Tiffany in ivory satin, and then, in jade with pale green point d'esprit lace, Ginger.

Ginger was one of Sweet Somethings' best showroom models. She was Irish, with creamy skin, green eyes, and that burnished copper hair that could never be duplicated by Clairol. But the thing that made her special was her presence. She sent out waves of good cheer, somehow, and anything she put on her body seemed to outsell anything else in the line.

Out she floated, graceful as a nymph, in the wispy teddy, wearing high-heeled green satin slippers to match. Out from behind the pink velvet draperies she glided, across the floor, to stand in front of the two women who sat at attention in their gilt chairs, listening as Howard described each garment and named each model. Ginger put a hand on one hip, made a half turn that was reflected in the mirrored wall behind her, then turned all the way around to show the low-cut back and the lace insert just above the buttocks, and turned once more to face her audience.

Shit! Elaine thought, fighting to keep the interested smile on her face. Next to her, at last, at last, was Sandra Goodman, the lingerie buyer from Nieman-Marcus, a sharp-eyed blonde who was gesturing even now for Ginger to come closer. Oh, Christ, for sure she'd notice the red-rimmed eyes, the puffy pouches. Ginger knew better than to show up for work in this condition! Dammit, Elaine thought, I don't care *how* much she loves that bastard, I'm sick of hearing about it and even sicker of having her arrive a total mess at least once each month! She was being paid—and very handsomely, too—to come into the showroom looking young and beautiful and sexy. Dammit, this was the fourth time and this was *it*. No more Mrs. Nice Guy! The way she looked today, Elaine figured they'd be lucky to sell a pair of panties to N-M!

When Ginger got close enough for the buyer to finger the fabric and take a close look at the lace and the workmanship, it was even worse than Elaine had feared. There were tears, actual tears in the model's eyes. She ought to dock the silly bitch ten bucks for every one of those tears. That was *not* the way a professional behaved in the showroom.

Meanwhile, of course, Elaine kept babbling on and on. A good thing she knew her merchandise so well, she could have sold it in her sleep. The tough part was to keep that smile in place and to keep her voice cheery and charming. Oh, just wait, Ginger, she promised silently, just you wait, you are going to find yourself on the line at unemployment *so* fast, your head will spin!

So it was blahblah, blahblah, and smile smile smile and yes, a discount for quantity might be arranged and hallelujah, if Sandra Goodman was talking about quantity discounts, then it looked as if Neiman-Marcus would be ordering several Sweet Somethings *in quantities*. No thanks to Ginger! So this time it was going to turn out all right, fine. But she couldn't have Ginger's private love life continually wreaking havoc.

There would be no softening, not this time. She didn't care *what* Howard said, this time Ginger was out.

Elaine could hardly contain herself until Goodman finally scribbled everything she needed to scribble and made her order and burbled about the beautiful line and how nice that they were designing for the . . . forgotten woman, and then sweetly added that she *could* expect the order as promised, couldn't she? And then she left and it should have been a moment of sweet triumph for Elaine, who'd been working toward this moment for eighteen months. Instead of feeling good, however, thanks to Ginger she felt only like kicking ass.

She looked at her wristwatch. She had so damn many things to do today; and at least two important calls were due to come in any minute. Sometimes she wondered if it was all worth it; and then, almost immediately, answered herself yes. What would life *be* if you couldn't cut deals! Of course, when Sweet Somethings had been just mail order, life had been a lot less complicated. No buyers, no big-production fashion show twice a year, no showroom, and, of course, no showroom models. When they had temper tantrums, they had them at the photographer's. Ever since she and Howard had decided to sell wholesale, it had been like this, just one damn thing after the other. Time-consuming, irritating, though it had a way of livening up the day, didn't it? But enough was enough, already!

She motioned to Howard to join her in her office, strode by the big dressing room, and peremptorily summoned Ginger. Their eyes met in the mirror. Ginger looked scared. Good. As far as Elaine was concerned, she had *better* be scared.

She and Howard were both already in her office, she behind the big desk and he standing, arms folded, leaning against the wall, when Ginger slunk in. As soon as she spotted Howard, she immediately wailed, "Oh, Mr. B.!" She didn't have to say anything else; Howard held out his arms —What a softie! Elaine thought—and gave the girl a big hug.

"Still with that Ted Fox," he said. "And still he makes you cry!"

Elaine viewed her husband with loving resignation. What could you do? There were six models, a bookkeeper slash secretary, two messengers, a seamstress, and a cleaning woman on the premises; and they all told him everything and he remembered every last little detail and he cared. He *cared*.

Ginger was still blubbering. "The worst part . . ." she choked out. Oh, Christ, what *now*? If the girl had gone and gotten herself pregnant!

"I've already gone through a five-pound box of chocolates! Remember when we broke up last summer and I put on ten pounds? I just know it's going to happen again if he doesn't get rid of that Miranda and come back to me!"

"Ginger." Elaine made her voice very hard. "Enough. Sit down and listen to me. You've pulled this stunt once too often. I'm sorry, but I'm letting you go. . . ."

"Oh, Mrs. B! It'll never happen again! I promise!"

"So you promised three times already! Enough! You've had plenty of warning. I can't allow Ted Fox's neuroses to screw up my business. If you don't have enough sense to get rid of this creep, then I can't do anything for you. As of this minute you've joined the unemployed. You'll get severance, don't worry."

But Ginger was no longer listening. She was crying loudly, like a small child, and Howard said, "Elaine!" in a tone she knew very well. It meant Don't be so tough, Elaine; it meant Give her another chance, look how miserable she is, after all, we're not dealing with a bolt of satin Charmeuse, we're dealing with a human being here. All of which he had already said to her, out loud, before Ginger came in. Dammit, she hated to cave in. How was the girl ever going to learn—well, never mind. In a few months all this might very well be academic. Why not keep Ginger on? If things went the way she hoped, she wouldn't be dealing with Ginger, or any other model for that matter, any more, ever. She'd be working full-time at Strauss Construction and Howard would have the whole responsibility and welcome to it!

"Oh, hell," she said. "Stop crying, will you, Ginger? Here,

have a tissue. Wipe your eyes, you're a mess. I'll make a deal with you, okay?" The girl nodded, blowing her nose. "You dump Ted Fox . . . no, no arguments, no next week, or next time. Either you dump that no-good bastard or we dump you. Period. Is that understood?"

Howard patted the model on her back and made soothing noises. "You'll see, honey. Elaine's right. Without him you'll do much better. Look. Take the rest of the afternoon off. In fact, take tomorrow off, go to the Vertical Club and have a good workout, a steam, a massage. You'll meet ten new guys within the first two minutes. You're too pretty—and too nice —to have to settle."

Ginger was full of effusive thanks, but Elaine was no longer listening. She was planning ahead: who could substitute for the girl tomorrow. Yes, call Model Temps and get a nice tall size six who needed a day's work. She made a note and turned to Howard. "Alone at last," she said with a smile.

"Never mind that mushy stuff." Howard laughed. "Feed me! I'm starving! A beautiful woman crying on my shoulder always makes me hungry, you know that."

Elaine got up instantly, going to the neat little pink and gray kitchen she'd had installed in one corner of the huge room. She went right to the freezer and announced: "We could have Swedish meatballs . . . or eggplant parmigina . . . or, oh, look, your favorite, sweetie-pie. Chili. How about chili?"

"Great." They moved together in easy, familiar patterns around the little kitchen. Elaine put two containers into the microwave, punched three buttons, and said, "I love cooking in this kitchen. . . . Why are you laughing?"

"When do you ever *cook* in this kitchen?"

"Exactly why I love it! And believe me, honey, when I'm over there at Strauss Construction and you're here, running Somethings all by your lonesome, you're gonna love it for exactly the same reason!"

They laughed together, and she thought, How lucky I am. She was still laughing, in fact, when Howard cleared his throat and said seriously, "Elaine?"

"What? Is something wrong?"

"No. Not exactly what you would call *wrong*. But, well,

I've been thinking. And as long as you're going to have *your* heart's desire—although why in the world you find the *tsuris* of the construction business in New York so appealing is beyond me—then I think I ought to have *my* heart's desire."

Elaine stared at him, her mouth open. "You've done it again! I'm completely floored. So tell me. What *is* your heart's desire. If it's not making Sweet Somethings even bigger, then I have no idea what it could be."

He patted her hand. "I haven't thought about it for years, actually. But when I was a young man, don't laugh, I wanted to be a psychiatrist."

"You *are* full of surprises! I'm not laughing; I think you'd make a wonderful shrinker. You won't believe this, but I was just thinking a few minutes ago, how sensitive you are. So? Go ahead."

"That's all. I want to go back to school and get a doctorate in psychology. I've even spoken to the head of the department of NYU. So if our friend Mr. Park of Korea comes through with a good enough offer, and you're set with Strauss, then I'll be taking Graduate Record Exams."

Elaine smiled at him. "Hey! Even if I'm *not* set with Strauss, why shouldn't you do it, anyway? I can handle this business alone. It won't be nearly as much fun, but what the hell . . . maybe I'll be your first customer. Ooops, excuse me. Client."

"Patient," he corrected her, grinning. And then added, "That's a damn good idea, you know that? God knows the models could use some help along those lines. I'll start with Ginger, poor kid."

"Who, Ginger? I used to feel sorry for her, but now I'm tired of it. It's the same story over and over. Doesn't that bastard realize? All he has to do is tell her a couple of little white lies and they wouldn't have any more trouble!"

Howard gave her a sharp look. "Elaine! You think people should lie to each other? You think that makes a relationship?"

There was a pause. Then, "Yes. Sometimes. There's nothing inherently wonderful about telling the total truth about every goddamn thing. The truth, the whole truth, and nothing but the truth can hurt horribly. Ted could save them both a lot of grief by hiding his other women." Another pause. "Like Daddy."

"Elaine!"

"I give him credit for that. At least he saved Sylvia the pain of knowing about his extracurricular activities."

"Elaine, you don't *know* anything, really."

"I know. Linda as good as admitted it."

"'As good as admitted it' is *not* admitting it. Maybe she wanted to give you a hard time. Or, maybe she got a little thrill from making you and Deena think that."

"And maybe it's true."

"Yes, maybe it's true. Even so, why not let it go?"

"Let it go? You're out of your mind! This changes everything, do you realize that?"

"No, it doesn't. Just because a man takes a roll in the hay once in his life . . . all right, twice maybe. Look. It doesn't change the fact that he was always a good husband and father. And still *is*, by the way."

The microwave beeped loudly and Howard brought the two steaming containers to the round table in the corner. They sat and began to eat.

"Good husband!" Elaine said bitterly after a few moments. "Good father! Oh, sure! Big bully, *that*'s what he was! Always shoving people around to get his way. Oh, I know, I know, he often did it with quote charm unquote. But he always got his way, always. Like what he did with me. He didn't want me in the business and, you notice, I'm not in the business. In spite of the fact that I proved myself over and over to him . . ."

"Please, sweetheart. Don't dredge up the past."

"Who's talking *past*? What happened a week ago, when I supposedly had a date with him to talk about the business, huh? You see what I'm talking about? One way or the other he always gets what he wants, the way he wants it. Except once," she added in a very different tone, and then laughed.

"When?"

"The den . . ."

"The time your mother redecorated while he was away on business?"

"Yeah, that time." Again she laughed.

* * *

What a pigsty that den had been. It always stank of cigar smoke; it was very dark in there because he loved his walnut paneling; the furniture was shabby and mismatched. It was finally broken-in the way he liked it he said. And to make matters even worse, whatever he was using got left wherever it was when he was done with it because this was *his* space and if he didn't want to pick up anything, he wasn't going to. Until he left for the office, when Sylvia and/or Earline marched in, flinging windows open and picking up his mess.

Jack's den was forever being loaned out to his cronies as a recovery room from angry wives, late meetings, heavy drinking, and other acts of God. The little girl Elaine found all those unshaven, cranky, unexpected men emerging from the den strange and scary; and for years she avoided going anywhere near the room, without even realizing why.

Sylvia pleaded with him to let her do something with it. "What something has to be done?" he'd say, laughing. "It's perfect the way it is."

"The girls are getting older; they need a place to take their friends." She meant boyfriends, even though Elaine and Deena were not dating. When Jack said so, Sylvia said pertly, "I believe in being prepared."

One morning at the breakfast table, when she had brought up the subject for several days in a row, he banged his fist down and said, "Sylvia. Stop it. Our daughters don't need a room to 'entertain' in. We moved here to this big apartment so they could each have a room of her own. And they do! So I deserve a room of *my* own, too, don't I?"

Sylvia retorted dryly, "Where's *my* room of my own?"

And her lips tightened when he laughed and said, "You have a room of your own. The kitchen."

And then the twelve-year-old Elaine piped up, "Daddy, we didn't move here to this big apartment so Deena and me could have rooms of our own. We moved here because you kept saying we're living in a manner that's beneath our means and you said it made you look cheap." She thought he was going to smack her, but instead, he just pushed his chair back angrily and stomped out.

She knew she was right; she'd heard them fight about it

often enough when they were still in Peter Cooper Village. Sylvia didn't want to move. "There's a playground right outside the building, and all their little friends are here. Wait a few years, then it'll be good." But he didn't want to wait, so they didn't wait. They moved. She and Deena got their own rooms. And he got a den.

For a man so intent upon presenting a particular image, he was surprisingly stubborn about his den—dirt, mess, and all. Maybe because it showed him to still be just one of the guys, in spite of his wealth and the lavish decorations he insisted upon in the rest of the apartment. Elaine had never quite figured it out. But stubborn he was and the battle raged on. When boys started coming around to see Elaine, Sylvia renewed her efforts. "You don't want her taking a boy to her *bedroom*, do you, Jack?" That struck home. He relented. Yeah, yeah, she could fix it up if she wanted it so badly. But somehow the money was never available.

So Sylvia saved—from her household allowance, ten dollars at a time—and made her plans and bided her time. And when he took a week's trip to look at some old factories upstate, she moved. In his absence, an army of painters, carpet layers, and furniture men led by a decorator-general called Philip invaded and attacked Daddy's den, emerging victorious.

What had been faded green, dirty beige, and nondescript brown was now a highly polished, very masculine place, in the style of an English library, with plaid carpeting—the very latest thing—nautical scenes in gold frames, a stuffed pheasant, black tufted-leather furniture. It was beautiful, at least to the three women of the house. But Elaine still remembered her mother, pink with excitement, nevertheless saying anxiously, "Oh, he's going to love it. Don't you think so, Elaine? Don't you think he'll just love it?"

"The very best things in that den, when it was all finished, were the lamps. Oh, Howard, the lamps! How we loved them, Deena, and I! Three of them, ships in full sail, with little tiny pennants flying and little tiny windows that lit up and glowed when you turned the switch. The *Nina*, the *Pinta* and the *Santa Maria*! Oh, God, they were fabulous! I wonder where they are now?" Elaine put her fork down, smiling at her memory. "Oh, no, wait a minute. Earline thought they were wonderful, too, and when Sylvia redid the den a few years ago, she gave them to Earline, all three of them."

"So they sailed north, to Harlem," Howard said with a smile, and Elaine got right up, walked over to him, and kissed his forehead loudly.

"That's for being clever and smart and wonderful," she said. Seating herself once more, she continued. "But, of course, he hated it."

"Who? What?"

"Daddy. The den. When he got back from his trip. He was *furious*. He told Sylvia she had been too high-handed. High-handed! He'd been promising she could do it for over a year. It must have have been over a year for her to save up enough money. He was so mad, he never noticed the WELCOME HOME, DADDY sign Deena and I made for him. He just turned on his heel and stomped out. I don't know whether he came home at all that night . . . and now, it strikes me, of course I know where he went."

Patiently, Howard said, "You don't know anything for sure."

"You're as bad as Deena. *She*'s ready to make all kinds of excuses. First, she says it never happened. Then, when you get her to admit it might have happened, she says, well then, it wasn't his fault." Elaine rolled her eyes. "She thinks he's perfect, that's her problem! And she doesn't want any dirty old reality to intrude on her picture of him, either. How naive can you get? Could she really believe for even one minute that he gave Linda those shares for being a 'loyal employee'? Give me a break!"

"Would you like to consider your sister might have a point?"

"No, I would not. I tried talking plain common sense to Deena for an hour this afternoon. Forget it! Deena will not face facts, she never has, she never will. She's never been willing to confront *anything*, head on, ever!"

"Elaine, not everything in the world needs to be confronted head on, you know. Some things are better handled with tact."

"To hell with tact! Daddy has to be faced with this!"

"Why?"

"Because finally, we're on equal terms. Well, almost equal terms. Finally, I've got something I can use!"

"Elaine darling, that sounds a helluva lot like blackmail."

"You've got it, sweetie-*piele*! You're one hundred percent correct."

"I don't think you really meant that."

"Oh, yeah? Well, I do. And if it's blackmail, tough. Daddy has always made up all the rules. Okay. So now it's Elaine's rules. Good. Let him see what it feels like to come up against someone with balls!"

CHAPTER TWELVE

Tuesday, December 24, 1985

"Deena and her husband went on a *what?*" Flo Edelstein poured herself another cup of coffee from the big urn and asked, "Anyone else for a refill?"

Four hands shot up and Flo laughed. Everyone in the Women in Judaism group had arrived early, as usual, so they could drink coffee and gossip before the Rabbi arrived and made them get down to business. "They went on a *what?*" she repeated.

"A windjammer," Sylvia said, and rolled her eyes. "Don't ask! It's a cruise, yes, but it's a cruise, no. You're on a ship but you're barefoot and they tell you don't bring any real clothes, just shorts and bathing suits."

"You mean you don't get to dress for dinner?" That was Molly Farber with the very strong Bronx accent that not even forty years of money and privilege had been able to erase. "Oy! That's the only time Herb'll take me dancing, when we go to the islands every February!"

"At least," Sylvia answered, "Herb does it then. *I* don't ever get danced with."

133

Molly made a face at her, over the tops of her half glasses. "I don't want to hear a word from you about that fabulous husband of yours. If my Herb looked like your Jack . . ." And she heaved a great sigh, holding her hand to her heart.

"Looks," Sylvia murmured, "aren't everything, Molly. Your mother never told you that?"

And Flo put in: "Come on, Sylvia, Jack's the most popular man in the entire shul. Everyone says so! Why do you think they made him president of the Men's Club—for looks? No. Because he knows how to deal with people, that's why. Murray told me."

"You know you're just being modest, Syl," Harriet Stone called out. "You got the best-looking, best-socialized husband. Never mind, Irene, 'socialized' isn't something I made up, it's a real word and if you read a few books from time to time, you'd know it . . . And Flo, you're lucky, too. Herb dances with you on a boat? Wonderful! Lou will take me fishing on a boat . . . but *dancing*? Forget it!" There was general laughter at this and Harriet acknowledged it with a gracious bend of her head. "Even at our Steve's wedding, he wouldn't get up to dance 'The Anniversary Waltz' with me—the *bride's* parents are already out there on the floor and he's sticking out his lower lip and saying 'Not me'—until his sister *made* him."

All five women laughed. The vagaries and childish nonsense of men were nothing new to them.

Into the laughter, Sylvia said, "Anyway, Deena and Michael are somewhere in the Caribbean and I hope they're having a wonderful time. It's their second honeymoon, Michael said."

"How romantic!"

"Yeah, yeah, romantic." Sylvia sighed a bit. "I hope so. Not too many marriages nowadays last long enough to *get* a second honeymoon."

And three of the women cried out in unison. "They should live and be well, *kayn aynhoreh*."

"What about the children? Who's looking after them?" Flo asked.

"What children? They're all great big galoots. The two college girls went skiing. What else? Everyone skis these days. In my time Jews didn't ski." Sylvia waited for the expected laughter, then went on. "And, as you all know, the oldest Nat, is in medical school, almost a doctor. He doesn't need a baby-sitter, at least not too often." Again, laughter from her friends. "As for Saul . . . well, Deena wanted him to stay with us." Here she put down her coffee cup and laughed. "Thank God he said no way José. Of course, I call every day and ask if he wants to come eat with us. But it's 'too far' from Brooklyn Heights. I ask you! Well, he's not a baby anymore and you have to let them do their own thing."

"Especially a boy. You don't want to make a boy into a sissy."

"Shame on you, Irene Katz, and you call yourself a liberated woman!"

"Well, you know what I mean."

"Well, all I know is my grandson the computer genius is probably living on pizza and ice cream. It's about time for the Care package from Granny." She laughed. "A nice piece of brisket, some potato kugel, a little chopped liver from Zabar's, what could be bad about that? If the mountain won't come to Sylvia, Sylvia will go to the mountain."

"Shame on you, Sylvia Strauss," Irene cried in a note of triumph. "If it was one of your granddaughters, I'll bet you wouldn't schlepp all the way over to Brooklyn with two shopping bags of food. And you tell me *I'm* not liberated!"

"I'm liberated. It's Saul who can't cook!"

"Oh, Sylvia, always a smart answer. Always a joke."

"Jack says if you can't joke, you're dead."

Molly Farber, always the peacemaker, quickly put in, "My grandchildren in Israel, when they come to visit me, which isn't often enough, they only want American food. You know what is American food? Pizza and take-out Chinese!"

From the doorway came laughter, and they all turned to smile at the young blond woman in her pleated plaid skirt and long fuzzy sweater. She looked like a schoolgirl standing there smiling down at the group gathered around the big round table.

"Well, well, it's the rabette," Sylvia said, managing to ignore the whispered remonstrances from Irene Katz. Irene did not approve of levity concerning her spiritual adviser. Too bad. "Good afternoon, Sally. We were just discussing women's liberation." Irene made a tight little sound. She didn't approve of calling the rabbi by her given name, either.

The rabbi smiled. "Oh, really? What I heard was 'pizza and take-out Chinese.' Although I suppose, in a way, they are part of the liberation of women. But I didn't think food was our topic for today."

"Well, don't we come here every single week on a Tuesday to discuss the modern Jewish female experience? And if that isn't food, I don't know what it is!" They all laughed at that, even Irene.

The young rabbi pulled her large desk chair over to the table, nodding when one of the women gestured at the coffee urn, pulling papers and pamphlets and books, all with neat colored markers, out of her attaché case. Now the women settled themselves into their chairs, waiting for the morning's business to begin. They were in the rabbi's study, a wood-paneled high-ceilinged room lined with books and in the corner a spiral staircase leading up to a small loft with a comfortable leather chair and more books. Three Tiffany lamps hung from the ceiling, and there was a much-worn Oriental rug on the floor. One wall was dominated by a huge Andy Warhol print of Golda Meir; and on the other long wall facing it were large reproductions of the Chagall windows in Jerusalem.

Sipping from her steaming cup, the rabbi said, "Now then. Today we're going to talk about Jewish marriage and divorce. And we all read our background material—I hope!—yes? Good. So then . . . what do *you* think?"

"*I* thought," Molly Farber put in, her plump face pink with emotion. "Here we go again . . . another case where the woman's rights, thoughts, and feelings don't count for borscht!"

And someone else answered, "That's not quite true, Molly. In a marriage contract, women have—"

"Never mind marriage! Divorce is what I'm talking about! A man can demand a get but can a woman? Three guesses! Divorce on demand, but only if you're male."

"What's the matter, Molly? You want a divorce?"

"Very funny, Harriet, very funny. As it just so happens, my

daughter, Inez, the one in Israel, does. But that no-good Gadi won't give it unless she signs over the house and the car. The house and the car Herb and I bought for her for a wedding present! And she should hand them over! To that bum! Agh! It's not fair!"

"Let her take the children and come back home," Irene said. "That's the answer."

"I know, I told her that, I said, Inez, come home, your mother and father will welcome you and your children, come home. And you know what she said? She said, 'Mama, my home is Israel now.'"

Now the rabbi raised her hand and said, "Ladies, please, we're getting off the subject. Remember what we all agreed at our first meeting? That we'd stick to the point?"

"I'd like to know the point," Molly Farber insisted. "There's *no* justice for us in Judaism!"

There was an outburst of shocked disagreement.

"Molly Farber's daughter, Inez, is having a problem in Israel," Sylvia said loudly enough to be heard over the others, "and right away she's ready to convert!"

"Not true, Sylvia Strauss! I never said I don't *love* Judaism—"

"Ladies, ladies, please. I think the point we're trying to examine here is that the female experience is missing in a great deal of Jewish law. But that doesn't mean it's totally missing. For instance, remember last week we discussed the sexual aspect of marriage, the obligation of the husband to satisfy his wife—"

"I told Lou and he said, sure, that's what you get when the rabbi's a woman."

"I thought you were going to say he had a headache!"

"That, too!"

"Ha! Mine has a permanent headache. He says to me, Flo, what do you want from me, I'm a grandfather."

"So how come we're not hearing from you, Sylvia?"

"At this stage of the game, sex isn't the most important thing in a marriage."

"So what is?"

"Your children," Molly said immediately, and there was a hum of agreement.

"A son to carry on the name," Flo added. She had four sons.

"To mourn for you, to say kaddish after you're gone." That was Irene, always the stickler for proper form. "That's right, isn't it, Rabbi? A girl can't say kaddish for you?"

Before the rabbi had a chance to say anything, Sylvia had risen to her feet, her face flushed. "That's nonsense! I was one of three sisters, and when my papa died, may his name be a blessed memory, my uncle, my mother's brother, came to her and said he'd be honored to mourn Papa for us. And me and my sisters went to Mama and said, '*We'll* pray for Papa. We don't need Uncle Charles to do it for us.' And you know, my mama was an old-fashioned woman in many ways; but that time she stopped and she thought about it and she said, 'Yes. We'll do it. I know your papa, *alevai shalom*, would prefer to hear our voices rising to heaven. He never *did* like Uncle Charlie.'"

The women in the group laughed at this; but Sylvia didn't. "This is serious," she said. "We're here to discuss the experience of being a Jewish woman. *This* is the experience of being a Jewish woman: that you're second class. All the way!"

"Every religion is the same. Aren't nuns complaining to the Pope?"

"Jews should be smarter than that," Sylvia said. "No, no, I'm sorry, now I'm doing it, making a joke of it. Rabbi, if you don't mind, I want someone to explain to me: Where is it written that boys are better than girls?"

Flo said, "In the Bible, that's where."

"Right. In the Bible. You know how smart the Bible is? The bible says Eve was born of Adam. Since when do men give birth?"

"Oh, Sylvia, that's not what that means."

"Oh, really, Harriet? Are you going to try to deny that in this world men are considered much more important than women?" She didn't wait for an answer. "When I was a young married woman, my father-in-law, that schmo, always gave me the heel of the loaf to eat. Who else had that? Ah-ha! All of you. Sure. That was supposed to what? Make sure you had a boy? And when I had my first—fourteen hours in labor, let me tell you, it was no picnic, even then Elaine was a big girl—what do you think my sainted mother-in-law said to me? She said, 'Never mind, Sylvia, next time you'll have your boy.'"

There were murmurs of protest around the table and Sylvia looked first into one face and then the next. They knew what she was talking about.

And then Harriet Stone said dryly, "Well, you showed them, Sylvia! Three girls!"

Sylvia made a little face. "I showed them, all right. Yeah, yeah." She gave a sigh, and sat down. "You want to know something? Something awful? The second pregnancy with my Deena, for nine months I prayed, even when I was in labor I prayed. Please God, I said, let it be a boy. Let it be a boy. You hear that?" Her eyes filled and she blinked rapidly.

"It's too bad you were made to feel that way," the rabbi said gently. "Particularly considering women have no control over the sex of their unborn children."

"That's right," Molly Farber put in. "I remember when I was pregnant the first time, my mother wouldn't even let me say I *might* have a girl. 'Bite your tongue,' she'd tell me."

"But that was the way everybody thought back then," Irene said. "Come on, why are we making such a big deal about it? We're all grandmothers here!"

"Once again you've missed the point," Sylvia said. "Dammit, can't you all see how horrible that is? That a woman should pray that the child in her womb is a male? There I was, a female with a female child whom I loved, and wishing only that my unborn baby should be male. What did that say about me? What did that say about my feelings of self-worth? Answer me that!"

"Didn't keep you from having your third daughter."

"Very funny, Irene, very funny. As it happens, I had my third daughter still trying to have a boy!"

"Sylvia! you're being overly dramatic!"

"Oh, you think so? Well, just ask your beloved Jack Strauss, Molly, the one you think is so handsome. Flo, go ask my wonderful husband, so popular at the synagogue, go ask him why he wanted a third child. For a son! What else? A son to carry on the name. What name? I asked him. What's so famous and wonderful about the name Strauss? If it was Ein-

stein, I told him, then maybe . . . if it was Freud. But Strauss?
What's the big deal about Strauss? I asked him."

"And? What did he say to that?"

"What do you think he said to that? Nothing. He got mad
and he walked away from me. And two months later I was
pregnant."

Flo said, "You made up."

Sylvia and Flo exchanged a look of understanding. "We
made up," she agreed. "I was almost thirty-five years old and
I was satisfied with my family just the way it was. Let me tell
you, Deena and Elaine were enough for any mother! But what
can I tell you? He wanted a boy more than he wanted a baby."

"And you?" the rabbi asked. "Did you pray for a boy this
time?"

"I don't remember," Sylvia said, her voice flattening. "But
I do know that I always felt differently about Marilyn.
Always."

"Oh, Sylvia, we're all different with each child."

"That's not what I'm talking about, Harriet, and you know
it! I just never was as attached to her, like I was with her
sisters."

"Hey, she came out all right. A doctor! That's not so bad."

"What do you think it was like all those years, bringing up
three little girls, knowing that Jack never stopped wanting his
son." She choked a little and said, "Never mind. I'm sorry
I've taken all this time talking about myself. So, where were
we, Rabbi?"

The rabbi smiled and said, "Someone asked what's important in a Jewish marriage and someone else said children."

Irene Katz now drew in a noisy breath, folded her hands
together, and looked as if she were about to pray. Sylvia
sighed inwardly; Irene was about to wax poetic, and when
Irene waxed, she expected the world to wait and watch. And
look appreciative. She was, as she never tired of saying, "a
very sensitive woman."

Now what she said was, "Our children are our immortality."

Worse than expected, Sylvia thought. "Oh, for God's sake,

Irene, let's have something a little more original, what do you say?"

Irene sniffed. "We're very good friends and I love you very much but sometimes we're quite different, you know. You have a tough attitude, Sylvia, I've always said that. *I* like to think well of everyone. I am a very sensitive person."

Agh, she didn't have the strength to try to deal with that. And besides, this was Irene, her girlhood friend, too bad her mind had stopped developing sometime in her teens, but there you were. Would it do any good to try to get her to really listen, to really think? Not at this stage of the game. And anyway, someone else took issue with her and that's how it went until it was lunchtime and the session was over.

The other four decided on Hunan Palace for lunch, but Sylvia begged off. "I have a headache," she said, but that wasn't quite true. More like a heartache. Why had she allowed herself to remember all that pain again? She had been so sure it was all put away. Once she had decided what she had to do, that had been that. What in the world had possessed her today, what made her say so many personal things, tell so much about her private life?

When the others had left, the rabbi put her hand on Sylvia's arm. "Sylvia," she said gently. "Is something bothering you?"

Sylvia paused, gazing at the lithograph of Golda Meir without really seeing it. After a moment she said, "You know, there once was a time when I thought very seriously about leaving my husband." Now she focused on the young woman's face, that serious face with the worried eyes. "A thousand times I *thought* about it but only once seriously. You know, it took me almost two years to decide about that. Two years and the whole time I had to keep it to myself."

"Yes, and?"

"In the end I went to the women in my life closest to me. My mother said, 'You made your bed, now you have to lie in it.' Nice? Well, that was my mother. And my gynecologist said, 'You want him back? Don't worry, he'll be back. They all come back.'"

"Well, it's obvious you didn't leave him," said the rabbi. A nice young woman. But young. Very young. "And it seems to have worked out very well." There was half a question in her voice.

"Oh, yes, very well. I have a beautiful home, a nice life, wonderful children, fabulous grandchildren, two doctors, even a computer genius, that Saul!" She laughed. "You might say I have everything a woman could want!"

CHAPTER THIRTEEN

Sunday, July 11, 1937

Sylvia Weinreb, twenty-one years old, healthy, and in her right mind, was feeling terrific. It was a beautiful Sunday, she was on the deck of the Staten Island ferry with a delicious cool breeze lifting her hair off her neck, and she knew a lot of fellows were looking at her. So what could be bad?

She was standing at the railing right at the front of the boat, leaning against it actually, a sister on either side. Funny, whenever they went out together—and that was every Sunday, because otherwise Mama and Papa wouldn't let *any* of them out of the house—she always ended up in the middle, with Helen on her right side and Ruthie on her left. It was the same today, and their squabbling was the same, too. If Helen said black, Ruth immediately thought white; if Helen said Brooklyn Botanic Garden, Ruthie only wanted Coney Island. That meant it was always left to Sylvia, who didn't mind a bit. Because it was such a hot day—well up in the nineties—she had chosen the Staten Island ferry and she was glad she had. It was very comfortable, even though you couldn't keep your hat on. And, if your sisters didn't pester you too much, you could imagine you were on the deck of the *Queen Mary*, going somewhere wonderful, where something wonderful might happen to you.

She loved going to new places and doing new things, loved excitement, loved carnivals and street fairs and weddings and bar mitzvahs, loved dancing and singing and carrying on. "Sylvia," her mother liked to say, "was born to be a Catskill *tummler*." And Sylvia could only agree. She thought it would be swell to have a job where you urged people to have fun, where you ran around the resort yelling that it was the exercise hour, the croquet hour, the cocktail hour.

The reality, though, was that she worked for her father, at his carpentry shop, a couple of blocks from Rugby Road, where they lived, and the only *tummling* she did was with Papa's account books. Actually, it was not so bad going to business; actually, it made her feel like she was taking care of herself, even though she was still living at home with her mama and her papa and her sisters. And it was a lot better than sitting around giving piano lessons and waiting to get married, like her older sister, Helen; or being in school like her kid sister, Ruth.

She loved going to business; still, it was nice to have Sunday off and to mingle with the crowds at Coney Island or Prospect Park or, like today, the ferry. They had decided to dress alike today in flower print dresses and white shoes and their new little hats that were practically all veiling. They were a good-looking threesome, the Weinreb girls, with their high cheekbones and dark hair and big round eyes; and Sylvia was very much aware of all the admiring glances that had followed the three of them all afternoon.

Especially one particular pair of admiring eyes, over there. Especially, she noticed, after the wind shifted and blew their skirts up and the three of them shrieked and quickly pushed them back down again. He was leaning against the rail, big and muscular, with thick dark wavy hair and eyes that twinkled. She *thought* they twinkled, but it could just be the light from the water. So she looked away and then, a minute later, glanced over at him again. He was still looking at them, his smile getting broader. He was so handsome. That man's for me, she thought. She leaned against the railing, tipping her head back so he could see the nice long line of her throat and the wind blowing her long black hair and, it shouldn't be a total loss, get a good look at her figure.

Boys liked her and she liked them. All afternoon she had been kind of making eyes at this boy, discreetly, of course. A nice girl didn't flirt openly, especially if she had a sister like Helen, but who could say anything if you gave a little smile in a certain direction? So she smiled a little now in his direction and he pushed himself away from the rail and her heart began to pound. He was coming over! No, he wasn't, he was going to walk right by to get an ice cream; no, he was standing there, right in front of them, shorter than she had thought, but strong, wearing cream linen trousers and a blue blazer. He swept the straw hat from his head, and grinned. What white teeth he had! What thick hair! What beautiful eyelashes!

"Hi, there, girls. Excuse me for being so bold; but when a man sees six of the most beautiful legs in New York City, all standing in one spot, well, it's irresistible!"

"You're pretty fresh!" Helen said smartly; but, even though her lips were pressed tightly together, her cheeks were pink.

"That's me, all right! Jack Strauss, fresh as the air on this boat and twice as breezy. And you?"

Sylvia said, "Which one are you talking to?" Helen jabbed her, hard, in the ribs, and Ruth tried to disappear behind her.

"All three of you. I have two shy friends standing on the other side, just dying to meet you. What do you say? We're nice fellows. Come have a Coke or an ice cream with us. Aw, come on, don't be shy. It's a beautiful summer day, just meant for boys and girls to make friends."

Talk about irresistible! He was so cheerful, so obviously good-natured and so obviously impressed with them. How could you say no to him? Helen hesitated—she *would*, Sylvia thought, the priss—but even she was charmed. After a few awkward moments, Sylvia held out her hand and said: "Sylvia Weinreb. And these are my sisters, Helen and Ruth." Helen gave her a dirty look. According to Helen, the oldest sister should always set the tone and Sylvia was constantly challenging her God-given rights and responsibilities. Well, phoo! If she had to wait for Helen all the time, nothing exciting would ever happen! She eyed this dark bright-eyed young man and promised herself that she wasn't going to let *him* get away so fast.

When he went to get his pals, Helen jabbed her again and muttered, "Awfully flashy, isn't he?"

"Maybe I happen to like that!" Sylvia retorted. "You *would*!" Helen said. Sylvia tossed her head, knowing full well that it made her long lustrous hair ripple down her back. Her hair was something else Helen didn't approve of. A young lady, according to Helen, was supposed to wear her hair shoulder-length and neat, like Helen did. She was not supposed to let it grow to her tush and wear it loose like some kind of streetwalker. Well, too bad, if that's what she thought! Sylvia Weinreb made her *own* rules . . . well, some of them, anyway. If she let her sister Helen rule her world, she'd never have any fun! The Lord knew Helen didn't! Just sat home, waiting for Prince Charming to ride up on a white charger. In the middle of Flatbush, Brooklyn, honestly!

The other two guys were all right, nice guys, but ordinary. Not like Jack Strauss, not broad and strong and energetic and handsome and just everything a man should be. And the personality! What a sense of humor! One joke after the other. She laughed so hard, the tears came. And she gave him back a couple, just about as good as his and he didn't get miffed and clam up like a lot of other boys did. He laughed. He put his big hand on her shoulder; she could feel the heat of it right through the thin fabric of her dress and he said, "You're okay, Syl!"

And when she knew all the words to *Three Little Fishies* —"Down in de meddy in a itty bitty poo . . ."—he couldn't get over it.

"You're real hep!" he laughed. Oh, she liked this Jack Strauss! She crossed her fingers behind her back and fiercely wished that he would ask to see her again.

Well, he did and he didn't. He asked to come visit them but it was *them* he wanted to visit. All three of them, Ruth and Helen, too. Couldn't he see that Helen was a boring old maid and Ruthie just a baby? Couldn't he see that she, Sylvia, was the live wire? Was he blind, or what?

Papa called her his rebel. She was the first one who had

insisted on taking a business course in high school and said
she was going to work, and when mama said, Oh, phoo,
you'll be married before you know it, and she said she wasn't
sure she wanted to get married right away like everyone else.
Mama said sharply, "Bite your tongue!" but Papa just laughed.
He was proud.

"That's my independent girl!" he said. "Nobody tells *her*
what's what, hey?"

And when he bought a Ford and she said, "Teach me, I
want to know how," he laughed again and said all right.

And then, when she didn't get her hair cut like her sisters,
like her mother, too, he said, "What's this? My modern
daughter, looking old-fashioned?"

And she grinned at him and tossed her head and answered,
"I don't have to follow the fashions like a sheep. Everyone
else is having their hair cut. I'll be different!"

And he applauded and said, "That's my girl!"

She loved being Papa's girl. She loved the role of the rebel
daughter. First of all, it made her different and she liked that.
As the middle sister, she was at a disadvantage. *Nischt a hein,
nischt a heir*, neither here nor there, neither the blessed firstborn nor the beloved baby but just the one stuck in between.
And the other big reason she decided to be nonconformist very
early on was Papa. From a very young age she realized that
Papa liked spirit. He always said, "I fell in love with your
mama because of her wit. Oh, and she was the prettiest girl in
the room, too." But Sylvia saw, every day of her life, how
Mama made him laugh and she resolved *she* was going to
grow up and be that kind of woman.

If she had been a boy, she'd have gone to college, to City,
like her cousin, Leo, and Become Somebody. That's what
men did, if they could. They Became Somebody. Women became the wives of Somebody. She knew that, ultimately, that
was to be her fate and she accepted it. But in the meantime,
she was going to be noticed. She wasn't going to be just
another girl. So she went to work with Papa at the shop and
she learned as much as she could about the work, and now she
could really talk business with him. She prided herself that
she wasn't just husband-hunting; she was a working girl. So

she worked for her father, so what? She could have had ten other jobs if she wanted.

On the hunt or no, as soon as she saw Jack Strauss she knew right away *this* she wanted. That's why she posed and preened and made sparkling conversation, thinking herself ever so clever and subtle. And when they all said good-bye at Battery Park, he did write down their address and asked if he could call. He lived in Brooklyn, too. "Not in your neighborhood," he said, "but I work not too far from Rugby Road, on Flatbush Avenue. Style-Rite Shoes. I'm the manager." The manager! Imagine! Even Helen had to be impressed with that.

And when he asked if they thought he might come calling on Wednesday, after supper, Helen didn't poke Sylvia when Sylvia said, "Oh, yes, that would be swell."

Of course, he hadn't gone three feet from them before Helen was hissing at her, "Sylvia Weinreb, you should be *ashamed* of yourself, the way you pushed yourself at that fellow!" Well, she wasn't ashamed and she said so and then she stuck her tongue out at Ruthie for looking so shocked and agreeing with every word Helen had to say.

"I do what I like," Sylvia told them. "I don't go creeping through life following everyone else's rules. *He* didn't think I was pushing myself. And anyway," she lied, "I don't care if he shows up or not on Wednesday night."

Well, he showed up, right on the button of eight o'clock, in time to sit with them in the living room listening to Fred Allen on their new Zenith console, while they all ate the chocolate ice cream he had brought. He said, "What a nice place you've got here," and he was right. Her father was a good provider, so there was an Oriental carpet on the floor, the furniture was all solid mahogany not just veneer like some people had, and the upright piano was a George Steck. Sylvia was very proud of the house she lived in and of the way she lived.

He was very polite with her parents, calling Papa "sir" and leaping up every time Mama moved, which was plenty because she had to make sure he wasn't going to die of starvation or thirst, God forbid, while he was a guest in her home. Finally, Mama laughed at him and said, "Jack Strauss, you'll give yourself indigestion jumping up and down like a jack-in-the-box." And then laughed loudly at her own pun. "Sit, sit already. It's all right, I'll know you're polite even if you sit still when I come back with the tea."

What Sylvia admired about him was that he enjoyed her wisenheimer mother. A lot of the boys who came over found her humor intimidating and tried very hard to avoid her. The fools! Didn't they think a woman could make a joke? But what Sylvia did *not* admire about him was that he paid equal attention to every single member of the family, talking business with her father in a very manly way, and also world events, like the rumors coming out of Europe that anti-Semitism was on the rise in Germany; complimenting their mother on her beautiful home; chatting about schoolwork with that baby, Ruthie; and asking Helen to play "Once in a While" on the piano and telling her how talented she was. Oh, he talked to Sylvia, too, very polite and very pleasant, asking her how she liked working and telling her how amusing he found her. She was going to give him a smart comeback to that comment, but old Helen, the killjoy, called out that she had the sheet music from the new Disney movie, *Snow White* and began to play "Whistle While You Work" and he got up and went over to the piano and that was the end of her one and only private conversation with him.

Three weeks later, after he'd come by twice each week, once on Wednesday, again on Sunday, it was still the same. This Sunday, he'd had his first meal with them, Leah Weinreb's best pot roast and potatoes with her special apple strudel for dessert. He expressed his pleasure at the meal, at the company, at the whole thing. "Thank you all so much for having me," he said when he left. "Coming to this house is such a high spot in my life."

After the door closed behind him, Papa sat down in his chair, unbuttoning his vest, and he looked around at all of them, laughing a little. "So, *nu*? What's it going to be, hey? Your mother just fed that young man a terrific meal, if I do say so myself, probably the best meal he's had in his whole life. But it's not your mother he's coming to see. The question is, *who*? Which one of you is going to be Mrs. Jack Strauss, hey?"

"How do you know he's not coming to see Mama?" Sylvia

quipped. "He spends an awful lot of time in the kitchen with her!"

"Sylvia!" Mama objected, as Sylvia had known she would. "Such talk!" Certain subjects were never mentioned by Leah Weinreb and one of them was It.

And then Sylvia noticed that Helen was blushing. *Gottinyu*, was *she* after him? Had he, God forbid, said something to her? She'd die, that's what she'd do, she'd *die* if it turned out Jack Strauss was after Helen!

He couldn't be. She wouldn't allow it, that's all. Maybe Papa didn't know who Jack Strauss was coming to see. Maybe Jack didn't know, either, not yet. But if Sylvia had her way, they were *all* going to know very soon.

How she longed after him! How she daydreamed about him: that he would secretly reach out for her hand under the tablecloth or that he would take her aside and say it's really you I like and kiss her. But, except for an occasional wink, he gave no sign that he favored her above either Helen or Ruth . . . or even above Mama, for that matter!

Obviously, she had to take matters into her own hands. She thought about what to do for four days, making first one plan and then scratching it out and making another. What she did, in the end, was stupidly simple: after Sunday dinner, she decided they all should have ice cream, it was so hot. And what could be more natural than to ask for his company? It was dusk already and no nice girl walked out alone after dark, especially in this neighborhood, where everyone was always gossiping.

She made sure they walked good and slow. If the old biddies behind their curtains wanted something to talk about, let them talk about Sylvia Weinreb and her handsome new beau! And she turned her head prettily to look up at him, very aware of how big and lustrous her eyes shone, very aware of the scent of his shaving lotion and of the bulk of his body only dimly seen in the lamplight. His shirt was so white beneath the linen jacket, it gleamed in the purplish twilight. The sodden heat of August had quieted everything but the crickets' shrill singing.

"It's like the country here," Jack said. "Really swell, you

know? With the trees and the grass and all. You're a lucky girl!"

"I'm lucky because I have trees and grass and all? Anybody can have that just by going to Prospect Park!"

"Aw, Sylvia, you're such a kidder!" He took her arm, as they went to cross the street; and she made sure to snuggle in as close as she could without being too forward. "What I meant was, your whole life. This neighborhood, your house —where I live, there aren't any houses like on Rugby Road; it's all apartment buildings."

"There's nothing wrong with living in an apartment."

"Agh! You don't know my neighborhood. They aren't those big fancy buildings; they're ugly brick boxes! People shouldn't have to live in places that aren't much better than chicken coops!"

"Jack Strauss, I can't believe a fellow with your pizzazz and charm comes from a chicken coop! And anyway, pooh, who cares? In this country, it doesn't matter where a person comes from, only where he's going... and *I* think you're going places!"

He stopped in his tracks. "Do you really mean it?" She wished she could see his face better.

"Of course I do," she said earnestly. "You're a go-getter; you're already the manager of a whole store and only twenty-two years old!"

"Yeah," he said, "you have a point there. I don't have to stop at managing a shoe store for somebody else, do I?"

"That's right! The world's your oyster, Jack Strauss. A man with your brains and excuse me for saying so but your good looks, why, there's no holding you!"

"Gee, Sylvia, that's the nicest thing anyone's ever said to me. You're really special, aren't you?"

"Sure. Just ask me, I'll tell you!"

He laughed. "And a live wire, too." They began to stroll once more. "But, no kidding, you've given me a lot to think about, Sylvia. I've been kinda worried lately." He took in a breath, then expelled it. "See, I didn't tell you, but my father ... he fixes shoes. He's a cobbler. It's his own business, but not like your father has, with half a dozen men working for him."

"And a young lady," Sylvia reminded him pertly.

"Yeah, and a young lady. But see, where I come from, it's . . . different than it is here. I mean, my father thinks I've gone as far as I can expect to go. He thinks managing that store for Sid Imberman is about the greatest thing that could have happened to me and what am I complaining about? It's white collar and it's secure. Agh . . ."

"Well, he's right as far as he goes. But you want bigger and better things, don't you?"

"You took the words right out of my mouth!"

"Then all you have to do is tell him," Sylvia said.

And he laughed and said, "You're a cute little thing, you know that? You don't know my old man—not yet."

She thought her heart would stop beating when he added those two little words. *Not yet.* Didn't that mean she was destined to meet his folks? She could not concentrate for a while after that and was grateful that they'd come to the dairy and had to busy themselves with their purchase.

When they walked out, she held her breath, so to speak. And then he did it: he took her arm again, just as natural as natural, pulling her in close against him. Elation rose in her like soap bubbles, light and airy and full of beautiful soft colors. They began to walk back, side by side, linked together, a real couple. She felt so proud to be seen with him. And when Manny Shapiro passed them and did a double take, she couldn't help giggling with her delight.

When they got to her corner, she said to herself, Sylvia, you've got to do it, it's now or never. She stumbled a little, accidentally on purpose, holding more tightly on to his arm and tipping her head to look up at him. Well, Jack Strauss was no dummy, he had the good sense to spot an opportunity when it clung to him and raised her lips to his. He gave a little smile and the next thing she knew, she was being smooched with a capital S.

The following Wednesday, when Jack appeared at the door and her father answered, this time he said, "Hello, Mr. Weinreb, I'm here to see Sylvia."

And her father just smiled sweetly and said, "I'll see if she's available." And turned to give her a wink.

CHAPTER FOURTEEN

Sunday,
February 8, 1942

"I love this house!" Jack had said, stopping in the middle of the sidewalk to point out the hand-carved gingerbread under the eaves to baby Elaine in his arms. "Look, *bubeleh*, see? your grandpa built this house. With his own two hands."

"Jack! It's too cold for lectures today. Look how she's shivering."

"She's not shivering," Jack said. "Are you, sweetheart? She likes hearing family stories, don't you, baby?"

Sylvia rolled her eyes heavenward and marched up the stairs herself. She didn't have to ring the bell; the door opened as if by magic and her father embraced her, drawing her inside.

Jack, now close behind her, handed the child to her grandfather and slid his heavy coat off, looking around, sniffing loudly—the house was redolent of chicken soup and a roasting bird—and making appreciative noises. "Mmmm . . . what a smell, if you could bottle it, you could get maybe five dollars an ounce for it. Eau de chicken soup . . ." He laughed, rubbed his hands together. "And am I hungry!" Still talking,

153

he walked into the living room and sprawled out on the plush sofa, looking around. "Love this house! I always did."

"I already told you, anytime you and Sylvia say the word, we'll build you a house."

"Yeah, yeah, but where? I don't want to go out by New Lots Avenue."

"How about Mill Basin?"

"Too far, too isolated. Nah, nah, I think we're probably going to head into Manhattan." Again, he laughed loudly. "Eventually. If my friend Marty comes through for me. No, it's just . . . this house. It always looks so comfortable, so . . . settled. There's something about it, I don't know."

Sylvia, carrying the baby, freed from her snowsuit and wriggling to be put down, said, "You make it sound as if we live in a slum. What's wrong with our place?"

Her father smiled at her. "Jack didn't say anything was wrong with your apartment, honeybunch. Can't he like our house? *I* do."

Sylvia sniffed. "It's more than like with him, Papa. Jack's in love with this house, with the piano and the dining room and the front lawn and the rosebushes and even the lamppost for all I know. This is perfect; ours is lousy; that's it, in a nutshell."

"Ours is a mess lately, Sylvia, and you know it. I ask you, Nat, what would you say if there was a diaper pail in your bathroom and bottles in your living room and toys everywhere? That baby has taken over our lives. We're supposed to clear the decks for her, for one little baby not yet a year old. I can't leave my cigars where I like them. There can't be heavy ashtrays on the coffee table. My magazines are hidden away because if they aren't, *she* eats them."

Mildly, his father-in-law said, "Jack, Jack, that's how it is with a baby in the house." He chuckled. "Three times we went through it. Don't worry, it passes. You're lucky she's not a boy. Believe me, boys are worse."

"Should one little *pitsel* disrupt everyone else? This week, she spit up all over the brand new sofa and now that she's crawling so fast, you can't read the newspaper even!"

He turned to give his wife an accusing look, but she was no

longer there. She had escaped, the baby still in her arms, into the kitchen.

"Maybe," Nat Weinreb said, "you shouldn't talk about her like that in front of her."

"Who?"

"Your daughter. Who else?"

Jack looked at the older man, amused. "Her? She's only a baby; she doesn't understand." Obviously bored with the subject, he quickly pulled a folded paper out of his jacket pocket. "I had a thought about that job on the Lower East Side. We could do it, Nat. We really could . . . and make a pile. Look, here are the figures."

Already Nat Weinreb was shaking his head. "I'd have to get another truck, Jack, and with the war on, you know that's almost impossible. Even if I could find one, with gasoline rationing, it'd be out of the question. Too far away. And anyway, it'll mean spreading ourselves too thin."

"We could do it, Nat! *I'll* be in charge of the Manhattan job. Don't look at me like that, Nat. You keep saying I'm your good right arm. And I've been in the business since before we got married. God, it's over five years. Don't you trust me?"

"Of course I trust you. It's just . . . I don't know, Jack, I don't think so. Too much, too big, too many problems. Manhattan's another world; it's not for us."

In the kitchen, Sylvia listened for a minute or two to the men talking. Again, business. More and more, Jack's attention was focused on the business. Seemed it was all he talked about anymore . . . when he wasn't complaining about the change in their lives since the baby arrived. Pushing herself away from the door, she took in a deep breath and let it out noisily.

"What is it, darling?" Her mother, sitting down for a change, with the baby on her lap, looked up. "Sit, sit for a minute. You look a little peaked." She bent to muzzle the infant's neck, laughing when the baby laughed. "And to think I didn't even hear you when you came in. What a bad grandma!"

"Mama. That's the third time you've said that. It's all

right, you don't have to come running the minute the door opens."

"But I *like* to come running. I wait all week for my treat ... now that your sisters are both gone, it gets lonesome around here. Too quiet. Oh! Did I tell you? Helen's pregnant, all the way out there in Chicago."

Sylvia began to laugh. "Mama, even in Chicago, they know how to make babies. And I hear they have a hospital or two, also."

Her mother broke off another piece of zwieback and handed it to the eager infant. "Hungry, *bubeleh*? They starving you over there on Westminster Road? Look at her, *kayn ayn-horeh*, what a beauty! A living doll!"

"I wish her father thought so."

"Sylvia! What a thing to say!"

"He really wanted a boy. He doesn't like her, Mama."

"Bite your tongue! Of course he likes her ... he *loves* her!"

"He *kvetches* about her all the time. She's not allowed to breathe."

"Sylvia darling, the first baby, it's always like this with them. With men. Look, they're like little boys. They get jealous. You have to give them a little extra attention."

"Don't you think I know all about that kind of jealousy? I pay attention to him. An hour before he's due home, she's in the tub, things are picked up, dinner's on the stove cooking, I'm brushing my hair and I'm putting on a little lipstick—just like it says in *Good Housekeeping*." She laughed wryly. "I'm a modern woman, Mama, I know all about the first baby and how it shouldn't get in the way of ... married life. Oh, Mama! I don't believe it, you're blushing! But listen, would you listen to me, please? I mean, really listen?"

Her mother had gotten up, depositing Elaine on the kitchen floor with a pot cover and a wooden spoon to keep her occupied, and was back at the stove, tending to her pots and pans. "I'm listening, Sylvia, but there are two hungry men out there to feed."

"Couldn't they just wait a minute? Anyway, they're talking business and you know what that means, you could serve dinner stone cold and they wouldn't notice. In fact, you could serve it *tomorrow*."

"Your father would notice, believe me, and he'd let me know about it quick enough."

"He's coming home awfully late these days," Sylvia blurted out.

Now Leah turned, her attention fully on her daughter. "Who? Jack? You think . . . ? I don't want to say it. But if he is, *you* have to try harder to make it nice for him at home."

"You mean running around? With who, the lumber dealer? The carpenters? Because that's where he is until all hours, at the office. The office! What's so wonderful there, that's what I'd like to know!"

The kitchen door flew open and there was Jack with a squalling Elaine held under one arm like a bundle. "Dammit, Sylvia, can't you keep an eye on your baby?"

Leah Weinreb wiped her hands and hurried over, holding out her arms for Elaine. "Now she's *my* baby?" Sylvia said, a sharp edge to her voice. "I seem to recall having some help from you in that department."

Leah Weinreb began to sing to the baby rather loudly.

"Do you know what she did, that kid? She crawled into the living room without a sound and before I knew she was there, she had chewed half a contract and drooled all over the rest of it. You can't make heads or tails out of it anymore." He broke off suddenly and began to laugh. "Drooled all over my figures," he repeated, laughing harder. "Oh, God, can you beat it? Can you just hear me, trying to explain *that* to tough old Al Schwab. Oh, Christ!"

Now they were all laughing, even Sylvia, and the baby, seeing everyone else convulsed, began to crow with delight.

Now Jack said, "Say, that delicious smell is getting to me, Ma. Dinner ready soon—I hope? All week my mouth waters, dreaming of how well I'm gonna eat in Leah Weinreb's house, rationing or no rationing." He bent and gave his mother-in-law a loud smacking kiss on her cheek.

Leah smiled and blushed. "Just because my butcher happens to be my brother Charlie, don't think for a minute we'd cheat the war effort!" And again, they all laughed. "But I'll *never* be able to figure out that crazy rationing! Books, tokens, stamps, red, blue, green . . . what next? Don't you laugh at me, Sylvia, how do *you* like shopping now that it's so many cents a pound, so many points a pound. And all those papers you have to carry around with you! Feh!"

"We come every week for dinner," Jack said. "It isn't fair you should bear the brunt alone. Let me give you some of our stamps."

"What are you talking about? You have a baby in the house. You need all your stamps. No. Thank you, Jack, I appreciate the thought. But it's our pleasure to have you for dinner. Only not," she added, "if you don't get out of here and let us girls finish up."

When Jack had gone back into the other room, the older woman turned and said, "There? You see? Everything's fine. He laughs at the baby's mischief. Believe me, Sylvia darling, there are men who *really* can't take it when there's a new baby in the house."

"Other fathers don't *kvetch* and complain all the time. My friends in the playground tell me—"

"Mothers in the playground!" her mother interrupted. "Bring me the soup bowls, will you? We'll dish up. Let me tell you about the women in the playground, Sylvia. They all make up fairy tales. Oh, sure, they have a perfect marriage, a perfect husband! According to them, their husbands come home smiling, is that right? And pick up the baby and make nice and never a harsh word? Yeah, yeah, sure. Don't you believe it, Sylvia. Every marriage goes through a period of adjustment with a new baby and anyone who tries to tell you different . . . well, all I can say is, she's lying. Don't listen to them, Sylvia, don't listen." She loaded a tole tray with the steaming bowls of soup and added, "And Sylvia?"

"Mmmmmm?"

"You haven't been talking to anyone about your problems, have you? No? Good. Listen to me, darling. Don't say anything to anybody. It can be embarrassing, you know, later. You don't want people to know too much about you. When it comes to family matters, believe me, Sylvia, nobody needs to know."

The elevator in the sprawling apartment house where Jack's parents lived was too small and too slow for such a large building and, as usual, they had just missed it going up.

"Well, there goes Sunday," Sylvia joked, only half-joking; and Jack chose to take the other half.

"Always a gripe when we come to *my* family," he groused. "Always something wrong!"

"Jack, that's not true. And anyway, since when do you love the elevator here so much. The last I heard, you wanted to replace it with a cart and a donkey."

"Da—da—da—" baby Elaine chanted.

Sylvia laughed. "Look how she's trying to say donkey."

"How about Dada . . . you think she might be saying Dada? Since I'm the one always schlepping her around?"

"Always, Jack? *Always*?"

"Well . . ." huffily. "On Sundays, it is."

"Tell you what, darling. You take the diaper bag and the bottles and the bananas and the toys and I'll take the baby."

"Men don't carry diaper bags."

This really amused Sylvia, and the baby, seeing her mother laugh, began to giggle, revealing six tiny white teeth and deep dimples. She was a very pretty baby, rosy, with large round blue eyes, thickly lashed, and tiny dark curls all over her head—enough hair for a little red bow to be fastened on top.

"Very funny, very funny," Jack said. "Now the elevator's here, how about it? Would you like to open the door for me, seeing as my hands are full?"

"Certainly, Mr. Bigshot." They got in, pushed the button for six and settled back as the ancient mechanism began its arthritic climb. "I hope your father doesn't throw Elaine up in the air and make her spit up like he did last week."

"Sylvia, I do my best to get along with your folks. The least you could do with mine is make an effort. For my sake, if for no other reason."

"Excuse me, Jack, I don't make efforts? I don't sit and make conversation? I don't ask after his health, his job, his lumbago, his sister in Russia? Come on, Jack, who're you trying to kid? 'Make an effort!'"

"All right already! Enough! It may not be a picnic in the country, but it has to be done."

The hallway on the sixth floor was badly lit and smelled of cabbage and damp. "What a dump!" Jack muttered.

"You grew up here."

"Exactly. I got out as fast as I could. Why do they stay here? I don't understand it."

When they rang the bell outside the apartment door, Saul Solomon's voice, a gravelly basso that could easily be heard for two or three city blocks, yelled, "Coming! Coming!"

"You'd think they didn't expect us," Sylvia said. "Every week, we ring and every week——"

"Lay off," Jack growled, and then the door opened and Saul Solomon Strauss himself loomed over them. He was not so tall as he was broad, but he loomed, he definitely loomed.

"So? It's you. Well? Don't stand in the hall like strangers. Come in, come in."

Coats were removed and hung in the closet, the baby was handed to her grandfather, whose mustache she immediately began to pull. He in return began to tickle her, making her squeal and scream and spit up. "What's with this baby, anyway? Always spitting up! They must stuff her over there at the Weinreb mansion." Sylvia glared at her husband. He steadfastly ignored her, and headed down the hallway to the kitchen, with the others right at his heels.

"How you doing, Ma?" He gave his mother, busy setting the kitchen table for supper, a kiss on the top of her head. She was, as usual, flustered. Dora Strauss was always in a state, struggling to keep up—with what, nobody had ever ascertained. There were always a few last-minute things she'd neglected to do, no matter how long she'd had to prepare. She slid her eyes up, checking with her husband before she put the silverware down and held out her arms for the baby. "Oh, *mammeleh! Shayner punim!*"

Saul Solomon grumped as he handed over the little girl. "What's the matter with you? You forget your English all of a sudden?"

She did not answer him but continued to talk to the baby in Yiddish, turning away from the rest of them as if they had all disappeared. Sylvia picked up the knives and forks and busied herself laying out the place settings, trying not to hear her mother-in-law. She knew darn well what was coming next and she didn't want to let it bother her.

Sure enough, Dora shifting to English, started in. "And look, look at those thin little legs, don't they feed you, my *shayner*? Never mind, I'll make you plump and healthy. I'll give you what to eat." Sylvia carefully said nothing, although she was infuriated. Dora did it every single time they visited. If there was one thing Elaine was not, it was underfed. She looked a little heavy to Sylvia, in fact. She was much plumper than the other babies her age in the park. The pediatricain said not to worry, she'd lose her baby fat when she started to walk. And as for healthy, well! There was absolutely nothing wrong with the way she took care of Elaine, and Sylvia couldn't understand why her mother-in-law kept up this carping, this constant criticism. Well, yes, she could actually. Poor Dora was bullied by everyone in her family. Sylvia felt sorry for her, sorry, but also disdainful. Catch Sylvia Weinreb Strauss letting anyone do that to *her*!

Moving around the porcelain-topped table, she tripped suddenly. "What in the world? Oh, look, Pa, there's a little hole down here. In the linoleum."

"Still that old floor, Pa?" Jack said. "I thought I told you to get it replaced! One of these days someone's gonna break his neck!"

"What? You think I'm made of money like some people?"

"I can get it for you wholesale. Whatever you want. Top quality."

"You think I've got nothing better to spend my money on?"

"I'll pay for it."

"Mr. Bigshot! I don't need you to buy me a kitchen floor."

Now Dora Strauss turned quickly. "Not so fast, Saul, if you don't mind. Jack wants to buy us a kitchen floor, okay by me. You don't want it? Fine, *I'll* take it!"

Jack shot his father a look. "First thing tomorrow morning, I'll send a man with it. What color, Ma?"

"What color you got?"

"Any color, just so long as it's green or tan." He laughed. "There's a war on, you know."

"While you're at it, how about *our* kitchen floor?" Sylvia said.

"What?" her father-in-law demanded. "You don't have the very latest, the top quality? Oy, Jack, am I ashamed of you! Don't you know that's no way to treat a rich man's daughter?" Sylvia very carefully did not look at Saul Solomon but she turned to her husband expectantly. He looked her in the eye and shook his head the tiniest bit, and her lips tightened angrily.

"The carpenter's wife!" Dora exclaimed. "Of course she doesn't have a nice floor! My shoes are always full of holes, *nu*?" But her good humor was restored and she put baby Elaine back into Saul Solomon's hands, tucked her graying hair back into the bun, and went to the small refrigerator, bringing out half a dozen flat oily packages, carefully wrapped in newspaper. "Whitefish," she announced. "A little belly lox, a little farmer cheese, and your favorite, Jack, herring salad. Oh . . . and a nice onion, let me slice it for you. Sit, sit, Saul, take the rye bread, Jack, bring the seltzer from the icebox."

"Fridge, ma, not icebox!"

"What do you want from me? Fridge, smidge, bring the seltzer! Elainele, come, you'll sit with Grandma."

"Ma, she ate. Please don't stuff her. And you don't have to hold her on your lap."

"Never mind, Sylvia, I'm a grandma, I'm allowed. My only grandchild and God knows when . . . oops, sorry, Sylvia, sorry, I forgot the rules. Don't ask when the next baby's coming, you'll be the first to know, am I right?" She smiled brightly at Sylvia until there was a smile forthcoming and then she nodded briskly and briskly set to the business of serving.

They sat and they ate, for the most part in silence, only speaking to ask that something be passed. Even Elaine quieted down and sat contentedly on her grandmother's lap, chewing on the heel of the rye bread.

Only when everyone had finished and the tea was being poured did Jack turn to his parents to say, "What do you hear from the girls?"

His mother smiled. "The twinnies love it in Washington. Twenty men to every girl, they say. They have plenty of boyfriends."

"Never mind boyfriends!" her husband said irritably. "Jack, I ask you. Your sister, Yetta, she's not satisfied to be two hundred miles from her family, no, now she wants to go and join the Wicks, the Wocks, the WACS, what do I know from this nonsense? I only know it's not for a Jewish girl. She says she wants adventure. Adventure! I ask you. Let her get married; she'll get plenty adventure!"

"Some adventure!" his wife said.

"Dora! *Shah!* I'm talking!"

"Excuse me, your majesty. I wouldn't say another word, not even if you beg me on your hands and knees."

"Wait a minute," Jack cried. "What are you saying? Yetta wants to join the Women's Army Corps? You're kidding! She just *went* down there two months ago. I thought she loved her job!"

His father made a face. "Job! They could find jobs here. What's the matter with Brooklyn, USA, all of a sudden? What kind of decent girl runs away from her mother and father—"

"Pa!" Sylvia objected. "The twins didn't run away and you know it."

"Same thing!"

"Hell, Pa, they *had* to get out of here!" Jack threw his head back and began to laugh. "You scared off every single boy in the neighborhood!" He turned to Sylvia, explaining, "You don't know what my father is like with them."

"Never mind, never mind," Saul Solomon said, flushing a little. "That's an old story, nobody wants to hear it."

"*I* want to hear it!" said his wife.

"I've never heard it at all. I'd love to." That was Sylvia.

"The twinnies were real cute when they were teenagers," Jack said. "Every boy for miles around wanted to take them out. They didn't care which one, well, who would? They were so much alike."

"And even then," his mother said with quiet pride, "I always dressed them alike. They were so adorable."

"They still are," Sylvia said, and Saul Solomon immediately had a comment.

"They'd be a lot more adorable right here at home where they belong."

"The boys used to hang around the shop, right downstairs," Jack went on. "Of course, not one of them was good enough for Pa's girls, not on your life! And if any boy got up the nerve to come in and ask if they could come out, if Pa didn't like the look of him—and you never did, did you, Pa?—he'd throw stuff at the poor schnook." Again, Jack laughed loudly.

"He could have been center fielder for the Brooklyn Dodgers, my old man. What an aim! What an arm! Right, Pa? Pieces of leather, half soles, a pot of glue, don't ask, if it was in reach, it got tossed."

"Those bums . . . they had one thing on their mind!"

Jack bellowed with laughter. "I've got news for you, Pa. So did the twinnies. All they needed to do was move out of the range of your throwing arm!"

"And now she wants only to go into the army. The army!" the old man grumbled. "Boy crazy, both of them."

"When a girl is over twenty years old, Pa, it's not boy crazy."

"They'll never get married, I just know it!" Dora suddenly burst out. "And it's all his fault! And now they've moved away to Washington, there are no nice Jewish boys down in Washington, they're not even going to be together, and next the army will come and take *you*, Yankele."

"Who, me, Ma? Not me! I promise you, if you have to put a star in the window, it'll be for Yetta and not for your little boy. Hey, everyone's enlisting; they don't need an old married man with a family. Don't you worry your head about it."

"When the tzar tried to take me into his army, you know what I did."

"Yeah, yeah, Papa, we know what you did. You came to America, the land of opportunity."

"Some opportunity. A shoemaker, me, who could have been a bookkeeper, an accountant maybe . . . a *shoemaker*."

"America's been very good to you, Pa," said Sylvia.

"Only the daughter of a rich man could talk such a way."

Now Jack rose to his feet, scraping his chair back and waking baby Elaine, who immediately began to cry. Sylvia also got up quickly, saying, "Let me take the baby, she'll need changing," and half-ran into the next room, a small room stiffly arranged with a matched suite of dark plush chairs and sofa, each with its starched antimacassar placed exactly in the center of the back. There was obviously no place for a damp baby on any of these pristine surfaces. Sylvia laid Elaine down on the carpet, putting a clean diaper under the baby's buttocks and, on her hands and knees, began to change and dress her for the trip home.

"Oh, Elaine," she said softly, looking with a tender smile into the bright blue eyes of the infant, "what a family, what a family! How they turned out your father, I'll never know, that grouch and that *kvetch*." Elaine stared back at her, unblinking. "Do you understand what I'm saying, baby? I wonder. You look as if you're listening so hard, and I'll tell you the truth, I think you probably understand much better than they ever will." She motioned with her head back into the kitchen, and sighed deeply.

"I wish your daddy would come home earlier, don't you? That's what I thought. We miss him, don't we? It gets lonesome being all alone. But I'll tell you a secret: promise you won't breathe a word? Because, Lainie, you're the first to know. See, in about eight months, you're going to have a new brother or sister, isn't that exciting? Anyway, I think so; I'm *almost* sure." She leaned on her heels, stretching her spine a little. "Oy, my back!"

"Why didn't I tell *them*? Because Dora would say it's bad luck to tell before the third month. So phooey on her! Next week, we'll tell Daddy, next week when I've seen Dr. Feinstock. And when we're a family of four—do you believe that, Lainie, a family of *four*!—then Daddy will *have* to come home earlier at night. Especially if—I don't want to say it to you, but it's true—especially if it's a brother, Elaine. Men want sons, that's all there is to it. And, you know, I'd like one of each. And you'd love having a brother. When I began to grow up, I didn't know what a boy *was*: I only knew from sisters."

Now she stood up, lifting the baby with her, kissing both chubby cheeks. "I'm sorry your grandpa made you spit up again. He's a pain in the neck, believe me, he won't listen to *anybody*. Everything has to be his way. No wonder his girls ran away from home. Don't tell him I said that, okay? Promise?" The baby gurgled. "And when *you* grow up, he isn't going to boss *you* around that way. And neither is your daddy. I won't let him. I don't care how many boys we have, I don't care how he feels or what he thinks, I won't let him. And that's a promise."

CHAPTER FIFTEEN

Wednesday, March 19, 1947

Jack Strauss, sweating and breathing hard, pushed his cock in and out of the woman's wet warmth. "Oh, baby," he groaned, "Oh, baby, baby, baby."

"You're so hard, honey!" She was panting, too, moving her narrow hips rhythmically to meet his. "Oh, God, it feels so good . . . wait. Let me . . ." And she pushed him away from her, moving down the rumpled bed quickly, taking him into her mouth and sucking avidly. A moment later, with a mighty grunt, he climaxed and then collapsed onto his back, breathing through his mouth, his eyes closed and a smile on his lips.

"That was terrific, Louise, really great." His eyes were still closed and he groped with his hand until he found her, pulling her in close to him.

"You're a helluva lover boy, Jack, anyone else ever tell you that?"

"My wife." He laughed and then, getting no response from her, opened his eyes and looked at her. "Hey! Only a joke, kiddo, only a little joke."

"Hell, Jack, you don't joke about stuff like that!"

"You're right, you're right." Now he stretched and yawned and, as he did so, turned his wrist so he could see the watch face. "Christ, it's after three already! I've gotta run!"

"Yeah, yeah, I know." She rolled over and stood up, a small, slight woman of about thirty, quite pretty although overly made up, and with badly bleached blond hair. She combed her hair with her fingers, allowing him to study her body, with its childish hips and small, neat breasts. "You had plenty of time before, when you were hot. Now, all of a sudden, you have an appointment you've got to get to."

"You know the old joke, Louise: 'When I'se hard, I'se soft, and when I'se soft, I'se hard.'" He leaned on one elbow, smiling at her. "Come on, kiddo, you know I'm a working man. Be nice to me, huh? Come on over and give me a little kiss, wadda ya say?"

"Oh, you." But she obeyed and when she bent over to put her lips on his, he opened his mouth and thrust his tongue into hers, kissing her passionately.

"That's to remember me by," he said.

"Don't you worry, I'm gonna remember you." The woman watched as he dressed himself. "I've had my eye on you for quite a while, ever since you first started coming into the luncheonette."

"Six months ago." Again, he laughed. "Jesus Christ, Louise, I nearly wet my pants when you leaned over and whispered in my ear, 'Any time, Jack, any time.' No woman's ever done that to me before."

She preened a little. "I know what I want when I see it, and I'm not afraid to say so. I'm only sorry I didn't say it a lot earlier. We coulda had some good times."

"Yeah, well, that's how it goes." It was obvious that his mind was no longer on her. "And we sure as hell had a good time today. You're one helluva lady. Oh, Christ, now I've really got to run. My 'appointment' is with none other than my partner—who happens to be my father-in-law. Which reminds me . . ." He went into the tiny bathroom and splashed vigorously. When he came back out, his face was still a bit damp. "Okay, kiddo, it's time to say good-bye. How's about a last kiss for the road."

"Sure thing." When the kiss ended, she clung a little and

then, without looking at him, said, "Uh . . . Jack . . . think I'll see you again?"

He pulled back, smiling, and said, "Hey! Louise! I'm a happily married man!"

Jack half ran the two blocks down Bedford to Warren. The first thing he saw was the line of six frame houses, small, neat, identical, and the neatly lettered sign that said WEINREB & STRAUSS, BUILDERS with the address and phone number and the big announcement ALL SOLD. It looked rather bleak right now in the middle of winter, the front patches of earth brown and frozen, and the trees bare. Come spring, though, there'd be grass and a couple of shrubs and the trees on the block would be in leaf and then . . .

"Shit," he said to himself. His father-in-law was already there, hunched into his pea coat, shivering a bit, tramping back and forth in front of the row of houses. He trotted, yelling, "Hey! Nat! Here I am."

"Where the hell've you been?"

"I stopped in at that little luncheonette on Bedford for something to eat . . . and the service was slow." He laughed.

"Well, Jack," Nat Weinreb continued as soon as Jack was close enough, "I gotta hand it to you. You were dead right. You said build six houses on Warren Avenue on speculation and I said no and you insisted they'd sell and I said no and here they are all sold. It worked out okay."

"That's right," Jack said. It was a bitter-cold day, with a raw wind blowing in from Sheepshead Bay and he, too, was hugging himself in an effort to stay warm, and stamping his feet. "We could have sold sixty, you know that? These vets are hungry for houses, Nat, hungry for houses. I'm telling you, the guys who recognize what's going on and who get in now . . . the sky's the limit!"

"Meaning?"

"Meaning it was a smart move, buying the land and building the houses on spec."

Nat said gently, "Too bad they're all alike. Cracker boxes, all in a row. Not like in the old days."

"That's right, Nat. 'Cause this isn't the old days; this is

1947, and we've got to move with the times or we're gonna be left behind."

"Behind who?"

"Huh? Behind . . . I don't know, behind all the other contractors. What's the matter, Nat, you don't like to make a big profit?"

"I like a big profit as much as the next guy, but I like also to take pride in what I've built. These houses . . . well, you know as well as I do, the walls are thin, the materials are cheap, the lumber was a little green, in a couple of years you won't be able to close a door in any of them."

"Not our worry, Nat. Look. They're not perfect, I grant you. But they were needed and they were needed fast and five thousand dollars is what these guys can afford. Believe me, after you've been overseas and you come back and try to live with your family in a Quonset hut like those guys out in Brighton . . . hell, a warped door is nothing. Nothing!"

"Maybe. In any case, right is right and you were right and I promised you I'd stop *kvetching* about workmanship and I'm a man of my word. In fact, I wanted to talk to you about the parcel out near New Lots Avenue. I'm willing to go ahead with that, too. Six more houses and—"

"Small potatoes, Nat, small potatoes. No, listen to me, we can do a helluva lot better than six more houses in the gut end of Brooklyn. There's a farm out at the edge of Queens . . ."

"Queens! Jack! We just finished moving the office to Manhattan. What do we want to go out to Queens for, hey?"

"Because, Nat," Jack said, his arm around the older man's shoulder, turning them both away from the houses and moving slowly toward Nat's shiny new blue Buick. The whole block was lined with brand new postwar automobiles. "Look at all the cars," Jack went on. "There's money out there, Nat, plenty of money and it's begging to be spent. On cars, on clothes, and on housing. Especially on housing. There's not enough to go around. In Queens there's an old farm; a bulldozer could level it in a day. And room for fifty little houses, just like these—"

"Whoa, Jack, you're talking much bigger than we can handle."

Jack laughed and walked to the passenger side of the car,

opening the door. "We'll hire more men, and we'll be big enough. Didn't Harry Truman tell us Americans to provide living space for our veterans? And isn't that exactly what we're doing? It's our patriotic duty, Nat!"

His father-in-law studied him, shaking his head. "Jack, I have to talk to you, and this is as good a time as any. It's about . . . well, our fifty–fifty partnership. Lately it seems like you're taking over."

"Wait a minute, Nat, that's not true. Don't we make all decisions together? Isn't that what partners do?"

"Yeah, well, it just seems that these days, it's always *your* ideas we're deciding on."

"Hey, Nat! Isn't that why you took me on? You said I had a head full of ideas, didn't you?"

"I don't know, Jack. I don't know how to describe it. I feel like I'm not really part of things anymore. Like a fifth wheel."

Jack threw an arm around Nat's shoulders. "Not true! Don't talk like that! It's Weinreb and Strauss, all the way! Look. You're how old now? Sixty-two? Isn't it time you took it a little easy? I'm just trying to take the heavier burdens off your shoulders, Nat. But listen, if it's making you feel uncomfortable, just say the word. We don't have to do the project in Queens. I'll do it on my own, on my own time with my own money, and you don't have to risk anything if you don't feel right about it. Whatever you say, Nat."

Nat Weinreb heaved a sigh. "When you put it that way . . . I must be getting old. But you know, Jack, the business is taking a direction that's a little bit strange to me and I'm not so sure I like it. Take that Queens thing; it sounds so impossible to me. Fifty houses! Hell, the entire shtetl my parents came from in Gonia, Poland, didn't have fifty houses!"

"We're a helluva long way from a village in Poland, Nat. The same way we've come a long way from building little additions and renovating kitchens. Weinreb and Strauss has to move into the future. The sky's the limit, Nat. I'm telling you, if there's one thing people are burning for, it's a place to live. The guys that get in first with housing are gonna clean up! Don't you want us to be those guys? Christ, we could be . . . goddamn millionaires!"

The older man shook his head again. "You make it sound so easy. You make me feel so out of date."

"Don't talk like that! I don't want to hear it from you! You've got plenty of good years ahead of you, and, goddammit, the company needs you, needs your experience. But the point is, if you're uncomfortable with our expansion, you can back off. I'll handle it. I don't mind the aggravation. And at this stage of the game, you shouldn't have to work so hard, you should be leaving a lot of the shit to me. Matter of fact, you could start coming in later, you could leave earlier. Why not? And come spring, take a month, take Leah, spend some time at the Concord, give yourself a rest. Who deserves it more?"

Nat smiled wryly. "Now I *really* feel old! Just kidding, Jack, just kidding. We'll do the Queens project, what the hell. But now, what do you say we get going. It's freezing here. I feel cold right down to my bones."

CHAPTER SIXTEEN

Tuesday, December 24, 1985

The phone rang on the other end, over and over, and Zoe's heart pumped harder with each ring. Where *was* he anyway? He'd told her in the office, when they were saying good-bye: "Call me anytime. Day or night." And he'd laughed in that wonderful warm way he had, looking into her eyes with that look so she thought she would faint. He was *so* good-looking, *so* sophisticated, so different from the boys at Cornell. Boys? Babies, that's what they were, boring and shallow. Not like Lawrence. Lawrence . . . even his name was beautiful.

Jesus, why didn't he pick up the phone? In about two minutes Judy was going to get tired of talking to that ski instructor—God, he was an airhead!—and come looking for little sister Zoe. That was a good way to excuse herself from him, and anyway, she thought her job here at Stowe was to be guard dog for her sister. Little did she know Zoe wasn't the least bit interested in *anyone* here. She'd have much rather stayed in the city, especially after Mom and Dad went on that trip to the Caribbean and she would have been all alone in the house. Hell, Saul didn't count; he was in his own world half the time, anyway. She could have come and gone as she pleased. Well, she and Judy had planned this ski trip back in September and she couldn't very well back down now.

Too bad she wasn't looking for boys; Stowe was packed to the rafters with them. With everybody in the world. This morning they'd had to wait over forty-five minutes for the lift! God! Almost an hour, just to get to the top of the mountain so you could ski down and go through all that waiting again! Judy loved it; she didn't care. She said that's where you met all the interesting people, waiting on line. But Judy hadn't just met the most exciting man in the world. Judy's life hadn't just suddenly changed, utterly and completely and forever. In fact, Zoe right now felt ages older than her older sister. *Ages.*

And then, in her ear, the sound of his voice, deep and lazy and warm. "McElroy here." McElroy here! Was there ever a man as sophisticated as this one? God!

Sweetly, but with her heart pounding like twenty jackhammers, she said, "And Zoe *here*, Lawrence."

"Well, hi there. What's up? Where you calling from?"

"Stowe. Of course. Or have you forgotten, in the past two days, where I was going?"

"Of course not. How could I forget?"

There was something . . . strange about his voice, but she couldn't figure out what. "Lawrence? Do you remember you told me to call?"

"Of course I do. You just . . . well, I was napping. I guess I'm still kind of half asleep."

"Oh, I'm sorry. Do you want me to call some other time?"

He chuckled and spoke softly into the phone. "No, no. No time like the present, as they say. This is terrific! So. What have you been doing with yourself?"

This was not the conversation she had imagined. Secretly, she had hoped he'd indicate that he'd like her to come back. Well . . . She took a deep breath and asked, "Have you been thinking about me, Lawrence?"

Now his voice dropped even further, deepened, became husky. "You bet! Every minute!"

That was more like it! Zoe's heartbeat speeded up and she smiled with delight, startling a young man in the lobby who was staring at her and who gestured to her, Did she want him to come over? She shook her head very hard and turned her back. The jerk! What did she want with a kid like that, even a cute kid, when she had a grown man interested in her, a man in his thirties!

She had hardly been able to believe he really meant it, the first time he smiled at her that way. It had been during Thanksgiving vacation. She and Noel were bored to death . . . they'd seen all the movies around, they'd been to a couple of discos and seen all the kids who were back . . . so they said yes when Papa invited them for a *really* good lunch, as he put it. That meant a steak house and she and Noel decided why not? Papa was a doll. He was a lot of fun for an old guy, and if you were his grandchild, you could have just about anything you wanted. Furthermore, they both knew that lunch with Papa would include a folded fifty-dollar bill slipped to each of them with the injunction, "Get yourself a little something."

So there they were, waiting in Papa's reception room, posing in all those mirrors, just hanging. And in walked Lawrence. She'd never forget it. He did an absolute double take, just like in the movies. Stared and stared at her, his jaw dropping. Well, he hadn't seen her in a few years. "I can't believe it!" he kept saying. "Could this be little Zoe?"

And when she came back with "It could be and it is!" he raised his eyebrows and came closer, looking right into her eyes, and said,

"Well, well, you really *have* grown up!" in a tone of voice that absolutely weakened her knees, just turned them to water, no fooling. He wasn't just talking like Papa's older employees, who always pinched her cheek and told her how cute she was and how much she looked like her mother—God, she was sick and tired of looking like her mother! Oh, no. This was different. He was *coming on to her*! He really was! She could hear it in his voice, she could see it in his eyes, and when he reached out and put his hand on her arm, then she *knew*. They always did that. The minute a guy started to touch you, no matter how casual the touch, you knew. Her chest had absolutely constricted when she realized he was flirting with her; she thought her heart would stop beating. He was so handsome, so sexy. And God, he wasn't just *anyone*, he was Papa's vice-president.

Lawrence had to leave then, but she was sure he let his hand linger on her arm for an extra second or two; and he said, "Let's say au revoir and not good-bye." It was to die!

At lunch she very casually brought him up even though Noel kicked her under the table to show he knew exactly what she was up to. Damn him, sometimes she regretted that he knew her so well . . . but not often. Noel was her buddy; he'd never, ever give her away to the family, never.

"Lawrence!" Papa laughed. "That man! What a life he leads! I'm telling you, young men today have it good. They don't think they have to get married the way we did! No, instead, it's bachelor pads and discos and trips to Europe and serial monogamy like you wouldn't believe!" And he laughed and laughed at his own humor. "Lawrence!" he repeated. "If I led the life he does, I'd be a basket case! A model on either arm, women calling him all hours, up till four in the morning, discoing, bar-hopping . . . don't ask! But he comes in eight in the morning every morning, chipper, good-natured, mind clear as a goddamn bell. I don't understand it. But who the hell cares as long as he does the job right? That's something both of you kids should learn; you can get away with a lot in life if you do the job right." And then he continued with one of his good-natured but oh-so-boring lectures on life.

She still wasn't quite sure exactly what it was that Lawrence did at Papa's company, but that didn't matter. Papa thought he was terrific, so he must be. And this man, who dated *models*, and drove a Porsche, a white one, and lived in a penthouse, and bought his suits in London and . . . and . . . and everything . . . *he* was interested in *her*, Zoe Berman. Unbelievable! Outta sight!

And it was even better when she got back to school and told Nancy her roomie all about it.

Nancy was thrilled. "Ohmygod," she kept saying over and over. "Ohmygod! What are you going to *do*, Zoe?"

"Noel said I should play it cool, said he'd kill me if I called him. Said to wait and see what happens at Christmas. We're going to go to the office one day. He promised." And then she and Stacey giggled with the excitement of it all.

"God!" Stacey said, "I'm so jealous! Thirty-four years old! I'm psyched!"

Now Zoe was glad she had played it cool. Because when she and Noel showed up at the office the second day she was home, Lawrence made a point of coming out of his office and talking to her and drawing her aside. And he held her arm the whole time; she thought she would die from it. It was like an electric wire on her, sending little jolts all through her.

"Listen, Zoe," he said, and then shook his head. "No, no, never mind."

"No, what? Really! Tell me! Please!"

"I shouldn't . . . but I can't help myself. I'd really like to see you sometime. I mean . . . *alone*."

Her mouth went dry. "Oh, yes. I mean, yes, I'd like that. That would be nice. That would be very nice." And then she could have sunk into the ground; honestly, her mouth! Now he'd think she was a baby, too excited to stop talking.

But he didn't. He smiled down at her, rubbed her arm a little bit, and said, "I'm glad. How about tomorrow night? For a drink or something. If you're not busy . . ."

Was he kidding! "I'm not busy," she said quickly, before he could change his mind and then, to her horror, he began to shake his head again.

"Oh, no, it's too crazy. Your grandfather . . . well, if he should ever find out . . . And he'd be right. This is not a good idea, as tempting as it is. As tempting, Zoe, as *you* are."

Oh, my God, it was really true! *It was really true!* He wanted her, he really did. Well, to hell with Papa. "My grandfather will never have to find out," she said. "Honest."

He regarded her very seriously. "Maybe we should think about this, Zoe, before we start up. It could . . . never mind. I don't want anyone to get hurt." Oh, my God, it really *was* all happening, just like her fantasy, *better*!

"But after Thursday I'll be in Stowe!" she blurted out. She could have bitten her tongue out.

"Maybe that's for the best, Zoe. Tell you what. You go skiing and you think about this and after you've done your thinking you give me a call." And he scribbled his number on the back of his card. That's when he had said anytime, day or night.

"I've thought about it, Lawrence," she said now, lowering her voice. "And I want to see you when I get back."

Better and better, thought Lawrence McElroy. He reached out his leg and, with a foot, eased the bedroom door closed. "I'm so glad," he cooed into the phone. "Because I want to see you, too."

And, hey! It happened to be true. She was just a bit young, that was true; but she was a luscious little peach, that Zoe. He always went for that type, always had, with the big tits and the tiny waist and the slim legs and those hot Jewish eyes. She wanted it. She might not even know it, but he knew. She wanted it and L. J. McElroy was just the guy to give it to her. Christ, just thinking about the possibilities gave him a hard on. That type always turned out to be wild in bed, writhing and screaming and shouting all kinds of stuff. Oh, man! And that young flesh, that smooth, smooth silky young skin, and everything still firm and solid and bouncy. Hey! He had to stop this, he had to pay attention to what she was saying.

Because getting this one into the sack wasn't the end of it. This one wasn't just your ordinary little teenybopper piece of ass. Hell, no. This was Uncle Jack's own granddaughter and you had to be careful. Because, speaking of ass, his would be in a sling if he did anything to her that made her run squeaking to the old man. He had to be damn sure she really meant it. If she didn't, if she was just playing college-girl games, if she was another cocktease like her mother, then messing with her would only mean trouble. So it was easy does it, this time.

At least he didn't have to worry about one thing: he didn't have to watch out for the love-and-marriage routine. When he was a kid, yeah, that was the way girls were. You had to be on your guard because, first thing you knew, they were wanting to know if you loved them, and if you said yes, then it was your fraternity pin and when was there going to be a ring and all that shit. But nowadays . . . hell, they were free as air, these girls. They fucked like puppies, didn't think a thing of it, moved in with a guy, moved out, moved in with someone else, like a revolving door. Far from the way *he* had been brought up.

But this one was still young. And she was a Strauss. A sweet little lamb, just waiting for Lawrence J. McElroy to lead her to green pastures. And, look, let's face it, would it be such a terrible thing if he ended up marrying her? Hey, what was he thinking about, marrying her? Come on, that was impossible. But was it, really? She was crazy about him, anybody could see that. She was crazy about him and if he was nice and polite and all goo-goo eyes, she'd *stay* crazy about him. A piece of cake. Why *not* marry her? He could do a helluva lot worse than marry one of the Strauss girls. So it was the next generation, so what? It would serve Deena right, all those years she lorded it over him and made him crazy. He'd be her fucking son-in-law! What a joke! And, hey, he wouldn't mind looking at that gorgeous little creature over the breakfast table the rest of his life . . . or at least until Jack Strauss kicked the bucket, if things didn't happen to work out.

But he was going too fast, letting his imagination run away with him. Exactly what he had to watch out for.

"Yes, baby," he crooned into the phone. "I miss you like crazy. Nuts, isn't it? Missing you, when we haven't even had our first date yet? But that's how I feel."

"Oh, Lawrence." He had her in the palm of his hand. If he had been wondering—and he had, he had—whether she was really interested in him or just doing a Strauss Girl number on him, he didn't have to wonder anymore. "I wish I was there with you right this minute, that's what I wish. And then you'd *really* miss me after I was gone!" Jesus Harold H. Christ on a pogo stick! She meant it, and now all he had to do was keep her feeling that way.

"Oh, baby," he said more softly. "If you only knew how much I want that . . ."

There were a few minutes more of that kind of stuff and before he knew it, *she* was making a date with *him*. Way to go! She talked about coming back early from skiing but he nixed that one; they'd all want to know why, he told her, and let's keep it our secret for now. Hey, she *loved* that! The idea of her family disapproving of them just made it all that much sexier. He knew his little girls . . . she might be a Strauss but she was just a broad like any other broad, when you came down to it. Forbidden fruit was always more delicious . . . and he knew one of the reasons she found him so attractive. He was an Older Man to her, all-wise and all-knowing. He'd gone this route before; he knew what it was all about. Take it slow and take it easy and before you knew it, he'd be set for the rest of his life. Might have to clean up his act when it began to get serious; nobody ever could accuse Jack Strauss of being a dummy, and if he was about to join the family, the old man's eye would really be on him. But time enough for that.

Now he had to get off the phone. It had been fifteen minutes, a bit too long for even an important business call—which is what he had told Tina when he chased her out to the living room. She'd be sulking now, waiting for him to come in and coax her back into bed.

Luckily, just then Zoe gave a little gasp and whispered into the phone, "Oh, shit, there's my sister, looking for me. Gotta go. Michael's Pub. Ten o'clock. Monday night."

And he said, "You got it, baby." And hung up, thinking *he* was really the one who had gotten it.

He eased himself off the bed, stretching out his taut muscles. Christ, he'd actually been a little bit tense there, during that conversation. Then he went to the door and opened it. Sure enough, there she was, wrapped in his robe, sipping at a drink, looking up eagerly when she heard him. He leaned against the doorjamb and gave her his best seductive smile.

"Hey, baby," he said. "Come on over here."

"Why should I?"

"'Cause I miss you," he said. "And so does Mr. Wonderful."

CHAPTER SEVENTEEN

Wednesday, December 25, 1985

The tropical sun was hot, even this early in the morning. According to the digital display on his wristwatch, the time was now 8:23:34. If they were back home, he'd be at the office now, situated comfortably at his desk, deep into work, a cup of hot tea at his elbow. Between eight and nine in the morning was always the best time for him: the phone didn't ring, the secretaries weren't even in yet, and a man could get some work done.

But he was not back home. He was, alas, leaning against the rail on the deck of a ship anchored somewhere in the Bahamas, hanging around idly, waiting for the captain to come on deck for Story Time. It happened every morning, right after breakfast. A bell clanged—as if they were children at camp—and they were given a supposedly humorous lecture on where they would be going ashore today, what dangers to watch out for, what activities were available. Since the ship went from one deserted island to another, the activities were so far always the same: sunbathing, snorkeling, swimming, drinking. In fact, the major activity, day or night, was drinking. Free Bloody Marys in huge sweating pitchers at breakfast. Free glasses of "grog" every afternoon. Free bottles of wine at each meal. No wonder everybody was drinking all the time. It didn't cost them anything, did it? And everybody, unfortunately, included his wife.

Ever since they'd come aboard, she'd been acting like an adolescent: laughing too loudly, throwing herself around, being overly friendly, drinking too damn much, chatting up anyone and everyone who came along. Right now she was deep in animated conversation with some woman she'd met last night, a bleached blonde from Florida whom Michael found silly. Deena liked to say that she found everyone interesting. Pah! That was a pose. He hadn't met a single person on board yet who could hold an intelligent conversation, who had anything to say worth anything. Why was she wasting her time? All these so-called friends she was making: she'd never see them again once they were back home.

If he'd known what a windjammer was really like, he might not have been so eager to take those tickets off Don Epson's hands, good price or no good price—not even to make Deena happy. He had hoped it would be a real sailing adventure, ten or twelve people serving with the crew, kept busy with the real business of sailing. What *he* would have liked was to haul the sails and swab decks and maybe do some steering. But there was none of that here. Oh, the dress was casual enough and there wasn't anything particularly formal about the ambience. But it was a luxury cruise cleverly disguised as a sailing adventure. Whenever the ship, the *Free Spirit*, upped anchor, a recording of bagpipes and organ playing "Amazing Grace" came blasting over the loudspeaker system, the first mate called for "help," and a dozen or so passengers pretended to heave on the heavy lines while their friends or wives busily took snapshots of something that wasn't really happening. Pretentious make-believe, that's what he thought of it all.

Deena, of course, was sucked in by the whole silly scene. She didn't see it as artificial, didn't care, either, as she took great pains to let him know. "Come on, Michael, loosen up. Everyone here—except you, apparently—is having a wonderful time." Damn, this trip was supposed to be bringing them closer together. She should excuse herself to that bleached blonde and come stand with him, where she belonged.

There was a little flurry of movement among the passengers, who were gathered in a tight clump, sitting and lounging on the deck by the stairs that led up from the boat deck. That meant the captain was on his way. Michael crossed his arms on his chest, heaving a great sigh. People were so predictable. They all thought the captain was so wonderful, so charming, so witty, so handsome. Michael knew damn well that if the captain had been a cross-eyed chimpanzee, the title would have given him glamour and authority, and most people would automatically think him wonderful and charming and witty and good-looking.

Of course, the fact was that the captain, whose name was James Ward, was a very tall, very tanned, rugged-looking man with a British accent and a pleasant offhand manner. He came up on the deck now, followed closely by Cara, his purser, a beautiful, leggy young woman. He looked around at them all for a minute or two, then said, "Who *are* all these people?" And when there was a ripple of appreciative laughter, he added, "These must be *your* friends, Cara."

And one of the passengers, a man, Michael thought, who looked old enough to know better, yelled out. "God knows I tried last night, but she wouldn't have me!" More laughter. Why, Michael thought, feeling hot and irritated and itchy between his shoulder blades, where he'd gotten a bit of a sunburn yesterday on the beach, why couldn't they just get on with it instead of doing a comedy routine?

Captain James Ward sat himself on a bulkhead. He was wearing white shorts and shirt, and sandals, and he looked very fit and very Colonial British. He smiled, flashing large white teeth, and said, "We didn't tell you, but Cara is a happily married woman." And to the groans that followed, he added quickly, "Only joking." Then he put on a serious face and said, "But enough levity. You're probably wondering where in the world we are *now*. The good news is that we sailed all night. The bad news is that we seem to have sailed into the Bermuda triangle." More laughter. Michael's sunburn itched even more fiercely.

Look at Deena, her head tipped back, the better to gaze up at the captain, smiling at every stupid thing that came out of the man's mouth, actually clapping and calling out: "Does that mean we get to stay forever? I hope!"

"No, lovely lady, but it does mean you'll be meeting Judge Crater . . . no laughs? Never mind. Tell me, am I losing my touch?"

There was, of course, a chorus of laughing dissent. "I'm losing my *patience*," Michael muttered under his breath. The fellow next to him gave him a look and said,

"Hey! this is a vacation, man!"

What did Deena mean, drawing everyone's attention to herself that way? The bathing suit she was wearing was quite enough. It exposed a great deal of her breasts—much too much. And she hadn't changed it, had she? Even after he asked her nicely. What was wrong with her? He couldn't figure it out. He had thought—he had hoped—that taking her away from the pressures of city life to the tropics would relax her. She'd been so moody lately, so out of sorts all the time. On the ship, surely, she would be more like the old Deena, the sweet, loving girl he'd married. But it hadn't happened. Instead of being grateful for this vacation, instead of being glad to be with him, she was more distant than ever. All he required of her was that she do her part in making this a second honeymoon. She might try being nice to him, maybe even cater to him a little bit.

As always, Deena was very aware of her husband's scrutiny. Why did he *do* that? It made her flesh creep. He felt it was his God-given right to watch her every move and judge her! Well, she wasn't going to let him spoil her enjoyment; she wasn't going to let him do that to her anymore. So she very carefully kept her profile to him, even turning away a little, and pretended he wasn't even there. She sat back against the polished wood of the long high-backed bench, loving the satin feel of it on her bare skin. Loving, too, the brilliant heat of the sun lying across her skin. The ship was moving smoothly with the warm wind and only if she really thought about it was she aware of the faint rocking beneath her. And yet, she had discovered yesterday when they went ashore at Gorda Key, that when she was on land, she missed that constant subtle motion. It was part of what soothed her sore spirit here—that, and the sparkle of light on everything, the soft *slurpslurp* of water moving against the side of the ship, the dolphins, the swooping gulls, the puffy white clouds in the sapphire sky, the tangy salt smell . . . everything, in fact, that was part of being on a tall ship in the middle of the ocean. *Everything* seemed good to her, the polished deck under her bare feet, the creak of the masts, the gentle flapping of the sails. She had become totally aware of every kind of physical sensation on this trip—even of the feel of ice water moving down her throat when she was thirsty, even something that simple and ordinary. It was wonderful and delightful in a way she would never have imagined. Or expected.

She hadn't wanted this trip, not really. She had gone around the house, reluctantly packing and reluctantly making lists . . . hell, *sulking*, that's what she had been doing. She hadn't wanted to break her date with Luke, not once she'd gotten up the courage to make it. She hadn't wanted to leave the kids, who weren't home that often anymore. And especially, she had felt it was a bad time to leave Saul on his own. She had groused and griped and bitched and moaned through the whole process of getting ready, prepared to hate this.

But, to her great surprise, she was enjoying everything about it. It was beautiful on the turquoise water. The ship was well run. Everyone was so friendly, everyone was Vacation Mode, ready to relax and have a good time. Everyone, that is, except Michael Berman, Esq. Dammit, he couldn't help ruining just about everything these days. This was just the final proof that she wasn't imagining it, she wasn't making it up, and—most important—that it wasn't *her*.

This was the trip *he* chose, the trip *he* wanted, the trip *he* sold her on. That being the case, why did he insist upon finding fault with every goddamn thing and everybody, including her own honey self. She should say, *especially* herself. Take this morning. Why couldn't he tell her she looked fabulous in her new swimsuit? Everyone else had. And the look on his face! It made her feel sick inside. She had tried on twenty suits at Saks, at *least* twenty, trying to find the one that he would think sexy. This *was* supposed to be a second honeymoon, wasn't it? Huh, Michael? And back about a million years ago, when they were first married, he had been crazy about her breasts, couldn't get enough of them, and loved it when she wore necklines that showed them off. He had told her back then that that excited him. Well, they were still the same breasts, still pretty firm and still in pretty good shape for an old babe who had had four kids. So what was his problem, anyway?

Even now, in the midst of her relaxation, she found tears stinging at her eyes. Damn him, if she let him, he was going to ruin this entire trip for her. Well, she wasn't going to let him. His negative attitude, she decided, was *his* problem. There had been a time, many years, in fact—up until very recently, in fact—when she had tried very hard to understand Michael. She had been ready to forgive a good deal of his sometimes rather egocentric and distant behavior . . . forgive it on the grounds that he was, after all, the child of Holocaust survivors, with problems she couldn't imagine; and that she, spoiled darling that she was of her indulgent father, owed it to him to be ultrapatient. If she couldn't understand him, she could at least sympathize, she could at least ignore a lot of what hurt her.

Okay, she'd done it. She had sympathized and empathized and ignored and taken it and rolled with the punches and tried to understand and made the best of it and counted herself lucky that he was such a good provider and all the rest of what one did to be a good wife. Even coming on this trip when she didn't want to—and doing the planning and packing and tending to all the details—even that had been part of being a good wife. Not to mention allowing herself to get sucked into his second-honeymoon fantasy.

Enough. She'd had enough. She was here and she was enjoying every single moment of it, whenever he let her, that is, and she was going to continue to enjoy it. The captain was grinning at her and gave her a little wink. So Michael found her wisecracks an embarrassment. Tough shit! as the kids would say. The captain found them irresistible! She loved making people laugh and she was usually good at it. Too bad her husband, the man who was supposed to be her intimate, her closest friend, and her ally, found this essential part of her so distasteful.

Dammit, even when he *wasn't* doing it, he was doing it to her! She had to make up her mind that for the duration, she wasn't going to let him jerk her around! She had to stop thinking about what he might think about her . . . and she hoped to hell that made sense.

Deena clambered down into the big launch, clutching her bag with all the necessities of beachcombing in it: the hairbrush, the camera, the suntan lotion, the paperback novel, the sunglasses. It was so super, not having to be Mommy, *not having to think about lunch.* It was now a bit before 9:30 A.M. They would lie around on the white sand or go exploring around the rocks or snorkel a bit and then, around 11:30, the launch would come roaring into the beach from the ship, loaded to the gunwales with rum swizzles, folding tables, gently steaming and delicious-smelling covered baskets, and five or six of the crew to set it all up and serve. She would not have to do a single thing except put the food into her mouth.

Heaven! she thought, and settled herself into the bow, her favorite place, where she could get the full force of wind and spray as the little boat cut through the waves on its way to the windswept empty island with its bright white sand and swaying palms.

Michael pushed his way forward and squeezed in next to her. "What's the name of this place?"

"Gun Key." She did not add that the captain had talked about it for ten minutes. She was going to be nice. "Someone told me the snorkeling here is absolutely marvelous. Oh, and look, there's a little hill we can explore. I wonder how big it is."

He grunted. So she continued. "And there's a nice little cove around the other side. You could take the snorkel gear and explore by yourself."

"There's not going to be any privacy on this trip—not with three hundred people all doing the same thing at the same time!"

She was going to be patient; she was *not* going to lose her temper. "Michael, there are only ninety-five passengers. And yesterday only a few of us did any snorkeling at all." In answer, he crossed his arms tightly across his chest. She knew what *that* meant; that meant the subject was closed, now and forever, amen.

It was a lovely little beach, rather narrow but with fine white very clean sand and a gentle surf that quietly pulled out and gently plopped big flat waves onto the edge of the sand. Deena took the brown hand offered her and jumped from the launch into thigh-high, pleasantly cool water. Michael even took her hand and waded into shore with her. Her heart lifted just the littlest bit. It would be so nice if it could be the way it used to be between them. Even in bed, no, especially in bed!

Last night he'd grabbed her and given her a hard, hot kiss, the likes of which he hadn't done for months and months. It had surprised and excited her; and she had been eager, anticipating a night of love. It was *really* going to be a second honeymoon. But there had been no drawn-out, romantic, delicious night of love and lust, not at all. He'd entered her quickly and eagerly and pounded into her almost frantically, his face screwed up intently, his eyes tightly shut. At first, it felt like dramatic passion, and then it felt like selfishness, and then, after he came suddenly—much too quickly, leaving her tense and frustrated—it felt like being used.

Maybe tonight, she thought, maybe tonight she could get him to slow down a little, to take his time. He always had been a bit too fast. When they were both young, and she was more naive, she had thought that it was wonderful, that he was so hot for her. Hell, when she was young, she had thought a lot of things!

But she didn't even see him again until lunch had been served; he just took himself for a long, solitary walk. And then, when he finally joined her, it was only to complain about the fat couple over there—the ones from San Diego or wherever. They had been splashing around in his cove, scaring all the fish away. And when he got back, where the hell was she? He thought they were on this trip together, pardon him for making that assumption. She kept disappearing all the time . . . wherever there was a man—

"What is that supposed to mean, Michael?"

"Exactly what it says. Your behavior is—well, I don't even want to say what I think it is."

"Dammit, Michael, I'm not doing anything except trying to have a good time."

He raised an eyebrow. "So I notice."

"That is absolutely not true and you know it. And, anyway, why am I being forced to explain myself and account for every minute?"

"Ask yourself that question, why don't you?"

"Michael, are you deliberately trying to start a fight, or is it just that you don't understand?"

He gave a little laugh. "Why in the world should I try to ruin a vacation that was my idea in the first place?"

"I'm glad you asked that question . . . because I've been trying to figure that out, frankly. And all I can figure is that somehow you expected something different and now you're disappointed and you're taking it out on me."

"Nonsense!"

"No, Michael, not nonsense. You know you're a perfectionist. You're damn proud of it! I think you had a particular picture in your head and now that nothing exactly matches that picture, you're determined to find fault with *everything*."

"You're wrong, Deena, you're totally wrong."

"Oh, really? Then how come the food is mediocre, the other passengers are all idiots, the bunks are too small, the cabins are too cramped, the saloon is too open, there's too much booze and too little sailing and too much sun and too little exercise and too much socializing and too little privacy and—shall I continue, or have you had enough, because God knows, Michael, *I* have!"

His lips tightened in anger and annoyance, and all of a sudden she had *had* it with him, right up to here. Why in hell did he schlepp her all the way down here in order to give her a hard time? And why in hell had she allowed herself to be talked into it? To think, she could now be in Luke Moorehead's arms . . . or something . . . instead of being treated like this!

"*You've* had enough!" His voice was as tight as his face. "I'm the one who's had it up to here, Deena. Ever since we got here, you've been drinking like a fish, dressing like a whore, and coming on to every man who even looks at you."

Very very quietly, she said, "Michael. Take that back. I'm telling you. Take it back." A tear or two, much as she hated it, leaked from her eyes and crept down her cheeks. It wasn't pain or hurt, not this time. It was rage. For him to pick on her was one thing; but how dare he make up things!

"When I see you, at eight-thirty in the morning, on your second Bloody Mary, in a bathing suit that shows half your breasts, smiling up at the captain and making a damn fool of yourself with your so-called wit—"

It was a good thing that the captain walked up just then, or she would have strangled him with her bare hands.

"I've been wanting to talk to you," he said, looking straight at her. "To say thank you."

"You're welcome. For what?"

He laughed. "If you knew how difficult it is some mornings to get people going. You see, we hope the passengers will give us a bit of a hard time . . . it gets everyone laughing and feeling good. That's what we're after on a cruise like this, you know, that feeling of camaraderie . . . we're-all-in-this-together sort of thing, you know. So you've been a wonderful help." He touched her arm briefly, and Deena made an effort not to pull away. Damn Michael, for making her so self-conscious!

"Glad to be of service," she burbled. "Deena Berman. Backtalk, wisecracks, and general foolery. Hours by appointment. Salary negotiable."

"Tell you what," the captain said. "Every morning, in return for your good services, you can have a free Bloody Mary." They both laughed at this. Deena deliberately did not look over at Michael.

After the captain excused himself and was walking away, she turned to her husband, unable to control her smile. "So," she said sweetly, "I'm making a goddamn fool of myself, huh?"

"If you care more about what *he* thinks of your behavior than what *I* think . . . no more need be said, need it?"

"There's something I'd like to tell you, Michael. You get ridiculously pompous whenever you want to make a point. It's a family joke!"

Color flooded into his face; he looked as if he might explode. But he simply turned on his heel and left her.

And, after they had returned to the *Free Spirit* at 4:00 and had—without a word to each other—changed and showered and put away the snorkeling gear and rinsed out their swimsuits, all the time being very careful not to accidentally brush up against each other, he pulled his big duffel from under the bottom bunk and began to load it.

"What do you think you're doing, Michael?"

"Packing." Very tight-lipped, very distant and calm. "We're leaving."

"Correction," Deena heard herself saying, feeling her heart begin to thump painfully. "*You're* leaving. I'm staying."

"You're crazy!" He gave her a look of such disbelief that she wanted to laugh, only her heart was pounding too hard. Surely, surely, he would do or say something and she would cave in.

Nevertheless, she lifted her chin and repeated, enunciating every syllable with great, exaggerated care: "You are leaving. *I* am staying. And I'm perfectly sane."

He didn't even bother to look at her this time, just kept emptying shelves and neatly folding his clothes. "You're out of your mind. Do you think for one minute that I would let you stay here alone?" And he gave that little laugh she hated more than anything.

That did it. Accelerated pulse or no, she was going to go through with it. "I'm not asking you for your permission, Michael. I'm telling you what I'm going to do."

"You're really hysterical."

"*Au contraire*," she said in her loftiest voice. She only wished it didn't remind her so vividly of her own teenaged daughters. "*I'm* having a very good time. I'm sorry you aren't, I really am." She paused and then decided to lie. "I wish you would stay. I had high hopes for this trip."

His eyes still fastened on the job at hand, he said, "I've made my decision."

"And, I," Deena answered blithely, "have made mine."

She was almost out the doorway when she heard his fist pound the wall. "Deena! Goddammit!"

Her master's voice. She stopped where she was and turned

to find him—at last, at last—looking right at her, all pretense at calm dissolved.

"I warn you, Deena, if you persist in this childish nonsense, if you don't get right back in here and start packing . . ."

If he could yell, so could she. "Stop ordering me around; it makes you sound like an idiot! This whole plan of yours to leave is idiotic anyway. Where the hell do you think you're going, anyway, in the middle of nowhere?"

"As it so happens, there's a boat from Bimini to Freeport and the captain has agreed to take us in the launch right now."

So it was true. He was really going. She waited for that empty, panicked feeling to hit her. It didn't. Instead, there was a tiny little glow somewhere in the back of her mind, a little warm feeling, and in a moment she would be able to put a name to it. And then she had it. Relief.

"Have a good trip back, Michael."

He clenched his fists.

"Deena, I warn you . . ."

She smiled at him. "No more warnings, Michael, no more threats. You're leaving, I'm staying. It's not the end of the world."

"It damn well may be the end of our marriage."

Her smile did not waiver. She was so damn proud of herself, of her calm and her control. "We'll see," she said, loving saying it, since it was what *he* always said when he didn't want to talk about something anymore. And she saw, from the quick dark flush in his cheeks, that he knew the words had been chosen deliberately. And that made her feel even better. "We'll see," she repeated. And left.

Deena sat at the bar just outside the main saloon, her back turned to the gangway but every sense tuned into the sounds of Michael leaving. The creaking of the launch being lowered. The crew shouting to each other. The ever-louder murmur as more and more of their fellow passengers gathered at the rail to stare, as the unheard-of took place before their very eyes. Who in the world, Deena heard someone say to someone else, would leave in the middle of a cruise? Who, indeed? She sipped deliberately at her gin and tonic, trying to quell the

rising anxiety somewhere just behind her sternum, and refused
to look.

She was deeply, coldly furious. It hadn't even occurred to
him to stay on because *she* was enjoying herself. Nothing had
occurred to him except what *he* felt and wanted. She had to
admit that this was hardly news to her. But seeing him react in
this different environment somehow made it very clear to her.

She saw suddenly, and felt sick with her knowledge, that
Michael Berman, from the very beginning, had always done
exactly what *he* wanted to do, period. And she had always
gone along with it. Of course, he allowed her a certain amount
of room—like a pet on a leash, she thought, and shuddered.
But now what? What was she going to do on her second honeymoon all by herself? What was she going to tell people?
How on earth was she going to explain why her husband had
taken off like this all of a sudden, and without her standing
there waving bye-bye. Maybe, she thought, she should go
make a show of it. But, she noticed, she didn't move from the
stool. She was finished with the charades, finished.

And then, as if reading her mind, Janet Lowe, an older,
sunburned rawboned British woman who seemed to know all
the officers and half the passengers and who was just gener-
ally nice and straightforward came over and sat down next to
her. "So now you're going to be on your own. I always travel
alone. Prefer it, actually."

Deena paused, unwilling to tell the easy lie she had
planned—that Michael had been called back on business—
but even more unwilling to go into the whole story of her
marriage. And into her momentary silence Janet said dryly,
"You don't have to tell me anything. I'm sorry if I seemed
prying. But you did look just a bit lost there . . . or maybe it
was my imagination."

"No. I was *feeling* just a bit lost. We had a terrible fight."

Janet put a hand on her arm and gently said, "I know . . .
voices do travel right through these thin walls."

Deena could feel herself blushing, something she couldn't
remember having done since she wet her pants in kindergar-
ten. All those nasty things they'd yelled at each other, while
everyone else sat on deck having their rum swizzles and looking at the sunset and hearing every shameful heated word! For

the first time since she was five years old she wished she could sink into the depths of the earth! Just disappear!

"Oh, dear, oh, dear, I've made you feel bad. Please don't. It wasn't anything most of us haven't heard before . . . or participated in, come to that." Now she smiled, adding, "You were actually very good, my dear, very articulate, very heroic."

And from the other side of her came another voice: "Yeah, kid, you really have guts." Mildred from Florida, drink in one hand and two lumps of deep-fried goodies in a napkin held out in the other. "He's gone now. Yep, on his way. You might as well eat, drink, and be merry . . . and here's some of the eats."

Deena was warmed. They were both being so nice. The knot in her chest loosened and she began to feel good . . . well, almost good. She took the proffered fritters—she hadn't liked them when she tried one yesterday, but what the hell, nice was nice—and thanked Millie from Florida very warmly, inviting her to sit down. But the two brothers from Milwaukee, the travel agents, George and Ray were already there, carrying on about a lady alone needing a drink, maybe two, and what did she think of the ship?

The time went whizzing back. Being alone, she was discovering, had its advantages. She always had been a good mixer, but when she was with Michael, half her mind was always casting about, wondering where he was, what he was doing, whether he was getting bored, looking bored, becoming impatient to leave. He had always said, "I leave the socializing to you. You're the expert." And she had always taken it as a compliment. But it really was putting her in charge of *his* social life. This was much nicer. She could talk and joke and laugh and not think about anyone else and not worry if she was saying or doing something he wouldn't approve of. It was quite lovely, in fact. And now she *was* feeling good, all the way good.

Dinner was fun, too. Janet said, "Come sit with me," and the people at Janet's table were a fascinating mixture and one of them, a Russian emigré doctor, spent most of his time flirting with her—in a most charming and understated way. And when the steel drum band came back in the launch from Bimini and piled onto the deck and the dancing began, Boris was at her side immediately, asking if she'd like to "dence." He wasn't very good, but who cared?—by this time, she'd had a few more piña coladas—and anyway, she hadn't been dancing with him very long, when one of the crew cut in, a tall, muscular brown man who spoke to her with a musical lilt, laughed a lot, and moved like an angel. And after him, either George or Ray and then Ray or George and then a college boy with a blond beard who was drunk enough to tell her very earnestly that he fantasized having a wonderful experience with a fascinating older woman and that she could be the one, she had only to—*hiccup*—say the word.

She danced and danced and danced, having an absolutely marvelous time, not caring whom she was with just so long as she could keep on dancing. And then someone cut in, and when she looked up, it was into the smiling sunburned face of the captain. Well, she liked *that* a whole lot. He smelled good, he looked good, he danced good. And now she felt very *very* good. And she told him so.

"Do you? How lovely. Because you feel very good to me." Could it be? Did his arm tighten around her? Did the look in his eyes become softer? And then she scolded herself because he was the captain and it was part of his job to dance with lonely ladies whose husbands had suddenly left ship, just as he was expected to be witty and charming at Story Time and all the time, come to think of it. That struck her funny and so she told him *that*, too.

"I'm so happy you find me charming, Mrs. Berman."

"Deena."

"Deena. That's an unusual name. What is it? Italian?"

That struck her as being extremely funny. "Far from it. Russian, I think. Yiddish. Polish. *Something* Middle European. Sorry, I'm babbling . . . what's yours?"

"My—?"

"Name. Or is it Captain?"

And that struck him as extremely funny, bless him. So there they were, the two of them, dancing and laughing and— she suddenly realized—having a very good time together. She was very conscious of his body close to hers, of his height and of the hard muscles in his back and shoulders. She was very aware of the scent of his aftershave and of the crinkles around his eyes, his very bright blue eyes, when he smiled. When the music stopped, she expected him to excuse himself politely and leave to spread himself around, and she found herself wishing he wouldn't. And lo, her wish came true.

A little rush went through her, leaving her with a light-headed feeling she rather enjoyed. The captain was coming on to her! If she wanted, she could . . . but right now she didn't want to think ahead. She was having too much fun right where and when she was. In between their laughter and their looks, he *had* managed to tell her that his full name was James Gordon Ward, that he had been born and brought up in Liverpool, that he was actually a merchant marine but that he had come to hate the cold and the long trips to nowhere and then he had laughed and said, "To a Liverpuddlian, the Bahamas are heaven." And then he laughed again and added, "And even though on the windjammers, we're underpaid, the job has its . . . shall we say compensations?" And when she, knowing damn well what she was doing, gave him her wide eyes, asking whatever did he mean by that, he just grinned at her and answered: "Well, one does get to meet many nice people."

And now he was putting his hand on her arm and asking her if she'd like a tour of the ship, "Unless, of course, you'd rather wait for the music."

Was he kidding? "The music can wait for us."

Up near the bow it was very quiet. Nobody came up here in the dark because of all the coiled lines lying all over the deck. Well, not quite everybody avoided this area; there was a couple nearby, in the shadows, closely entwined. He just chuckled and drew her on, still talking about how this worked and that worked and telling her all the nautical names for things and she just went along with him, enjoying the sound of his baritone voice and the feel of his dry, warm, callused hand holding hers, and the certain knowledge that any minute now, she was going to be kissed.

They stood together right in the center of the bow, leaning over the quietly lapping water below, watching the schools of tiny bright-colored fish that swarmed around the ship's lights, looking over at the island, a darker hulk in the darkness, with some pinpoints of light here and there, and gazing up at a clear inky sky filled with stars. His arm went behind her back and he rested that hand on the rail right next to her elbow. But not quite touching her. Well? she thought. Well?

"Mr. Berman had to leave very suddenly, didn't he? Business, he said. Exactly why I left that rat race."

"Oh, he told you it was business?"

"Yes. Something about an emergency . . ."

"It was an emergency, all right! If he hadn't left, I'd probably have thrown him overboard!"

"That bad, was it?"

Deena laughed. "Oh, you heard it all, too! Then I don't have to explain how my husband found this ship too confining and the passengers too low-class and the islands too deserted and the booze too free-flowing and his wife too . . . too everything."

"I must say, I don't agree with any of it. Especially not that last bit. *I* find you just about right."

He turned to her and brought his face down, brought his mouth down to hers. Deena found herself clinging to him, kissing him hungrily. He tasted wonderful and he felt wonderful. His arms were tightly around her, pulling her in close. He wanted her! They would keep kissing and then he would ask her to come to his cabin and, yes, she would. She wanted it and wasn't she into doing what she wanted?

It was like being in a dream, flowing in and out of focus in a very lovely way. They kissed and kissed, more and more avidly, his tongue in her mouth, and hers searching his. Deep in his throat he made hot little grunting sounds. His hands dug into her back and he thrust his loins into hers and she nearly fainted with excitement. And then he said something to her, she couldn't hear all of it, but she said yes because her entire body was screaming yes, yes, yes and her mind was saying yes, yes, yes. And then she was saying it aloud: "Yes, yes, yes . . ." And they had made their way to his cabin and he had locked the door and they had torn their clothes off and they were standing together, locked in an embrace, skin to skin, his avidly erect cock a thick bar of heat against her belly, both of them exploring the other's nakedness with hands and mouth and both of them pulling the other over to the bunk and falling on it, clutching at each other and yes yes yes, she was going for it, he was in her, he was big and hard and quivering and moving like a piston and now she was crying out: "Yes, yes, yes, *yes!*"

CHAPTER EIGHTEEN

Thursday, December 26, 1985

On Tuesday night, when Michael got out of the cab in front of the house, he was exhausted. Furthermore, he was still furious with Deena. How dare she stay on without him? What was he going to say to people when they asked? Goddammit, she had no right to humiliate him in this way! And look at that, goddammit! Every light in the house blazing! Disgusted with everything, he hefted the big suitcase, and humped it up the goddamn stairs, up to the front door. Since Saul was home—by God, you couldn't *miss* that Saul was home—why the hell couldn't he come out here and help for a change?

Michael was really steaming, ready to explode, as he unlocked the front door and let himself in. He kicked the damn bag inside, already bellowing "Saul!" at the top of his lungs, when he had to stop dead in his tracks, startled. Because Saul was there, standing in the hallway, directly in front of him, looking defiant, somewhat sick, and, above all, guilty. There was a beat or two while Michael took it in and then, trying to keep his voice down, to keep it calm, he said: "Saul, what's the matter? Why are you standing down

198

here looking like that? What's going on?" He couldn't help it; his voice just got angrier and angrier. But goddammit, the kid looked *guilty*.

And then the stranger came trotting down the stairs. The policeman. Michael knew he was police even though he wasn't in uniform; something in his gut told him. And it set off a warning bell in his head. He found himself thinking, my God, they've come for me! His heart began to beat very very fast, a panic reaction he was powerless to stop. He hated it when this happened. *Hated* it! He had no reason on earth to fear the police; he was an American, a law-abiding citizen and in the United States, where the police were protectors of the law and of law-abiding citizens' rights. In this country the police did not come in the night to take you away because you were Jewish.

He forced himself to stand perfectly still, to look up the stairway, his face calm, sucking in two deep breaths. He was even able to say, with every evidence of control, "I think you'd better explain your presence in my house."

"Detective Fatullo. The eight four. You're Michael Berman?"

"Yes. And this is my property, Detective. Have you a reason for being here? Has there been some trouble?"

By this time Fatullo was all the way downstairs and they were on an equal level. He held out his hand with a leather case in the palm: the shield on one side, his identification on the other. Michael didn't need to see it but he couldn't tell the detective *that*.

"Trouble, yes." A slight pause while he glanced over at Saul, and Michael immediately said, "Trouble with my *son*?"

"I'm afraid so. We've been investigating credit card theft and—"

This was ridiculous! "Stop right there," Michael said, feeling more and more confident with every passing moment. "My son is not a thief. He has no reason to steal." Michael's gesture took in not just the hallway with its original oil paintings and its Oriental rug, but the entire house, the lovely quiet of Monroe Place, the whole neighborhood with its wealth, its resonances of power and privilege. "As you can see. There's been some kind of mistake."

Detective Fatullo looked at him with what seemed to be pity. How dare he! "I'm sorry. The subpoena says this is the place and this is the young man and this"——he glanced up the stairs. Following his look, Michael saw two other men hefting Saul's computer, the monitor, the printer, the works—"is the computer."

Now Michael looked at Fatullo, really looked. The man had a perfectly ordinary Italian peasant face, broad, with deep grooves at the sides of his mouth, tired brown eyes, thinning dark hair. He looked like the neighborhood greengrocer Michael remembered from his boyhood. But he wasn't, that was the hell of it, he wasn't Tony of the fruit stand, he was a detective in the eighty-fourth precinct.

"Just what are you doing with my son's computer?"

His answer was a proffered warrant. Michael scanned it quickly. It gave the police the right to seize this particular computer from his son's room at this address. It was perishable evidence.

"Perishable evidence? Evidence for what?"

"I'm sorry, sir, that's confidential. It has to do with a continuing investigation in which your son may be involved. I'm sorry," he repeated, "that's all I can tell you. If you want to discuss this further, I suggest you get in touch with the district attorney's office. Okay, Farrell? Got everything?"

"Gotta go back up and get the software and that'll be it."

And then suddenly they were gone. Or so it seemed to Michael, who felt very much as if he had come in on the middle of someone's bad dream. His? No. Saul's. It was Saul's doing. He glared at his child, his son, his last born. Saul stood slumped against the banister, arms crossed on his chest, shoulders hunched.

"For God's sake, stand straight!" Michael snapped.

Saul obeyed, his face sullen and his eyes averted, moving as slowly as he dared, in defiance of his father. Goddammit, Michael thought, rage rising in his throat, this child had been nothing but trouble for him almost since the day he was born. Always temperamental, stubbornly resisting any attempts at reason, going his own damn way no matter how it affected anyone else in the family! Goddammit, he'd *always* been a disappointment. Had there ever been a school report that

didn't say Negative Attitude or Bad Work Habits or Not Working up to Potential or some other damn thing? He'd been in
three different schools and each time he got kicked out, he'd
looked his father straight in the eye and promised to do better
. . . to try, at any rate. "Dammit, Saul, that's all I ask of you:
that you at least *try*." And Saul had always said, "Yeah, okay,
I'll try."

But goddammit, he never had! What was the matter with
him? What was the *matter* with him? He had everything a boy
could want . . . *more*! His brother and his sisters all were doing
beautifully, always had. There'd never been any trouble with
them.

Of course, they had their moments. Nat had originally
wanted law school and then, suddenly, at the last moment,
chose med school and there had been all the trouble about
making up three sciences. But that was nothing. And the girls
. . . well, the girls were, after all, female, and prone to whims
and fancies.

But none of them had given him any *real* worry or heartache. Certainly, he'd never had the police invade his home,
looking for them, saying they might be involved in an investigation! Of theft!

"What's this all about, Saul? What've you done?"

"Nothing."

"That's patently false. The police don't arrive with a warrant and take away your property if you've done nothing."

"*I* don't *know* what it's all about! They wouldn't tell me
any more than they told you."

"I'm going to have to call the D.A.'s office. You know
that, don't you?"

"Go ahead, call them!"

"Before I do that, Saul, let me ask you again, because I'd
much much rather you told me yourself. What have you been
up to with that expensive toy of yours?"

"I got into the Sears database," Saul mumbled. "And, anyway, you always call it that expensive toy of mine. Why does
that bother you? *You* didn't buy it; Papa did. So why do you
care so much how much it cost?"

"Keep a civil tongue in your head when you talk to me!"

Saul gave him a belligerent look. Why couldn't he talk to

this child? Why couldn't he get through to him? He loved Saul, loved him every bit as much as the others. So why was it always so difficult with Saul? He couldn't understand it. He had always tried so hard with this one. He was the one child they hadn't planned and it was Michael, in fact, who had really wanted him! Deena had been ready to go to Puerto Rico or wherever to have an abortion. An abortion! An abomination! No Jewish child, he told Deena, should ever be murdered again. He gazed at his son now, standing with obvious impatience, waiting for his father to finish talking and set him free. He longed to say to him, "I saved your life, Saul, before you were even born. Your beloved mother, the mother you think so highly of, *she* was the one who didn't want you."

He had been ready to cherish this child, cherish him—or her, if it came to that—*especially* because of the circumstances. He had always thought of this son as a gift; and that's how he had always treated him. And this—*this*—was his reward!

He felt as if a leaden weight had been placed in the middle of his chest, making it difficult to breathe. Now he knew what was meant by a heavy heart.

His son stood in front of him, not moving, his head bent, his eyes down, his face sulky. "Look at me, Saul." And when the head came up, Saul's face, slightly swollen, petulant, defiant, angered him all over again.

"What in the world could make you do a thing like this, Saul? To *steal*? Goddammit, you've been brought up in a household that values honesty, decency, and integrity. You've never known anything else. So, why, Saul, *why*? Answer me. Answer me, dammit!" He itched to grab him by the shoulders and shake an answer out of him but was able to restrain himself. "Saul! I'm speaking to you!"

"I hear you."

"I'm waiting for an answer."

Saul stared at him and shrugged. *Shrugged!* "What's the big deal, anyway?" he said, his eyes daring Michael to do something. "Everyone does it. It was just my bad luck to get caught, that's all."

"That's all? *That's all?* Is that what I heard my son say?"

"That's what you heard your son say." Saul sneered, his eyes bright with combativeness.

Rage rose in Michael's chest, into his throat, and filled his mouth with a sickening bitter taste. This child, this child of his loins *dared*! Michael was filled with one overwhelming urge: to strike down this insolent brat, to show him just who made the rules around here. But of course, no civilized man would strike his own child.

And then Saul's lips curled in a self-satisfied little smile and that did it. Without volition Michael's arm shot out and he heard the sound of his hand cracking on his son's face, felt the jolt, and saw Saul's head snap back, and was horrified.

It was over in an instant. There was the mark of his hand emblazoned on Saul's cheek. "Saul! Saul, I didn't—" he started, but the boy did not wait. He turned on his heel, went up the stairs three at a time, and ran into his room, slamming the door with such force that a painting on the stair wall was knocked askew.

Michael put his face into his hands and allowed the bitter tears of his rage and disappointment to fall.

CHAPTER NINETEEN

Saturday, December 28, 1985

The plane finally taxied its slow way into the gate and the voice of the chief stewardess came over the loudspeakers, saying how wonderful it had all been and how she and the captain and the entire crew hoped they had enjoyed it, too, and would choose this particular airline forever and ever amen.

Amen, Deena thought. Standing up was its own particular pleasure after four hours of being squinched into an airplane seat. But on the other hand, there was the matter of her hand luggage and her fur coat. She'd forgotten all about fur coats during the past four delicious, superlative, magnificent, satisfying, sex-filled, sun-filled days. She'd forgotten about snow and New York City and winter and her job and her family and what's-his-name, the man she was married to. Four fabulous days of floating through life, not thinking about much of anything except maybe the next drink, the next meal, the next time she'd be in Jamie's bed, making love. His hands on her, his mouth on her, his tongue on her. He was a wonderful, imaginative, and tireless lover. She'd forgotten how good sex could feel.

She shivered with delight at the memory. And he'd said he'd never forget *her*, either. What's more, she believed it. She'd spent almost the entire flight, drifting and dreaming, reliving her own private windjammer in her head, her eyes closed to keep the harsh realities from intruding.

But here at JFK Airport was reality . . . and it was pretty harsh. A glance out the window showed a bleak darkness with a half rain–half snow spitting against the glass and piles of dirty snow edging the runway. New York, New York, a helluva town—but not in the middle of winter—the Bronx is up and my spirits are down.

It always took forever to get off the damn plane; couldn't they figure out some better way of doing it? Like letting women with heavy fur coats over their arms and long squinched legs whose names began with D get out first. How was that for an idea? She giggled to herself. Probably she should have stopped at the second vodka tonic; she was just the littlest bit high. But so what? She didn't have to drive and it would give Michael something to complain about. He should be grateful to her. What was life to Michael Berman if he couldn't find fault?

She smiled and said a cheery good-bye to the flight attendants, unable to resist adding "And my compliments to the chef." They laughed, perhaps politely, perhaps not. She didn't care; getting a laugh was something she had to do. Maybe, she thought, she was a joke junkie.

And that reminded her: she had to plan her entrance, her greeting to Michael. It was not something she looked forward to, but if she handled it right, it could go off without a major battle in the TWA terminal. A hug, a kiss, a friendly open smile, maybe even a humorous comment: that was the ticket. Make like nothing had happened, like he *hadn't* left her alone in the middle of their second honeymoon, like he hadn't said all those awful things to her, like she hadn't said all those awful things to *him*.

Like she hadn't spent the past four days having the first affair of her life . . . getting her brains fucked out, isn't that what they said nowadays?

Walking not too fast and not too slowly along the corridor to the big customs area, she heaved a great sigh. Yes, she'd had a wonderful time, it had been lovely, but that was then and this was now and in just a moment or two she had to give her husband a great big happy smile and a great big happy hug and save her memories for later. Maybe tonight, in bed, after Michael had turned his back on her and was snoring.

It was much faster, getting her bags and passing through Customs, than she had anticipated. It was only 8:35 when she walked through the big doors followed by the porter with her luggage. Michael was not among the eager people crowding either side of the walkway. He was also not standing apart from the others, disdaining close contact with strangers. He was not in any of the phone booths. He was not coming in the door. He was not there! The bastard had not come to meet her!

For a few minutes she allowed herself the luxury of fuming and calling him every name she could think of. And then the anger died down and she found herself feeling hurt and abandoned. The one emotion that was missing, however, was surprise. She found she was not at all surprised. It was very Michael-like to punish her this way. Well, tough luck, Michael! She was a big girl now; she knew how to tell the porter she needed a taxi and how to be handed into a cab by the starter. She knew how to say "Brooklyn Heights" and "thank you" and pay the driver. She didn't need him.

It would have been gratifying if he'd missed her; hell, what did she mean, *gratifying*? It should have been normal, it should have been natural. If Michael were just a bit more sensitive, a bit more tuned in to other people. And if my grandmother had wheels, she thought, smiling a little, remembering how often Daddy said this to them when they were small. If my grandmother had wheels, she'd be a cart. And that made her start thinking about Daddy again . . . and Elaine . . . and *that* whole mess. Later, she thought, tomorrow maybe.

She had to struggle herself and her luggage up the front steps by herself, find her keys in the dark, and let herself into a house that was so quiet, she was sure nobody was home. It wasn't quite 10:00; they *could* be out to dinner, or at a movie.

Except that, of course, Saul and Michael never did anything together except nitpick and wrangle. So they were both gone; some welcome-home! I guess that means I'm *not* welcome, Deena thought, pushing herself in and shoving the bags across the foyer. She'd unpack later. Right now she was starving to death. Maybe there was a piece of cheese in fridge, or a chocolate chip cookie in the cupboard.

She made her way to the back of the house, turning on lamps as she went. Living room, dining room, and then she opened the kitchen door, and *surprise*! There was Michael, forking scrambled eggs into his mouth while reading from a thick book.

"You're home!" she exclaimed, her voice sounding more wounded than she would have liked. So she quickly added, "Is Saul home, too? God, there wasn't a single light showing when I got here, I was sure you were both out."

The look he gave her could only be described as cool. "So," he said, "you're back."

Deena bit back any kind of cute comeback. Not now. It was time to try to make some kind of peace. "That's right!" in her brightest voice. She stood by the doorway, her smile becoming strained, waiting for him to go on, say something else. Instead, he simply bent his head and continued to read. Or *pretended* to continue to read.

She began to boil. "Is that it? Is that all you have to say to me? 'So, I'm back?' Is that *it*?"

His head came back up and now he really looked at her, eyes narrowed, lips thinned out. Oh, my God, Deena thought, he's *angry*. Still! Even after he had made his point by leaving. Her heart sank. So there was not going to be even a makeshift attempt at peaceful coexistence. She suddenly felt very tired. She didn't want to fight with him; she didn't want to even talk to him. But when she turned to leave, his voice shot out at her: "That's right! Walk away! It's just like you!"

"Just what in hell does *that* mean?"

"I'm supposed to be grateful, I suppose, that you finally decided to honor us with your presence. Well, you're a bit late to be of any use, Deena."

"Michael, excuse me, *you* left *me*. On a boat. Remember? So would you please make some sense?"

"Sense? Ha! The scene I walked in on, when I got home, was far from sensible! It was a nightmare!"

"Michael, what—?" Oh, my God, something dreadful had happened! Why was he playing with her, teasing her? "Goddammit, Michael! If something's happened to one of the children, you *have* to tell me!"

He held up a magisterial hand. "I don't suppose you've seen today's *Times*. Well, here, here's where your permissiveness has brought us all!" He pushed at a carefully folded newspaper.

Heart thumping wildly with anxiety, Deena reached out for the paper—who was dead?—but even before she could drop her eyes to see what it said, to find out the worst, Michael began to recite in a harsh emotionless voice: "BROOKLYN YOUTH INDICTED."

"Saul?" Nobody was dead. Thank God. But . . . *indicted*? Deena's hand flew involuntarily to her heart. And indeed her heart felt this moment as if it might burst out of her chest. "What? Why? What's he *done*?" Tears began to form under her lids. "Where is he?"

Michael's tight smile smacked of something she didn't like. "Not in jail, thank God. Upstairs, in his room, where he'll be staying until he gets put on the train for Concord Military Academy next Thursday."

"Michael, dammit, you can't just—"

"Oh, yes, I can. I let you do it your way all those years and obviously, your way was lousy. So now we're going to do it *my* way. If the district attorney's office will let us."

"Michael, for the love of God!"

"All right, then. I suppose you have a right to hear the whole sordid story. Last Tuesday, when I got here, every light in the house was on . . ."

And she sat, listening, feeling worse and worse with every word. It *was* her fault! No, it wasn't; of course it wasn't. But it *felt* like it was her fault. If she'd been here, if she had come back with Michael. But it was already done by the time he got back, so that wouldn't have changed anything, either. Still, she had been down there, lying in the sun, lying in the captain's arms, acting like an irresponsible girl, when she should have been home, tending to her child. But what good would it have done, four more days of tending to her child? She tended to her child all the time. She'd been taking care of him forever! Dammit, why did she feel this way? Why did every detail of Michael's story make her feel as if she alone were responsible? She knew damn well he was making her pay for daring to defy him. Dammit, all she'd done was what she wanted to do. She had a right. People did what they wanted to do all the time. Why couldn't *she*? Well, for the first time in her life—that she could remember—she'd tried putting herself first. And, of course, she was being punished for it.

"... and he hasn't spoken a word to me since." Michael finished his recital and sat back, looking aggrieved. She pushed down her immediate reaction, which was annoyance at his self-centered view of what had happened. But it must have been very difficult for Michael to admit he had slapped Saul in a fit of temper—Michael, who espoused self-control and discipline and furthermore thought of himself as a totally rational man, unswayed by easy emotion.

"Oh, Michael," she said, putting extra warmth into her voice. "I'm so sorry. I'm sorry you had to handle this all by yourself."

"You don't have to be sorry for *me*. My eyes have been opened, once and for all. I've said for years that you're too permissive with him ... no, no, Deena, don't get defensive. I blame myself. I was too busy to check on you, to see what was happening with him. I never even went into his room to see what the hell he was doing in there with all that fancy equipment. I was too busy. Well, that makes me responsible, doesn't it? At least as responsible as you; maybe even more so." His tone was even and reasonable.

Deena stared at him, speechless. He was a wonder, Michael Berman. He had just managed to blame her and make her feel even worse than she had before—and managed to do it while ostensibly absolving her. She looked at him, waiting to feel the old familiar need for his forgiveness, but it was no longer there. There was nothing but bleak emptiness. She didn't care whether he ever forgave her. She didn't care whether he blamed her or didn't blame her. She didn't care what he thought, period.

Poor Saul, she thought, spending these last three days

locked in his room, alone in the house with his judgmental, unforgiving father. Of course, Michael would never see it that way. And of course, Michael saw nothing strange about banishing his son in a totally arbitrary way. To a *military* school, of all the damn things! The man who could bore you to tears, arguing against military regimes, who hated the unquestioning obedience that was trained into the military mind. Oh, sure. But he demanded that same unquestioning obedience from his own son. He would be stunned if she pointed that out to him. But she was certainly not going to let *that* stop her; and she was absolutely not going to let him send Saul away. She drew in a breath, prepared to do battle.

The phone rang. Saved by the bell, she thought inanely; and then, who would be calling at this hour? "I'll get it," Michael said. Good. She didn't feel like being cheery on the telephone right now. "They think they found von Erdheim, in Bolivia. Oh, and by the way," he added casually, "they call at all kinds of crazy hours. So I'll be sleeping in the den. No sense your being disturbed."

So he was leaving their bed. She didn't care about that, either; let him do as he wanted. She was going upstairs to her son.

But in a surprised voice, Michael said, "The phone's for *you*."

It was Elaine. As soon as she heard her sister's familiar warm slightly husky voice, Deena began to cry.

"Deena! What's the trouble? Tell me!"

She could barely get it out. "Saul . . ."

"Oh, God, is he hurt?"

"No." She swallowed hard, to get her voice under control. "He's . . . oh, God, he's in terrible trouble, Elaine! With the *police*!"

"I'm coming right over. Don't move!"

Through the tears Deena couldn't help smiling a little. "Where am I going, Elaine?" Her sister's concern felt so good after Michael had as much as told her she was a lousy mother. He was taking her child out of her care, taking her child *away* from her.

He wanted to send Saul away and in spite of her outrage, she wasn't at all sure she could stop him.

She felt so goddamn helpless, and, let's admit it, guilty. She needed a kind word right now, a hug, a kiss, a warm smile. And here was her sister, her big sister, who didn't even hesitate a minute, not for a *second*, but whose immediate response was to come over and take care of her.

"Oh, Lainie," she said, her voice quivering. "Thanks so much. You'll never know how much your offer means to me. God, I was feeling so alone." And then she stopped, unable to continue in front of Michael. "You'll never know," she repeated.

"Glad to be of service. Does that mean I *shouldn't* come over?"

"It's not the best of all possible times. The offer, all by itself, was comfort enough. Honestly."

"You know I mean it. You know I'll be happy to do it."

"I know. And I appreciate it. *Believe* me, I appreciate it."

There was a longish pause. Then Elaine said, "Actually, the reason I called . . . but never mind, I don't suppose you'd feel like coming up to Daddy's office with me tomorrow afternoon. About that matter we discussed."

"Oh, Lainie, I already told you how I felt about that. And now—"

"Say no more. Just thought I'd mention it. My appointment's at four . . . just in case you change your mind."

Funny, Deena thought, how her perception of Elaine was able to change completely from one minute to the next. First, it had been Elaine, the strong big sister, ready to give aid and comfort. And now, suddenly, Elaine sounded forlorn; she sounded suddenly like she sometimes had, back when they were kids together, and she and Daddy had been tangled in one of their endless battles. How could she say no to Elaine after Elaine had, without even thinking about it, offered herself to Deena. They were *sisters*. She knew Elaine as well as anyone in her life . . . maybe better than anyone else in her life. She hadn't grown up side by side with anyone else, hadn't shared her childhood with anyone else, not in the same way. Hadn't shared her parents with anyone else; Marilyn was so much younger, she was like another generation.

Deena didn't really understand why her sister felt she *had* to confront Daddy with this. As far as she herself could see, it wouldn't serve any useful purpose. But, there you were. Elaine had to have everything out in the open, discussed, and *settled*. Elaine would feel at loose ends until she had it all finished. And, in a way, she was right to object to an outsider owning shares—their mother's shares, at that.

That's the part of it Deena didn't want to even think about. *All* of it was the part she didn't want to face. But an injustice had been done to her mother. And besides, Elaine deserved her support.

"I just did," Deena said now.

"Did what? Changed your mind? Oh, Deena, you are a darling. I know how hard this is for you, I really do. But, goddammit, I *need* you."

Deena surprised herself by laughing. She hadn't thought she had any laughter in her right now. "Oh, Elaine! You know that's the way to get me, with my social-worker's heart!"

"Yeah, I know it. But that's not why I said it. I said it because it's true. I do need you and I appreciate, and . . . I'd better hang up before I start sobbing over the telephone. Talk to you tomorrow, kid."

Deena hung up, bemused. You know, she thought to herself, Elaine hasn't called me kid since I was in second grade and saved her from the playground bully. Interesting. Is that how Elaine saw *Daddy*—as a big bully? Could it be that she had lived 43 years and only now was realizing that maybe Elaine had had a different father than she had? And she'd just been congratulating herself on how well she knew Elaine.

She sat, slumped, at the kitchen counter, carefully not looking at Michael. If she met his eyes, he'd be sure to ask her what *that* was all about. She didn't want to talk about Daddy, about Saul, about them, about Elaine. She didn't want to talk about anything. She didn't want to *think* about anything. Maybe if she pretended he wasn't even here, he'd go away.

And to her surprise, it worked. When she finally looked up, she was alone.

CHAPTER TWENTY

Monday, January 6, 1986

When Elaine stepped off the dimly lit elevator into the jungle glare of the Strauss Construction reception area, she had to blink a little. Maybe skylight plus mirror plus up-lighting was just too much, she thought, and when she had more to say about what went on here, she'd do something about it. You could have electrically controlled shades; you could—and then she stopped thinking about decor, surprised to find Deena already waiting for her. She looked gorgeous in her fur coat, but so weary, so worn out, in spite of the glowing tan.

Poor Deena. The worst thing in the world was to have your child in trouble, any kind of trouble. And to have the police involved! She still recalled her own exhaustion the year Noel was sixteen and decided to become a dropout. She had thought she wouldn't live through it with her sanity intact . . . and she might not have without Howard there. It was Howard who kept talking and talking and talking to Noel until finally he got through. Too bad Deena had always had to do all the tough stuff all alone. Well, she knew what she was getting before she married him, although she was so infatuated, who knows how much she allowed herself to see.

She gave Deena a big hug, saying, "Bless you for coming. I'm itching for a fight... yeah, yeah, I know, what else is new? Thank God I can always count on you, no matter what. Speaking of which, how *are* things?"

Deena sighed. "Saul is sulky and uncommunicative... and so is Michael. I tried to talk to him, but he wouldn't."

"Which one?"

A brief laugh. "Both. But I meant Saul. I pounded on his bedroom door, I pleaded with him to let me in, to talk to me. Nothing doing." She paused and then burst out: "Oh, God, I don't know my own child, Lainie, he's a stranger to me! He's been stealing, that's number one, and number two, he can't even see anything *wrong* with what he's done! He's only sorry he got *caught*. Where did he come from? That's not how I brought up my children! I'm sorry, I'm carrying on, aren't I?"

Elaine pulled a bit farther away from Miss Harvey's desk and positioned them so that she was shielding her sister. "Carry on, Dee Dee, it's okay. I know how you feel. It's too bad Michael can't be of some help, that's all."

"Oh, give the devil his due. This morning he's talking to somebody in the D.A.'s office. Did you hear what I just said? *The D.A.'s office.* I just can't deal with it, I can't make it real. My son, involved with the D.A. and with the cops? I mean, he's had his problems, but... my son?" She stopped and took a deep breath. "Enough. I don't really want to go over it again right now. One problem at a time, I always say."

"I want you to know how grateful I am that you're taking on mine this afternoon."

"What else are sisters for, except to use?" It was an old joke between them, not very funny anymore, but it let them both know that they were there for each other in spite of their considerable differences.

Miss Harvey had apparently already buzzed the sanctum sanctorum; because she now told them they were to go right in, Mr. S. was waiting for them.

He did his usual number: jumping up the minute he saw them, throwing out his arms, flashing a great big smile, yelling across the room, "The two most beautiful girls in New

York City! Come, give your old Daddy a great big hug and
kiss!" All this, followed by noisy kisses, and bear hugs, and
cheek pinches, and smiles of delight. Elaine could understand
why everyone thought him so marvelous, why all her mother's
friends openly and noisily envied her her handsome, outgoing,
charming, sexy husband. She could even, when it wasn't annoying her, understand Deena's persistent unquestioning devotion. After all, she was his favorite. Elaine guessed that
when you were someone's favorite, you repaid them with total
devotion. She guessed it; she wouldn't know.

But now, down to business. Daddy could prance around his
office from now till kingdom come; he should know by now
that she was immune to his considerable and well-practiced
charms. And anyway, today she had no patience for this.
Today, she just wanted some straight talk, for a change. Let's
see if she could get him to stop performing for five minutes.

Smiling at him, she said evenly, "We know how busy you
are, Daddy, so let's get right down to it."

"That's my Lainie, always in a hurry! But you could sit
down first. You could even have a cup of coffee, no? All
right, then, no. Sit down, sit down, both of you. Elaine, I
know what's griping you and I don't blame you. Linda overstepped, seriously overstepped. Why she wouldn't take your
word and give you the records you wanted, I don't know. But
look, see? I have them all right here." He picked up a thick
pile of file folders, brandishing them before slapping them
back down onto the desk. "I've pulled out everything on the
Ninth Avenue Project and you can take it all right now into the
conference room or even take it home if you like." He sat
back in his chair, beaming at his own largess. "How's that?"

He thought he was going to get away with that garbage!
Well, think again, Elaine thought with asperity. I'm not one of
Sylvia's graying friends, to be cosseted with a show of chiv-
alry! She shook her head. "Too late, Daddy," she said, smiling
into his puzzled eyes. "It won't wash."

Now he looked hurt. "How can you talk to me like that?
You're interested in the business and here I am, offering you
carte blanche . . . total access to all these files. So, what are
you talking about this time?"

"How do I know it's total access? You could leave out anything you don't want me to see."

"Why in the world would I do a thing like that?"

"Oh, I can't imagine! Since I know so well how thrilled you are at the prospect of letting me into the business at all."

"Come *on*, Elaine," Deena objected, "taking that tone isn't going to accomplish anything." Always Daddy's girl! But Elaine needed her. So she gave Deena a grin to show her she was listening.

And then he had to do one of his numbers on her; he never could resist. He laughed heartily and turned to Deena, saying, "Your sister is in the habit of using female tactics in the *shmatte* business, so don't cramp her style."

"You're a fine one to talk about tactics!" Elaine snapped. "Making fun of my industry doesn't diminish me. And belittling my success doesn't take away from the fact that Sweet Somethings grossed twenty-two million last year." She gave him a hard look. "You can't make me feel stupid by calling me names, Daddy, not at my age." And then watched, with great satisfaction, as he visibly switched gears, leaning back in his chair, replacing the steely-eyed look with a kindly smile, throwing his hands up. "Okay, okay, sweetie-*piele*. You win. I apologize. How's that? So let's get to the point already." He glanced at the big gold wristwatch. "We're both busy people."

If he thought he was going to soft-soap her . . . Oh, shit, Elaine told herself, of course he thought he was going to soft-soap her. What he didn't realize was that things were very different now. She had a little surprise for him.

She smiled back at him and said very sweetly, "Okay. Here's the point: you took shares that belonged to our mother and you gave them to Linda." Was it her imagination or did he cringe just the littlest bit? He was an old hand at negotiation; he certainly knew how to stonewall. "And we want to know why."

"It's actually none of your business. But you're my daughters, my children, and by the way, shareholders in this company. So I'll tell you. Gladly! Linda has shares in this company because she earned them. She is my most trusted business associate. You know how close a man and his personal secretary become...excuse me, Ms. Woman's Lib, how close a *person* and his *administrative assistant* get to be when they work well together. Linda knows more about this business, in some ways, than even I do. She has all the details at her fingertips. Jesus, I don't have to tell you girls how long and how hard Linda has worked for this company! She *deserves* those shares. In fact, I was at fault that I didn't think of it earlier. There...now you have it all." And he sat back— smugly, Elaine thought, so sure he'd taken care of everything.

"Correct me if I'm wrong," Elaine said evenly. "What you're trying to make us believe is that you gave Linda our mother's shares because she's a devoted employee?"

"Didn't I just say it?"

"Well, I have a word for that and the word is *bullshit*!" She could hear the little gasp from Deena—dammit, when was Deena going to wake up and get smart?

Jack paled perceptively. "That's how you talk to your father?" he demanded, but there was something shaky in his voice; so she pushed further.

"That's how I talk to a father when he's telling me a bullshit story! *Trusted employee*! Give me credit for a little intelligence. Linda as much as admitted to us that 'employee' is hardly an adequate description of your relationship." He really was looking chalky under that tan. Good. So it *was* true. She couldn't help feeling a little self-congratulatory zing. She had been one hundred percent correct and Deena, with her baby notions about beloved perfect Daddy, was all wet. She pressed on. "Perhaps 'mistress' would be more apt?"

His face changed with that word. It sagged, that was the only way to describe it. All the life just drained out of it for a split-second. And then, just as swiftly, he put a smile on his face and said, "Come on, Elaine! Deena, talk some sense into your sister! So I gave Linda some shares! So what? Everything I own is also your mother's and she knows it. She'll get it all when I'm gone. Who was I supposed to take shares from, my girls?"

That's right, Deena thought, he was just taking care of his girls, as he had always done. But when she started to say something, Elaine shook her head fiercely and said, "Bull.

Shit. I'm forty-five years old, Daddy, give me a break, will you? We *know* all about it, so stop pretending!"

Deena fully expected him to explode: to pound the desk, turn red, and give Elaine hell. But he didn't. He sucked in a deep breath. He sagged, dropped his eyes, stared at his clasped hands. And then, to her astonishment, he looked up and said calmly, "Okay, Elaine, what do you want from me?"

Deena hated her sister's little smile. Was taking over the business so all-important to her that she was ready to sacrifice her own father? Ready to do or say anything, no matter how hurtful? She stirred, uncomfortable, and Elaine turned to her. "Why are you looking that way, Deena? *I* haven't been dishonest! *I'm* not the liar and the cheat!"

And he still didn't defend himself, just muttered, "Get on with it, get on with it."

Elaine stood up, the color high across her cheekbones. There was no doubt about it; she was triumphant. And Deena did not like her at this moment, not at all.

"One. I want the Ninth Avenue Project. Complete control . . . oh, don't get excited, you're still the boss around here. But I want to be project manager, reporting straight to you. No Lawrence, no Linda."

"Done."

"What I'd really like is for Linda to get out of this office."

Now his face came to life. "I can't do that to her! Don't ask it of me!"

Then it was all true, Deena thought. Linda really had been his . . . girlfriend. Maybe she still was. How disgusting. All those years, when Linda was so sweet to his three little girls, it had just been her slimy way of showing off for him, letting him know how motherly she was. Ugh! How sickening that she should have thought for even one moment that she could replace Sylvia!

Oh, God, did Sylvia know? Did she have an idea? No, she couldn't. She couldn't have known and gone on all these years, joking with him and holding hands and smiling at him when he patted her fanny and acting as if everything was so nice and normal. It just wasn't possible.

She found it almost impossible to focus on what was happening in the office now. They were talking numbers and dates and her head was aching. In any case, they seemed to be finishing up, and if she'd missed anything important, tough.

"And I want it in writing," Elaine was saying.

"Come on, baby, this isn't IBM you're dealing with, this is your daddy." He held his hands out, supplicating, and the sight of the twisted smile on his face made Deena's heart turn. He was a frightened man. She couldn't remember ever having seen him afraid of anything, ever.

"Exactly." Elaine's response was said in a very cruel, ironic tone.

"Elaine!" Deena burst out. "Enough! You got what you came for! Let it go, for God's sake!" She couldn't stand this! This was terribly wrong. Things were being done and said here that nobody would ever be able to fix. "You don't know—"

Jack held up a hand that she should stop talking, his eyes fastened on Elaine's. "And if I won't put it in writing? If I insist you should trust me?"

"Then I'll be forced to go to Sylvia."

"Elaine!" Now she was horrified. "For the love of God! Quit it! You couldn't hurt our mother for the sake of a piece of paper!"

"*Shah*, Deena," Jack said in a very subdued tone. "Elaine, listen to me. Your mother knows nothing, do you hear me, *nothing* of this! I'm sure of that. The most important thing is that she should never know. She should never be hurt. You'll get your piece of paper if it's so important. Do I care? What's another piece of paper to me?"

"When?"

"When I have a minute. In a few days. *Soon*."

Elaine was so stubborn. From his first words, she had begun to shake her head and she was still shaking it when he finished.

"Thursday morning," she said, implacable. "That gives you two working days. Surely, you don't need more than that, not with such a *devoted* and *efficient* administrative assistant."

Deena watched her father flinch just the littlest bit. It clutched at her; a vulnerable Jack Strauss was new to her. She sat where she was, not obeying Elaine's imperious fling of the head to follow, letting her sister make her swooping exit without her company.

She looked at him for a long moment, feeling very sad, not knowing what to say. What *could* she say? Her whole world was changing before her very eyes. The man sitting across from her, avoiding her eyes, staring at his knuckles, that was the man who, up until a few minutes ago, she had admired extravagantly, trusted utterly, loved unquestioningly. Now he looked up, trying to smile at her. He looked pathetic. Sighing, she said, "Oh, Daddy, I'm so sorry."

"Hey, baby, no big deal! You understand: your daddy's just a human being, a man with a man's frailties and weaknesses and needs—just like any other man. It's true, there was a time when I needed . . . there was a time when Linda . . . she needed me and I guess I needed to be needed. I don't know, she was a widow, she was all alone, I don't know. It happened. I'm sorry my girls had to find out now and take it so hard. You *do* understand, don't you? Deena? Dee Dee?"

Where was his regret? Where were his feelings of remorse? Where were his feelings, period. She was assailed with a sense of irretrievable loss. What was going to happen to all of them now? She'd read somewhere that the bonds of relationships are forged, not in chains, but in threads . . . and it was true. She saw herself, connected with all her loved ones in a kind of cobweb, delicate but strong. And now, sitting here with Daddy, where she had always felt safe and protected and loved, she could feel those threads breaking. "Understand?" she repeated, "I'll try. I don't know if I can. But Elaine—"

"Aw, Elaine! You know Elaine, always a short fuse. Elaine will come around, don't you worry. She'll calm down soon, you wait and see. Like she always does. She's a practical woman. And anyway, hey, it happened a long time ago, what meaning can it have to you now?"

"Oh, Daddy!" Could he really think that because it was long ago it didn't count? Would she ever feel the same about him again? She looked at his rugged, handsome face, with its deep smile grooves and lively eyes, and remembered suddenly how proud she had always been as a girl when he came to pick her up anywhere, because he was so strong and handsome and full of fun. She had been so sure that he was a rock: dependable, honest, straightforward. And all the time he had been cheating them . . . not only her mother, but all of them!

She gazed at him, not moving, not answering his implicit plea that she come to him, embrace him, let him know nothing had changed. It had changed all right, and she had changed. Everything had changed and nothing would ever be quite the same again.

When Elaine saw her sister emerge, five minutes later, from Daddy's office, she was shocked. Deena had aged a year for every minute. She looked awful. So Elaine went and took her by the hand and got her into the elevator and downstairs and into a taxicab, talking the whole time. "Come on, kiddo, I'm taking you to my house and we'll jump into a nice cold bottle of wine together."

Finally, when they were on Central Park West, Deena spoke. "It's too damn much for me. I can't seem to take it all in." And she lapsed back into her remote, self-contained silence.

What was her problem? Elaine wondered. So Daddy fooled around a little when he was young and foolish! What man hadn't? Especially a man with a curvaceous, beautiful young secretary who openly adored him. Was it so surprising that he might find it appealing, even irresistible? She could write the scenario of how it happened. First a few little brushings up against each other; then exchanged glances full of meaning and longing; and then a little lunch and then a little dinner and then a little hanky-panky. The way it happened with everyone. And could Sylvia have been that easy to live with? God knows she had never been averse to handing out orders or giving you a piece of her mind whenever she felt like it; it didn't matter who you were. Maybe it could be tough on a man. She had reason to know it could be tough on a little girl. So he fooled around with his secretary; it was nothing to get this upset about. She only wished she could say all of this out loud to her sister.

She personally knew a little about this sort of thing. There had been two or three rocky years, not so long ago, for her and Howard. She stared out of the cab window, not really seeing as they turned on Central Park South, heading for the

West Side; but instead, seeing the face she had promised herself never to think of again. Dave. He had cried, actually broken down and cried when she told him she wouldn't see him anymore, that she was married to Howard and intended to stay that way, and she couldn't do it anymore. "I thought you and I had something special, Elaine, something really special." Well, they had. It was just that it ended up being more special for him than it was for her. She was forty, Dave was thirty, it couldn't have worked even if things had been different. He was a romantic dreamer. A sweet man, that Dave, but not too much between the ears.

That thought made her laugh aloud—God, what a thing to think in the middle of a reverie about your one and only extra-marital lover!—and, finally, finally Deena came out of her blue funk to ask her what was so amusing. So she told her a lie: "I just saw a streetwalker over there, fatter than me, and wearing gold short shorts, would you believe!"

Well, here they were, in her apartment, shedding their coats and making small-talk while Elaine got out the bottle of chilled wine and the two oversized goblets. "You don't want to spoil this good wine by having anything to eat with it, do you, Deena?"

"God no, I think I'd like to get looped."

"I'll drink to that!" They laughed, Deena a bit wanly. "Come on, Deena, it's not the end of the world."

"I don't think it's the end of the world. But it's the end of something."

"Your naïveté, maybe?"

"Elaine! He lied to us, for years and years. We trusted him and he betrayed us!"

"*I* haven't trusted him for years, Deena. I never made a myth out of him."

"Stop saying that! I haven't made a saint out of Daddy! But I can't believe he really used to . . . carry on with Linda."

"Used to? I'll bet you a hundred bucks they still . . . carry on, as you so delicately put it. Don't look at me like that. I'm only being realistic. And anyway, hey, don't think for one minute I forgive him! I'm mad, I'm mad as hell, but not because I'm disappointed in him."

"Then why?"

"Because he thought it was fine to run around with his little playmate and come home to his family late and seldom! Do you realize that by the time Marilyn was born—and we were just little kids—he was hardly ever around? But when I began to date Howard, suddenly he was the heavy father, calling Howard names, giving me a curfew at the age of twenty, demanding to know every goddamn detail . . . oh, and snide little remarks like, I hope you don't let that half-pint get away with anything! I knew then that it was all phony. It had nothing to do with morality or with his love for me. It had to do with power, Deena, power and control. By God, he owned me and my virginity, that's what it was all about!"

Deena took a large gulp of her wine and said, "Why didn't you ever tell me any of this before?"

Elaine laughed. "There was no way you were ever going to believe me, Deena. Think back. I'm right. Because he was very different about Michael. Michael, he fawned over. Michael was the prize. Michael could do no wrong. As hard as he fought against Howard, that's how eager he was for you to marry Michael."

"But why?"

"I don't know. I never could figure it out. He was in awe of him for some reason. Maybe because Michael was in law school? I just don't know."

"Well . . ." Deena raised her glass and gave Elaine a wan smile. "He made a good choice for himself, all right. Michael's devoted to him. At Thanksgiving—did you notice?— when he was taking movies? The minute you and Daddy began to fight, Michael stopped taking pictures. Nothing bad for the record. I think he loves Daddy much more than he loves me."

"Well, to tell you the truth, I never *did* understand why you were so crazy about him . . . he was so cold, so unemotional. Brrr . . ."

"Not to me. To me he was mature and sophisticated and brilliant and gorgeous and out of reach. Oh, above all, Lainie, out of reach. I pursued him relentlessly until he caught me." She gave a bitter little laugh. "As a consequence, I've never, in all the years we've been married, ever been sure that he really loves me, or that he ever did. Well, at least he used to lust after me. That I had proof of. And now I don't even know *that*." She looked her sister straight in the eye. "That's right, he's moved into the den."

Elaine pondered a moment, then poured them each some more. "I always thought you'd end up with Paul Mankewicz. He was a doll, remember? God! Talk about gorgeous, talk about brilliant!" She heaved a great theatrical sigh. "I'd have taken him—gladly. How come you dumped him, anyway? I've been wanting to ask you that forever."

"Easy." Deena's speech was becoming just a trifle slurred around the edges. "He was nice. I always wanted him to take his nice and go away . . . funny, isn't it? I thought nice was so boring; and now, now I think I'd give a year of my life for just a little nice." Her eyes welled up. "Look how lucky you've been. You know, I never told you, but I thought Howard was a jerk. Shame on me!"

"I hope you don't think that comes as a surprise to me. I knew very well what everyone thought of Howard. You want to know why I married him? I'll tell you why I married him. I wasn't madly in love with him, I wasn't even *in* love with him, period. Don't look like that; it's not a crime punishable by death, you know. But he was the very first man who didn't, after knowing me a few weeks, just very casually, out loud, let me know how fabulous, *really* fabulous I would look if I just lost ten, twenty pounds. I could be better than Elizabeth Taylor! Yes, Deena, they *all* did, sooner or later every last one of the bastards! And Howard's *never* . . . and what's more, I know he doesn't even think it, not even in his most secret thoughts. Howard loves my body the way it is and my mind the way it is and my personality the way it is and it didn't take me too goddamn long—because after all, I *am* a Strauss and that means I'm goddamn smart—to realize what a prince I had.

"Not that we've always had El Perfecto marriage, Dee Dee, that's not what I'm saying. We've knocked quite a few rough edges off each other; we've had our share of disagreements, battles, and just plain riots. But in the end it worked out."

She leaned back in the chair and then said, "You know, it's like in the old country, with arranged marriages. I didn't fall in love with my husband until after we'd been married for several years. Remember that ectopic pregnancy I had, the year after Noel was born? Well, not only did he take care of me and the baby, but he was terrific when the doctor said I couldn't have any more kids. Howard's dream was a house full of kids, you know. I thought he might leave me . . . you know, I was a fat lady and now I was a barren fat lady, so who in the world would want me?"

"Oh, Lainie!"

"Hey, that was a long time ago. You don't see me suffering, do you?" They gave each other a long look of understanding and raised their glasses.

"So, a baby is why you fell in love with your husband," Deena said, giving herself more wine. "Funny, a baby is why I'm not in love with mine anymore."

"Are you planning to explain?"

"It's very simple. I didn't want Saul. Michael did. You don't have to guess who won. When I look back now, I can't believe I allowed Michael that control over my body, I just can't believe it. But, of course, Michael had everything on his side: the Holocaust, his own arid childhood, not to mention the prevailing social climate that said abortion was murder, and women shouldn't argue. Oh, hell!"

"Poor Deena!"

"Poor Saul, you mean! That's why this latest escapade of his is making me crazy. I didn't want that baby, I never focused on him the way I did with the others, I kept the nurse on for months. I always had somebody there to take care of him while I went out and made shopping my career." She stopped and they both laughed a little. "I'm feeling guilty, Lainie, I feel that probably Michael's right and it *is* somehow all my fault . . . and then that makes me furious with Michael."

"Don't be ridiculous. Noel always had Jessie, from the time I brought him home from the hospital. What's wrong with having full-time child care? *I* did it! And Noel's no lousier than any other rotten no-good spoiled kid of his age! The only reason, probably, that he never got into trouble with a computer is he didn't have a computer when he was sixteen! You were a very good mother to Saul, Deena, come on, don't beat yourself up like that. It's not going to help Saul. Or your marriage."

"I'll tell you something. I'm not sure I care what happens to my marriage anymore. Michael's pushed me right against the wall; I have no place to go. I have nothing new to try; I've tried everything. *He* doesn't give a damn!"

"Ah, Deena! I wish I had a magical answer for you. But who knows anything about someone else's marriage? As Daddy always says, 'You never know what goes on behind the closed bedroom door.'"

Deena winced. "Oh, swell, Lainie, quote Daddy some more about happy marriages, why don't you? Some expert *he* turned out to be!"

"There you go again. I happen to think that Daddy and Sylvia have a very good marriage. I happen to think they're both quite satisfied with the bargain they made. What you don't know, Dee Dee, can't hurt you; and I think that our mother is blissfully ignorant." She laughed. "He may have been a liar and a cheat and a skunk. But he seems to have successfully kept her in the dark all these years. The important thing," she said, leaning forward and looking suddenly serious, "is to keep it that way. At her age, Sylvia doesn't need to confront this sort of thing. Agreed?"

"Of course, agreed!"

"Good. But there is one person who should be told."

"Who?"

"Dummie! Who do you think? Marilyn."

"Marilyn!" Deena nearly choked on her wine. "Why? There's no reason for this to go any further. Why involve Marilyn?"

"Because she's our sister! How's that?"

"But she's three hundred miles away and she doesn't really care all that much what happens to us and she and Daddy have never gotten along anyway. And you know Marilyn: she'll insist that we tell Sylvia. You know how she prides herself on her quote honesty unquote."

"I think you just talked me out of calling her. Anyway, to tell you the truth, I never know what to say to Marilyn. I was going to ask *you* to talk to her."

"Me! Come on, Elaine, remember me? The placator and the peacekeeper and above all the coward of the family?"

Elaine laughed again. "I remember you. I remember you always running into your room to put your head under the pillows whenever the scary parts came. And that included everything from radio programs to the mildest kind of disagreement at the dinner table."

"Yeah! Well, I wish I could do it now. I wish I could put my head *somewhere* and make all this go away."

"Well, you can't, Deena."

The two sisters looked solemnly at each other and, in unison, pulled in deep breaths. "I know that," Deena said. "I know that. But, Lainie, what are we going to *do*?"

Wryly, Elaine said, "What women always do, Dee Dee." She gave her sister a grin. "Take it like a man!"

CHAPTER TWENTY-ONE

Saturday, January 21, 1961

Deena had been out of breath as she opened the apartment door—very quietly because she wasn't supposed to be here. She stood leaning against the door, trying to calm her heavy breathing before she was confronted by her mother, who would be furious on two counts. One: Elaine had uninvited her to this party and Deena was supposed to be sleeping over with her friend Ellen. And two: she had run up the stairs instead of taking the elevator like a lady. Well, too bad. She didn't care what Sylvia said to her. Elaine was having a big party with lots and lots of college boys and it wasn't fair to leave her out!

Elaine had been talking for weeks and weeks about all the grad students and law students and med students she had invited. ". . . . And they're all coming, too," she announced proudly at the dinner table a couple of days ago.

"And why not?" Daddy wanted to know. "It's the chance of a lifetime! I know how I felt every time I went to the Weinrebs. All those beautiful sisters . . . and a piano, too!" He rolled his eyes and winked at Sylvia and made them all laugh.

228

And then Elaine looked over at Deena and said, "Well, at *this* party there'll be a piano, all right. But only *one* beautiful sister."

"That's not fair!" Deena cried. This was the first she'd heard of that particular plan. And Marilyn only made it worse by adding her protest. "Sylvia said I could stay up late and see everybody. Does that mean I don't get to come, either?"

Elaine gave Marilyn such a look! "You can take coats at the door, Moo Moo. But don't you dare say anything to anybody." And then Marilyn did a little number about being a mute doorman and that made everybody laugh, too.

Except for Deena, who was boiling. "Excuse me," she said in her loftiest tone, "but if you expect me to pass the hors d'oeuvres, Lainie, you've got another thing coming."

"You," Elaine announced, "are not going to be here."

"What?! Sylvia!"

"Now, now," Sylvia said soothingly. And then, to Elaine: "It doesn't seem quite fair, Elaine."

"Sylvia, listen. These aren't just the same old guys. These are *men*. This is my first real grown up party, with drinks and hors d'oeuvres and stuff. I don't want Deena hanging around . . . and my friends don't either."

Rebellious, Deena muttered, "What do I care about your stupid friends? They're all a bunch of phonies anyway. They think they're so special and sophisticated because they're *juniors* and *seniors* . . . to tell you the truth, Lainie, I'm not too crazy about your friends always giving me a hard time about being a lowly frosh."

"Oh drop dead!"

"DDT!"

"Girls! Shame on you, and after what Hitler did! I never want to hear that expression again! As for you, Deena," Sylvia said, "Elaine's been planning this party for a long time. In fact, young lady, you were never invited in the first place so—"

"Daddy!" Deena turned to her court of last resort.

But he shook his head, saying: "Don't look at *me*! I'm getting the hell out of here, believe me! I'm playing cards at the club and I'm not coming home until they throw me out!"

So he was no good to her, darn it. And then Elaine said,

"And anyway, I can have this party anyway I want it because someone at this table had two hundred of her closest friends at the Pierre, whereas someone else never even got a Sweet Sixteen."

"Just because you weighed two hundred pounds and were afraid nobody would dance with you!"

Elaine looked as if she'd like to kill, but Daddy ordered silence. "Enough already! We've now spent the entire dinner hour fighting over this party and I don't want to hear another word about it!"

There was silence for a little while. Deena hated that little smile on Elaine's face; she was so pleased with herself for getting her way! And then, after dinner, Daddy pulled her aside and said, "No more sulking, now, Deena. Here." And he reached into his pocket and pulled out his wallet. "Saturday, you'll invite your own friends and make your own party, eat Chinese, go to the movies, or maybe even take in a Broadway show." As he spoke, he counted out more bills. He handed Deena a thick wad, folding her hand around it. "There. You'll have a better time that way than you'd have hanging around Elaine's graduate students, believe me! You're a beautiful girl; you meet plenty of boys on your own, I notice. One party you won't miss. There! Now give Daddy a big hug and kiss. All done? All done."

There was no sense talking back. She'd do what she always did, pretend to go along and then, very quietly and in her own time, do what she wanted. The important thing was to show Elaine the Pain that she couldn't uninvite her own sister. They'd always had their parties together and shared their friends. No way was she going to be forced out of it this time! The more Elaine didn't want her there, the more she was determined to show up!

So, tonight, after she and Ellen and Susan and Karen finished with the movie and had their dinner at the Great Shanghai, she did not go back to Ellen's house. Instead, a bit nervous over her own derring-do, she came right back to the house and ran up the stairs before Tom the elevator man could see her.

Now she tiptoed down the hall to her room. There was already a lot of noise from the living room and she recognized

her new Chubby Checker record playing on the phonograph.
So, her records were invited to the party even if she wasn't.
Well, she'd told Elaine not to take them and Elaine hadn't
listened. So now she had a *right* to come to the party.

In her room, she brushed her hair, put on dangle earrings,
and quickly changed out of her slacks into her new skirt and
then unbuttoned the top three buttons of her angora sweater,
then changed her mind and buttoned one of them back up. No
sense in causing a commotion; it was going to be bad enough
just showing up. Maybe Elaine would be too busy to yell at
her; that's what she was counting on. Well, let her try; if she
started up, Deena would just very calmly and very coldly pick
up all her records and take them away! The thought made her
giggle.

Uh-oh. One of Elaine's older men had spotted her and
there was a gleam in his eye. And now she recognized him.
Oh my God, it was David Baum, the worst drip in the world.
Why had Elaine invited *him*? But of course, he was a med
student. Maybe medical school had taken some of the drippi-
ness out. But she didn't feel like finding out. And here he
came, a big dopey grin all over his stupid face, calling her,
saying, "Hey! Let me get a good look at you!"

Not if she had anything to say about it! She wasn't going to
let David Baum close enough for a good look . . . or for anything else. So she pretended she hadn't seen or heard him and
beat it into the kitchen.

There were six or seven people already in there, leaning
against the counters, sipping on their drinks and smoking and
talking a mile a minute. There was a strong smell of perfume,
cigarette smoke, and beer.

And, most important, there was a boy there she had never
seen before . . . a man, really, the handsomest man she'd ever
seen, tall and dark with startling light eyes, his lean cheeks
deeply shadowed. He was talking intently and everyone listened to him. He was gorgeous; she couldn't take her eyes
from him, he looked so much like an actor. Not even Susan,
who got all the really interesting boys to call her, had ever
come up with anyone like *this*.

She inched over closer to his group, looking as casual and
as mature as she could manage. With the earrings she could

pass for twenty, easily. Now, how could she get his attention? Without making a fool of herself. The best way, she figured, was to stand there and listen to him. If she kept her eyes on him, sooner or later he'd feel it and he'd look at her. And after he looked at her . . . well, she'd figure that out when it happened.

Oh, rats, he was talking *politics*. She didn't know anything about politics; politics were boring. Politics and business: that's what Daddy and his friends always talked about and whenever she heard a conversation about politics, she could almost smell the cigars!

" . . . the end of apathy!" he was saying. "Just like Jessica Mitford said. I tell you, there's a new feeling in the air and it's all due to Kennedy!"

One of the other men laughed rudely. "Kennedy! If you think he's really idealistic, you're naive, Berman! He's a Boston politician from the word go. Jesus Christ, you know who his grandfather was—"

"I don't want to hear any more Honey Fitz stories. I'm getting sick of them. I believe in this man. I think there's a new day dawning and I'm sorry if that sounds corny!"

And someone else said, "You can't believe what these guys say, Michael. They have speechwriters!"

And someone else added, "He's just young and better-looking than the usual president; that's what gets most people."

And the handsome boy whose name Deena now knew was Michael Berman turned and said in a cool tone. "Brains are what get *me*, Alexander. And I defy any man here to tell me that he heard our new president say, 'The torch has been passed onto a new generation of Americans' without a chill going down his spine!"

"Not me! All I thought was, 'Well, at least it's not Tricky Dick!'"

Several of them laughed at that; but not Michael Berman. Deena crossed her fingers and said loudly, "I'm not a man, but I felt a chill. Does that count?"

They all turned to look at her. She wanted to die; but it was very important that he notice her, so she stood her ground and smiled brightly. The boy he had called Alexander put a hand

on her shoulder and said, "Well, well, and who have we
here?" but she couldn't be bothered with him. Would Michael
Berman smile at her?

Yes. Michael Berman smiled. "Have we met?" he said.
"I'll want your name when I tell President Kennedy you're a
fan."

Oh, joy! "Deena. Deena Strauss." And she heard one of
the guys laugh and say, "I'll be damned, it's the kid sister! I
haven't seen *you* since you were in third grade. My, my but
you're all grown up!"

Oh, go dig a hole and bury yourself, she thought. Who
invited you? But she smiled and answered smartly, "Wish I
could say the same for *you*!" And he laughed, Michael Berman, the handsomest boy she'd ever seen in her life, thought
she was funny!

For a few minutes it was great fun, with two or three of
them fighting over who would get her a drink and making her
a part of the group. But when she looked at Michael Berman,
he had already turned and was deep in *another* discussion!
This time about public defenders and poor people and Southern sit-ins and bar exams! He was obviously a brilliant boy
and he had ideals and he was willing to get involved ... but,
really, didn't he like girls? Didn't he like *her*?

And then several of them drifted off to get more beer or
something and he looked right at her—right at her!—and he
spoke to her, *spoke to her*!

"And what do *you* think? Is our justice system fair ... or
does it need a major overhaul?"

Was he making fun of her because she was young? Well,
she didn't care. She gave him one of her best sophisticated
smiles, tossing her head a little, and said, "You're a very
convincing speaker. But Morty had a point. If people didn't
get into trouble, they wouldn't need lawyers, would they?"

"When you're poor, my dear Miss Strauss, it's too damn
—excuse me—too difficult *not* to get into trouble with the
law. That's the kicker, you see. And that's why Morty is full
of horse manure. He's dealing with his own privileged world
and not with reality."

He didn't talk down to her a bit, not even after he found
out she was only a freshman at Barnard and eighteen years

old. She wanted to tell him she was twenty but he'd find out from Elaine . . . or from Morty, if it came to that . . . so she decided on the truth. He didn't seem to mind. They stayed there in the kitchen for an hour and a half, talking. About poverty, and the Negroes' fight for equality, and government . . . real things, adult things. That is, *he* talked. She mostly just listened and nodded and looked agreeable, while she memorized his face, feature by feature, taking it all in so she could describe him to the girls tomorrow.

Later on, when Elaine came in and saw her and began giving her hell, Michael came right to her rescue. He put an arm around her shoulder—she thought she would fall to the floor in a faint—and said, "My fault entirely, Elaine. She just came in to get a drink and I've been bending her ear ever since. And she's a terrific listener, too." And he squeezed her shoulder.

It was nice to have him on her side, but even he wouldn't have stopped Elaine on a rampage. But luckily, just then, Elaine's latest came into the kitchen looking for her. Howie Barranger, a nice enough guy, but kind of jerky, not with it. Elaine seemed to think he was wonderful. Deena didn't get it; there had been plenty of guys after her sister who were much better-looking and had more on the ball. The minute he appeared in the kitchen, Elaine was all sweetness and smiles. She'd give it to Deena later, but good!

Michael Berman spent the rest of the night with her, talking to her, even dancing with her. He wasn't a good dancer but he smelled divine and it felt wonderful to be held by him. He was tall and that was nice and he was big, like Daddy. He bent to give her a light kiss when he left at 2 A.M. and said, "I'd like to see you again some time, Deena."

And she went floating to bed, hugging those parting words to herself, thinking of the witty things she'd say when he called. Because, of course, he would call.

But he didn't. She gave him a couple of days leeway and then it got annoying. Why wasn't he calling her? Boys always called her. It was maddening, and here she was, grounded by Daddy. "I'm sorry, Deena darling, but you defied me. Me, and your mother, and yes, your sister, too. You gave us your promise not to appear at that party and you lied." Her secret thought was, Well it was worth it, to meet Michael Berman. And anyway, who cared? She wanted to be home so she wouldn't miss his call.

And then it was two weeks and she was on the phone with Ellen, stamping her foot, her eyes filling with tears of frustration. "Dammit, he told me he wanted to see me again. So where is he?"

"Can't take it, can you, Deena?" said Ellen. "If he *had* called you the next day, you'd have broken up with him already!"

"Would not!"

"Oh, yes, you would. That's what you do all the time. If they like you, you can't stand them; and if they don't—"

Loftily, Deena answered. "Phoo. They always do."

"Up until now..." said Ellen, and Deena was plunged once again into the depressing certainty that Michael Berman had forgotten her existence. But he couldn't have! He wouldn't dare! Well, but if he had, she'd have to forget him. But she couldn't! She couldn't get him out of her mind. He'd seemed so interested in her, he'd spent so much time with her that night. He wouldn't have spent so much time with her if he were just being nice to Elaine's little sister, which is, of course, what Elaine kept saying. Nevertheless, he didn't call.

So she called him. It took more nerve than she thought she had . . . and she had plenty. But calling a boy was a great big no-no. Nice girls didn't do that. According to Sylvia, Deena always thought, nice girls didn't do anything that was fun. Nice girls didn't: call boys; chase boys; let boys know they liked them; flirt with boys; order the most expensive thing on the menu; try "to peel him like an orange"; talk about what she was interested in, only what he was interested in; let them "get away" with anything which meant s-e-x, of course. By this time she had already broken most of those rules. But she had never, ever, called a boy first.

Her heart pounded and pounded; she could feel it in the ear that was pressed against the phone. And when he picked up and said, "Hello?" she nearly hung up. But dammit, she wasn't going to back off now. She looked down at the notes she'd written, took a deep breath, and plunged in.

"Michael, this is Deena. Deena Strauss. Elaine's sister.

You met me at her party? Two weeks ago?" And then she waited. Forever.

"I remember you. Well, hi there." And then *he* waited. Dammit!

"Did I do something to make you angry?"

"Angry? I don't understand."

Oh, dammit, she really *was* dumb! She should have had something to invite him to, an extra ticket to something . . . some good reason to call him. Well, too late now.

"You said you wanted to see me again. And you haven't called. Well, I'd like to see you, Michael, but I don't like waiting so long. If you're angry about something or you're just not interested, please tell me and I won't wait anymore." God, she'd really done it; she couldn't believe it. She thought she'd feel relieved but she didn't; she felt awful.

"Well, gee, Deena, I do want to see you again. I've been very busy." He sounded puzzled and she cursed herself again for acting like a dopey little teenager. Probably none of the older girls he knew would dream of calling and saying a dumb thing like "Are you angry?" She wished she'd never even had this stupid idea. And then he went on. "I'm in the middle of studying for finals but they'll be finished in another couple of weeks. How about . . . February sixth? Would you like to go to dinner with me?"

She thought she'd faint; she thought she'd die of joy. But she let him wait a minute, so he shouldn't think she was *too* eager. And then, in her coolest, most adult voice, she said, "Dinner? Let me see . . . yes I'm free on the sixth. That would be very nice."

As soon she hung up, she dialed Ellen's number. Wait till Ellen heard that he'd asked her out. And that was all that Ellen was going to hear. She certainly wasn't going to tell Ellen she'd done the unthinkable and called a boy. Oh, no! She was not going to tell anyone, not even her best friend, not now, not ever, not as long as she lived.

CHAPTER TWENTY-TWO

Saturday, May 6, 1961

They had made a charming pair, the dark-haired burly man with his broad smile and the dark-haired husky little boy, throwing a ball back and forth in the park, laughing together as they kept a running score. Father and son? Perhaps. But perhaps not. They did not actually look alike. The little boy, though, was obviously eager to copy the man's every move and gesture.

"That's great, Lawrence! You're a regular Willie Mays! Where'd you learn to peg the ball like that?" He caught the tossed ball and threw it back, saying, "Here comes a high fly to deep left field and Lawrence McElroy is going back and yes, he's got it! And now hold it a minute, Lawrence." He reached into his jacket and brought out a cigar, unwrapping it and twirling it in his mouth.

"I love my new ball and bat and glove, Uncle Jack. Wait'll the guys in my troop see them! Our scoutmaster is real neat! He says city kids have to learn city sports. We play stickball, too. Uncle Jack, did you used to play stickball when you were a little boy?"

"Did I play stickball! I was a three-sewer man!" He glanced at his big wristwatch. "Uh-oh, I'm afraid we just had our last out, kiddo. We have to get you back to your mother by four o'clock."

"Aw!"

"Never mind that. A man does what he has to do first . . . then he does what he wants to. Always remember that, Lawrence."

The boy ran to his side and took his hand. "I will. Uncle Jack?"

"Mmm." They began to walk out of the playground.

"The Boy Scouts are having—"

"Oh, look, Lawrence, there's the Good Humor man. Don't I remember you telling me before how you wanted a toasted almond?"

"Yeah! Yeah! Come on, let's hurry."

"You hurry. I'm an old man in my forties, I don't hurry anymore." He laughed, reaching for his wallet, pulling out a bill. "You can get me one, too." The boy muttered something and Jack, impatient, said, "What? What? Speak up."

"I don't like to do that."

"What? You don't like to get your own ice cream from the Good Humor? What kind of talk is that. You're ten years old. Go on. Let me see you do it. Just say, 'two toasted almonds', and give him the money."

"I don't know how much it is!"

"Don't worry, I gave you more than enough. He'll give you the change."

"What if he doesn't?"

"Lawrence, I'm losing my patience. You don't sound like the fine big boy I know. You sound like a sissy."

Stubbornly: "I'm not a sissy."

"I know that. Now prove it. Go on. You're going to have to learn how to deal in business one of these days." He laughed a little and patted the child on his rear end. "Listen to me, Lawrence, you'll never get *anywhere* in this world if you don't learn to speak up and say clearly what it is you want. That's how I got where I am."

"Yes, Uncle Jack."

"Okay then. Go!" He watched as Lawrence, feet dragging

a bit, forced himself into the line of children at the back of the truck. A few minutes later he was back, flushed with success.

"Good boy. And as a reward, you can keep the change. How's that?"

They walked slowly east on Fourteenth Street, which was busy and bustling as usual on a Saturday afternoon, with all the shops putting thier goods out on the sidewalk, many family groups strolling all across the sidewalk, and dozens of children riding up and down on bikes.

"Look, Uncle Jack, a red Schwinn. I wish I had a new bike like that."

"You have a bike."

"It's too little."

Jack laughed. "You're not so terribly big yourself."

"It's too small and it's rusting and all the other kids have brand new bikes and I never get to have—"

"What's this I'm hearing? Whining? Be a man, will you! Only girls whine!"

"Do your girls whine?"

Another laugh. "All the time!" The boy hesitated, frowning, and then he laughed, too. "Still, Uncle Jack, I do wish I had a nice new bike."

"You know that change I gave you before? Put it in that bank account I opened for you last Christmas and begin saving for a new bike. That's what a good businessman does. You're never too young to learn how things are accomplished in this life, Lawrence."

"Yes, Uncle Jack."

"And you know what? If you learn all the things I'm trying to teach you, I'm going to take you into my business when you grow up and finish school. Maybe I'll even let you work summers when you get into junior high. How would you like that, huh?"

"Oh, Uncle Jack, that would be great! Do you really mean it?"

"Would I lie to you? Of course I mean it. But you have to show me you have the right attitude."

"Oh, I will, Uncle Jack, I *will*."

Jack looked down then at the face turned up to him so trustingly. He smiled and reached out, rumpling Lawrence's hair. "You're a helluva good kid, you know that, Lawrence? A boy a man could really be proud of."

"Uncle Jack?"

"Yeah?"

"Could I ask you a favor?"

Jack took his arm and they began to cross the street. "Sure, sure. What is it?"

The boy took in a deep breath and let the words rush out in a tumble. "Well, see, our Boy Scout troop is having its father/son dinner. It's next week and I know you're probably too busy, but I'm getting three merit badges and everybody else has their father coming with them and I'm always the only one—"

"No, no! It's a father/son thing. You can't bring me; I'm not your father."

"I asked. I can bring you, I can bring anyone."

"I'm not the right one, Lawrence. No, no, I can't do it, I absolutely can't do it. Period. *Fartig*. Finished. Now, stop that sniveling. Men don't cry over something so unimportant. Ask one of your teachers. You must have a man teacher you like."

"Maybe I'll ask Uncle Fred," Lawrence muttered. "Uncle Fred likes me. Uncle Fred takes me lots of places."

Jack's tone changed subtly. "Uncle Fred? Who is this Uncle Fred who takes you lots of places? I've never heard of him before."

"He lives in our building. Right across the hall. He comes over a lot."

"He does, does he? Well, that's interesting. I'll have to ask your mother about him; I want to make sure he's okay to take to that very important dinner."

They entered the curved paths that led through Stuyvesant Town, walking in uneasy silence. When they got to Lawrence's building, Jack cleared his throat and said, "Well, kiddo, I guess here's where we say good-bye." And then, with an intake of breath, "Oh, for—look, Lawrence. You still fussing over that father/son thing? I'd do it if I could. No more tears now. A man doesn't cry over every little disappointment that comes his way in this life. Come on now, you don't want to upset your mother, do you? Dry your eyes. Enough already! Okay? Okay. That's much better."

Once more he tousled the boy's hair and added, "Who knows, there might be a bright red two-wheeled surprise waiting for you one of these days very soon. How's that? Okay? Yeah, that's right, even though you already got your birthday present from me yesterday. So, how's about a nice big hug? Okay! That's my boy!"

CHAPTER TWENTY-THREE

Sunday, October 29, 1961

Golden autumn sunlight had been slanting in the windows of the Strauss kitchen that morning at 11:22, and there was a crisp tang to the air that sent the red and white curtains swaying and three pages of the Sunday *Times* flying across the room. Jack took a sip of his coffee, laughing a little as Marilyn went chasing the fluttering sheets, scrambling among them, tripping as she tried to fold them.

"Look at her, fighting the power of *The New York Times*! Listen, Marilyn, first step on them. That's right . . . now, when they're lying still, now you can fold them." He took another gulp of his coffee, motioning to Sylvia with his head that yes, he'd like a refill, "Never mind, *bubeleh*, it took your daddy five full years to learn how to fold the *Times* the way the subway riders do." And he demonstrated, folding the paper lengthwise, two columns at a time. "And sometimes, even with me, the paper still wins." He was in a good mood. The day was beautiful, yesterday they had closed the deal on that group of buildings on West Sixty-sixth, the bagels were really fresh for a change, and in another hour or so, having showered and shaved, he would be heading for his weekly pinochle game at the club, so what could be bad? Even Marilyn who, at twelve could drive a person crazy with endless medical discussions about the crippled animals she kept dragging home from the streets, even Marilyn seemed delightful to him this morning. Before, he had even been able to act interested in a bunny with one ear, the latest, found yesterday in Central Park on the bridle path. Yes, everything was falling into place lately.

"Oh, what a beautiful morning..." he began to sing, riffling through the thick pile of papers for the sports section.

And then Elaine walked in, freshly showered, her damp hair already beginning to curl into little ringlets all over her heard, wrapped in a thick terry-cloth robe with the initials JS embroidered on the breast pocket.

"Your mother doesn't take you shopping often enough, you don't have your own robe to put on? So how come every month a bill from Saks, a bill from Bendel, a bill from Bloomingdale's?"

"It was hanging on the hook," Elaine said. "In our bathroom. Do you want me to take it off?"

"Elaine. Why take that tone? Your daddy didn't say take it off. He didn't mean anything." Sylvia soothed.

Elaine grunted and said, "Oh? Sorry." And poured herself a cup of coffee, going to the counter where Sylvia had laid out all the usual brunch items: bagels, pumpernickel, cream cheese, lox, jams, sliced tomato, sliced onions, a chafing dish with scrambled eggs, juice, and a bowl of fruit. She began to help herself.

"You were out awfully late last night with what's-his-name."

Without looking up, Elaine said, "His name is Howard— as you damn well know."

"Elaine!" Sylvia protested. "That's no kind of language to use to your father."

"Forget that. Where's your sense of humor gone, Elaine? Home with what's-his-name?"

Elaine's back was to all of them, and it visibly stiffened. She did not answer the jibe and came to the table, pulling out a chair.

Her father leaned forward, examining the contents of her plate ostentatiously and then went back to his paper.

"All right," Elaine said after a moment or two. "What *else* is on your mind?"

"Nothing, nothing. Only I thought I heard a lot of talk from you about cutting down—"

"I am."

"That you call cutting down? There's enough on your plate to feed the entire Russian Army."

"Jack!" Sylvia said in a pleading tone. "You promised!"

"Never mind, Sylvia," Elaine said, still in the same cold monotone. "That's his idea of fun: getting my goat. I don't let it bother me anymore. Howard likes me just the way I am." The words were spoken bravely, but she pushed the plate away from her an inch or two.

"Howard! That pipsqueak! He's only half a man, the *pitsel*. What does he know, spending all his time in that hole in the wall on Orchard Street?" Then he laughed. "Maybe that's why he likes you just the way you are. After all, the man sells girdles all day long!" He laughed richly at his own joke, ignoring Sylvia's hand on his arm, her warning shakes of the head.

Marilyn busied herself, pushing herself away from the table, fussing with the food on the counter. In a minute she was back with a plate which she presented to Elaine. On it was a bagel cut in half with the curved sides facing each other, butterfly fashion. She had spread cream cheese on it and put little bits of lox to represent the spots on the wings; and two long pieces of onion made the antenna. "Here, Lainie." Her voice was very quiet. Then she leaned closer and whispered into Elaine's ear: "I love you the best and I think you're beautiful."

"You little darling!" Elaine grabbed the little girl and squeezed her. "Thank you. It's a beautiful butterfly and if you don't mind, I'm going to eat it right this minute." And she pushed a healthy chunk of bagel into her mouth, making dramatic yum-yum sounds.

"I rest my case," Jack said. "Now you're happy."

"Dammit—" Elaine began, "Lay off me, will you? For just one minute of just one day?"

From the doorway came Deena's sleepy voice. "I'm going to leave," she said, her hands over her ears, "if this fighting doesn't stop. I could hear the voices all the way in my room. It's enough to kill a person's appetite."

"Not your sister's!" Again, Jack laughed at his own witticism.

Deena said, "Oh, Daddy! That's not funny!"

At the same moment, Elaine snapped, "He doesn't care about my feelings!"

Now everyone's voice was raised, and again Deena clapped her hands over her ears. "I'm leaving; I'm going back to my room."

Jack leaned back in his chair. "A houseful of prima donnas I'm living with! *She* can't take a joke . . ." and head inclined in Elaine's direction, "*She* feeds her . . ." That was for Marilyn. "And *you* threaten to run and hide your head under the pillow. When you were four, that was cute, but now? Come in, sit down, eat your breakfast, and let's have no more of this. *Fartig*. Finished. The end."

Deena filled a plate then, heaping it with some of everything, and sat down. Her father waited until she had lifted the first forkful of eggs to her lips and then said, "So, Dee Dee? You were out awfully late last night. I looked at the clock, it was after two when I heard the key in the lock."

Deena laughed. "What were *you* doing up at that hour, young man? If you don't start keeping more regular hours, I don't know what's going to become of your complexion."

"So where did Michael take you last night?"

"That new Israeli nightclub, with the dance troupe. You know, I told you about it. *The New York Times* gave it a rave review."

"That Michael! So cultured! So up on everything new!"

"Huh!" Elaine said, disgusted. "If Howard took me to the new Israeli nightclub, you'd demand to know what he meant by taking me out drinking all the time!" She ignored her mother's entreating look, saying, "Well, it's true. Michael can do no wrong, it seems!"

"Michael's a lovely boy," Jack said. "A lawyer, a professional, you know how many Wall Street firms wanted him? He's just starting out and he's already earning a good living.

Why shouldn't I think highly of him? He's obviously going places, he's brilliant."

"You don't have to fawn all over him all the time!"

"I don't fawn all over him, and furthermore, he's a wonderful young man. I'm sorry, but I can't help saying it over and over again. He's a wonderful young man and your sister's a lucky young woman to have caught him."

"Deena's had plenty of nice boys coming around, Daddy, as have I, I might add. In case you hadn't noticed, the Strauss girls are popular." Elaine's cheeks were flaming with indignation.

"Michael is more than a nice boy. He's a man and, like I said, he's going places. Deena could do a lot worse, and if she's smart, like I think she is, she'll make sure he doesn't get away."

"Jack!" Sylvia protested. "What are you talking? Deena's not marrying *anyone* for quite a while! She's only eighteen. Deena has to finish college before she even thinks about marriage . . . and you know it, Jack."

"I don't see why! Just look at that face. She doesn't need a degree to get whatever she wants in this world! All she has to do is ask!"

Deena interrupted this, a pleased smile spreading over her face. "Oh, Daddy! You mean you'd let me get married now?"

Elaine gave a short laugh. "It's the only way you'll ever get your own apartment, Deena, the only way you'll ever be allowed to leave."

"Again, Elaine? You want to move out? Go. Move out!" Jack was enraged. "Get your own apartment! Be my guest! Let the whole world know what kind of girl you are! Break your mother's heart!"

"Jack! At least Elaine wants to finish college. She doesn't want to end her life before it's even begun! You, Deena. Listen to me. When I was your age, the best thing that could have happened to me was my father would send me to school. I've always been sorry I wasn't able to go to college!"

"Then I have a terrific idea, Syl. *You* go to college!"

"Don't talk back to your mother!" Sylvia laughed a little, lips only. "You're not too old to be spanked, you know. I'm serious and I'm telling you: You'll wait until you're finished college. *Then* you can get married, if you still want Michael so badly. And if he wants you so badly, he'll wait. Promise me."

Deena looked straight into her mother's eyes. "I don't want to make any promises I can't keep." Her voice was stubborn.

"Get off her back, Sylvia. Can't you see the girl's in love?" He got up to stand behind Deena, his hands on her shoulders. "Sylvia, Sylvia, don't you remember what it was like when we were in love and couldn't wait not even for a minute, never mind three, four years? Of course you do," he added quickly, moving to her and bending to give her a kiss on the top of her head. "Of course you do!"

"What about me? Elaine asked. "I'm almost finished with college and I'm in love and we're planning to get married."

"Over my dead body!" Jack roared. "I won't allow it. He . . . he's shorter than you, Elaine!"

"That is the most pitiful objection I've ever heard! It's not even intelligent!"

"And you outweigh him, too!"

"Jack! No more! Enough!"

"You b—!" Elaine bit off the word, her eyes filling. "You're not being fair, you know."

"You asked for it. You came in this morning, spoiling for a fight. Well, you got one. I forbid it. No daughter of mine is going to marry a *faygeleh*, a fairy!"

Now Elaine began to laugh, not a pretty laugh. "Oh, boy, are you way off the track! You think Howard Barranger is a fruit? Oh, boy, are you ever wrong!"

Her father's face darkened. "And how would you know so certainly?"

"How do you think? We've been sleeping together for the past six months!"

She ran out of the room, ignoring her parents' shocked faces and Deena's gasp of surprise, ignoring even Marilyn, who ran after her yelling, "Wait Elaine, wait, what is it, what's wrong?"

CHAPTER TWENTY-FOUR

Tuesday, January 14, 1986

At two o'clock of a January afternoon, the streets of hell's kitchen deserved the name: crowded, noisy, dirty, clogged with traffic. Elaine had her taxi stop a block and a half from the corner of Ninth Avenue and Thirty-eighth Street—her destination—because she could see it was going to be twice as fast to walk it. The cabby was philosophical: "New York City!" he offered, and shrugged.

She stepped out of the cab, spotted the pile of dirty snow just in time, and smartly jumped over it—right into ankle-deep slush. "Oh, shit!" she burst out.

A delivery boy zipping by on his bike laughed and called out, "Give it to 'em, mama!" She, however, did not find it very funny. She found it cold and dirty and disgusting. Furthermore, her new Joan & David calfskin boots were now soaked with filthy, salty New York slop and probably ruined. Where in hell had her mind been—to wear fancy boots in this weather, in this season, in this town! Ruefully, she eyed the damp leather . . . three hundred bucks, down the rathole. That was more than her secretary made in a week.

248

But right now her feet were of relatively little importance. She had taken time off from her own piles of work to check up on a few bothersome—she didn't know what to call them exactly—discrepancies. Yes, that had a nice ambiguous ring to it. Better than thievery, larceny, or stealing, all of which she had a feeling she was dealing with here.

She pushed through the midday throngs, much worse at this time of year, even on grungy old unpopular Ninth Avenue. Which, if Jack Strauss had his way, was shortly going to become gorgeous, gentrified fashionable Ninth Avenue. And he probably would have his way, Elaine thought with admiration. Give him credit. He had already done the trick on Lower Broadway, the financial district, Park Avenue South, and his last wonder, Old Seaport Village down near the South Street Seaport.

She'd just come uptown from Old Seaport Village, more convinced than ever that Daddy—say what you would about him—had the touch when it came to predicting the public mind on housing. How he did it, she would never know; but he was unerring. One day at breakfast or over a cup of tea he'd look up from his paper and make a remark like "You know what would make a real good neighborhood for all the yuppies?" And then he'd name it: an impossible, usually horrible, rundown area. Old Seaport Village had begun that way. He'd even taken them, Elaine and Sylvia, one sunny Sunday afternoon, for a stroll through the area. Elaine remembered very clearly because she had been absolutely adamant that this would never, ever go. "My God, Daddy, just look at it. It's dreadful! There are no services, not a single place to shop, no place to go at night, and, worst of all, the whole place stinks of rotten fish!"

And she couldn't have been wronger! O.S.V. had been sold out before it was completed, with the smallest apartment, a studio with a kitchenette along one wall and bathroom tucked in a corner, going for $150,000.

"How do you do it?" she asked him.

And, give him credit, he laughed and said, "It's a skill, *bubeleh,* I could even teach it to you." Pretty soon she was going to call him on that one. She was going to forget that oinky "even" and she was going to sign up for the course.

And here it was: the Ninth Avenue Project. What used to be 575 Ninth Avenue but had been reborn, according to the large announcement posted on the front of the building, as The WestView: luxury condominiums—terraces, fireplaces, river views, model apartments ready for inspection, sales office ground floor open 8 AM-8 PM, beginning February first.

She walked right into what would be the lobby one day soon. Outside, the building looked pretty much finished, with all new windows and air-conditioning sleeves in place. And the lobby, although not completed, was at least neat and clean, with clear directions to the sales office. Would *she* buy an apartment in this building? Would *she* find it inviting enough to walk in here off the street? Hard to say. It wasn't a turnoff; but, on the other hand, it wasn't the Upper West Side, either. It was Ninth Avenue, and just a generation ago it had been one of New York City's most notorious slums.

She made herself stop. She was not in a position to judge. She was just learning about this business, and anyway, she thought with a laugh, the building was nearly done. Another month and a half and they'd be ready for occupancy. It was a waste of time, conjecturing about the wisdom of this project; what she had to do, first and foremost, was find a certain party called Frank Malone. The Invisible Man: that's how she thought of him. She'd been here twice in the past week, trying to talk to him, and he was always somewhere else. She had a list of invoices and a big question about them. And he was in charge. He was the man she had to see.

It had all begun when she was studying the books. She saw that this job was costing quite a bit more than the Seaport project, which was very similar in size and scope. When she took a closer look, she found that certain costs—concrete, for instance, and metal lathing—were up a bit, probably inflation. But the increased cost of lumber was out of sight.

She had to do some research. *Research!* A funny word. Before it had mostly meant asking Daddy. But not this time. Even after she found out that lumber prices had increased ahead of inflation, she was still bothered. And so she went back into the files on the Seaport project and lo and behold, Joseph & Co., Lumber Dealers, had been the original and only vendor; suddenly there were bills from another outfit,

Downtown Lumber & Supply. Why? The prices were no different according to the invoices. Why split the business? It certainly looked as if Joseph & Co. had always done well by them. Daddy had told her that business was split only when a supplier couldn't give you what you needed; and she couldn't believe that was true of Joseph & Co. They were the biggest in the metropolitan area.

And then she discovered there were no delivery tickets for Downtown—not even one. She went to Daddy and, as casually as she could manage, asked him, "Why would a whole bunch of delivery tickets be missing?" And he just waved her off.

"Oh, God, delivery tickets! Lemme tell you about delivery tickets. The truck comes in, they unload, Malone checks it over, and the the driver has him sign for the load and gives him a receipt the size of a betting slip. Malone shoves it in his jeans and if he doesn't have a hole in his pocket, and if it doesn't by accident go through Mrs. Malone's laundry, and if he doesn't get drunk at lunch on Friday . . . well, then maybe, *maybe*, I said, that ticket finds its way into the office. Yeah, yeah, I know, in a perfect world every delivery ticket would be matched to its invoice. But Lainie, honey, this ain't a perfect world. Delivery tickets! If I had a nickel for every lost delivery ticket, I could have retired twenty years ago!"

So she smiled at him, didn't bother him with smelly little details, and went quietly about her business. Which, she decided, was going to be a thorough check on the invoices and matching delivery tickets for another vendor, *any* other vendor. And she found out by and large what she expected: that the file, for instance, for De Luca Sons, Doors and Windows, was missing half a dozen delivery tickets and that many of the tickets looked exactly as if they had been through a Friday afternoon drinking session plus a trip through somebody's washer/dryer combination. But they were *there*. You couldn't read them easily, but they were there. That was the point, wasn't it? To answer her own question, yes, that was the point.

And that was the big question she had for Mr. Malone. How come there were no, repeat *no*, delivery tickets anywhere in the world for Downtown Lumber & Supply. Well, maybe she wouldn't put it quite that bluntly; she had been here three times already, and if there was one thing she had found out about construction workers, it was that they wouldn't answer questions, period. She had never been so frustrated in her life; they wouldn't even tell her the time of day! Nobody knew nothin'.

Of course, she should have been forewarned. All her life she had heard Daddy say, "My men don't talk to outsiders. They all know, if you don't open your mouth, you can't get into trouble!" And he'd laugh. So, she might be the boss's daughter, but she was first and foremost a woman, an unknown quantity. An outsider as far as the men were concerned.

What they did was keep telling her she had to talk to Malone. But when she said, Fine, show me to him, he was either out to lunch, in a meeting, at the office, or somewhere in the building and they couldn't find him. Today she had finally done the smart thing: she had called Mr. Frank Malone on the telephone and made a date with him. He was either going to be here or he was going to be in deep shit!

He was here, as it turned out, deep in conversation, as it turned out. One of the other men pointed to him when she asked for Mr. Malone, but offered nothing else by way of help. Elaine didn't know quite what she ought to do. She could see that he was engaged in business . . . something to do with the half-completed kitchen she could see through an open doorway. He and two other men, all in hard hats, were bent over blueprints. From her earliest childhood, she knew that you never interrupted a man involved in a blueprint. So she cooled her heels and looked around instead.

It was going to be a nice apartment, with more space than was usual in a conversion in this town. She had to smile at herself; since she had begun this project, she had become almost obsessed with apartments, walking into buildings posing as a prospective tenant, looking around, measuring everything with her eyes, deciding yes or no, good or bad . . . a regular self-made expert, that was Elaine Barranger! The more she looked, actually, the more she realized how little she knew about this business. But that wasn't going to hold her back; she was learning all the time. Even today, even right now. One long wall of this living room had been faced with brick. She had been with enough real estate salespeople lately to know what a selling point *that* was. That goddamn wall was worth an additional ten thousand dollars.

She glanced at her wristwatch: two-thirty already; and she'd told Howard she'd try to get back to the showroom this afternoon before four. Well, maybe she'd make it and maybe she wouldn't. He'd already told her to take all the time she needed. She didn't want to take advantage of his good nature. On the other hand, if she did a half-assed job on this, Daddy would *never* give her another chance. If she screwed up on this, she'd be lucky if he gave her the time of day!

She shifted a little, uncomfortable in the high-heeled boots, one soaking wet, and stared at the back of Superintendent Frank Malone. When she was a kid, everyone knew that if you stared at someone long enough, they'd "feel" it and turn around to look straight at you. If she remembered correctly, it had always worked.

And it worked now. He straightened up and turned around, a quizzical look on his face—a look swiftly replaced by a smile fairly dripping with charm.

"Well, Mrs. Barranger. Hello."

"Hello yourself, Mr. Malone. I can hardly believe my luck, finding you."

Now he came over, his hand outstretched. "Yeah, they told me you'd been here a coupla times. Sorry about that." They shook hands briefly. "Now. What can I do for you? Your old—your father told me I should give you every cooperation."

It was wonderful, Elaine thought, how totally chauvinistic this business still was. In the *shmatte* business, a woman didn't need her father, her husband, her son, or any other man for that matter, to have credibility. But in construction . . .? Forget it! If you were female, you practically had to have the entire Marine Corps standing behind you before anyone would pay attention!

So what did she need this for? One: she wanted her piece of the action. And, two, before she was finished around here there'd be at least *one* woman in this business who got respect . . . and it wouldn't be Leona Helmsley, either!

She answered his question. "You can tell me a few things . . . but privately."

"Agh!" He gestured to the two others, still poring over the big sheets. "They won't hear anything. Go ahead."

"Tell me about Downtown Lumber."

He shook off the hard hat and scratched his head, frowning. "Downtown? You sure that's the name?"

"Downtown Lumber and Supply, Inc. On Gansevoort Street."

He shook his head. "Never heard of it. Why?"

"Never heard of it? You sure?"

"Positive."

"They haven't been supplying you with, say, two-by-fours on this job?"

"We use Joseph. Old man—Mr. Strauss has always done business with them. They're the best!"

The belligerence tinging the last three words made her smile. "Don't worry, Mr. Malone, I'm not out to replace anyone."

He looked a question at her which she was damned if she'd answer. Then he shrugged and said, "I'm not worried. But, for what it's worth, Joseph's is big, they have the stuff, it's good quality, and they're on time. Believe me, in this business that's worth something! Those guys over there? They shoulda been finished with the kitchens last week. But try to get delivery on time from the plumbing supplier!" He laughed a little, and shuffled his feet in the direction of the two workmen.

"I realize you're a busy man, Mr. Malone. But it's taken me three trips to find you. I have just a couple more questions."

"Shoot."

"Who signs the delivery tickets?"

"You're lookin' at him."

"And if some are missing?"

"Aw . . . if you've seen them, you know they're the easiest thing in the world to lose." He laughed. "Not to worry, though. I check personally on every single delivery. You're never going to be shortchanged if Francis X. Malone is on the job!"

"So I've heard," Elaine said sweetly while her brain began busily to work on this latest information. "Well, and I won't keep you any longer... oh, wait. Just one more thing." He turned, midstep. "Do you write the orders too?"

"Never! That's Lawrence's thing. Of course, I have to tell him what we need; I mean, I'm here on top of everything, right? But the way it works with your old—Mr. Strauss, nobody puts in orders for materials except either him or Lawrence. And it's usually Lawrence, I'll tell you that right now."

Elaine smiled at him. As Alice said of Wonderland, "curiouser and curiouser." But she was feeling well rewarded for her patience and diligence.

"Well, thank you very much for your time, Mr. Malone. I'll be sure to tell my *old man* you gave me your full cooperation."

His lips twitched but she could see he didn't dare laugh. Not sure whether she really meant it to be funny. He'd learn. A few months on a job with her and he'd know.

Downstairs again, she didn't even pause a moment. Howard was going to have to do without her today. She had something she had to do.

It was three-thirty by the time the cab fought its way to Strauss Construction's office near Rockefeller Center; and she fought *her* way past Linda McElroy's ever-so-sweet and ever-so-gentle but ever-so-stubborn efforts to find out what she was up to. Elaine smiled until it hurt, literally, went to the file cabinets and got what she wanted, while Linda danced and hopped behind her, insisting that it would be much faster if Elaine would only tell her what she needed. She managed to hide the files from Linda's darting eyes and, still smiling, took herself into the small conference room, which had a lock on the door and used it.

Now. Right to the source, that's where she had to go. She pulled out the big Manhattan business-to-business directory and went to the D's under "Lumber." Up and down the list she went. There was Doric Lumber and then there was Dynamic Building Materials. She looked again. Doric, then Dynamic.

No Downtown. She looked under B for building supplies and under C for construction and under W for wood for Christ's sake. Maybe it was a new outfit, although she was beginning to have her doubts. She called information and she got first an operator and then a computer voice and neither one of them had ever heard of Downtown Lumber & Supply.

She sat at the big polished table and stared for long moments at the wall opposite her covered with photos of the company's most prestigious jobs. She was thinking and she didn't like what she was thinking. But, being Elaine Strauss Barranger, she wasn't going to sit here very long with nothing but vague thoughts. Being Elaine, she picked herself up, carefully put away the files, fielded Linda's flurry of inquiries, smiled some more, and managed to smile her way out to the elevator bank.

When the elevator doors slid open, she nearly jumped out of her skin. Talk about willing somebody to appear! Here she was, thinking about Lawrence McElroy and here *he* was, before her, handsome and debonair as always, turning on the old charm in front of her very eyes.

"Elaine! What a surprise! What brings you here?"

"What else, Lawrence? Business. I'm learning this business, remember?"

"Remember! I told Malone to be sure to be there when you came around this time. Did he follow instructions?"

The phony little worm! She tried very hard to look pleasant, while talking through gritted teeth. "I saw him, if that's what you mean."

"I hope he was helpful to you." There was a question there. Like mother, like son. They were both dying to find out what she was up to. Well, *gurnischt helfen*, as Sylvia always said. Lots of luck, folks! Nobody was going to get anything out of her until she was damn good and ready to give it.

She smiled. Again, with the smile. She was going to be all out of smiles when this day was finished. "Malone's a good man, no question about it," she said, sliding quickly into the elevator. She gave him a flip little wave, letting the doors close, and then leaned back into the corner of the cage, composing a list of questions she was going to put to them at Downtown Lumber & Supply. When she got there.

But when she got there, it wasn't there. In a way, she wasn't surprised. But, thorough was thorough. She made the cab driver go up the street and around the block and through again, while he protested: "Lady, you're killing me! I'm down here all the time . . . thirty years I'm driving a hack . . . and I'm telling you, there's no such place. Never has been!"

Elaine stared out of the cab window at the old buildings on Gansevoort Street. No Downtown Lumber & Supply existed. That meant that no supplies had ever been delivered to either Old Seaport Village or WestView by nonexistent Downtown. And *that* meant that somebody had been falsifying invoices and pocketing the payments. Somebody who had been systematically stealing and she thought she knew who it was. Immediately, her mind began making lists: things to check, proofs to find, papers to read. She had to make sure of this one. Should only take a week or two and then . . . well, Daddy would be in for a nasty surprise. And Elaine would be in, period!

CHAPTER TWENTY-FIVE

Friday, January 24, 1986

There was nothing as sweet as a young girl, Lawrence thought, running his hands over Zoe's smooth, silken flank. Everything solid, firm, deliciously yielding under his touch. And she smelled so good, all clean and fresh. But best of all, it was all new to her, new and wonderful and exciting. Everything he did made her moan and wriggle around. He liked them eager and pliant and not too aggressive . . . hell, that was the man's part, wasn't it? . . . and he liked them innocent. He loved that smile of delight, he liked to push himself a little away from a girl so he could watch and see how her eyes widened when he hit on the right spot. Like now. He rubbed gently over her clit and was rewarded with a very loud gasp as she arched her back to bring herself closer. Lawrence smiled at her, even though she was incapable of seeing it. Her eyes were closed, her cheeks were flushed with heat, and she was wet, wet, wet.

Now she was really into it, thrashing around and begging him, "Please, please give it to me, darling, give it to me." Lawrence allowed himself a groan. . . . he hadn't wanted to scare her, innocent lamb, it was her first time, so he had been taking it real slow, real easy.

But now . . . way to go! This is what always got him . . . the transformation from little lamb, all melting eyes and hidden heat into this: a moaning, writhing *woman*, hot and demanding.

"You sure?" he whispered into her ear, gently easing himself on top of her. She felt so fragile under him, so . . . *little*, in spite of the big tits and the sweetly curving hips. So close to him, it was creepy how much she looked like her mother. He might be about to fuck Deena. Whoa there, none of *that!* He had to stop that; it was too weird, screwing the daughter and fantasizing the mother. This was serious stuff here, this was sincere. This wasn't going to be a one-night stand, no way. Not with someone from the family!

"You sure?" he repeated, and her answer was to take in a deep breath, wind her arms around his neck, and pull his face down to hers, pushing her tongue deep into his mouth. Oh, she was ripe! She was ready!

"Oh, yes, Lawrence. I love you. I want you. Please."

Okay then. He was pretty hot himself, hard as a fucking rock. If he didn't get into her pretty soon, he might come before they even started.

She was no virgin. He slid right in. And she cried out, like they all did, because he was so big. She was tight and warm and wet, pushing herself to meet his thrusts, and in a minute he stopped all thinking, became all cock, pulsating, getting to the edge, climbing over the edge, trembling, swelling, pumping, sweating, shouting, coming. Coming, coming, coming, *coming!*

As he collapsed over her, he heard her fervent whisper, "Oh, I love you, I love you, I love you!" She really was a baby, wasn't she? A sweet baby, but a baby. She hadn't even come; he knew that. She didn't know it, though. She had a lot to learn. Well, she could do worse than learn from Lawrence McElroy. And she'd end up being fabulous; she was a typical hot Jewish girl, just like he'd figured. Yes, she'd be very good in bed in the end. And if it turned out she wasn't, hell, there were plenty of women out there dying for it.

But he was getting too much ahead of himself. Time

enough to find out what was going to be; time enough to figure out what to do about stuff *after* it happened, right? Right.

He rolled off her, groaning a little, and gave her a kiss. "That was wonderful, sweetheart."

She melted. He could see it, she just melted right away. She was a goner; she was in love. She was his for the taking.

"Oh, Lawrence, I do love you so! Was it really good? I want to be good for you."

A light kiss on her lips. "You are, baby, you are."

They lay there for a few minutes while he felt himself relax, felt that old familiar drowsiness slide over him like a nice warm blanket. Then she said, hesitant: "Um... Lawrence?"

"Um."

"Don't... don't you love me?"

"Of course I do." He reached out for her and she snuggled into his chest with a sigh.

"You didn't say so."

"Um."

"Lawrence?"

Dummy! "Of course I love you, baby, of course I do. It's just that I'm so sleepy."

"Oh, honey! I'm so dumb! Of course you're sleepy and here I am, bothering you. But, you know, my mind is going around and around. I can't help but think about what's going to happen when I tell my parents about us."

Sleepy or not, he had to say something. "Zoe, baby... um ... do you have to tell them anything yet? I mean, what's wrong with the way we're going right now? Soon you'll be back at school..."

"I'm sick and tired of sneaking around like some kind of criminal! I mean, it's been easy right now because Saul's in so much hot water. They've both been running around like chickens without heads, arranging a school for him and yelling at each other and yelling at him and slamming doors, and Mom.... well, half the time she's out of the house and the other half she's in another world. She could care less about what *I'm* doing. But that's not going to last forever." He was drifting away, starting to fall asleep, he couldn't help it, it always happened to him after sex. But he really should pay attention to what she was saying. It was his future. Anything that was going on in that family might turn out to be important to him.

That family. Look how intertwined his life was with the Strausses . . . from before he was born, even. And yet, what was he to them? He didn't know. Sure, he had called the old man Uncle Jack—for years—but what did it mean? Once he'd thought of Jack as a kind of substitute father, but that was just a kid's pipe dream. Oh, yeah, Jack used to come around —pretty regularly, come to think of it—and throw a ball with him and play Monopoly and stuff. Jack taught him how to play pinochle and how to pitch like a man and how to ride a two-wheeled bike . . . bought him his first two-wheeler.

Bought him his first Brooks Brothers suit, too. Didn't take him, Mom took him; but Jack told them to ask for Mr. Samuel, his own salesman and Mr. Samuel, small, dapper, with a hairline mustache, had been expecting them. Lawrence got not only a dark blue suit, but a pair of gray slacks and a Harris tweed jacket, three button-down shirts, and a couple of rep ties. Brooks Brothers: that was the epitome! He never had clothes that good again until he was working and earning his own money for them.

But he had had to learn the hard way that Jack *wasn't* his father. Damnit, he never *had* a father, never! When all the other kids were doing things with their dads, he was alone. Alone in the Cub Scouts and alone in school. Always alone. Mom was glad to do stuff with him but, shit, she didn't know; it wasn't the same. No mother, no matter how terrific, could take the place of a real father. He could still remember his shame, in the first grade, when Sister Loretta asked everyone what their father did and he had to say, "I don't have a father." He mumbled it and she made him say it louder and he thought he would die right then and there. All the kids laughed and it didn't even help when Sister asked more questions and then explained that his dad was a hero, killed in the war. He was marked forever: the boy without a father.

For a while, when he was ten or eleven, he hated Mom because she was never going to get married. By that time he realized something was going on with her and Uncle Jack; he was too young and naive to know what that something was, but Jack was the only man she ever talked about. He prayed every night that she'd find somebody to marry and then he'd have a real dad. He even prayed for a short time that she and Uncle Jack would get married—that's how stupid he was, that he didn't stop to think that his uncle Jack was already married. Of course he knew it. He knew Uncle Jack's family—his wife and his daughters. Dummy!

She was a devoted mother who sacrificed all her own comfort for him so he could have a good education and nice clothes and summer camp. But, damnit, she should've gotten married. She should've given him a father. Damnit, she cheated him out of a normal childhood. Because when push came to shove, Uncle Jack wasn't any kind of father, not even any kind of substitute, not even any kind of uncle. A couple of times Lawrence decided to ask him to do something that was important to him, like the Father and Son Canoeing Weekend the year he was fourteen and still an avid scout. He prayed and prayed and then got up his courage and asked Uncle Jack to please go with him. He just didn't want to be the only boy alone again, always being teamed up with the assistant scoutmaster. Always the poor pitiful thing. He hated it!

And Uncle Jack said no. He gave some kind of weak excuse and he slipped Lawrence a twenty-dollar bill and said, "Here, kid, go out and get yourself something nice." But that didn't make up for the disappointment. He'd cried himself to sleep that night. That was the last time he'd ever cried. Because, that night, in his bed in the dark, he clenched his fists and he made himself a pledge that he'd never ask anyone for anything again . . . except maybe Mom. That he'd never cry again. He knew damn well, that night, that he couldn't count on anyone ever again. He'd just have to count on one person: himself. Look out for numero uno. That was still his philosophy of life. You had to look out for yourself because if you didn't, nobody else would. If his father had lived, that's what he would have told him. Because that's what it meant to be a man.

He hadn't done so badly, taking care of himself. He'd worked damn hard, even though his boss was Jack, *damn* hard. Jack wasn't going to do him any favors, he knew that. And he was hired because he was damn good. He had his degree in civil engineering plus two years working for the Port Authority. Jack had never had any reason to be sorry, either. If the business had expanded in the past ten years, it was at least half the doing of L. J. McElroy, if he did say so himself. Jack had given him so many raises, he'd stopped counting. "Damn-it," Jack said, "you're good, my boy, even better than I thought. Of course—" But he never finished the "of course" and when Lawrence asked him "of course what, Jack?" he acted like he'd never even said it.

But when push came to shove, blood was thicker than water, right? Didn't matter how damn good he was! Didn't matter how many years Mom had spent being nice to Jack Strauss, going to bed with him, making up to him, soothing him, cooking for him all those nights he came over, never asking him for a damn thing in return.... and that wasn't even mentioning what she did for him at the office. When the time came and he wanted to sell the business, Jack didn't consider his mother or him. Like all those years of loyalty were garbage.

It was Mom who picked up hints here and there and finally figured it out. Even when she was making appointments for him to see possible buyers, Jack *still* had the goddamn nerve to keep it a secret. Lawrence had waited and waited to be told that at least he'd be kept on in a good position, that he'd be given some stock... *something*. But there was nothing but silence from Jack. Nothing mattered to him but his family. In the end, everyone but members of his family could just go to hell as far as he was concerned! It wasn't fair, goddamnit, it was unjust! And... well, that's why Lawrence began to take what was his by right. If Jack wasn't going to give him what he deserved, by Jesus, he was going to get it somehow. And it was so fucking easy; he couldn't believe it. Type out an invoice, get yourself a mail drop somewhere, and collect the checks.

That was going to stop now, of course. If he was going to be a member of this family, hell, he couldn't do that anymore. And anyway, he'd been getting nervous, with that fat bitch cow Elaine snooping around the office. She was nasty but give her credit; she was shrewd, the way some of those Jewish bitches were.

He never *liked* doing it. He had to! He was relieved, to tell the truth, that he could stop. Today, he'd gone for the last time to Gansevoort Street, picked up the check—this one was twelve thousand dollars, that's all, he didn't believe in being too piggy—walked up the street to the bank, and put it right into his Downtown Lumber account. Downtown Lumber, L. J. McElroy, President. Next week he'd withdraw the last of it and Downtown Lumber would just disappear off the face of the earth. Made him laugh.

"What is it, sweetie?"

He turned to look at Zoe, wide awake again. Pretty little thing, sweet, crazy about him, rich . . . and big tits, too, just the way he liked them. He bent his head and gave one of the pink nipples a little kiss and she giggled and pressed him even closer. She really was adorable, he thought. She wanted only to please him, only to give him what he wanted. There wasn't a selfish bone in her body. She'd done all the hard work on this relationship, all the lying and the sneaking around and *happy* to do it as long as she could be with him. He could see the look on her face the minute she caught sight of him and it was pure happiness. There was something wonderful about that, about knowing for sure that somebody really loved you.

Oh, yeah, Mom loved him; there was nothing she wouldn't do for him. But Mom was an angel, and besides, she was his mother and that's how mothers felt about their children. But this thing with Zoe, now, that was a different thing, a special thing. She lit up when she was with him; even *he* could see that. He knew that as far as she was concerned, he was the smartest, the handsomest, the sexiest, the biggest and the best.

He ran his hand down the indentation in the center of her smooth tight back. God, she felt good. And she made him feel good, too. She had that nice old-fashioned attitude—that a woman should be there for her man and everything else was secondary. The hell with that woman's lib crap. He liked it this way. He could just hear his friends now, giving him the business about robbing the cradle and like that. Well, fuck them. He liked the way she made him feel. He liked calling the shots. He'd always noticed how women treated Uncle Jack, like he was king of the world; and he'd decided long ago that that's the way he wanted it, too. And by Jesus, he was going to have it, he was really going to have it!

The soft, curvy little thing nestling in his arms, cuddling up to him, so trusting and so sweet . . . she was his! His for the asking! His for the taking! Maybe at last he had really lucked out. He was, he told himself fiercely, going to be a good husband to Zoe, he was going to try not to cheat on her, to always be a good lover to her. He was going to take care of her because she loved him. He wrapped his arms even more tightly around her and held her very close.

Zoe wriggled a little. "What is it, honey?"

"Just thinking how lucky I am," he said.

"Because of *me*, honey?"

"Because of you, my sexy little . . ." He let the words trail off into a growl in the back of his throat as he kissed her neck, right under the ear, chuckling as she turned to fit her smooth young body into his.

She giggled. "Oh, Lawrence, Daddy's going to have a *fit* when he finds out about us."

They could *all* go to hell, Lawrence thought, the whole lot of them. Because he was going to win whether they liked it or not. He was going to give Jack Strauss his first grandson . . . and that would be the biggest triumph of all!

CHAPTER TWENTY-SIX

Saturday, January 18, 1986

When the phone rang, Deena fully expected it to be her mother asking her to bring something she needed to the party; or Elaine, or maybe even Marilyn, who had come in for their parents' big anniversary open house but—Marilyn-like—had chosen to stay with a friend thirty miles away, way the hell up in Westchester. Rye, for God's sake! First of all, as far as Deena was concerned, nobody real lived in Westchester, and secondly, of course Marilyn didn't have wheels and she and Michael were scheduled to schlepp over to Grand Central to pick her up at the train.

If Marilyn thought for one minute that they were going to drive all the way up to Rye to get her. . . . that's what Deena was thinking as she went for the phone. Plus, she didn't want to spend a whole hour alone in the car with Michael, not the way she was feeling about him this morning.

But it wasn't Marilyn. It was Dick Seltzer, *Dr.* Dick Seltzer, fellow Clayton parent, father of Saul's friend Kevin, psychiatrist, and helluva nice guy. She had called him yesterday at his office and left a message. But she never expected him to call back during the weekend.

"Dick. How kind of you to call back so quickly. Happy New Year," she burbled, "a little late, but sincere."

"The same to you, Deena. I heard about Saul. I assume that's why you called. And, well, Kevin's already moaning about what is he going to do without Saul to hang out with and . . . well, Deena, if there's anything I can do. Hell, Saul's been at my dinner table a thousand times, and I like the kid. Like him a lot. So. How can I help you?"

Tears pricked behind her eyes. "How can I help you?" Such a simple phrase and probably said without much thought; and yet nobody else had thought to ask her what they could do to help her. No. Change *nobody* to *Michael*.

"Oh, Dick, you have no idea how grateful I—" she began, and he interrupted.

"Yes, I do. Deena, I have a very good idea. You don't have to thank me. Just tell me what's on your mind."

It was such a relief to pour out the whole story, leaving out nothing, including her horrible arguments with Michael, their battle on the windjammer, his leaving, her staying, her coming back alone to find disaster and Saul's future all planned out without her having been consulted.

"I don't think this is a good idea, just packing him off to boarding school like this, Dick. If anything, he needs our attention more than ever, don't you think?"

"Well, Deena, I don't want to get too specific because I don't know enough about all the circumstances. But it seems to me, from the sound of things, that perhaps Saul needs to get away from home . . . perhaps only briefly." He paused delicately, and then went on. "It may be the tension at home. . . . I mean, he may possibly be acting out his anxieties about you and Michael. Mind you, this is only an educated guess."

"Well, Dick, I dare say your educated guess is as close to the truth as anyone can get right now."

"I do think it's important for you and his father to let Saul know that he's going away not because you're rejecting him, not because you're punishing him, but because—"

"But that's just the trouble, Dick!" Her voice began to climb the register as her agitation mounted once again. "As far as Michael is concerned, this is all punitive. He doesn't give a damn for his son, he doesn't give a damn for me, he cares only that *he* be vindicated."

"Who the hell do you think you're talking to?"

If they hadn't been alone in the house, she wouldn't have recognized the rage-strangled voice as her husband's. Startled, she whirled around, clutching the phone protectively to her shoulder; and as soon as he saw that, he strode over, snatched it away from her, and slammed it down onto the cradle. "How dare you!" he gritted between his clenched teeth. She could see that he was literally shaking in his rage. "How *dare* you! You may *not* go behind my back and talk about our personal business. Not to anyone!"

"Don't worry, it wasn't just anyone. It was a shrink and it was about Saul."

"I didn't hear Saul's name, I heard mine! I didn't hear Saul being belittled and betrayed, I heard myself! So don't try to tell me it was about Saul." The last couple of words were said in a grating falsetto, an imitation of her without doubt.

It was that condescending mimicry more than his words that made her slap him. He looked as shocked as she felt; she hadn't even known she was going to do it; it was as if her arm had a mind of its own. And then he slapped her back, hard, hurting her. Without volition, tears began to pour from her eyes in frustration and fury.

"You fuck!"

"Typical, Deena, to call names like a child instead of taking responsibility for your own actions. I can't deal with you anymore!"

"Maybe that's why Saul did this thing, did you ever consider that? Maybe Saul is trying to tell us something, tell *you* something?"

He curled his lip in the disdainful way he had and gave that little laugh. "Is that what your fancy shrink pal told you to say?"

"Oh, Michael, stop being such a schmuck! It was Dick Seltzer. You *like* him, even though you'd never talk to him when Saul was seeing him. Remember?"

"You had no business talking about our private concerns. To anyone."

"Well, Michael, if *you* had talked to *me*, maybe I wouldn't have to call a professional. You left me out of the whole thing. Well, I've taken care of Saul, all by myself, with very little goddamn help from you all these years. And I'm not going to entrust him to you alone just like that!"

"I can't do any worse than you already have, can I? A boy needs the close supervision of a *man*, that's all that's wrong with Saul."

"Oh, Michael, you really take the cake. You believe that a brilliant and wealthy child steals because he simply needs male supervision! Nothing in this life, Michael, is that simple! Especially not a child. Especially not a child who had to grow up with an uninterested father . . . don't bother to give me that hard look! You've never been able to find time for *any* of your children . . . never changed a diaper, never played a game, never went to a school play! All you want is that once a year we all sit down together in the den for the photographer. All you want is for people to come in and walk down the front hall and admire those beautiful color photographs of Michael Berman and His Perfect Family. Don't you dare tell me what I did wrong with Saul! At least I did *something*.

"You went crazy at the mention of an abortion! But, Michael, I carried the child for nine months, and I've been taking care of him ever since! By myself! I'm so damn tired of doing it all alone! In spite of the fact that I could cheerfully murder you for sending him away, and in spite of the fact that I'm going to miss him, I'm *glad*, Michael, I'm relieved. I'm going to have four months for myself, and it's *wonderful*!"

"Ah-ha! Now the truth comes out!"

Deena sprang to her feet, quivering. Her voice, which a moment ago had been strong and ringing, now came out in a thin whisper. "Michael. Don't say anything else. I warn you. One more condescending word—one more 'ah-ha!'—and I won't hold myself responsible for my actions." And, with barely a pause, she added in a totally different voice: "And if we don't get going right now, Marilyn in going to be standing out in the cold, waiting for us."

* * *

As soon as she had settled herself into the backseat of Michael's black Mercedes, Marilyn knew she had made a mistake. The anger in the car was almost palpable, and now she regretted allowing Michael to insist that he pick her up. She'd told him, "I'll take a cab, Michael, I know how to take a cab!" But he wouldn't hear of it. Michael was such a Good Boy, always intent upon doing the Right Thing just in case God happened to be looking. She didn't know how Deena stood it.

Today it looked as if she wasn't even trying. Marilyn attempted to make cheery social conversation. She asked after their health, their holiday, and their children. Very short shrift is what she got, especially about Saul. She knew what had been going on—Sylvia always kept her posted on family gossip, whether she wanted it or not—but she wondered how Saul felt. Forget it . . . they just didn't want to talk about it.

She gave up after a few minutes and looked out the window. Not a pretty sight, not to her. A wind was howling down the canyons of skyscrapers and a low pall of dark gray clouds smothered the tops of the tallest buildings. On its best days New York was not her favorite place, and today was not one of its best. Coming down on the train from Westchester, she had looked out and thought how disgusting it all looked, bleak and grimy even up there in the wealthy suburbs. The old snow next to the tracks was brown with filth, and the glimpses of towns showed empty little streets and empty little stores, and as far as she was concerned, empty little lives.

It was so different in Mt. Hebron. There was space and light and air. Even in filthy weather like this the countryside looked clean. When she left, day before yesterday, when she walked out in the morning on fresh snow that had fallen during the night, the world was white and her footprints were the first to disturb the thick drifts. And quiet! That's what she really loved about Vermont. Growing up on Central Park West, she'd always hated the noise and the tumult. She'd always thought there was something wrong with her—her big sisters were so sure they lived in the best place in the world—until the first summer at camp, the year she was eight. Camp Thoreau was in Vermont, and from the very first day she knew she'd found her true home. She knew then that one day when she was grown up and on her own she would come back to Vermont to live. And so she had. Of course, her family found this choice bizarre . . . but then, they found most of her choices bizarre.

She knew her mother, for instance, would have something to say about what she was wearing. Sylvia never gave up. And Sylvia was at a loss to explain how she had brought up a daughter who would choose a denim skirt and a red and black checked shirt for New Year's Day when she knew she ought to be dressed up, like everyone else at the party. Marilyn hadn't thought to look before, but now she leaned forward to see what Deena had on. High heels, bright red dress Marilyn would bet had a designer label, and a fur jacket. She looked lovely; she always did. Deena was a pretty woman and she was interested in clothes. Marilyn just didn't care what she had on as long as it was comfortable. She never picked out anything *ugly*—at least, she didn't think so. And if she did pick out something ugly, well, to hell with it. She couldn't be bothered with the nonsense of fashion and style and what was in and what was out; she didn't have time. She shopped mostly from the L. L. Bean catalog and she was well satisfied with the results. Whatever Sylvia had to say. . . . well, that was *her* problem.

And then, when they all walked into the apartment, over-heated, overcrowded, as it was *every* anniversary as far back as she could remember, Sylvia gave her a big hug, pushed her at arm's length, looked her up and down the way she always did, and then said, "What a nice outfit, Marilyn dear. I love your buffalo checks. But of course, a woman with a bust like mine could never wear that . . ." And then she turned to Deena, and Marilyn was left wondering what in the world her mother was talking about. Until she got into the huge living room and looked around and saw not one, not two, but three women wearing shirts just like hers. Well, look at that! she told herself. I'm in style, of all the damn things! What was surprising was how pleased it made her feel, that and her mother's approval. She thought she'd outgrown that, years ago.

It was the typical Strauss party. Too many people in the room, all trying too damn hard to have a wonderful time and there, holding center stage as usual, her father, his voice louder than anyone else's, telling a story complete with gestures and a great deal of hearty laughter, just like a borscht circuit comic working the crowd. He was good at it; they were all doubled over.

She didn't find him entertaining. She knew him too well; she knew that all his gallantry to women and all his expansive hospitality were part of the role he played, the role of Warm and Wonderful Jack Strauss. She felt like the kid who insisted the emperor had no clothes. . . . except she'd never had the guts to say it aloud. No use wondering if Jack had seen her; it wouldn't make any difference. If he had an appreciative audience, no one else existed.

Not that she cared, not anymore. She'd made her peace with that particular thing a long time ago. She knew who her father was. A phony of the first order and a sexist bastard to boot. Why nobody else seemed to see it was beyond her. Sylvia was a fool to have put up with all his shit all these years and do nothing about it except make a few wisecracks and go to her women's meetings and socials at the temple. To be fair, her mother was probably a woman who needed to be married, but, dammit, she could have demanded some changes in his behavior. At *least* that! Or she could have gone to get that college degree she always talked about and done something for herself. What kind of role model did she think she was for three daughters!

She made her way to the bar, which was always set by the dining room door, and got herself a glass of champagne. Now what? She looked around the room. Was there anyone here she felt obligated to say hello to? No. But then, she had long ago dissociated herself from this whole milieu. Look at them, dressed to kill and for what? To stand around at Jack and Sylvia's, look rich, drink and eat, and size one another up. How well she remembered the day-after conversations between Sylvia and her friends. They would price everyone's outfit, analyze everyone's hairstyle, decide who had had a face-lift, guess whose marriage was on shaky ground, and complain about how everyone else in the group did nothing but gossip!

Yes, Marilyn decided, there were far too many diamonds in

this room, too many Saks Fifth Avenue labels, too many furs heaped on her parents' beds, too many meaningless conversation about too many meaningless lives. She hadn't been here more than ten minutes and she was already fed up. She felt the same every year, and yet she continued to appear every year. Why? Because they asked her to, and she seemed unable to say no.

It was time to find Saul, who happened to be her favorite. Another misfit in the family; God, she'd recognized that in him by the time he was six years old. Her nephew Noel was a spoiled Jewish prince, with all his brains, and the others were ciphers to her. But Saul had an oddball intelligence that stubbornly refused to conform—even in his family of strong-willed parents. She could relate to *that*!

She'd have to go find him. He wasn't in the living room. Nor were any of the kids, come to think of it. Probably all watching television, gorging on the caviar or the miniature spinach strudels. Christ, the food in this house! There was enough uneaten gourmet garbage to feed her whole town.

The conversation in this place was garbage, too: golf scores. Tennis scores. Cruises. Fashion shows. Deals. Stock tips. Household help. Sales. Bullshit! She never should have come. She had left too many things behind that were *really* important. Her friends. Her little house in the woods. Her pets. Her work. Her quiet peaceful satisfying life. Her patients, especially. There was a little girl she suspected might have been infected with AIDS last year when she'd had a transfusion. She was showing most of the symptoms—though she'd had pneumonia a few months ago and had recovered—the final test results were not yet back from Boston. The entire family was in a state of shock and needed her support. They didn't dare tell anyone else. Marilyn sighed deeply. There would be hell to pay in Mt. Hebron if word ever got out that there might be a child with the dread disease. So they had this burden to bear all by themselves and Marilyn had found herself on the phone at least once a day with the distraught mother. This kind of emotional support went with the territory when you were a family practitioner in a small town; and it was this kind of medicine she was deeply committed to. To be in this city, in this house, in this company, was to be in alien country. She wished she had stayed home.

But as long as she was here, maybe she could be of some help to poor Saul. She poked around and finally found him, hiding in the breakfast nook, nibbling gloomily on a brownie and pretending to be engrossed in a football game on the tiny television set.

"Well, here you are!" She made herself sound cheerful, even though she found the sight of his pale, drawn face distressing. He needs vitamins, was her immediate thought, and some exercise, for starters. And then, when he focused on her and life sparked in his eyes, he needs someone to talk to. She slid into the banquette next to him.

"One more extra pound and I won't even be able to get in here."

"Tell me about it!" He gave a rueful glance down to his soft belly. He was right; he was too heavy by far.

"So, my friend . . ."

"You're the only person in the world who still thinks I'm their *anything*." He gave a brief little laugh. "After my terrible crime against humanity! You heard, didn't you, they're sending me up the river!" He changed his voice to a mock growl. "Fifteen to life."

Marilyn regarded her nephew. Overweight, unhappy, pasty, angry, helpless. And trying to joke it all away. "Have you considered that maybe it'll be good for you to get away? That maybe you'll even *like* it?"

"I've considered it. But, Moo Moo, how would *you* feel if your parents wanted to get rid of you? And didn't bother to hide it? You think you'd be able to tell yourself that you were gonna like it?"

"You think your parents want to get *rid* of you?" She spoke carefully and he laughed, this time in genuine amusement.

"God, Moo Moo, you sound like my psychiatrist, you know that? Always repeating the patients' statements back at them. Yeah, my parents want to get rid of me. They're dying to get rid of me . . . *him*, especially."

"Saul, is that fair to your father?"

"My father doesn't give a damn about me! He never has! You know what he cares about? *His* standing, his shame. His goddamn *name*! That's what he kept saying to me, that he was ashamed to have me bear his name." Saul made a face. "He's never cared about *me*. He doesn't even know who I am. He's always too busy, he's never home. Him and his Nazis! And if it's not that, it's his work. I've never had a father, not really!"

"I'm sure your father loves you very much," Marilyn said, thinking very fast, wondering what in the world she could say to comfort him. The truth. Why not? The truth, she had found after years of struggle, was the only thing that kept you sane. "On the other hand," she added, touching his arm, "I know where you're coming from. I had the same kind of relationship with *my* father."

That surprised him. "Papa?"

"Yes, that wonderful, warm human being! Your doting grandfather! Believe it or not, he ignored me, he was too busy for me, he was never home for me. So I showed him! I moved to Vermont!" She laughed and, after a moment, Saul did also. She could see by the look in his eye that he was still chewing over this brand new information. "But, Saul, listen. A distant father is tough to deal with; but it forces you to find your *own* way. And that's all to the good."

"Some way I found!" He rolled his eyes back in a way that vividly reminded her of the young Deena.

"You want to talk about it? About why in the world a bright young man like you would choose to do something so dumb?"

Saul stared at her with troubled eyes. Yes, Deena's eyes, she realized, with the same softness in them. He looked so vulnerable. Well, he was, wasn't he? He wasn't a hardened criminal; he was a troubled teenager with a workaholic father.

Finally, he shrugged. "I don't know, Moo Moo. Stupid, isn't it? But . . . I don't know."

"It seemed like a good idea at the time?"

"Yeah." Then he smiled a little, the first since she'd come in. "Not *everyone* could do it, you know. If I hadn't rented that post office box so close to home, they'd never have found me."

Marilyn frowned. "So maybe now you'll use your smarts to do something *smart*? How about it, pal. We all know you're brilliant, you don't have to prove it by breaking the law.

Going away to school may be a golden opportunity for you to prove—yes, Saul, to your father—that you can do wonderful things."

Now Saul really laughed. "Come off it, will you? That's not why they want me up there! They want their big mistake out of sight and out of mind. *And*," he insisted as she opened her mouth to answer him. "And, Moo Moo, they also don't want me around to see what's going on with them."

"What's that supposed to mean?"

"Christ, they fight all the time. I hear them. They think I'm safely shut away in my room, but I hear them. They hate each other! They aren't even sleeping in the same room anymore! I don't know why they bother to stay together! So they're taking it out on me. Good old Saul, let's make him the scapegoat, let's send him away to a prison. . . . no, wait, how about a school? Well, if I can't stand it at that military school, I'm telling you right now, I'm running away. And I'll go where they'll *never* find me!"

"Oh, Saul . . . running away never does anyone any good. Tell you what. If you really hate that whole idea . . . well, think about maybe coming up with me, staying with me, and going to school in Vermont?"

"Honest?"

"Honest," she said. And at that moment Michael came into the kitchen, his handsome chiseled face tightening at the sight of his son. Marilyn immediately made up her mind. "Michael," she said, "come for a walk with me, will you? I need to talk to you about something important."

It was after four o'clock by the time she and Michael got back, and she was nearly frozen by the icy wind that was blasting through Central Park. A glance in the hall mirror showed flaming cheeks and nose and she made a face at her reflection, knowing that her mother would find something to say about it. Oh, well. *She* thought it looked healthy and attractive, and to hell with it. She followed Michael through the now-empty living room, through the now-empty dining room, and into the den, which is where Jack and Sylvia's parties always ended up, with all the casual friends gone, and everyone else smashed into the smallest room in the place, shoes off, feet up, schmoozing and kibitzing and telling old family stories. The whole family, except for Nat, of course, was there—even Saul—and someone had brought in platters of desserts. Marilyn realized she was hungry, and saying hello to the assemblage, went right to the plate of her mother's home-made apple strudel.

Sylvia smiled in approval at that and said, "What the two of you had to go outside into that horrible weather for, I don't know."

"You probably don't want to know," Deena cracked. There was an acid edge to her voice, Marilyn noted. Deena was miffed. Well, she was right; she should have been asked along. But Marilyn had figured, hell, Michael was the tough nut; and if they weren't getting along, she'd never get either of them to agree to her plan. As it was . . .

"Michael and I had important business," she told Sylvia, "which you will all be told about as soon as I've talked to Deena."

"Good." That was Elaine. "You want to talk to Deena, and Deena and I want to talk to you. So long, everyone, we're going into my room."

"You hear that, Sylvia?" Jack laughed. "For twenty-three years she hasn't lived here and it's still her room!" He was, Marilyn realized with a start, proud of it. He *liked* playing Daddy. It suited him. Maybe he missed it. Well, she'd missed it, too.

Elaine's room had been redone recently in the very latest English country garden mode, and when they were walking in, she spread her arms wide and said, "Welcome to my bower. Couldn't she have picked something a bit less . . . girly?"

And Deena said, "Anyway, it's better than mine." She rolled her eyes. "I ask you: red, blue, purple, and green stripes? On *everything*? I don't know what in the world was in her head. She tells me it's the thing: *I* call it instant headache. Be grateful for pink and lavender cabbage roses, my dear Lainie."

"You didn't drag me in here for a private conference on wallpaper," Marilyn said. "I *hope*. Because here's what I know about wallpaper. As long as it's already on the wall, it's fine by me. And now that we've gotten aesthetics out of the way, do you want to tell me what you really want to tell me?"

"That was funny!" Deena said appreciatively. "Really funny."

"Once every visit," Marilyn said dryly. "I feel I owe it to my family."

"That's two!"

"*Deena*! I already asked what's really going on. Let's have it."

"Yes, Deena, let's tell Marilyn what we brought her in here for," Elaine said.

She stopped, waiting for Deena. What in the world? After she'd told her taciturn New England friends that none of the women in her family was the least bit shy or backward or reserved! She decided it would probably be fun to just wait and let her sisters trip all over each other for a while. There were a lot of false starts and a lot of interrupting each other. But at least, two words emerged from all the *fumfering*: *Daddy* and *Linda*.

"Oh, that!" she said, staring at them in disbelief. They were really stumbling around, unwilling to tell her. "Is that still going on? I would have thought that two people their age and one of them having had prostate surgery. . ."

And, of course, Deena could not resist. "Which one?"

While at the same moment, Elaine was saying, "What do you mean, *still? You knew*?"

Why, she had just created a sensation. It was incredible. "Sure I knew. For a long time. Didn't you?"

"Oh, sure," Deena said dryly. "A long long time . . . since maybe last month."

"I can't believe it. Yes, I can. You really *didn't* know!"

"If we'd known," Elaine said angrily, "don't you think we'd have told *you*?"

"Don't get that tone, Elaine. I've already said I thought that of course you were both aware of it."

She had been thirteen. It was a Friday during Easter vacation and she had been visiting her friend Angela's grandparents in little Italy, down near the Village. It was always great fun to go see the De Vitos because they ran a pastry shop and they were warm and loving and there were always a couple of boy cousins around to flirt with and tease them. Later, she was able to understand that it was the closeness of Angela's family, the authentic closeness they all felt to each other, that's what was so seductive and compelling. As always, on her way home, she felt sad and lonely, wishing she had that at home.

On an impulse she decided to go by Daddy's office, which was five blocks away. Maybe this time it would be different; maybe this time he'd really be glad to see her, instead of kissing the air next to her cheek and quickly handing her over to Linda. Maybe.

She was a block away when she saw them: Daddy and Linda, arms tightly around each other, kissing. Even though they had put themselves in the shadow of a deserted entranceway, it was unmistakably them. She stood frozen where she was, unable to move, almost unable to breathe. No, no, no, she kept repeating to herself idiotically. But yes, yes, yes, it was her daddy and Linda, kissing each other in a way she had seen only in the movies and so knew it meant the two people were in love. In love! It was that thought that was unbearable, and she did the only thing she knew to do: turned and ran away. She shouldn't have been there! She shouldn't have gone where she wasn't even wanted! In a way, she thought it was her fault.

She knew it was awful; she knew it was wrong; she knew she must never tell. She was convinced that this was the end of her parents' marriage and she waited, clammy with dread, that night and for many nights thereafter, waiting for Jack to come home and announce that he was leaving. He would leave them and they would be all alone and then what would they do? She could hardly bear to think about it . . . and yet, she could not stop thinking about it.

After two weeks of this horrid anticipation, waiting for the ax to fall, she was a nervous wreck. Even Jack noticed something, and at the dinner table one evening, he turned to her angrily and said, "Again with the sour puss, Marilyn! I don't know what in hell's wrong with you, but it's ruining my appetite. Shape up, will you?"

She burst into tears—it was just too much, coming on top

of everything else—and ran into her room, slamming the door and flinging herself across her bed.

Sylvia came right after her, knocking first and asking if she could come in and then coming in anyway. Marilyn smelled her mother's Chanel No. 5 and felt the wonderful warmth of her arms around her, the release of just crying and crying and Sylvia's cool hand on her cheek. "What is it, *shayner kind*. Tell Mother, I'll understand. Is it a boy?" The question was so close yet so far off the mark, it brought fresh tears.

And all the time her brain was clicking away, racing ahead, trying to figure out what she could tell her mother that would have the ring of truth. Finally, when the sobs had turned into hiccups and she was able to talk, she said, "I feel so terrible. My friend . . . my friend Carla . . . she saw her father kissing another lady and now she's so afraid they're going to get divorced. She can't get it out of her mind, and it's making her afraid and . . . she talks to me and it makes *me* afraid."

Was that good enough? Marilyn wondered, feeling Sylvia's arms tighten convulsively around her. Then her mother said, sounding irritated, "She shouldn't have told you that; that's a terrible thing to talk about." And then her hold loosened and she absently began to pat Marilyn on the back. "Look, *bubeleh*, let me try to explain," she said, in quite a different voice. "Men . . . how do I tell you? . . . men sometimes, when they feel they're getting older, want to prove to themselves that they're still handsome and attractive, so sometimes, they kiss another lady. But you tell your friend Carla not to worry, a kiss doesn't mean divorce. A kiss is just a kiss. Maybe she saw a friendly kiss." Marilyn shook her head wordlessly. "No? Well, does a twelve-year-old know what she's seeing? Probably. But it doesn't mean divorce, *bubeleh*, and she should never tell anyone, not anyone at all. Besides you, I mean. And that goes for you, too. Not a word, not to anyone. It could cause a lot of trouble, Marilyn, and for no reason. As long as her father is coming home at night to her and her mother and is taking care of his family the way he's supposed to, she should forget what she saw and stop worrying. You understand?"

That was fine by Marilyn, who really was tired of dealing with it all by herself and wanted only to forget the whole thing. Of course, she didn't. She stopped agonizing over it;

having put it onto her mother's shoulders she felt freed; but she never forgot. Every time she saw Linda, she remembered. She hated Linda, hated her. And hated him, too, for making her so afraid and then yelling at her. And for kissing Linda. For loving Linda and not her, his own daughter. For everything.

"I was thirteen when I discovered it," she explained to her sisters. "You guys were so much older, so much smarter, I naturally assumed you didn't tell me."

They looked at one another for a moment or two and Marilyn wondered what they were thinking, each of them. She hardly knew them. By the time she was twelve years old, they were both married. What did she have in common with them?

"Well!" Elaine finally said. "I guess that takes care of *that*!" She laughed a little. "You know, I think I was actually looking forward to breaking it to my baby sister gently."

"How can you joke about it, Lainie? How awful for Marilyn! I know *I* feel adrift—and I'm forty-three, not twelve! Poor Moo Moo! Poor baby! And you kept it to yourself all those years!" She came across the room and put her arms around Marilyn. It was nice, Marilyn thought, but unnecessary. Gently, she said, "Thank you, Deena, but it all happened a long long time ago and I'm not suffering anymore."

"Okay, then," Elaine announced in her best business voice. "Now that that's settled, let's get on with the agenda. First of all, I think we're all agreed . . . Sylvia never gets wind of this." They all nodded solemnly. "Next . . ." And she launched into a tale of dealings with Daddy's business and the books and irregularities of some sort and a guy named Malone and a non-existent lumberyard and a whole bunch of stuff Marilyn wasn't really too interested in. "I want to go into the office when Linda the watchdog isn't anywhere around and I want to make copies of all the pertinent stuff."

Marilyn couldn't help smiling. "Sounds like a spy thriller to me, not a family business."

"Oh, really? Well, it just so happens I want both of you with me when I do it . . . just in case."

"Whoa," Marilyn interrupted, envisioning days of being

trapped here, cooped up and bored to death, while Elaine did something or other. "What do you need *me* for?"

"I never want anyone to say that I cooked up any of this. You two are my witnesses."

"But you have Deena!"

"Look, Marilyn, it's time you took a little interest in the family business, you know that? I realize that being a doctor is the next best thing to being God; but you *are* a shareholder, you know, and we're involved with theft here! I have a very good idea who's stealing from the company, and there's going to be a showdown and it's not going to be pleasant. Instead of crapping out on us, like you usually do, I'd like you to stick around this time. It's only a day or two. Surely, your patients can spare you for such a short time."

How dare she? Coldly, she said, "You know nothing about my patients and their needs."

Deena, wringing her hands, pleaded, "Elaine, Elaine!" but Marilyn kept talking through her voice.

"And I want an apology for that crack about thinking I'm God."

"That's not what I said. . . . oh, all right, all right, I'm sorry. I really am sorry. I'm upset; I've been handling this all by myself and it's getting to me." Silence. Then Elaine said, "But will you?"

"Hang out here and stand behind you while you do your spy stuff? No way! I'll stand behind you from Vermont; but I have work to do and yes, I have patients who can't spare me. I have patients who need me *today*." At that moment it struck her that she was telling the plain truth. It also struck her that she didn't have to stay here. She could go. She was a big girl now, she could do whatever she felt was right.

And then it hit her: Saul. Oh, God, Saul. And she hadn't even talked to Deena yet about his coming up to Vermont to live with her and go to school and breathe fresh air and maybe get a fresh start on his young life. How would Deena react? Michael had proved surprisingly receptive.

"So you're leaving again, running away." Elaine was really mad; well, too bad.

Marilyn managed a tight smile. "Yes, Elaine, I'm leaving.

But it's not running away, as you so sweetly put it. I live there, remember? And that means I'm going home."

"You're still a member of this family."

Marilyn couldn't help thinking, it might surprise you, how little connection I feel to anyone here. Anyone except that poor confused kid. "In fact, I have a family matter to discuss with Deena. Right now. And *alone*."

Elaine tossed her head in a familiar gesture. "What do you have to say to Deena that you can't discuss in front of me? This *is* my room, you know." She tried for a laugh but it didn't quite make it.

"It's personal."

"If it's a family matter, then it concerns all of us." God, she was a pain in the rear end, Marilyn thought. Couldn't take a hint, wouldn't hear a direct request even!

"It doesn't concern you, I said." Marilyn heard the edge go on her voice. It was a sound that appeared only around her family. Well, to hell with it, she didn't care. Let Elaine make of it what she wanted. She went on. "You've always bullied Deena and I need *her* decision, not yours."

"What the hell do you mean by that? It's absolutely not true! I don't bully anybody. I'm a strong person with strong opinions, admitted. But I don't force my opinions on anyone. Ask Deena." And, typically, without waiting for Marilyn to do so, she turned to Deena and demanded: "Do I bully you, Deena? Do I?"

"No, no. Of course not. Wait, Marilyn, don't get that look. Elaine was my mouthpiece a lot of times, true. But I feel she stood up for me, not bullied me. Unless you have your own reason for sending her out of the room, I feel comfortable with her here. And don't worry, I'm capable of making my own decisions."

Shit. She'd said all the wrong things, of course, managed to antagonize both of them. Well, it was done. So be it. "Okay," she said. "Here goes. I've had a long talk with Saul. He's very unhappy about being sent away."

"You think I don't realize that?"

Marilyn waved her off. "Of course you do." She paused. How to put it delicately? There was no delicate way. "Look. He's miserable at home, he told me. He's very bothered by what's going on with you and Michael." Here she waited for the inevitable denial—which, surprisingly, didn't come—and then went on. "He says you fight all the time and you're not sleeping together. He says the tension is unbearable."

Marilyn watched Deena's face as her sister struggled to hide her uneasiness. You asked for it, she thought. You said let her stay, so here she is, hearing it all. Somewhere inside she felt smug. All her childhood those two had told her what she had to like and dislike, what she was supposed to wear, how she ought to behave, and, goddammit, even what she should think! All those years of trying to do it their way, all those frustrating, idiotic years, until she was finally old enough to realize that she wasn't like them and didn't want to be like them.

"In any case," she finished, "Saul feels beleaguered at home. You can't expect a teenage boy to be able to handle marital difficulties. Adolescence is—"

"I know about adolescence! Saul is my fourth child, not my first. What do you know about it? You've never been married. You don't know what it's like. And anyway, marriages have ups and downs; it goes with the territory. Every marriage has rough spots; we just happen to be in the middle of one right now." She paused for breath and then, frowning, plunged on. "Saul has no *right* to talk about our personal family matters to anyone! Oh, my God, I can't believe I said that," she added in an entirely different tone. "That's exactly what Michael said to *me* when he discovered me talking to Saul's shrink!" And she began to laugh. "And *I* gave *him* hell!"

Tightly, Marilyn said, "Apparently nobody around here listens to Saul."

"You've got a hell of a nerve. You show up for a day or two, once a year, and you have all the answers! You don't know a goddamn thing about real life, Marilyn."

"I'm trained to take care of people; and Saul, in case it had escaped your notice, is a person. And, by the way, I happen to know from experience what it feels like to be a teenager living in a home where things are wrong." To her horror, her throat suddenly constricted and her eyes filled.

Deena was immediately at her side, arms around her again. Marilyn suffered the hug for what she considered a decent amount of time and then pushed Deena away. Too late, she thought. Aloud, she said, "The point right now is Saul and what we can do to help him. After five minutes with him I could see that he needs a change of scene and rules to live by. But I think I have a better way." And she outlined her plan to have him join her in her house, live with her, go to the district high school, and even help around the clinic.

And then she mentally sat back and watched them react. Elaine, of course, was miffed as hell. *She* was supposed to be the one with the answers. She put out a few weak objections ...Saul was a city kid, he'd die up there in the wilderness. Marilyn was too busy to really keep an eye on him, he hated the cold ... garbage like that.

At last, when Marilyn decided she'd had enough, she said, "Elaine. Shut up, will you? This is exactly why I wanted to talk to Deena alone. Look. Here's how it is. I've made an offer. I meant it. I want the kid, the kid wants to come with me. Even Michael has agreed. So, Deena, what do you say?"

"Do I have anything to say about it? It sounds like a fait accompli, to me." But she was smiling. She was going to go for it. Good. Marilyn had already decided she'd take him anyway; but it was much better for everybody if Deena approved.

Deena held up a hand and said, "Okay, here's how it is. If Saul went to military school, the world would think that was a punishment very fitting to the crime. I would get points for that. *But*, if he goes up to Vermont, where he'll probably be happy, it's going to look as if his mother couldn't handle him. And how would *that* look, since his mother counsels other people's children at the Clayton School! Sensitive, understanding, intelligent, compassionate Mrs. Berman! I ask you, how could this person admit that she screwed up so badly with her own son!" Tears openly ran down her cheeks, but she was still smiling. "So, Elaine? Nothing to say, for a change?"

"Stop blaming yourself, Deena, you're a wonderful mother. Teenagers are like that. He's going through a stage and if you want my opinion, living in Vermont might be fun, but it won't work miracles, he'll grow out of it no matter where he is."

"Elaine," Marilyn said quietly. "Shut up." She turned to Deena. "Then it's settled? Good." She pushed herself away from the wall where she'd been leaning. "Then we'd better get going. I do have patients waiting for me."

"Wait, wait. There are things you should know about Saul. He won't eat fish. You have to fight him into the shower and then he stays there for hours. He shouldn't have chocolate. And—"

Now it was Marilyn's turn to laugh. "Hey! I'm not becoming his slave, Deena. I'm not even becoming his mother. I'm merely taking him into my house; and once he's in my house, believe me, he'll shape up or ship out. He'll eat what's put on the table, he'll do his chores, he'll go to school and do his homework and he'll stay out of trouble or I'll kick ass. So . . . stop, okay? Come. Kiss your baby good bye, Deena. And, Deena, let go, will you? Let go."

CHAPTER TWENTY-SEVEN

Monday, May 5, 1952

It had all been worth it, all of it, Linda thought. The three months of morning sickness, the swollen ankles, the loneliness, the moments of terrible aching doubt, even the agony of labor and birth. Why didn't they tell you how much pain there was? Why didn't Dr. O'Brien warn her? But never mind now, it was all over and she was the mother of a beautiful baby boy. She'd already seen him this morning; just after dawn they brought him in, all sweet and clean, wrapped in a little blue blanket. Baby Boy McElroy: that's what it said on his bracelet. He was her baby, her son, her beautiful little boy, hers to love forever, a son to love her forever. Baby Boy McElroy . . . it rhymed, she thought sleepily, it rhymed.

The first time she had missed her period, all she could think was no, no, it couldn't be. She couldn't be pregnant, just couldn't. And then she made herself calm down; she'd skipped periods before. No sense in creating tension; she wanted to be her usual serene and competent self for Jack. But when she missed again, she knew. She was already thickening in the waist, already feeling sick at the smell of meat, already sleepy every afternoon. She knew, and it terrified her. She didn't want to go to the doctor, didn't want to know for sure. But she had to! If she was carrying Jack's child, she had to tell him—and right away. After she came out of Dr. O'Brien's cool, dim office that hot September Saturday, feeling sick to her stomach, feeling panicky and lost and desperate, she knew exactly how she was going to do it. Every Saturday afternoon Jack went to the office for a few hours. Sometimes he brought Elaine with him. Sometimes it was just the two of them and they made love on the leather couch. She had told him earlier in the week that she was busy this afternoon and, although he'd given her a puzzled look, he didn't question her.

All the way over to the office she prayed he would still be there when she let herself in, that she wouldn't have to wait until Monday to talk to him. She'd die if she had to wait until Monday, just die! But he was there and as soon as he saw her, he frowned and said sharply. "What's wrong? You look awful. Sit down. What is it?"

There was no way to tell him except to tell him, right out. "I'm going to have your baby, Jack."

"The hell you say! You told me you always use your diaphragm!"

"I do, Jack, I didn't lie. I don't know what happened. I swear. I don't know how..."

"Damn! Damn!" He got up from his chair and began to pace. She wished he would come over to her and give her a hug or something to show he wasn't hating her. It wasn't her fault.

"It's not my fault, Jack. The doctor said . . . he said even a diaphragm isn't one hundred percent effective."

"So you *have* been to a doctor and he says you really are . . ." His voice drifted off.

"Pregnant, Jack. I'm pregnant. The question is: what are we going to do now?"

"Do! I'll tell you what we're gonna do! *You're* gonna get on a plane to San Juan, Puerto Rico, and get an abortion. Don't look like that. I'll arrange it, I'll pay for it. Stop crying, Linda, I'm not going to send you to some filthy butcher. Down there, they have these nice little clinics where that's all they do. They're real doctors and real nurses, it's not anything like what you read about in the *Daily News*. Stop it, will you?"

"But I thought . . . you said . . . I was sure we'd get married."

"Married! You crazy? I never said anything to you about getting *married*. Jesus Christ, Linda, I'm already married, remember? With three little kids and a wife I happen to love."

It hurt so much. She knew he hated any kind of fuss, but she couldn't help it. She began to sob loudly, like a child. All her hopes and dreams crushed in a moment. Now he came to her, lifting her to her feet and putting his arms around her.

"There, there, no need to cry, Linda. You'll go to Puerto Rico, and as long as you're there, why not take a week, you'll stay at a fancy hotel on the beach and maybe I'll be able to come down for a few days and be with you—why are you shaking your head?"

"No," she managed to choke out. "No abortion!" She pushed away from him and forced herself to stop crying. "Never abortion."

"Come on, Linda, there's no other way."

"But it's a mortal sin!" And to her own surprise, she crossed herself.

"Hey!" Jack protested. "Where'd *that* come from? I thought you gave up all that stuff!"

"You don't have to be a practicing Catholic to know that abortion is murder, Jack."

"Well, I'm sorry," he said after a few minutes of silence. "I just don't see any other way. Because there's no way I can marry you!"

Tears spilling from her eyes, Linda said, "Never?"

"Not a chance."

"Then we're finished. " She turned on her heel, numb and fighting back the tears that threatened to fall. This time she wasn't going to give him the satisfaction! She couldn't figure out where she found the guts to walk out, but she did. She turned on her heel and walked right out, paying no attention when he called after her. If he wanted her, he was going to have to change his mind. And if he changed his mind, he knew where to find her. Because she was never going to set foot in this office again.

She got into the elevator, blinded with her own tears, and —once in the street—began to run. She didn't care where she was going, she just wanted to get away from her misery. But when she ran out of breath, panic and pain still weighed her down and she just plodded along, sweating, her hair sticking to her forehead, trying not to cry anymore. And there it was: a church, St. Ignatius, right in the middle of a row of tenements. She went in, breathing deeply the familiar smell of church: candles burning, dust, furniture polish, and the faint lingering aroma of incense. There was a statue of the Virgin, with rows of votive lights flickering at her feet, and that's where she knelt, to the most understanding mother of them all. She said her Hail Mary and then prayed her own prayer, asking for guidance. What should she do? Could she keep her baby and live in shame the rest of her life? Could she give it up for adoption, her own flesh and blood? And Jack's, she reminded herself, and that brought on a fresh outburst of sorrow. How could he be so callous, so cruel? It was his child, too. But look how easily he was able to give *her* up! Men were horrible. She looked up at the serene face, at the sweet chubby Infant, and it came to her that motherhood was blessed by God. It was a sign to her. She would have this baby and, somehow, some way, she would keep it.

She was strong in her resolve. She knew that soon she'd have to find work, but for the moment she was very busy figuring out how she was going to do this thing, how she was going to manage it. All week the phone rang and rang. Most of the time it was Jack, and each time she heard his voice, that beloved deep rich voice, she hung up, her pulse hammering in her throat and temples. She was *not* going to go back to him, not as his secretary, not as anything, no matter how much she suffered.

By Thursday she was no closer to finding an answer. She even considered calling her mother in Norfolk. Her mother! God, her mother would kill her! And then, on Thursday, an envelope came in the mail from Strauss Construction. She almost threw it away unopened, but something told her not to; and when she opened the brief note, in Jack's handwriting, of course, a pile of twenty-dollar bills fell out. And her paycheck. The note said only that he was sorry she felt this way, that he'd told everyone in the office that she'd taken a medical leave, and that she would be getting her paycheck in the mail regularly. It was really over! He wasn't going to change his mind and come back to her. She thought her heart would break. No more his strong arms around her, no more his sweet urgent love, no more romantic dinners, no more secret rendezvous, no more, no more! She put her head down on the little kitchen table and wept bitter tears.

When the phone rang, her heart leapt up. It had to be him, saying he was a fool, that he realized she was his one true love. But it was only Frannie, calling from Long Island.

"Hey! You never called me yesterday. And now you're not in the office and they say you're on leave. What's up, Doc?"

"Huh?"

Fran laughed. "This weekend. With me and Ed. Our house. Garden Village. Remember? You were supposed to call and tell me what train you were getting. Say! Is something the matter?"

It was such a relief to tell Frannie the whole thing, such a load off her mind. And she was even able to smile when Fran said, "Well. Now we have to figure out what to do. You just come out as planned. Don't you worry, I won't tell Ed a word, not a single word." It was so nice, feeling that someone else cared.

Fran had married her cop, the one they'd met in the park. He was nice enough, red-headed, slim, with a ready laugh, but he wasn't Linda's type. And anyway, her plan was to marry somebody with a lot more class than a New York City policeman. But Frannie loved him and they seemed very happy together. To each his own.

They lived in one of the houses in Jack's Garden Village development out on Long Island. On Deena Road. There was a Linda Court, too, and a Sylvia Street and an Elaine Way. Linda was the one who got Fran and Ed on the top of the waiting list, and by the time Fran had her first baby, Barbara Linda, they were already living there.

She packed just any old thing and got herself on the right train somehow. Her mind was whirling around. Ed picked her up in the station wagon. He took her bag from her, gave her a hearty kiss on the cheek, and said he hoped she didn't mind him just dropping her off, but it was his bowling league night. "And anyway, I shouldn't even apologize. You girls always have plenty to talk about!" And he laughed. "Even after you spend ten hours a week on the telephone."

Frannie's living room was comfortable, early American maple with a big oval braided rug in front of the fake brick fireplace. But no originality. No class. Even so, Linda exclaimed over the new coffee table and over baby Barbara, who, as it happened, was screaming her pretty little head off.

"She's exhausted," Frannie said, and Linda privately thought that Frannie looked exhausted herself, pale and a bit pinched in spite of the big belly. But, when her friend came back after putting the baby down in her crib, she was full of smiles. "Let me get some nice screwdrivers and then we can go sit on the new patio and really talk."

"Screwdrivers! My, aren't we getting sophisticated! Vodka!"

"They're so much better than martinis. I never really did like *them*, you know. Gin, ugh!"

Linda smiled. "I always felt like a hick if I didn't order a dry martini."

"Me, too." They looked at each other fondly and Linda thought, We always could talk to each other about anything.

Sitting down together, Fran leaned over, putting her hand on top of Linda's, and gave her a look of sympathy. Her question was unspoken, but Linda answered it anyway. "I'm going to have the baby. And keep it."

"Oh, Linda. Is that smart?"

"I don't care what it is! I went to church and I prayed and that's what I've decided. I can't give it up, Frannie. It's my baby!"

"And his," Frannie said with meaning. "And what's he doing about it, I'd like to know?"

"He's sent me a bundle of money, Fran, almost fifteen hundred dollars. And he says my paycheck will come every week. I can do it."

"That creep! I'm sorry, Linda, but as far as I'm concerned, he's buying you off. I hate to say I told you so, but I told you so. I said, when push comes to shove—"

"Please, Frannie . . ." Once again the tears welled up in her eyes. "Not now. I know what you said, and you were probably right. But I love him."

"You don't *still* love him; you can't! Not when he won't even take responsibility for his own child!"

"Frannie! You seem to forget! Jack's got a wife and three children. He can't just leave them, not a chance!" It astonished her to hear herself defending him—and with his own words, too. "You can't understand, Frannie, your life is different. You have a nice husband, a lovely little house, a sweet little baby, another one on the way . . ."

"You could have all those things, Linda. You're still young. And beautiful."

"Don't you say abortion to me, Frannie! Or adoption either! Don't you dare!"

Frannie sat back in her webbed chair and heaved a great sigh. "All right. You're going to have this baby and you're going to keep it. Now, what we have to do is make up a really good story for you, one that everyone will believe."

Now Linda relaxed. They sat talking earnestly until it got very dark and then they went into the kitchen and sat at the table with paper and pencils. And by the time Ed Hollister got home at 11:05 P.M., Linda had become the grieving widow of brave Master Sergeant Lawrence McElroy of the U.S. Army Tank Corps, killed in action in Korea less than a month after his unit got there. "You only had one weekend together," Frannie intoned, her eyes wide with the drama of it all, "and then he was shipped overseas." It had been a quick City Hall wedding . . . hell, lots of people did that, Linda said, and Frannie agreed. "You don't have to give people a reason. All kinds of things happen in wartime." Oh, they had every detail worked out: he came from Oklahoma, he was twenty six when he was killed, he had dark eyes and dark hair. "You know why," Frannie said, giving Linda a look, and Linda nodded, dropping her eyes. She didn't want to think about Jack right now. Right now it was very important to believe in Sergeant Larry McElroy, aged twenty six, not terribly tall, with broad shoulders and a big grin. It was important to believe that she had fallen in love with him and that he was now dead. That way, if people caught her crying, she'd have a good reason.

They sat with their heads together, sipping their drinks. Frannie had made a whole big pitcherful; and every time Linda's drink got halfway down the glass, she'd top it off. By nine o'clock Linda was beginning to feel real good, real secure about everything. They got a little silly about Sergeant McElroy, making up three sisters for him—Suzie, Margie, and Ellie, all models and actresses. They decided the McElroys of Tulsa, Oklahoma, were oil-rich snobs who had a huge ranch and a private plane and tons of money. "So, of course, they won't ever have anything to do with *me*!" Linda said.

Frannie giggled, agreeing, and added, "They're mad he got married so fast and without their permission."

"They cut him off without a cent."

"Wrote him right out of their will."

"Boy, do they feel crummy now that he's been killed!"

"But you're too proud to contact them and tell them you're pregnant 'cause they'll think you only want their money."

This wonderful invention tickled them both, and they began to laugh hysterically, unable to stop, doubling over, gasping for breath.

Finally, Linda said: "Shame on us, laughing like this, when my husband's just been killed in action, fighting for his country."

Frannie got up and came over to give her a hug. "Oh, Linda, you're going to do it, you really are. You're going to be fine as long as you can laugh."

But she'd cried as much as she laughed; she'd cried plenty during those next months all alone in her apartment. But now it was all over and it was all worth it. Because here, by the side of her hospital bed, on his knees, tears filling his eyes, was Jack. He was kising her fingers and gazing at her with such tenderness!

He kept saying, "A son. My son. You've given me my son. I promise you, I'll always take care of him. Of you, of both of you." He was back, as she'd always secretly known he would be, as he had to be! "My son," he said again. "My son." He kept saying those words, in a tone of awe, as if she'd just given him the best gift of his entire life. And she had, by God, she had!

"Have you seen him?"

"Just before. He's beautiful."

She felt such a surge of love for him, for both of her men. "What shall we name him, darlin'?"

"Name him? Whatever your heart desires."

"Then I'll name him Jack."

"No!" The word exploded from him and he came to his feet in one swift motion, letting go of her hand.

"Jack!"

"I forbid it. No, absolutely not. Do you want people to . . . to think . . . to guess . . . to wonder? No!"

"Nobody will suspect anything, Jack. I'm a widow, remember? And you're my generous boss. What could be more natural?"

"Maybe. But anyway," he went on in a calmer tone, easing himself down on the edge of the bed, taking her hand once more. "Jews aren't allowed to name babies after anyone who's living, see? So I'd always feel funny about it. No, pick something else."

Now she was a bit hesitant. "Well . . . maybe I should give him my father's name—or yours. Say, Jack, how about *that*? What was his name?"

"No, Linda! You can't do that either! It would be so damn obvious. I can just imagine. Saul Solomon McElroy!"

Well, it *was* funny in its way; but she couldn't help feeling a little hurt. A minute ago he'd been kissing her hands and saying "my son."

He must have seen something in her face, because he quickly bent to give her a kiss and said very seriously, "Linda, I meant what I said before. I can't claim him, you can see I can't claim him. But I *will* always take care of him. He'll have everything a boy could want. I'll come and see him regularly and be like an uncle to him. He'll have a college education, and he can come into the business with me whenever he's ready. How's that?"

"Well . . ."

"And listen to *this*, Linda. I've got it! About the name, I mean. What's his name . . . the sergeant's. Your . . . *husband*. Your late husband, I should say."

"Larry."

"Lawrence. Perfect. What could be more natural than naming your little boy after his dead father? Come on!"

This decision seemed to make him very happy and he kissed her a lot, all over her face and her neck. She loved having him kiss her. "Jack?" she said.

"Mmm?"

"Are you glad Frannie called you to tell you about the baby?"

"Glad! I'm goddamned euphoric! I may send her a little present! Of course I'm glad."

"Because it's a boy?"

Was there the tiniest little pause? She couldn't really tell. And then he said, "Of course not! No I can't lie . . . I'm happy to have a son, finally. But what's with all these questions. I'm here, aren't I? I'm here and I'm so glad to see you. I really missed you, you know." He burrowed with his nose into her neck and then said softly, "I can't wait to get you into my arms again—if you know what I mean."

She knew, and her heart lifted. He still loved her, he was still her Jack, and he'd promised to take care of them forever and ever. Everything was going to be just perfect!

CHAPTER TWENTY-EIGHT

Sunday, August 10, 1952

Riding up the Taconic Parkway, Sylvia had opened the window of the station wagon and let the hot dusty wind blow her hair. It felt so free and the Westchester hills were heavy with greenery and brilliant summer blossoms. The day was typical of mid-August, lit with golden sunlight, somnolent, heavy with heat and the perfume of flowers past their prime, just on the edge of spoiling. Riding along, breathing in deeply, loving the feel of heat all over her body, she thought briefly that maybe she had made a mistake, not taking a bungalow at Wicopee like Flo and the rest of her friends this year.

But no. She'd done it for three summers, when Deena and Elaine were very small, and she had never really liked it very much. It didn't seem natural, somehow, only women and children, alone all week without men. And then the herd of men came up by bus late Friday, tired out, sweaty, expectant. And what they expected was a picture-perfect weekend, complete with picnics, ballgames, swimming parties, golf, tennis, sweet-smelling obedient children—and wives, too—not to mention perfect weather. And this was all to be presented to them, finished, complete, no work attached. God forbid a dish should need washing, or a child should be sick, or it should rain!

She didn't know what happened with the other women, but she hated it when Jack paced up and down, peering out the windows when it had the gall to rain, stinking up the whole place with his cigars and grousing about the rotten weather, the missed golf game, the spoiled pleasures. She always felt he was blaming her. Oh, he never said it in so many words, but she knew in her heart and in her soul that it was all her responsibility. After three summers of stomach-knotting tension every time a gray cloud appeared in the sky or a piece of meat burned or a child *kvetched*, she decided no more.

And besides, although nobody in the world knew but her and she'd never tell a soul, the worst bellyache of all came from the certainty that Jack was seeing other women in the city during the week. She didn't know it for sure, but she knew it for sure. So at the end of the third summer she made up a story that the girls were allergic. They needed to stay in the city. He found it very amusing—"I've got to be the only man in Manhattan who has to keep his children in the hot city for their health!"—but he never questioned anything medical.

The annual company picnic was compulsory. That's where they were heading right now, up to Mohansic State Park. Jack had gone up early in the big truck with the keg of beer and the boxes of hot dogs and cold cuts and charcoal and paper plates, while Leroy, who usually drove the truck, chauffered Sylvia and the girls and the potato salad and the cole slaw in the station wagon.

Sylvia turned to check on her daughters. All three of them were crowded into what they called the Back Back, playing some game or another with the baby and making her laugh. Sylvia smiled. She loved the open, unselfconscious sound of Marilyn's laughter; it was infectious. And it was pure happiness. Lucky baby, to know that innocent kind of happiness.

She used to be happy that way. When she was young and

full of dreams, she had believed everything her parents told her. They told her she was beautiful . . . that she would one day fall in love and get married and live happily ever after . . . that she was witty and charming and unusual and special. And was she? No, not really. But she fancied herself all those things, and more. Oh, sure. Papa called her his rebel and she loved it. What a swell sound that had. It made her really different.

But really and truly, had she ever rebelled against anything? No, not really, not truly. So she went to business—she had thought that such a big deal—but let's face it, it was her father's business, and the salary she earned from him he could just as well have handed her as an allowance. She lived at home, she behaved herself, she walked out with the right young men or with her sisters, she never dreamed of breaking any of the rules, not really. She was fooling herself, thinking herself such an independent woman! She was, in the end, the middle sister of three, who stayed in her father's house until she went to her husband's. *Independent*! Ha!

She learned how far she was from rebellion or independence as soon as she was married. Jack Strauss ran his household, period *fartig* finished. And he expected her to keep right on behaving herself. He, too, bragged about how funny she was, what a rebel; and he, too, was only talking. Jack made all the rules and her only way around them was to use her wits. So she used them. Like inventing allergies, for instance. At least, after that, she was able to keep an eye on him in the summertime. No more summer bachelor! Men! Why their minds were so often on sex, she didn't know. For the most part, it was messy and sweaty and why all the fuss over five minutes of heavy breathing? Men never seemed to care how a woman was feeling. They only wanted what they wanted when they wanted it. But she knew that if she was going to keep her wandering boy at home, she had to act receptive. Sometimes, in fact, she really felt eager, but how did a woman tell that to a man? *She* didn't know. But she tried to show him how much she loved him in other ways. He mustn't leave her.

She needed him. Why? Because she was so afraid. Afraid

of what? Better ask what she *wasn't* afraid of. She feared that
her children would get hurt; that something would happen to
Jack; that there wouldn't be enough money one day; but
mostly that Jack would become bored and leave her and then
what would she do? Because the biggest fear of all was *divorce*.

How could she make her way alone? How could she face
her family? Her parents? Her friends? How could she manage,
all alone, with little children to take care of? How could she
live without him? Divorce! Even the sound of the word was
frightening. Everyone knew what happened to a divorcee. She
was prey to every hot-blooded man and that meant all of
them. None of her married woman friends would dare to have
her around, afraid she'd seduce their husbands. She'd have to
move to a smaller apartment in a cheaper neighborhood. Who
would her daughters have for friends? No, divorce was unthinkable. Impossible.

So he didn't come home every night for dinner; lots of
men had to miss meals during the week. She could handle
it. Every once in a while she found a napkin or something
like that in one of his pockets, from a bar or nightclub. And
when she did, she crumpled it up and threw it away and put
it right out of her mind. It wasn't important. And who
knew? Maybe it really was business, like he said. When
you had small children, it was best just to believe. As long
as it didn't get out of hand; just as long as he didn't embarrass her in front of their friends. And he didn't. Oh, Jack
Strauss was clever and careful. When they were together, it
was "Sylvia darling" this and "Sylvia darling" that and hugs
and noisy kisses and jokes and presents. Jack was a big one
for presents, making his girls search in all his pockets for
what he had hidden, or making them all close their eyes and
put out their hands. Her, too. And it wasn't as if he brought
home cheap trinkets. Oh, no. Her pearl earrings were a
Thursday-night gift, brought home after he'd been out very
very late on Wednesday.

But he was not often out very very late . . . surely not more
often than most men. They had what she considered a good
working marriage. She left him to his business and he took
care of her. Men had their needs; they were different from

women, she knew that. What was important was that they loved each other and they loved their children and that the family stayed together.

Days like this were important, when she and the girls got all dressed up and went to Westchester to be with everyone from the office, to eat together and play ball and laugh and talk, something her daughters would have for a memory. They should grow up remembering how important their daddy was to so many people, how much he was loved and admired. They would be the center of attention all day long and she, for one, felt that was good for children every once in a while. Their daddy was the president of the company, and why shouldn't they have all the good things that came along with position? Why else was he working so hard, spending half his life out in the wilds of Long Island, arguing with suppliers and dealing with the unions and having all the heartaches and headaches of trying to build up the company if not to make a better life for his family?

When Leroy pulled into the big parking lot at the park, seven people appeared as if by magic out of the grove of trees to carry the salads and help them all out of the station wagon, crying out "Welcome, welcome!" and fussing over the girls and saying how beautiful they were and how adorable they all looked, dressed alike.

Well, they *were* adorable, wearing yellow pleated skirts with white middy tops trimmed in yellow and yellow ties. Elaine and Deena wore white socks with yellow trim and tan sandals, whereas the baby, Marilyn, still a toddler, had to wear her high-topped white shoes. How Marilyn had cried, how heartbroken she had been that she couldn't have "stwap shoesies" like the big girls. But now, being lifted out of the back of the wagon, the center of a cluster of admiring women, she was all gurgles and giggles, the insult of being considered a baby forgotten for the moment.

The best table under the leafiest tree had been saved for them, and within minutes of her seating herself, it was without doubt the head table in the grove. The secretaries and wives were more than happy to unload the food and set it out at Sylvia's direction. And someone was always fussing over Marilyn; she was passed from person to person like a living doll, making everybody laugh at her loud comments on everything. Like her sisters, she was a precocious little mite, full of notions and with a vocabulary, at the age of two that was really astonishing. And in the meantime the two older girls were charming everyone in sight. They were funny, those two, full of jokes and smiles. But always respectful, nothing of the wisemouth about *her* daughters!

She looked around, thinking how lovely this was, this beautiful day and the big old trees and the dappled sunlight and the women with their pastel dresses and bare shoulders and the sounds of laughter and friendly talk . . . just like an Impressionist painting, she thought. And when Jack appeared from the ball field with the other men and came up to Sylvia with a big smile and a big kiss, she felt so proud, she felt so complete, so secure. He might run around a little bit from time to time, but when push came to shove, she was his wife. And that's what counted in this world. Position was everything. She could still recall, years later, the smell of him, a bit sweaty, a bit dusty, but not much, and his aftershave over it all, and the feel of his rough cheek and his muscular arm around her, squeezing her. Let them all see what he thought of his Sylvia!

She was surprised to see Linda appear suddenly at the edge of the grove, carrying her brand new baby. "What's she doing here?" she asked, quickly adding, "Not that I mind, of course, but I thought she was taking a leave of absence." Linda had been Jack's personal secretary since she got out of Katie Gibbs and that had to be at least ten years ago. Jack would never hear anything bad about her although Sylvia had never really been able to warm up to her. She seemed a bit of a cold fish, behind that drawling Southern charm, a bit tight lipped and altogether too possessive of her boss and his time. Sylvia, for many months, had had to almost fight her to get to talk to him on the phone, until she spoke to Jack about it and told him he'd better put that young woman straight. "I only call you if it's important and you know it," she told him. "When *I* call, I should be put right through." And there hadn't been any more of that particular monkey business after that. She understood that a man and his secretary had a particular kind of closeness, that he depended on her and she knew all of his business, she had to. She didn't want to annoy him by acting at all jealous. So she was always warm and friendly to Linda— and in fact had bought a lavish baby gift when the little boy was born.

So now she said quickly, "It'll be so nice to see her baby . . . what's his name again?"

"Lawrence."

And no sooner was the word out of his mouth, than Linda was walking up to them, smiling her tight little smile. She said hello to Jack, and Sylvia didn't give her the chance to say anything more. She went right up to her, arms wide, saying, "Let me hold that beautiful Lawrence!"

Later, she wondered if Linda really had hesitated for just a moment . . . or whether it was something she made up. In any case, she held the bundle in its pale blue cotton blanket out to Sylvia, saying, "And where are those pretty little girls of yours? I've brought three lovely jump ropes with me."

The girls were already running over to her; they loved Linda. Well, you couldn't blame them; she always made such a fuss over them and she had the patience to play their little games with them for hours and hours. More power to her; Sylvia didn't have the *zetsflaysch*.

So it was a few minutes before she really looked down at the sleeping infant in her arms, pulling back a corner of the blanket so she could see all of his face. She loved babies; they were nothing but good. And those sweet chubby little faces, so innocent, so delicious.

Baby Lawrence opened his blank baby eyes just as she looked down at him and she stared at him while her brain froze and the world stopped dead. She had no idea how long she gazed down at him with her mind whirling around and around and the sounds of the picnic blurring together like a bad dream.

It was the face of all her babies, the same face! It might have been any of her girls there in her arms, chubby fists aimlessly waving, infant mouth making a little bubble, the round eyes already turning dark gray, shaded by incredibly long thick curling black eyelashes. She knew instantly, without the slightest doubt, not even a tiny shadow of a hesitation. This was Jack's child. *This was Jack's son.*

Her next coherent thought was no. No, no, no. It couldn't be; she was imagining it. She closed her eyes tightly and opened them again. Surely, this time, the resemblance would turn out to be a trick of the light and her jealous fancies.

He wouldn't have, he couldn't have. Not with Linda. Not after he begged and pleaded with Sylvia to have a third child and she had done it, done it for *him*, carried that baby for nine months, vomiting every morning and evening for the first three, feeling her legs swell up again, not able to sleep on her stomach, watching her belly and her face balloon slowly into shapelessness. For him she'd done it. For him, because he wanted so badly to try for a son, an heir, a man-child who would take over the business, who would work with him someday.

Every man wanted a son, and the male child she had conceived, she had lost, so she'd already felt a little guilty. He was convinced, when she became pregnant again this last time, that it was another boy. And she'd thought it might be nice, having a baby in the house again. Deena was already six and in school all day, a big girl with a mind of her own. As for Elaine, she had had a mind of her own since birth! They were very busy most of the time with their own little lives. It might be pleasant to have a little one following her around, asking those adorable questions, saying those adorable things, looking at her in that way they had.

She managed to forget completely that she always tired of toddler talk after a few minutes and hated playing kiddie games. She managed to convince herself she really wanted another baby. Because *he* wanted it. And, all through this pregnancy, she prayed only that it should be a boy, please dear God. When the doctor said it was another girl, she wasn't able to hide her feelings. She burst into tears and Dr. Lewis said, "There, there, now, Mother. You're just excited. She's a fine healthy baby. As soon as you hold her in your arms, everything will be fine."

Later, Jack insisted, "Sure a boy would have been nice, but

the important thing was that both mother and child were doing well."

She believed him. Of course she believed him; she had to believe him. She was weak with gratitude and relief. It was only another girl, but he wasn't going to leave her because of it. And until this moment she'd had no reason to think any different. He always called Marilyn his Golden Girl; told everyone the father must have been the mailman or the egg man because how did this family of gypsies, with their dark hair and flashing eyes, come by a little blonde? He loved to show her off, loved all the admiring comments. Her thoughts gave her a shooting pain in the middle of her chest that made her catch her breath. She couldn't bear it, she couldn't bear it! Such betrayal! Not only of her, of their marriage vows, of everything she'd thought she had and held dear; but of all of them, her *and* the girls. No matter what had gone on, no matter how bad he had made her feel, no matter how much shame he had given her, she had always been so sure that he loved her. So sure. And it was a lie, it was a lie!

She looked down at the sweet baby face there in the crook of her arm, so innocent, so sweet, so trusting, so unknowing, *so familiar*, so horribly familiar that she could no longer bear to look at him or hold him. She gazed down, unwilling to look up for fear she would reveal herself, her hurt and her rage. *What was she going to do, for God's sake?* But now was not the time to think about that; now she was in public, in front of all his employees and their families. She couldn't make a scene, not now and not here.

She did not know how she was going to look at Jack or talk to him or behave in any normal way with him. She did not know how she was going to live the rest of her life with him. With her pain.

Dimly, the sounds of her daughters' laughter and, in the distance, a ballgame, with its shouting, reentered her consciousness. She must do something. She must get this baby away from her. She moved rigidly to the carriage, bending over to lay him down, feeling like a puppet, feeling wooden and yet going through all the familiar motions, putting him on his belly, smoothing the covers, arranging the pillow, pulling the mosquito netting back over the top of the carriage, rocking the carriage for a moment and then, only then, turning and moving away as quickly as she could without looking as if she were running. *His child.* That was his child lying there in the carriage, his son. And she could not bear it, she could not bear it. What was she going to do?

She heard Deena's husky laugh, the sound of which had always made her smile. Deena had such a funny deep voice for a little girl, always had had and it had always amused her. Jack, too. Jack loved that voice; he always said, well, if he didn't get his boy, he at least got the voice. And that thought sent the pain lancing right through her, so that she had to stop and stand very still and take in a deep breath. The girls were sitting on a blanket on the grass under a tree with that blond bitch, that man-stealer, that whore. Even Moo Moo was sitting still for a change, babbling away but sitting still as they made daisy chains. She longed to run over there, to grab her daughters, her babies, and snatch them away. Linda rubbed her filth off on them by playing with them. Tonight they would all get baths!

She discovered, that afternoon, how difficult it was to play her part, even with such high stakes. But she found that she could do it. She smiled and she laughed and she joked and she chatted with everyone, even that whore. And Linda smiled back at her and gushed on and on about her girls and even talked about the baby's dead father, killed in the war. *Killed in the war!* And the bitch had the gall to squeeze out a few tears, totally overcome with her grief. Sergeant Lawrence McElroy of the Tank Corps, killed in action in Korea before he even knew he had fathered a son. A terrible tragedy.

How she had cringed inside, being forced to listen to this pack of lies, this garbage! There was even a snapshot, blurry and wrinkled a bit around the edges, of a handsome young man squinting into the sun. It could have been anyone, anywhere. Had Linda really known this young man in his neatly pressed uniform? Or had she picked up the photograph somewhere? Sylvia remembered looking at the snapshot of the anonymous soldier, feeling chilled to her bones. Someone had taken that picture, somewhere, and he had smiled at the person behind the camera. Maybe his real wife, his real sweet-heart. He had been a real person and that whore had stolen his life to use for her own purposes!

Enough! Enough! She had to pull herself together. After all, she was the boss's wife, she had a position to maintain. She was the hostess here, the mother of those three beautiful girls and it all had to be protected. The guilty would be punished in the end. But for now, *enough*. She drew in a very deep breath and smoothed her hands over her skirt. They were clammy with sweat. She would push it all away for now, push it down deep into her brain, where she wouldn't have to think about it. Later, she would figure out how to go on living.

CHAPTER TWENTY-NINE

Friday, January 31, 1986

The kitchen was aromatic with a mixture of sweet dough, cinnamon, and melting butter. Sylvia moved from place to place, sniffing and patting and stirring. Strudel always smelled good, from beginning to end. It also took a lot of time and mindless work, stretching the dough carefully so it didn't break, draping it over the edges of the clean table evenly; and this morning she needed a lot of time and mindless work to help her think. God knows she needed to think, badly.

Elaine had called last night. Sylvia knew she wasn't supposed to know anything about it; Jack had taken the call in his den, barking at her to hang up the kitchen phone. But she heard enough. Elaine had found someone stealing from the business, and Jack didn't want to know from it. How he had hollered! She knew that noise and she knew what it meant. The more cornered he felt, the louder he got. Elaine must have discovered something really big, the way he was bellowing and carrying on. He didn't realize it, but she had been able to hear every word, right through the closed door, the long hallway, right into the kitchen.

"Business should be kept in the office . . . I don't want to hear about it now . . . how many times do I have to tell you . . . you're going to spoil my dinner . . . how can you be sure

. . . I don't want your mother bothered by this kind of *narrishkeit* . . ." That kind of thing.

Usually, Jack talked with her about the business. After a bothersome phone call, he would normally come to the table and grouse and grumble and tell her all about it. But this time he sat down and began to eat without a word, pretending nothing had happened in there with their daughter. Not a peep out of him. So it was some kind of secret; she knew right away what *that* involved: that woman and her son. He couldn't fool her!

Over dessert, one of his favorites, her own homemade coconut custard pie, she asked him, innocent as a newborn lamb, "What was that, with Elaine?"

He shrugged. "Your daughter Elaine! One day, you mark my words, she's going to go too far with me, too far!"

She knew better than to argue with him. Elaine never knew how to handle him, never had. From babyhood she had always gotten under his skin. Not like Deena, who could wind him around her little finger. It wasn't that hard to do, God knows. Be sweet, make a little joke, give him a little kiss, let him know he was still king. How many times had she told Elaine? A hundred? A million? But it was like talking to a wall. Elaine only wanted to do everything *her* way. Sylvia heaved a great sigh. Elaine wasn't a little girl anymore, needing her mother's protection from her father's wrath. She was a grown woman, and a smart one, too. Mind your own business, Sylvia had told herself.

She took the sweet-smelling damp dough and began to pound it, grateful for the physical release it allowed her. Elaine was smart, yes. Maybe too smart. If she was going to be at the office so often, she was bound to come too close to the truth. And then, oy, *then* would there be questions! More than questions, there would be hell to pay! And what would become of all of them?

After all these years of hiding it, was the whole disgusting mess going to be exposed for the entire world to see? Was she doomed to relive all that pain again? She didn't know if she could take it this time. It had been so hard, keeping all those secrets. She had had to pretend to hear no evil, see no evil, speak no evil, *feel* no evil . . . like four monkeys in one.

Every summer at the company picnic after that first time, she had to look at that child and know what she knew and keep quiet, even keep her face from showing anything. And all the time her knowledge was a knife in her heart. When she didn't see him, she didn't have to remember that he existed. She could forget, then, about Jack and that woman. But through the years she was forced to face it, again and again, to feel that lance of pure pain shooting through her.

That Lawrence! Jack *had* to bring him into Strauss Construction, didn't he? Why? Why couldn't he leave well enough alone? Why couldn't he find him a job in another company? Keeping Linda on, well, that she understood. Sort of. She didn't like it but she couldn't ever say anything about it because then Jack would know that *she* knew. She didn't want to rock the boat. It hurt her, knowing about Jack and that woman. But on the other hand, she had three little girls; he was nice to them, he took care of his family. So why make trouble? Why start up? Why risk everything? So she kept her mouth shut and reconciled herself to Linda staying in the business, Linda being in the office every day of the week, Linda buying birthday presents for them in his name.

But why drag Lawrence in? They didn't really look *alike* but there was a definite resemblance. He was taking such a chance that someone would notice, that someone, someday, would put two and two together and get four. And she never believed Lawrence was all that valuable to the firm, not for one minute! He was there because Jack wanted him there, period, *fartig*, finished. You see, Jack? she told him silently, you see what you did to yourself by being such a smarty-pants? You helped him up the ladder and you see how you're repaid? You made sure he got to the top and that just made it easier for him to lie and cheat and turn on you. Agh!

She hated Lawrence. He had always been the true child of his conniving, seductive mother: smiles and wiles and practiced good manners. Oh, butter wouldn't melt in his mouth, that Lawrence! "Please may I, Mrs. Strauss?" and "Thank you, ma'am" . . . she knew how the two of them, the mother *and* the son, calculated every smile, every dimple, every "please," every "thank you." There was nothing genuine about either of them! As far as she was concerned, they were two leeches pretending to be decent human beings. It wouldn't surprise *her* to find out that they had been stealing from Jack! And never mind Jack, how about all of them: her, her daughters, her grandchildren even!

She marched around the kitchen table, pulling with practiced hands at the dough, stretching it evenly, not even thinking about it. None of this would be happening now, she thought angrily, if Jack hadn't been such an idiot about that woman. No, wait a minute. None of this would be happening if she hadn't had that miss between Elaine and Deena. She'd never forget it, never. All alone in the apartment, Elaine napping, and suddenly such pains in her belly, she staggered to the toilet, doubled over. She thought it might be food poisoning, and that scared her because she and Elaine had both eaten the same tuna fish for lunch. But it was so bad, she couldn't even check on the baby first.

She sat on the toilet, with waves of cramps rolling over her, pain after horrible pain, sweating, and becoming more and more frightened. If this happened to Elaine! And what if she couldn't get in to her. But the baby never made a peep. She never knew exactly how long she was there in the bathroom, dizzy and soaked in her own sweat. And then when she looked down, she saw the umbilical cord and the tiny baby in its sac and she began to wail. Her baby! Her new baby, dead! She had had a miscarriage, and all the time she thought it was a bellyache!

It was a little boy; you could see it. Jack's son, her son. If only she hadn't miscarried that baby boy. It had taken her years to get over that lost child—that was understandable, she had carried him for a full four months, she had felt life—but she *did* get over it. She never loved her daughters less because of it.

The moment that woman became pregnant, Jack should have sent her away. But no! By that time he was obsessed with having a male child. There was no sending her away at that point. He had to wait and see if *she* would produce a son for him. And what was wrong with his beautiful bright girls? she cried silently for the one-thousandth time.

Not a good idea, dredging all this up again. Sylvia stood still in her sunny kitchen and held a trembling fist to the center of her chest. It still hurt. Elaine and Deena had not been enough for him; no, he had to have that third child so much later. And then Marilyn, beautiful, golden Marilyn, hadn't been enough to satisfy him, either!

Once she had looked into the chubby cherub face of Linda's baby boy, once she had recognized him, then she had really steeled her heart. Nobody knew; nobody would ever know, not from her. But from that day she had tried very hard to make her girls strong women who would never, never need a man to make their lives complete. Maybe she'd done too good a job with Marilyn. Marilyn was a doctor, yes, independent, her own person, solid, substantial, doing important work. But deep in her heart Sylvia couldn't help feeling that her daughter was missing a big part of life, not having the joy of her own children. In a way, even though she knew it was probably old-fashioned, Sylvia felt a woman without children was only half a woman.

That was why she got married, really, to have a family. Oh, yes, she wanted a handsome man and a bright one . . . like her father. She certainly wanted to be in love with her husband. But the important thing was having children. And as for the *personal* side of marriage, that was something girls of her time just didn't think about very much. Certainly her mama never talked about it, except in very vague terms. The night before her wedding, Mama had said, carefully not looking at her, "Sylvia, about your wedding night . . ."

"Yes, Mama?"

"You love Jack, don't you?"

"Of course I do! You know I do!"

"Good. And he loves you. Remember that, tomorrow night, when the two of you are alone. Together. In bed. He's going to want you to do . . . men have certain appetites, you understand, that women don't. I'm talking about the marriage act, Sylvia darling. At first it's going to seem strange to you. But no matter what he does, it's all right. I know Jack, and he's a good boy."

That had been her sex education, sum and total. And, of course, it made her terribly nervous. *What* was going to be so strange? And how? And the answer was: everything was strange: the big double bed, her fancy white nightgown, Jack undressing in the bathroom and coming out smelling of shaving cream. And then him climbing in under the covers and turning to take her in his arms. And all she could think was: And now what do I do? But she didn't have to worry; he did everything.

Now when she thought back on it, she had to laugh. Today in the movies you could see more in five minutes than she and Jack did in the first five months of their marriage! But back then, oy, she wanted to die, she was so embarrassed. For a long time it hurt her, but, of course, she couldn't tell him. And then, every once in a while he cuddled her and stroked her gently and then she would find herself responding when he pushed into her, find herself feeling pleasure. There were certain ways he sometimes moved and certain things he sometimes did that she especially liked; but there was no way she could bring herself to tell him. My God, she didn't even know the words!

But I was a good wife, she told herself, understanding and patient and loving. And her girls were good wives, too, look at them, in their forties and still married to the same men. In this day and age, that was a miracle!

Of course, she added with a little pang, who knew how long she could say that about Deena and Michael? Something was very wrong there. Look how he left her on that cruise and came back early. From a second honeymoon yet! Rolling her strudel slowly, carefully, patting in into place, Sylvia shook her head. Not good, not good at all. Still, it was a good thing he came back in time to deal with Saul. And that was another heartache, that Saul. Such a lovely, smart, loving boy, to all of a sudden get into such trouble! She couldn't understand how Deena had missed the signs; she'd always been so good with the children, such a devoted mother.

Not like Elaine going back to business right away, leaving a year-old child with a *shvartzeh*. Not that Elaine was a bad mother, she added quickly. Noel might be a bit of a wise guy, but smart! He was at Princeton, a handsome boy, an athlete, and very popular. His mother's looks and his father's sweet nature, how could he go wrong? Deena never went to work at all until her baby, Saul, was almost thirteen, and then it was only part-time and in the neighborhood. In his own school!

But it was plain as the nose on your face that something was bothering Saul a lot.

She slid the aromatic, shiny roll of strudel onto the baking pan, curving it around itself, sprinkling it with cinnamon sugar and chopped walnuts. Yes, there was something very wrong in that household. Another woman? No, never! Not Michael! He could send you to sleep talking about ethics and morality! She remembered thinking that at least, with him, Deena would never know the heartbreak of an unfaithful husband. Still, at nineteen Deena was so pretty, so lively, so full of fun, so popular with the boys . . . what had been her hurry? Why had she thought she *had* to marry him so quickly? Why had she thought she would die if she didn't have *him*? To Sylvia, he had always seemed a bit of a stiff . . . extremely good-looking, without a doubt, and smart. But distant. She'd never said it to Deena, she never would. But she had never stopped wondering what in the world her beautiful sparkling witty daughter saw in such a prig.

Jack was at least partly to blame, and she had told him so. "Why are you pushing that young man on Deena?" she had demanded all those years ago. "One, she's too young to tie herself down; and, two, I don't think he's the right man for her." But would he listen? One, she was only a woman, and, two, Jack saw him as mature, steady, solid, safe. And maybe, Sylvia had often thought, maybe Jack saw Michael as a man who would never be a real rival for his daughter's esteem.

In the end, though, a woman picked her own husband in spite of anyone's liking or hating him, in spite of anyone's advice or opinion or good intentions. Deena had been utterly taken with him, just completely wrapped up in getting him. The more he backed off, the more she wanted him. You couldn't talk to her! She didn't want Paul or Hal or Jerry or any of the cute young fellows who came around. She wanted only Michael Berman.

Sylvia slid the pan into the oven, wiped her hands on her apron, and stared blindly into the blank oven door window. If only she had been able to really talk to her daughters, to tell them the truth about everything. But in her day you told a little fable to your children about your marriage. Come to that, you told the whole world that fable, including yourself. You told yourself a story; you told yourself that you had a good marriage, it was better than most. You told your daughters that a good marriage was a matter of give-and-take.

What you didn't tell was that you gave and he took and if anything went wrong, it was your fault. Of course you didn't say that to a young woman in love. Would she hear you if you did say it? Of course not. And where did it all end up? In her day, you stuck with it, through thick and thin and anything else that came along. Now? Now was different. Didn't she read in the *Times* the other morning, there was an epidemic of divorce in this country. She had a premonition that Deena was going to get a divorce. And then what? Could a woman be better off all alone to make her own way? After all those years with the same man?

If Deena came to her, Sylvia thought with a bit of self-disgust, and asked what she should do, she wouldn't know what to tell her. She'd have to say, "I don't know one divorced woman who's happy, who isn't miserable and lonely and looking to get married again." She'd have to say, "Better the devil you know." She'd have to say, "Don't ask me, Deena, what do I know from divorce? I'm a happily married woman."

CHAPTER THIRTY

Saturday, February 1, 1986

Up out of the subway station and right into a blast of icy wind cutting across Fifty-first Street. Brrr! Dreadful! Linda McElroy pulled the sheared beaver collar of her new coat, a Christmas gift from Jack, up around her ears and cuddled into it. Somehow she felt no warmer. The subway had been over-crowded and smelly and disgusting, as it always was these days; how she hated it. For years Jack had yelled at her, "You could afford a cab, goddammit, Linda! It's only a couple of bucks, for God's sake. What the hell is wrong with you, any-way, always playing poor?" Playing poor! She wasn't playing anything. It was only a couple of bucks to *him*, sure, he had plenty. But she was a working woman, on her own, with no-body to depend upon. She had a fine son, but she'd never in this world, ever, ask Lawrence for anything. He had his own life to live.

Another gust blew dirt into her eyes, and she ducked into a doorway to get a tissue from her bag. This coat, she decided, was a mistake. She should have gotten a fur. He should have given her enough money for a fur; in fact, he should have *suggested* a fur coat. This was one present from him she didn't like, didn't even like the way he'd given it to her. Handing her five one-hundred-dollar bills and saying, "Get yourself a new coat." She'd felt so cheap, so hurt, she couldn't even speak, could hardly look at him. He'd never given her cash before, ever. It was always a beautifully wrapped box . . . even the year he gave her a new refrigerator, oh, years and years ago, he'd gone to the store, he'd picked it out, he'd had it delivered, and he'd come up before she got home and put a big red ribbon around it. He used to be so romantic, so thoughtful.

She stuffed the tissue back into her bag, feeling that familiar clutch of panic around her heart. Don't say *used to be*, she told herself, don't even think it. But she couldn't stop herself. Lately, he'd been so . . . different. She didn't know what to make of it, and every time she started thinking about it, she got a sick feeling. He'd come by only two or three times in the past six months or so. The sex part had slowed down a long time ago; she had gotten used to the fact that he hardly ever wanted to go to bed. That was all right with her; she had never liked it all *that* much. Sex was something men wanted awfully bad and they were willing to do many things just to get it. Once she'd learned that, she knew what to do . . . when to hold back, when to give in. And didn't it get her Jack? Once again, just thinking about him, that pain grabbed at her. Because maybe she was losing him, and the thought terrified her. It made her feel the way you felt when you stepped down, expecting more stairs, and they weren't there. She couldn't lose him, what would she do without him? It would be unbearable!

She wasn't going to lose him and that was the end of it. She couldn't and she wasn't going to. That's why she was on her way to the office today, on a Saturday in February, when she should have been on her cruise. She always took a cruise, every February, into the sunshine, into the Caribbean, saved her own money for it. She always went with a girlfriend, usually Marian Clemente, a widow living down the block. It was her time of freedom and, okay, so if she met a nice man and he wanted to get romantic, buy her dinner and nice little souvenirs, she wasn't going to say no. She had had

a couple of shipboard romances over the years, but she had
always ended them at the dock and come back to Jack. She
was his lady, he always said so, "You're my lady, Linda darling, my special lady," that's what he'd say. That's what he
used to say. Oh, Christ, she had to stop this!

Now she was right in front of the office building. Now her
heart started pounding and her hands began to sweat. She
didn't like this, didn't like it a bit. Why was she sneaking
around, trying to catch him in the office with a woman? Those
other times, when he got a crush on someone else, she'd never
done anything, just waited patiently and made believe she
didn't see he was behaving any differently. And he always
came back to her. She knew he would. They had something
special. They loved each other. She'd given him his son.
Once, he'd said to her: "If I'd only met you first, Linda . . .
who knows?"

So what was she doing, at this stage of the game, trying to
spy on him, canceling her vacation, even, because she was
scared that when she got back, he'd call her in and look serious and clear his throat and tell her they were finished. Oh,
God, no! Please no!

What she ought to do was turn around and take herself
right back to the subway station and go back down and get the
Number Four to her stop and go home and forget this nonsense.

But she couldn't. She couldn't. This time was different.
This time there was something icy cold about the way he was
treating her. Oh, he was all surface sweetness, but she knew,
she knew. A woman always knew. He forgot their dates. Their
regular Wednesday dinner wasn't regular anymore. Or she'd
catch him looking at her, just looking at her, in a way that
made her blood run cold. Things like that. And when she tried
to talk about it, to ask him what was wrong, what had she
done, he had only said that he didn't know what she meant.
He never promised her a rose garden, and she knew how
complicated his life was.

Monday, after the others had all left, she went into his
office, and when he lifted his head from the papers and saw it
was her, there was such animosity in his eyes! What had she
done? "Jack! What is it?"

"What's what?" he said. And when she began to tell him her fears, he interrupted her. "Haven't we always had a rule, about the office?"

"But you've been acting so cold and strange to me. . . ."

"Dammit! We'll talk another time!" And he went back to his work. She might as well disappear from the face of the earth for all the attention he was going to pay her.

That's the way it had been. After she'd had that little to-do with the girls, with Elaine and Deena, she'd thought maybe *that* was it. Maybe he was mad at her, that she didn't deny their love outright to his daughters. She'd had many bad dreams about that confrontation, wondering if she'd admitted too much. But he'd never said a word to her, not one single word, and if there was one thing she knew for sure about Jack Strauss, it was that he wasn't shy about saying whatever was on his mind.

So it had to be another woman. Another woman. Impossible! Unthinkable! And yet, and yet . . . it had to be. There was no other reason for him to snub her.

That did it. Her mind was made up. Right into the lobby and right into the elevator and up, without another backward look or thought. After forty years—*forty years*—of being totally committed to him, of sacrificing her life to him, her body, her devotion, her very soul, she was not going to give him up, not without a battle!

On the way up she examined herself carefully in the mirrors that lined the walls, smoothing the soft shiny hair which she still wore in a pageboy because Jack loved it. Fifty-nine years old but nobody would ever guess. No face-lift either, just Ivory soap and Oil of Olay and a light hand with the makeup. That was the ticket, once you were past forty: subtle and careful and soft colors. Feminine.

She smiled at herself to make sure there was no lipstick on her teeth. Nothing looked worse on a woman than stains on her teeth when she smiled. It looked careless, sloppy. Grooming was everything. She looked . . . well, pretty. Yes. Pretty. Even more than pretty. A lot of blondes went all wrinkled at an early age . . . that fine, delicate skin . . . but not her. And she was a natural blonde, born blonde. She colored her hair now, of course, but its honey color was an almost exact match

for the curl her mother had cut from her hair at the age of three
and saved. She was proud of being a blonde, of being born a
blonde. Proud of her green eyes that slanted just the tiniest
bit... and the long curling eyelashes. Her mom and dad
called her their little beauty and that's why they named her
Linda because it meant "little beauty."

She was as pretty now as when they first met; there wasn't
another woman her age who looked as good. If she'd gone on
The Norway this year, as she and Marian had planned, there
would have been a dozen men buzzing around her, just like
always. Jack would have to be a *fool* to give her up... even
for a younger woman. What woman, no matter how young,
knew him the way she did, cared about him the way she did?
No other woman could take her place! Surely he realized that!

And now it was really happening and her heart was hammering painfully in her throat and she could hardly swallow.
She could still turn back. Sometimes it was better not to know.
But she couldn't. This was how it started with them all those
years ago, on a Saturday afternoon, the two of them alone in
the office, carefully not touching as they handled files and
correspondence. And so aware of each other. She remembered
every moment of it, every step they took, every glance, every
indrawn breath.

And then Jack had suddenly stood up, banging his fists on
his desk so that she turned, startled. She'd never forget the
glittering look of him, never, not as long as she lived.
"Linda!" he said in a strange voice. "Come here." She didn't
stop to think, even for an instant, just went, and as soon as she
was close enough, he reached out with his strong arms and
pulled her into him, almost crushing her, and kissed her. She
could still recall the little electric shock she got at the touch of
his mouth on hers. And when he lifted his head, he said, "Oh,
God, we can't, we can't!" and pushed her away from him.
And then that summer he sent his family away and then it
really began.

But it had started on a Saturday in winter in the office in
the middle of dreary day, just like this. She crept down the
hall as quiet as a mouse on her tiptoes. There was a light
slanting from under the door of his private office. Now her
throat really went dry. She didn't want to believe it. He was

there. Now she was going to put her hand on the doorknob and swing the door open and—

Oh, Jesus, what *was* she going to do? If he was alone, she had it all planned out. She'd act surprised that he was there and make like she'd forgotten something and was just in the neighborhood so she thought she'd drop by and pick it up. That was easy. But what to say if she found him with someone? Her mind always dithered around when she tried to rehearse what she'd say then. She'd just have to wait and see what *he* had to say for himself. She'd know then what she had to do. It would come to her.

She stood still for a moment, drawing a breath and preparing herself for the worst. And then, just as she'd thought it so many times, she put her hand on the knob and she turned it and that moment she heard the murmur of voices and *it was a woman*! And then she didn't even have to think, it was as if she were propelled. She pushed the door open with a might shove, yelling as she strode in, "Just what in hell—?!"

And then stopped dead still in amazement. Holy Mary Mother of God. Not Jack and a woman. Elaine. And Deena. "Just what in hell," she continued, "do you think you're doing here?"

Elaine and Deena had been completely engrossed, sitting one on each side of Daddy's huge rosewood desk, marking and collating the copies they'd made. It was tedious idiot-work, not really needing any thought; so they were talking.

They'd been in the office since eleven o'clock, letting themselves into a strangely dim and silent space. Deena was nervous. "I feel like a thief," she said as Elaine groped around for the light switch.

"Really, Deena!"

"Well, that's what it feels like, like sneaking in."

Elaine laughed. "It feels like sneaking in, because it is, dummy! Oh, Dee Dee, don't look at me like that . . . there's a good reason for it."

"I have to think so, don't I? Since I don't understand half of what's going on."

"You said thievery before? *That's* what's going on:

thievery. And we're here to catch the *ganef*! The lousy little thief! Oh, when Daddy sees what I've found—!"

"You're enjoying this, dammit, Elaine! You're having a good time!"

"Damn well told." And why shouldn't she? She was the smart one who discovered it. Daddy didn't think she was good enough or tough enough or man enough for his business? And El Crooko Lawrence *was*? He'd soon see what was what and who was who! She couldn't help it . . . she had to laugh with excitement and sheer pleasure.

Deena of course hated *that*. "You sound so damn gleeful. Someone's been stealing from Daddy—from *us*—actually—and you're chortling and rubbing your hands together."

"I am, I am!" By this time they were in the file room and she was digging for what she wanted, so she didn't see the look on Deena's face. But she heard the disgusted snort.

"Well, I don't like it."

"I know you don't. And I'm sorry. But you keep forgetting, Dee Dee, that you and I had two different fathers. I've been waiting for a chance to prove to him that he's all wrong about me. You think I'm happy he's got problems! No, no, you're wrong! I'm happy all right, but only because it's *me* who's uncovered the mess and it's *me* who's going to fix it up. This time, I figure, he'll have to stop condescending to me. He'll have to admit, in front of the whole world, that I may not be a son, but I'm perfectly capable of taking over the business anyway."

That got to Deena of course. She was so tenderhearted. "After all these years . . . you *still* feel the same way about him?"

"Doesn't *he* feel the same way about *me*? And, by the way, Deena dear, don't *you* still think he's king of the world?"

"No! Well . . . yes, maybe." And then they both had to laugh.

"The only thing harder than being someone's kid," Elaine said, hoping this way to end the subject once and for all, "is being a parent. Noel shows up from school, hugs me and kisses me, tells me he's missed us, he only wants to sleep and eat and be with his family, right? So he's in and out at all hours and I never even *see* him and I come home the day after

New Years's from the office and there's a note saying he's gone up to Cambridge with his friend Josh. My God, he just got back from California, two days before New Year's! So what I'm trying to say, Deena—Deena, what's the matter?" Her sister was scowling and twisting her hands together as she had always done when something bothered her.

"Noel's been out of town so much?"

Elaine laid out the papers she needed, glancing at dates to put them in order. "I didn't know you cared," she quipped.

There was a pause, and then Deena said in a worried voice, "Dammit, Elaine, something's going on with Zoe. She's been out very late every night since she got back from Stowe . . . no, no, that doesn't bother me. But she's let me think she's been with Noel. Of course I believed it; you know how those two are."

"You know what that means. She met someone skiing, that's all."

"Yes, probably, but . . . she's never been secretive. If anything, she's been perhaps a mite too forthcoming. I mean, I know more about her sex life than I really want to. But this time . . . I can't describe it, but it makes me uneasy. And if it's just a new boy in her life, how come she hasn't told me? I've heard about every last one of the *others*, God knows!"

"So you think. Deena, Deena, you can't remember your own teenage years and believe that your kid will tell you everything!"

"It's not that I want her to; she just does. Or, anyway, she *did*. I even asked Judy—they were at Stowe together—and she looked blank and said, 'Zoe? Hell, no. She wasn't into partying at all. You aren't going to believe this, Mom,' she told me, 'but it was Judith Eleanor Berman who was the popular one this time. Zoe went to bed early every night and was practically the first one on the slope in the morning!' So . . . now I don't know what to think, Lainie. And I don't know what to do about it."

"Do? That's simple. Ask her!"

"You don't understand . . . it's not so easy. I think she's lying to me and I'm really afraid she'll lie again."

"A kid is lying to her mother? So what else is new? Come on, Deena, get off the Perfect Mother bit, will you? Kids really bring themselves up, you know. We only *think* we're doing it. God, I can't remember even toilet-training Noel; one day he was wetting his pants and all of a sudden, he was saying wee-wee and taking himself to the toilet. And I haven't asked him where he's been late at night since he was sixteen and had his first girlfriend."

"Well, you're different from me."

"You want to know what I think, Deena? I think you're overly involved with your kids, I really do. You worry about every goddamn thing and it doesn't do a bit of good! When they're ready to grow out of a thing, they do. God, I remember a year when Noel didn't say two truthful words in a row . . . just made up whatever sounded good to him. And one day, it just stopped." For a split-second she felt that little ping of doubt. There were still times when Noel was charming her, telling her tales, when she wondered if he knew where truth ended and fantasy began. But that was silly. He was just a bright, creative young man with an excess of energy, that's all. After all, he was at Princeton, wasn't he? You didn't make it in the Ivy League without being a cut above the average.

Deena asked, "Don't you *ever* worry about Noel?"

"Never. Why should I? He's doing just fine and, look, Deena, you're the one who's always going on about how children have a right to their privacy and dignity and individuality . . . ha! Gotcha, didn't I? Zoe's fine. She's probably in love for the first time and it's too beautiful to spoil by telling *Mom*, for Christ's sake!"

They were laughing, in fact, when the door banged open and there was Linda, all slicked up, red in the face, screaming her head off. "Just what in the hell do you think you're doing here?" She looked ridiculous.

Very very calmly, in the hopes of bringing Linda's blood pressure down somewhat, Elaine said, "Working. Daddy gave me a key, remember?"

Oh, she was a cool one, that Elaine, thought Linda. Turning the papers over in case I should walk over there and see what it is she's doing. If she thought she was fooling Linda McElroy, she had another thing coming.

"Working?" she repeated sarcastically. "Well, all I can say

is, the two of you sure look guilty for people who are merely working."

Elaine gave a dramatic sigh. Lawrence was right, Linda thought, she was a bitch on wheels. Always so infuriatingly superior, always had been. And never the manners to hide her disdain. Even as a little girl she could give you a look from those blue eyes, calculating and scornful, trying to make you feel small. Something she'd learned at her mother's knee, no doubt.

They *all* did it, looked down their noses at you. How many times had Jack said it to her: "Sylvia married beneath her, oh, yes, she did." Of course, he laughed when he said it; he pretended it didn't matter to him. But she knew her Jack. It must still rankle; it had to. Imagine living with four of them, all putting on airs!

"Wrong," Elaine said. "We were surprised, that's all. I mean, Linda, you *did* make quite an entrance. You can't blame us if we were startled. And, come to that, what're *you* doing here?"

"I? Well . . . I . . . I forgot something. I came back to look for it."

"In Daddy's private office?" Oh, that smarmy smile! How she'd love to slap it right off Elaine's face. Thought she was so smart!

"No, not in your father's private office. But when I saw a light, and I know that no one's supposed to be here, well . . ."

"You just happen to be wrong, Linda, that's all. I'm supposed to be here. And I *have* to be here on a Saturday because I have another business that I run during the week."

On and on she went. Linda didn't really *care* why they were there. Jack had made a terrible mistake in the first place, putting his daughter on a big project when she didn't know diddly-squat about the business. That's what Lawrence had said, and he was right. It was Daddy giving his little girl a new toy to play with and, as far as Linda was concerned, it was wrong. And it was so unjust! Lawrence should be in charge of all the projects. He'd proved himself over and over again. It just wasn't fair to give that cow the right to come in any damn time she wanted and trample all over everyone, acting as if she owned the place, going into private files. But you couldn't say a word to Jack; he'd snap your head off.

After all those years she'd spent, being nice to his spoiled brats, smiling at them, playing endless stupid games with them, bringing them presents she couldn't afford, when all the time she was hurting inside just at the sight of them, his "real" family! After all the years she'd spent with him, listening to his sweet words and believing all his promises about "some-day," giving totally of herself and asking so little in return!

All she ever wanted or expected was that her son, *their* son, should get his birthright. Those little girls always had so much, everything they wanted, *more*—while her beautiful, brilliant boy had to scrape along on the leavings. And as if that weren't bad enough, they snubbed him, they made him hurt and they made him cry . . . he, who was worth a hundred of them!

"Look," Elaine was saying, "my father put me in charge of the Ninth Avenue Project and I've got to do a superior job. You know that. I have to *prove* myself." She rolled her eyes and smiled. You almost couldn't help smiling back. They did have charm, the lot of them. That, they got from Jack. "So here I am, on the weekend, going through papers with a fine-tooth comb. We're just about done. So you don't have to worry. We'll lock up. And turn out all the lights."

Miss Superior was not going to get rid of her so easily. "I hope," Linda said in her coolest tone, "that you're not sug-gesting that Lawrence doesn't do his job properly."

"We're not implying anything," Deena said. Oh-ho, an-other county heard from! "Don't get so excited. Elaine's not trying to take Lawrence's job."

Linda couldn't believe her ears. "The hell she's not!"

"Linda!" Deena and her big innocent eyes! Well, they couldn't fool Linda McElroy. She knew that she and her boy were being pushed out, after all their years of devotion and hard work.

Lawrence had told her to stay out. "Ma, Ma," he said the other night, "quit, will ya? It's no big deal. I have too much work as it is and this project has been a royal pain in the ass since the beginning. *Nobody* wants to spend that kind of money on a place on Ninth Avenue! You know what's across the street? A whorehouse . . . a *busy* one!" How he laughed. "I say let the fat cow moo over it and chew it with her cud and let *her* try to get the damn thing finished and sold. It's fine with me."

But she didn't care *what* he said. Lawrence was a saint, so patient and sweet and long-suffering; but a mother knows her son and she knew that inside he was deeply hurt.

"You can both stop with the innocent act!" she said. "What do you take me for, anyway? A *complete* fool? By all rights Jack should be handing over the entire business to Lawrence!" She could hear her voice rising and she wanted to stop it but she couldn't.

Elaine stopped smiling and her voice became syrupy sweet. "Now, Linda, take it easy. We all know how hard Lawrence has worked and how very valuable he's been to Daddy. . . ."

What the hell did the bitch mean, he *has* been valuable? How dare she? *How dare she!* If she and Lawrence were to be thrown aside, then, by Jesus, Jack Strauss could have the guts to do it himself! Not send those overdressed, overstuffed, self-important snobs!

"Goddamn you!" she shrieked. In a corner of her mind she knew she was going out of control, but it was only a corner, and she was able to ignore it. She was shaking in her anger, yes, and in the joy of finally, *finally* doing the right thing! "Very valuable, very valuable, you *bitches*! The *most* valuable! That's what he is, the most valuable. Yes, yes, and more than that, he's the most valuable person in the world to Jack, the one Jack *loves . . . the . . . best.* Don't either of you say a word, not one more word, do you hear me?" The heat was climbing in her face, burning on her cheekbones, burning her from from head to foot. Take his birthright away, would they?

"Yes, he's the one Jack loves the best and he's the one who should be taking over the business, and would you like to know why? I'll tell you why. Because he's Jack's own child, his son, his only son!"

She heard herself laugh as she watched those two pretty, vapid faces pale and crumple. "And what," she demanded triumphantly, "do you have to say to *that*?"

There was a terrible silence for just a minute and she felt a surge of panic. She didn't really know these women; what if they got violent? Jews were a volatile race!

But all that happened was that Elaine said, in a flat voice, "You're a liar."

"Liar, am I? Well, I can prove it."

"And what about Sergeant McElroy?"

Again, Linda had to laugh. It was wonderful, the way she'd had everybody fooled, all these years. Even Lawrence. "Sergeant McElroy!" she repeated sardonically. "I made him up. I invented him. An old wallet, thrown in a trash can: that's where I found the snapshot. It was perfect; you could hardly see the face, but it was a soldier and I had something as proof. It's wonderful, you know, how people accept pictures. Oh, yes, my dear girls," she repeated, eyeing them carefully. They seemed rooted to the spot, frozen. "Oh, yes, Lawrence is Jack's. And mine. He's *our* child, the living proof of our enduring love." That sounded good, she thought, that sounded right. "So you can start rethinking all your plans, Elaine, you *and* your mother. Because it's *me*, Linda McElroy, who gave Jack Strauss the son he always wanted!" And she couldn't seem to stop it, she had to laugh at them.

One minute, they were halfway across the room; the next, Elaine was towering over her. And then, *crack*! her hand smashed across Linda's face, snapping her head back on her neck.

"Whore!" Elaine cried. "Whore! How dare you!" She grabbed her sister's arm and said, "We're going, Deena. We have business to attend to. As for *you*, Mrs. So-Called McElroy, keep your mouth shut! If my mother hears one syllable of this, even a *hint*, I'll kill you, do you understand, I'll put a knife in your heart!"

And then they were gone, and suddenly she had to sit down because her knees had turned rubbery and all she could think was, Oh, sweet Jesus, what have I done?

CHAPTER THIRTY-ONE

Saturday, February 1, 1986

"No," Deena said. "I can't. Don't make me."

"You have to."

Deena kept shaking her head, no. It was all she could think, it was the only thought she could keep in her head. "No," she said again. "Not now."

"Now." Elaine was adamant.

"But why? Why can't we wait? I can't even think straight. Why can't we wait until we're calmer and have time to figure out what we want to do?"

"Because, Deena, this is a mess that's needed cleaning up for forty years. I don't want to wait even ten minutes more!"

They were sitting in a cab, a cab Deena didn't even remember getting into. She didn't recall leaving the office, or putting her coat on. But it *was* on; she knew it was on because she was curled in a corner of the taxi, clutching it tightly around herself, wishing to God Elaine would stop talking and let her go home. But Elaine with a notion was an irresistible force.

"It's not our mess, Elaine," she said finally. "I don't want to deal with it now."

"You never want to deal with anything painful. But this involves all of us. like it or not." She gave a harsh little laugh. "All these years I've been saying Lawrence is a bastard. Little did I know!"

"Elaine! How can you turn it into a joke, for God's sake?" Deena huddled herself deeper into the corner, putting her forehead—it felt burning hot—against the cold windowpane. She felt sick. If this part of her father's life was so different from what she had thought . . . if this part of his life was a lie . . . how could she trust the rest? Everything about him was called into question. And that meant everything in her childhood, all her best-loved memories. It was such a strange thought. "I feel lost," she said to Elaine. "Lost in a strange place."

"Small wonder! He's a liar! A liar and a cheater! You feel lost? I feel conned! All this time, all these years, I've known that he wished for a son. I laughed about it even; I mean, it's so typical of that generation. Why do you suppose I went and got a CPA I didn't want? Because it proved I could think like a man and achieve like a man and maybe even be as good as a man! And all the time he *had* his son. And all the time he led me on and lied to me and made me promises! Shit, he *knew* he was never going to give me a break. And why? Because he already had the son he wanted. That bastard! That no-good cheat! How could he do it to all of us . . . how could he do it to me? And always with his hugs and kisses and fucking *charm*! Oh, Christ, Deena, when I think about his glib performance as the doting father and the doting husband and the decent human being, I want to puke! I want to kill him!"

Deena heard her sister's words from a great distance. Somehow she couldn't seem to connect to it. "Poor Marilyn," she said.

"What—poor Marilyn? Why poor Marilyn, for Christ's sake?"

Now Deena opened her eyes and turned to look at Elaine. Her eyes felt scorched; there were tears behind them but somehow they would not come out. "If it's true that Daddy just wanted a son, then . . . well, Marilyn's borne the brunt of it, really."

"Oh, you think so? Well, Marilyn isn't here! Marilyn's never here! Fuck Marilyn. It's just you and me, kid. Like it's always been."

Deena sighed. God, she was weary. She felt as if she'd been through a war. Glancing at her watch, she was amazed to find that it was only one-thirty in the afternoon. "Why, Elaine? Why do we have to do it now? Just what do you plan to say to him?"

"Say to him? I've got plenty to say to him, and none of it words of love, believe me! He lied to me and he cheated me and I'm going to face him with it, right there in his club in front of all his cronies who think he's so wonderful!"

Deena winced. Once Elaine got started, she sped on like an express train. "Oh, Elaine, that's not necessary. Look. You're mad at him. I'm not. I'm hurt and disappointed and . . . a lot of things. But I'm not angry. I'm certainly not angry enough to be a part of a big scene. So *you* go and *you* yell, and later, I'll face him myself in my own way. Whatever he's done, I don't think it's right for us to go in there and humiliate him in public. I won't have any part of it."

Elaine took in a deep ragged breath. "Okay, Dee Dee. If you don't want a 'big scene' and if you don't want him humiliated publicly, then I suggest you come with me. Because if you're not there to hold me down, I'm gonna crucify him. I swear it. You know how I get."

Deena indeed knew how Elaine got. She thought of Daddy, so unprepared and open, staggering as Elaine poured her poison all over him. "You win," she said. "I'll go. But only if you promise to behave decently."

"I'll try. That's the best I can do."

The West End Club was in a handsome old town house, full of leather chairs and oak paneling and old Persian carpets —and, even these days, Deena noted, the strong smell of cigars. The club's elderly concierge, George, was dozing in his usual seat, right near the front door; and he looked startled at the sight of two women entering the sanctum sanctorum. The West End was men's-only. And then he recognized them. "You're Mr. Strauss's little girls, aren't you? Well, he's taking a steam."

Elaine, paying him absolutely no mind, stood on her tip-toes and craned over his shoulder. "No, he's not," she said in an irascible tone to match his own. "I can see him from here. He's in the lounge."

George grimaced just slightly. He had to let them go in, there was no rule against it; but he didn't want to, that was clear. In her best imperious way Elaine sailed on by him and Deena followed, feeling very like a small tugboat caught in the wake of an ocean liner.

They stood in the doorway to the lounge. Not that they weren't *allowed* in; but it was uncomfortable for a female. It was so obviously a male preserve, with heavy furniture, a big polished mahogany bar, spittoons from the year one, dark oil paintings of dogs and horses and guys with mutton-chop whiskers . . . the whole urban macho *megillah*.

Deena heard her father before she saw him. He was laughing. And then she saw him, leaning back on his stool against the bar, his white hair still damp from his steam-and-shower, his face tanned as always—from here, you couldn't see the lines—so that he almost looked young. He was telling a story, making everyone laugh. Deena stared at him, distancing herself from him, studying him as if she had never seen him before. And, in a way, she hadn't. He was a different man from the one she had always believed in. He had become alien. It was like having double vision, the man she didn't know superimposed over her familiar darling Daddy. I don't know him, she thought, I don't know him at all.

And then he caught sight of them. He stopped talking mid-sentence and pushed himself off the stool instantly, coming quickly toward them. "What is it?" he was calling out, "What's happened? What's wrong? Is Sylvia—?"

"No, no, don't worry. Nothing's happened to Sylvia," Deena said in a rush. She couldn't stand seeing that look of alarm on his face. But when she glanced over at Elaine, Elaine was glaring at her. I guess, Deena thought, I'm not supposed to be nice to him.

"Let's get on with it," Elaine muttered to her and, turning to Jack, said gruffly, "We need to talk to you. Now."

"Here I am!" He held out his arms. "So talk. But first . . . how about a hug and a kiss for the old man?"

"Not this time," Elaine said, but Deena had already stepped up to him, automatically lifting her lips for his kiss. Funny, she felt so terribly cold, so unmoved by his embrace and by *him*. "Dammit, Deena," Elaine went on. "You *know* we have business to do."

"Is there someplace more private?" Deena put in quickly, before he could ask any embarrassing questions.

"This isn't private enough? There's only my friends. Nobody will bother us."

Elaine said, "No, this isn't private enough. We need absolute privacy for what we have to discuss."

He frowned briefly, then grinned. "The last time you wanted that kind of privacy, Elaine, it was boy troubles. You got maybe boy troubles?" And then his smile faltered as he noted the undeviating set of Elaine's grim expression. Quickly, he looked to Deena and then, perplexed, said, "No smile even from *you*, Deena? No? Okay, then, you want absolute privacy, I'll give you absolute privacy."

They went down the hall and short way, where he led them into a small empty room, devoid of the plush trappings of the front of the club. Here it was white walls, tile floor, venetian blinds, vinyl chairs and tables. "A meeting room," he explained. "We rent them out to neighborhood groups." He gestured them to chairs but nobody sat. He didn't sit, either, but took a stance next to one of the tables, leaning against the back of a chair. Elaine stood, legs slightly apart, as if planted; and without thinking about it, Deena moved until she was midway between the two of them. She felt terribly awkward. She didn't know what to do with her hands, so she stuffed them into the pockets of her coat.

Before Deena could think of how to begin, Elaine started her story, beginning with wanting to come into his business, then backtracking to her childhood, then up in time again to her three visits to Malone, back to her CPA, up to her wedding day, when he had said something to her . . . Deena couldn't keep track of it. Daddy kept interrupting, saying, "Wait a minute, you lost me there," or "Where were we? At your wedding? Or at the project?"

Deena suddenly knew, very clearly, that this was an act, that he wasn't interested in getting it straight or in clarifying anything. He was trying to stall Elaine and he was getting a charge out of her growing frustration. "I can't understand what you're trying to tell me, Elaine. If you'd calm down and get to the point . . ." Deena longed to tell him to quit it, to stop pretending, to play straight with Elaine. And for the first time, she had just an inkling of what it was about him that Elaine found hateful. He was playing with her, baiting her.

So it was she, after all, who blurted it out. She just couldn't stand watching him do that for one more minute. "Daddy," she said very clearly and loudly, "we know all about it. That's what Lainie is trying to tell you. We know it all."

"What—*all*?"

"Oh, Daddy. Don't make it more difficult than it is."

"I don't know what you're talking about. I couldn't make heads or tails of what she was saying. And now you're talking riddles, too."

Deena gave Elaine a shut-up signal. I'm handling this now, she told her silently with her eyes. "Linda came in this morning while we were in the office—later we'll explain—and one word led to another and in the end . . . we know all about it, about everything. About *Lawrence*."

As she watched, he shifted mental gears—she could see it, she could actually see him, like an actor changing roles, and she went cold. He arranged his face to be chastened, serious. And then he began to talk. He was very good at talking, Deena thought, and wanted to weep because she was aware of him being very good at talking with warmth and sincerity. This must be how he did business, how he did family, how he did life. And she had never seen past the performance until now. Until now.

"Look, girls, I'm not perfect, I never said I was. I'm just a human being. And I've always tried to live my life in a decent, humane manner. And I think I've succeeded. Never mind that laugh, Elaine, you still owe me respect. I always tried to do the right, the decent thing. She was Catholic. She was all alone. She was afraid. I was never going to leave your mother, never! She's the most wonderful woman I've ever known, she's never uttered an unkind word, never had an evil thought, never called a person a name. How could I even think of leaving an angel like that? I loved her. I still do."

He stopped then, looking at them, and Deena thought, He's waiting to be congratulated on his sensitivity! Elaine laughed out loud, not a pretty sound. "If she was so goddamned wonderful and if you loved her so goddamn much, how come you cheated on her?"

"I'm only a man, like all men. I'm no saint. We worked together all day long and she was young and she was pretty, and, yes, she was crazy about me and maybe I liked that and there she was, a lonely widow—"

"Bullshit! She told us already: she made up Sergeant McElroy. He never existed."

"All right, all right, forget that. But all the rest . . . that's exactly how it was."

"Okay, so let's say you were carried away. You screwed her. Okay. But why didn't you stop there? Why didn't you find her another job, in another city? Why didn't you end it?"

"How could I send her away to a strange city, a woman alone, with nobody? She cried. I can't stand it when a woman cries. And then she got pregnant. When I suggested abortion, she nearly went crazy. I was afraid . . . and it was so dangerous, back then! She could have died, having an abortion. Lots of women did, you know. I couldn't treat another human being like a piece of garbage."

"How about me?" Elaine demanded, and then made a face. "Never mind, never mind. I don't expect you to understand what you did to me. Why did you keep her around after she had the baby, her and her bastard both?"

His lips thinned. "Careful, Elaine. Careful how you talk to me."

"Why the hell should I be careful with you? You've been cheating me all these years . . . cheating all of us! Favoring your bastard over your own child, giving him the business that I wanted and deserved, taking him under your wing and teaching him everything, that egotistical, womanizing shit!"

"I warn you, Elaine. You're going too far."

"Warn away. You've destroyed your credibility. Okay, let's say she couldn't have done it without your help, let's say the world made it awfully goddamn difficult for a woman alone to raise a child back then. Given all of that . . . dammit, you didn't have to keep her in *your* office, you could have gotten her a job somewhere else, anywhere else! And then, on top of it, you bring *him* in? Why? Why in the name of God keep them around where we all had to see them and deal with them?"

"It just seemed the right thing to do. And, in fact, Elaine, not that it's any of your concern, but it *was* the right thing to do. I still believe that."

"Bullshit. You kept her around so you could fuck her whenever you wanted!"

Oh, my God, Deena thought, no, don't. But before she could get the words out, before she could move a muscle, Daddy had, in three long strides, come up to Elaine, and smacked her across the face open-handed. Elaine cried aloud, "No, Daddy!" but it was already too late. He was standing there, purple in the face, and Elaine was staring up at him, blinking rapidly, trying not to cry. And across her cheek was the imprint of his big blunt-fingered hand, blazing like a brand. Never, never before, never in her life had there ever been even the threat of this kind of thing. Screaming and hitting: that was for the goyim. And now both of them had struck out at another person, both of them. Deena hated it, it was horrible. The whole family was careening out of control.

She marched up to him, putting herself between him and her sister. "Don't you dare!" she grated out. "Don't you touch her!" She surprised herself; she had never in her life even thought of confronting her father in anger like this.

They looked into each other's eyes. At first, his glared, filled with anger, and then they went glassy—with shock, she thought, shock that his sweet little Deena would dare to holler at him—and then kind of blank. She knew what that meant; he could see that fury would get him nowhere and now he was preparing to try to charm her with sweet reasonableness. He needed her on his side. But she didn't think so, not this time.

Then he shook his head a little, as if to clear it. "Strange," he said, "I just had a little dizzy spell. . . ."

From behind him Elaine said, "Oh, no, you don't! You can't pull that on *us*."

As if she hadn't even spoken, he moved to sit down in one of the vinyl chairs, continuing in a conversational tone of voice, "Don't worry, I've had them before. It's nothing."

"I'm not worried," Elaine spat out. "Don't worry about *that*. But you and I have to come to terms with this . . . this shit."

"Elaine!" Deena protested. Really, it wasn't necessary to inflame the situation.

"*You* be quiet, Deena. You're always ready to kiss and make up, no matter what's been done to you. You like to smooth the cover over the mess, hoping it will make the mess go away. Well, I'm here to tell you: it doesn't. The mess stays right there, underneath. So butt out."

Deena was jolted into total silence. Elaine was on the warpath and anyone in her way—even the sister she had brought along to control her—was going to get scalped, too. So she watched as Elaine advanced on their father. Funny, how much smaller he looked, sitting down, with Elaine looming over him, like the wrath of God in sweater and jeans.

"Hear me, Jack Strauss, and hear me good. You are going to get rid of them. Both of them. Now! God knows it's long past due!"

He waved a hand at her. "I'll take care of it. I'll take care of it."

"Linda goes, is that understood?"

"I'll take care of it, I said."

"No, that isn't good enough. *Is that understood?*" And she stood and waited until he nodded, then went on. "As of Monday . . . out. O-U-T."

"All right. I'll take care of it."

"Lawrence, too."

"Now, wait, Elaine, let's not get too damn hasty here. You can't believe it's right to punish *him*. All he did was get born. And anyway, I need him. I've trained him and he's damn good, he's loyal to me; and lately, he's been taking over more and more . . ." His voice trailed off and Deena didn't blame him. Elaine was looking as if she could kill.

"I know he's been taking over more and more, Daddy dear. That's my big complaint. You didn't want to hear me when I called you Thursday. But he's been stealing from you for at least a year. Probably longer! And I have proof. Think of it: Your loyal little boy has been kissing your ass and robbing you blind!"

Jack flinched and put his hand over his face. Too bad, Deena thought, too bad and too late. There was no hiding from any of it anymore.

Stubbornly, Elaine went on. "Lawrence is *out*, as of Monday. Say yes, damn you!"

"I'll take care of it. I said I would and I will. I'll do what you say . . . for your mother's sake."

"And I never want you to see either of them—your whore or your bastard, ever again!"

He pushed himself to his feet, looking more tired and lined than Deena could ever remember; he looked broken. "Enough, Elaine," Deena said. "You made your point. You got everything you wanted. Enough."

"It's okay, Deena darling. I'll survive even your sister." There was a hint of the old Jack as he tried for a grin and almost made it. "Even her, I'll survive."

CHAPTER THIRTY-TWO

Saturday, February 1, 1986

It wasn't my fault, Linda thought. None of it. I didn't ask those two to come snooping around the office on a Saturday. If they hadn't been there, it never would have happened.

As soon as she got into her own little apartment, she ran for the kettle. She felt frozen; a nice hot toddy would hit the spot. And that's what she was doing, bustling about in her own kitchen, with her own things, when the front door just burst open and there, smelling of the cold and looking *gray* and *awful*, was Jack in the doorway of the kitchen.

"Jack! Darling! What's wrong? Sit down, sit down." Those bitches; did they really run right to Daddy like the two spoiled brats they were, to whine to him and turn him against her? Yes, they certainly had, she decided as she fussed over him, trying to get him to take off his heavy coat and calm down a bit. The look on his face told her he knew everything. Oh, sweet Jesus, what now? She hadn't had a chance to think this out, to figure out what to say and *how* to say it. She had to be very careful.

"Jack?" she said again, moving away from him. "I'm mak-

339

ing a hot toddy this very minute. I just got in, would you
believe? Five minutes earlier, and you'd have missed me, but
oh, dear, don't think I mind, oh, no, I love seeing you anytime, you know that . . . it's just you haven't been here on a
Saturday for, I don't know how long . . . months. Maybe a
year. So I'll just get you a glass—" And then she stopped
scurrying around and turned to look at him and her voice just
withered in her throat. He was looking at her as if . . . as if he
wished her dead. It was pure hatred in his eyes, and it put
chills up and down her spine. "Oh, Jack, it can't be *that* bad."
She turned away to pour their drinks, saying, "Come sit with
me in the living room, where we can be more comfor—"

"*Linda*. Shut the hell up." She froze where she was, her
heart pounding painfully. Holy Mary Mother of God pray for
me now and at the hour of my death Amen. "I have something
to say to you. You have betrayed my trust. Don't interrupt me,
don't even open your mouth. I trusted you never to mess with
my family. You knew that was rule number one: don't mess
with my family. I made that clear to you from the very beginning. And I promised to take care of you and the boy and I've
kept that promise all these years. And you couldn't keep your
mouth closed, could you?"

Linda stared at him. Suddenly she remembered that old hot
look, back when he couldn't keep his hands off her, years
ago. He'd come charging in that door over there, bellowing
her name, like a great bull, and when he found her, his arms
would go around her and he would half-drag, half-carry her to
the bedroom. Sometimes they didn't even get all their clothes
off before he was plunging into her, snorting, his eyes glittering. No snarl on his face *then*, like the one now, that showed
his teeth and made him look dangerous. No spots of dark red
on his cheekbones.

Ah, but then he got angry with her only if he thought she'd
shown any interest in another man. Once she'd made friends
with the fellow across the hall, just friends, they had a cup of
tea together and sometimes went to the movies on a weekend
afternoon. It was *nothing* and what was she supposed to do
with herself all the times Jack was with his *real family*, doing
his *real family* things? She had a right to friends.

But he would have none of it. "You're mine!" he growled,

crushing her to him. "I need to know that you're always here waiting for me." And later, in bed, he said, "You don't understand, Linda, the thought of you with another man, just smiling at him, makes my heart stop." Oh, the idea that he was that much in love with her, so besotted that he couldn't even bear the thought of her talking to another man—it melted her.

But that was a different time and that was a different Jack from the red-faced fury who stood, still in his tweed overcoat with his fists clenched, glaring at her. "Listen to me, I've always played straight with you. I've never promised anything I couldn't deliver and I always delivered. I thought of sending you to Chicago after Lawrence was born. . . . I never told you that . . . but I didn't, did I? It would have been easier for me, but I always tried to do the best by you. You and him, both!"

Oh, yes, the best, Linda thought. When Lawrence was born, you fell on your knees by my hospital bed and kissed my hands for giving you a son. And he looked like you, too, and that pleased you. She could remind him right now that the day he knelt by her bed, he made her promises she'd never called him on.

"You took my youth from me, Jack!" she said, her voice trembling a little. "You needed *me*, not the other way around, but I don't suppose you remember that, do you? You strung me along for your convenience, for years and years, Jack, and don't you deny it! You strung me along, made me stop seeing anyone else, made me think that one day we'd get married. I was a convenience to you, that's all I was!"

"I never said I'd marry you, never! The fact is that right from the beginning I warned you! I wasn't one of those guys whose wife didn't understand him, none of that! I told you then I couldn't ever desert Sylvia and the girls and you *know* it."

"It's not worth arguing about now, Jack, what you said and didn't say back then! What's most important is, you've never acknowledged your son and *that*, I know quite well you promised. Oh, yes, Jack, don't you remember how you felt when Marilyn was born and it was only another girl? The end of your name? How you came to me and said, If only I could have a son!

"And I did it for you. I had your son for you, and what did

your son and I get in return? Second-class treatment and second-hand attention. I couldn't tell him who his father was, oh, no, he wasn't good enough to know! I wasn't *allowed* to give him your name, oh, no, he wasn't good enough. And—"

Ugly color stained his face. She'd seen him furious, many times, but never like this. The man looked apoplectic. "You're damn well told! That son of yours has *proved* he's not good enough, not for the Strauss name! That no-good son of a bitch has been stealing from me . . . did you know it, did he come home and tell Mama all about it? Huh?" He was advancing on her and Linda backed up. She didn't know what he might do.

"Stealing!" she said, lifting her chin up defiantly. "Not stealing! He's your *son*. He hasn't gotten half of what he deserved from you, and he's had to settle for second best his whole life. Because you didn't think a boy who was half Irish was good enough to take your name. Don't tell me what you think he's done, I don't care, do you hear me, I don't care! But whatever it is, I know one thing: it's not stealing."

He started at her, the muscles by his jaw jumping in spasms. "You . . . *knew*?" he finally said hoarsely. "You knew all the time. You knew your precious boy was robbing me left and right and you never breathed a word of it to me. You've betrayed me in *every* way, you whore!"

"Whore, is it, you dirty little Jew!" It was too much, *too* much. He had just made her life a total waste, all of it. She hated him. Hated him! She glared at him, wishing him dead.

And then, just like a nightmare, it began to happen. He stared at her with that glittering hatred and then his eyes glazed over. For just an instant she thought he looked panicked and then there was emptiness. He was looking at nothing. That terrified her: the absolute blankness in his eyes. She knew that the soul was in a person's eyes and it had always been especially true of him.

And then, worse than a nightmare, he toppled to the floor, boom, just like that, one minute standing, his fists clenched, his eyes full of fury, the next minute, falling over like a stone, crashing on his face.

She heard herself shrieking, "Ohmygod! Ohmygod!" over and over again, rooted to the spot, unable to move, her heart pounding and pounding with fear. No, no, it couldn't be, he couldn't be ... she could not even think the word. And then she forced herself to kneel next to him, to reach out, to lift his head. He was a dead weight. No no, mustn't think that word. He couldn't be, he mustn't be. He moaned a little and she found that she had been holding her breath. Now she let it out on a sigh of relief. Oh, thank God. His eyes were rolled back but yes, he was breathing. He had only fainted.

She pushed herself up and went to the kitchen sink to wet a towel with cool water. But rubbing it on his face didn't do a thing, didn't bring him around. She kept calling his name, asking him to speak to her, speak to her, but he would not answer. "Why won't he answer me?" she sobbed. "Why won't he answer me?" She was beginning to feel scared again. She did not know what to do.

She had to do something. Hospital. Yes, that was right. Call an ambulance. What was that emergency number? Why had it gone flying out of her mind just when she needed it? One one nine? No. Nine one one.

She got up, took a deep breath, and backed over to the phone so she never had to take her eyes off him. The woman who answered was calm, didn't ask embarrassing questions, just what had happened and where. "An ambulance will come as quickly as possible," the woman said. "We'll take him to the nearest hospital." St. Joseph's, that was. Good. She had to get him out of there. Oh, God, what was wrong? Why didn't he wake up? It had been so long; it was terrifying to watch him lying there so quiet, so still. Jack Strauss, who had always been so vibrant and exciting and full of life! No, stop it; she mustn't think that way. She must calm herself and figure out what to say, what to tell people, what to tell Sylvia.

He had come here this afternoon to pick up some work she had taken home. Those two would *never* tell their mother what had really happened, *never*. She could count on that. No matter how upset they were, she knew how they felt about their daddy. And their mother, for that matter. They were a close family, you had to give them that.

Her hand hovered over the telephone buttons. She knew his home number, of course. "He came here to pick up some work," she rehearsed, "and, I don't know, had some kind of fainting spell. Don't worry," she went on, satisfied that her voice betrayed none of her feelings, "He seems okay now. They're taking him to St. Joseph's just to be sure." That sounded okay. She'd say that.

And then what? What if he died? What if he didn't? In either case, what was she going to *do*? When he came to, sooner or later, he'd remember why he had come to see her today. Jack was not a forgiving man. And there was Lawrence to think of, and the trouble he was in. With her help he could fix the records so nobody could prove anything. Or he could throw himself on their mercy, maybe say he was doing it for the good of the firm. Yes, wait a minute, he could say he was putting the money aside, not for himself, but for the company. For Jack, because Jack had been spending too much lately. Maybe, even, he could say that Jack had asked him to do it. Why not? Jack wouldn't deny it; the thing he hated most was to be showed up for a fool. He'd never be able to admit that Linda and Lawrence, the second-class citizens, had taken him for a royal ride. They'd be perfectly safe forever.

But don't let him die, please don't let him die, she prayed. What was she going to do without Jack? He had been the center of her existence for so many years, just the thought of losing him made a great pit yawn before her, made her feel as if she were falling through a trap door. She had loved him so much for so many years . . . what did a woman do without the man she loved? She answered herself by dialing a familiar number.

When a voice and not a machine answered, she gasped her relief. "Oh, God, I'm so glad I got you! Listen Lawrence darling, something dreadful has happened. It wasn't my fault. . . ."

CHAPTER THIRTY-THREE

Monday, February 3, 1986

It was only four-thirty, Monday afternoon, but it was already getting dark outside. The hospital room was mostly in shadows, only the one light on now, next to the chair where Sylvia sat, pretending to work on a needlepoint pillowcover. Pretending to work, but really gazing at her husband, her Jack, as he lay asleep on the bed. She ignored the slim plastic lines leading from him to the monitors out front, in the nursing station of the ICU. Those, she didn't want to see.

Look at him, she thought, doesn't look a day over sixty with that tan and the thick wavy hair. He still had all his hair . . . most of his teeth, for that matter. He was a young and vigorous man; he was going to recover from this stroke. Completely. With her help he was going to come out of it and be himself again. Sleeping, with his head thrown back, he actually looked even younger than sixty, all the lines and creases erased. He looked so much like he had when they were courting. She remembered a picnic in Prospect Park with their crowd, when he was napping after the softball game. She had sat under a tree then, looking at him, happy just to see his face. He still looked the same. And she was still content to just sit here and look at him. That was love, Sylvia thought, that's what it really was, not the lust of youth or the breathlessness of wondering whether he felt the same or even the romance of the first couple of years of married life, when everything was new and miraculous. No, it was this: it was caring about each other over the long haul, through all the ups and downs . . . through *everything*, and that meant *every thing*. God knows she had gone through enough with him and yet, here she still was, still by his side, still caring about him, still able to look at him and feel tenderness.

Sometimes she wondered if she had done right all these years, keeping the truth hidden. But of course it was the right thing. Her girls had never known, had never had a moment's suffering. That was reason enough. And anyway, the truth, in her humble opinion, was a greatly overrated commodity. Look at Jack's sister Dot, for instance. Such a beautiful girl, so vivacious and charming. But she had to marry Jonah Golodny. Not bad enough he was a Red, an agitator, always shooting off his mouth about the working class. But he couldn't lie a little, take the silly loyalty oath and *fartig*, finished? Not Jonah Golodny! No, he had to stand up and tell the truth, no matter what, even to McCarthy! So, of course he got into trouble.

Lucky for him, Jack gave him a job . . . for good money, too. You'd think the man would have been grateful—Dot certainly was—but no. Jonah Golodny was going to be true to his principles if it destroyed them all . . . and it very nearly did. The FBI came after him, and the whole family was forced to disappear. They even had to change their name. So much for the truth! Sometimes it took a lie to keep life happy and serene. Sometimes, a *lot* of lies.

On the bed, he stirred, already *kvetching*, even half asleep. "Oy, God . . . a drink." His speech was a bit slurred . . . a slight paralysis in his tongue, the doctor said.

Sylvia jumped up, sat on the edge of the bed, poured Jack a glass of water, handed it to him, soothing him with a shower of words. "It's me, sweetheart, Sylvia, don't worry, here's a drink, take it easy, there you go." Just like dealing with a child. He drank noisily, he sighed noisily, he lay back noisily.

Men! They did not know how to deal with sickness, especially their own.

"My arm! I can't feel it."

"*Shah*, Jack, the doctor told you it would feel a little numb for a while."

"A little! I can't feel it, I'm telling you."

"That's why," she continued, as if he hadn't interrupted, "they're going to send you to physical therapy . . ."

"Like hell! I ain't going!"

"Oh, Jack! You know if the doctor tells you to do it, you'll do it. Stop carrying on; it only keeps you from getting better."

"I'm too sick," he *kvetched*. "Listen to me, my tongue won't work!"

"They don't mean right away, Jack. When you're ready. Just take it a day at a time. I'm sorry I brought up the physical therapy. It's too soon to talk about it."

"I'll never get out of here."

"Nonsense, of course you will. Already you're talking so much better. You're a very lucky man. You had a stroke, but it was only a little one."

"Little stroke! Like a little pregnant!"

"You see? Already you're joking, how bad could it be? And no, the doctor explained it to me. There are all different kinds of strokes, and you had a mild one. Look at you, you're coming along just beautifully. You're very lucky, Jack."

"So how come I feel so crappy? With a dead tongue? Lying here like a lox!"

"Oh, Jack, you're such a *kvetch*! But don't worry, I'm going to make sure you come out of this just like you were. You'll see."

"Well, hello there, Mr. Strauss! And Mrs. Strauss." It was the specialist, the neurologist assigned to Jack's case, standing in the doorway, larger than life. Sylvia quickly got off the bed—she wasn't sure what the rules were—and backed away.

"Mrs. Strauss! Don't disturb yourself. I'm just here for a minute, just checking to see how my patient is getting along." He was extremely tall, handsome man with a shock of pure white hair and thick horn-rimmed glasses. Dr. Kopmar. Sylvia remembered after a moment of searching her mind. Dr. Joseph

Kopmar. A nice personality, always pleasant, like now, always full of energy. You felt good, having him to take care of you . . . at least she did. Jack, of course, was full of gripes. Why did the man talk so much? Why did he keep saying things were all right? Why did he wear that sissy aftershave? Why was his hand always on Sylvia's shoulder? Why couldn't he have his own doctor, for Christ's sake?

She told him. "Nate Levinson is a wonderful doctor, Jack, but a neurologist he isn't. He isn't even affiliated with this hospital. But he knows Dr. Kopmar, he says Kopmar is the best in the city if not the world, so come on."

Now the doctor held Jack's wrist, talked to him a little, rolled back his eyelids, asked him to do this, try that, all very quickly and very gently. "Very good," he said. "Very good indeed. You're making a rapid recovery, Mr. Strauss. That should make you happy, eh? I'll see you again tomorrow on rounds . . . and then perhaps we'll talk about moving you out of intensive care. That shouldn't bother you, eh?"

"Oh, doctor, that's such good news," Sylvia said, but Jack's voice covered hers.

"Leaving already, Doc? What's your hurry? Isn't it kinda dark for golf?" And he laughed a little.

"I have golf balls that glow in the dark." He grinned at his patient, gave Sylvia a wink, and left.

"That *is* good news," Sylvia said. "And you know it. You see? I told you; it isn't as bad as you want to make out."

"I don't like the way he flirts with you," Jack grumped. "Because he's a bigshot . . . doesn't give him the right. Now when I'm not feeling so good."

"Of course you aren't, my dearest. Of course you aren't. That's to be expected. But you're better today than you were yesterday and that's what counts, isn't it? Certainly it is." She sat back down next to him, holding his hand and feeling pleased in spite of everything. After all, it wasn't every woman aged seventy who could say her husband was jealous if another man paid attention to her. "There, there, soon Marilyn will be here, your daughter the doctor; she already talked to Nate, so she knows what's what. Deena was here before while you were sleeping. Elaine's been taking care of the business. All your girls are doing their best to make sure you get all better."

He grunted, somewhat mollified. He even smiled at her and she decided to take advantage. "Jack," she ventured after a few minutes of companionable silence, "the doctor keeps asking."

"Asking what?" His voice was almost sleepy again.

"About what happened just before. *You* know, before you blacked out . . . before the stroke."

He kept his eyes closed. "Nothing. I told you already, nothing. Getting some work from Linda, it happened. Out of the blue. He should stop talking already. Enough!"

"But, darling, it's important that—"

"I'm so tired, sweetheart, so tired." His voice slurred more heavily.

"Of course. I'm sorry. . ."

She was sorry, sorry for him, but she was also sorry he couldn't bring himself to tell the truth. He was such a fool, her smart Jack. He knew he was marrying an intelligent girl; he had said so often enough, bragged about her to his friends. So where did he think all those brains disappeared to, huh? If it weren't so awful, it would be funny, him going to Linda all those years, "working late at the office" all those times, thinking she was buying his stories. Thinking she could look at that baby and not know a Strauss when she saw one!

She knew why he had been at Linda's place on Saturday, and it wasn't to pick up work. It hurt. It still hurt. She had been so certain that part of it was long over. It had been quite a few years now since he had made excuses about coming home late. She had been so sure there was none of that between them anymore. But he had been there on a Saturday afternoon, after he had told her he was going to be at his club. Suddenly he was up to his old tricks again! It hurt. It hurt worse than it had the first time.

Never mind, Sylvia, she said to herself. The man is lying helpless in his bed. There's no time for your hurt feelings. He needs you now more than he's ever needed you. She would take such good care of him! Nobody could take care of him like she could; nobody knew him like she knew him. Nobody loved him like she loved him. And now he would see for himself how true that was.

She felt a presence in the doorway and turned. "Marilyn!

You're here!" In spite of herself, she could feel the tears gathering, it was such a relief. Elaine and Deena were wonderful girls, but they had no experience with something like this. She got up and embraced Marilyn, whose tweed coat was still cold from the outside.

"Sylvia, Sylvia, don't squeeze me to death. I'm sorry I'm late. I was lucky enough to bump into Dr. Kopmar in the hall, so we had a chat. And then I had to call home. Saul made me promise. God, is he a worrier, just like Deena, I swear. He was convinced my plane would go down over Totowa. There was a little flurry of snow when I left," she explained. "So. How is he?" Even as she spoke, she was moving to the bed, her face solemn and professional.

She gently picked up her father's hand, her fingers on the pulse. Just like Dr. Kopmar, Sylvia marveled. She knew, of course, that Marilyn was a doctor; but this was the first time she had ever *seen* it and it was a revelation. That woman over there, the one she remembered as a baby, as a twelve-year-old sobbing alone in her room, she was a *doctor*. A physician. When she held her father's wrist, she wasn't only looking at him and worrying Daddy are you going to be all right? She was checking him over, she was looking at him professionally, she was deciding if he was going to be all right. The thought was so new and overwhelming that Sylvia found she had to sit down.

After a minute or two Marilyn looked at her and said, "He looks good."

And a voice from the pillow said, "How else should I look? You're always with sick people! Half alive looks good to you!"

"So, Daddy. You really are okay. Dr. Kopmar told me we had every reason to expect a good recovery."

"And what does that mean? No doctor can promise, right? You're all so closemouthed I can't stand it! Tell me: *what's going on*, how about it?" He had lifted his head from the pillow, propping himself on one elbow. Suddenly, he tired and collapsed back down; and Sylvia ran to him.

"It's all right, darling. Don't tire yourself." And to Marilyn, she added, "You see how he overdoes. And then he *kvetches* how lousy he feels."

She and Marilyn smiled at each other, and Marilyn said, "That sounds normal to me."

"Some daughter!" he grumped. "I had a *stroke*, not a little cold! Give me a break!"

"Give yourself a break," Marilyn said, "and stop fussing, okay? Sylvia's right: you'll wear yourself out complaining. No, no, don't talk back to me. Remember, I'm a doctor." Her lips twitched a little. "You have a fine neurologist taking care of you, you're in a very good hospital, and if you don't drive Sylvia crazy, you should be out of here before too long. And as for you, lady," she said to Sylvia, "you stop rushing to his side every time he makes a sound. He's perfectly capable of letting you know when he needs you."

Sylvia said nothing, but she thought, A lot *you* know, my daughter. When you've been married as long as I have, then you'll understand. She smiled at Marilyn. Smart, very smart, my daughter the doctor, but still dumb about some things. In some ways, children never grew up.

"Your sisters said I should let them know the minute you got here," she said. She excused herself and went to the phone booth in the hall. She dialed, first Elaine and then Deena. But neither one of them answered. Funny. It was dinnertime. They should be home. At least *one* of them. Well, they'd been spending a lot of time here, so maybe they needed to get out. But still, they'd asked to be called and they were usually so dependable . . . where could they be?

CHAPTER THIRTY-FOUR

Monday, February 3, 1986

Howard walked into the showroom of Sweet Somethings with Noel at seven-thirty P.M., so of course the place was quiet. Even the cleaning crew had come and gone and all the lights were off. But at the far end of the showroom a shaft of light sliced through the darkness.

"Your mother!" Howard said with only a touch of asperity. My poor Elaine, he thought, she has much too much to do these days. Her whole family always turned to her whenever they felt the need for her strength. And she never said no, not his Elaine. Talk about Wonder Woman; she was the original.

"I'm hungry," Noel said.

"Me, too. You understand why she needed to work late. She really feels she has to do everything she's always done, even with all the added responsibilities that she has now that Papa's in the hospital."

"Is Papa going to be okay? I mean, *really.* Tell me. *Before* I see Mom," Noel said.

What a great kid! Howard's heart swelled with pride. Look how thoughtful he is! Well, Noel always got along with everyone, everyone liked him. And who could blame them? He has smart, he was good-looking, he was a fine athlete, a fine student, really everything a father could wish for. He might have hoped for more children; but no use thinking about that. Poor Elaine, she had cried so hard when the doctor said no more. "I should be able to give you as many babies as you want!" she said. Howard had told her then that Noel was such a great baby, he was enough. And by God, he hadn't thought of it again until now, but it was the truth. Noel was *more* than enough for anyone!

"Your Papa is making a very good recovery. Hey! It's only two days since he was taken to the hospital and already he's *kvetching*!" They laughed a little; better than crying.

They had picked their way in the semidarkness across the familiar showroom, and Howard opened the door to her office. There she was, illuminated in a pool of golden light, head bent, the hand holding the pen moving rapidly. It had always delighted him, how quick she was at everything . . . and that it amazed people who didn't know her. The deals she had cut because they had figured a big woman like her would be ponderous and slow! He chuckled a little to himself, remembering the times when Elaine had put on her fat-lady act, especially for people she didn't like.

"Darling," he said. Her head came up and a smile lit up her face.

"Saved!" she said, and then she saw Noel and she got to her feet. "Welcome home, sweetie." She kissed him on both cheeks, then held his face between her two hands, gazing at him with undisguised pleasure. "You're such a good boy to come see your Papa."

"Hey, Ma, it's only from Princeton, New Jersey, you know. And how could I not come after Papa's had a *stroke*, for Pete's sake?"

Elaine sighed. "Don't worry, sweetie pie, your papa is one tough cookie."

She looked quickly and meaningfully at Howard, who mouthed, "What news?" to which she shook her head.

"Sylvia was supposed to call me," she said. "I hate like hell to bother her at the hospital with phone calls. I'll call her at home later."

Howard went to her and gave her a kiss and a pat. "She's probably been calling you at home, sweetheart. Which is where you really ought to be."

"Howard, what can I do? The catalog has to be printed, I still have that project to finish for Daddy, not to mention I have to familiarize myself with everything over there before" —she stopped herself, glancing at Noel, and then continued with hardly a hitch. "—before it gets too complicated," she finished. Howard understood. She meant before she got rid of Linda, finally, Linda, who was stubbornly coming into work every day and sitting implacably at her desk, waiting for something to happen. Linda must know what was inevitable just as soon as Elaine no longer needed her. "And then," Elaine went on, "I have to take my turn at the hospital."

Howard laughed, but lightly, lightly. He had to be very careful with Elaine these days; she was doing too much and had a tendency to see ill will where none was intended. "You don't have to do *everything*, sweetheart, really you don't. Let Deena spend more time with your father; *she* doesn't work full-time."

"Denna has problems of her own. Worse than the office." They exchanged another look.

This time Noel caught it and said, "What's happening at the office? What's happening with Aunt Deena?" And then he laughed. "I know, I know. 'Later, later, we'll talk when you're older.' You never did tell me how old I had to get . . .!"

That changed the subject nicely. They laughed and then Elaine went for a bottle of wine in the little refrigerator. "Let's all have a drink," she said. "There are a couple of things I'd like to glance at, Howard, if you don't mind. Noel, it will only take a minute." Her voice was warm and bubbly. Howard knew she did not like talking about Linda and Lawrence. They were a double thorn in her flesh . . . or, as she liked to put it, she was forced to eat shit and smile by having them stay in the office. But they were necessary to her right now. Howard had spent a lot of time convincing her that necessity was more important than any personal vendetta.

"You'll get him," he promised her. "You can bring charges anytime you want. If that's what you want. You can punch him in the nose. Just wait another week or so. Then you can do whatever you think is right."

Soon the three of them were gathered around her exquisite carved fruitwood desk, the one he'd given her for her fortieth birthday because she saw it in an antique store during one of their trips to Paris, fell in love with it, and said no, no, it was too much money. It was. But she loved it and he loved her and so he snuck back to the shop and arranged to have it shipped to New York. The look on her face, the day it arrived at the showroom, was worth every franc.

She was going over the "blues," the photographic blueprints, for their next catalog, checking for errors in the copy or prices. The sheets were already covered with her neat penciled notations. He pulled up a chair, took a good swig of his wine, and looked over the pages while he listened to her. Prices had shot up, the printer was getting old and careless—those were complaints she had made every year for the past twenty years. About the same printer. And she was unhappy with one of the models. "Look at her. Grim, grim, grim. Where does she think she is? In a Ralph Lauren ad?" She was right. Madeleine was looking particularly sullen in page after page. Then he looked a bit more carefully and then he leaned back and chuckled.

"What's so funny?" Mother and son spoke as one.

"Nothing. I think I know why Maddie looks unhappy. Elaine, look, see how she's sucking in her belly? She's never had to do that. She's pregnant, or I'll eat the page."

Elaine bent closer; then she laughed and said, "You know? I think you're right. Oh, shit . . . now you're going to have to have a long talk with her and find her a good doctor and maybe replace her. Do you realize how long it's going to take to rephotograph all that stuff?"

"Aw, Ma, come on, she looks wonderful." Noel had gotten up and come behind them to look. "Very sexy, very cool. You're not selling only to the little old ladies who want a smile all the time. And she doesn't *look* pregnant. Give Maddie a break!"

"Yeah? You think so? What do you think, Howard? Let it go?"

He nodded. The model looked a little pouty but didn't they

all, these days? Nobody would notice. As long as the merchandise looked good, who cared? And he said so.

Noel laughed at that. "Some people," he said, "think the *models* are the merchandise. God, the guys at school think I get lucky all the time! When *I* visit Mommy and Daddy at the office, I get a showroom full of beautiful women in sexy underwear!"

They all laughed at this and Howard wondered whether Noel realized that his mother and father were well aware of how he lost his virginity when he was seventeen years old. Sandra, an older model, one of the "big" models—what could Sandy have been? Howard thought now, a size fourteen? Probably a size twelve—had taken Noel into her bed. A very good start for a teenage boy; Sandra was warm, voluptuous, imaginative, and eager. As Howard had reason to know. *That* had happened the year Elaine had strayed. Well, neither Noel nor Elaine would ever know about him; nor that Noel's father had asked Sandra to give the kid a break. God, Noel had been such a mess of repressed passion and boyish lust; if ever an overgrown, oversexed seventeen-year-old had needed a good lay, it was him. How many dads could have done that for their sons?

He still missed Sandra sometimes. Poor gal, she had hated being a big model. Never mind that she was beautiful and good and very attractive, and that she had plenty of work. She only wanted to weigh 110 pounds. Well, she made it. She damn near destroyed herself doing it, too. Anorexia nervosa . . . what a horror. She ended up with her hair falling out, her teeth falling out. But thin. Oh, Christ, yes, thin. God, what a strange business this was. When a normal-sized woman was considered heavy . . . and here, running the whole show, was the most beautiful woman in the world, as far as he was concerned, and she was a size sixteen. Maybe more. He could care less!

When they finished with the blues, Howard pulled Elaine to her feet and said, "*Enough*. You stood us up, and now I'm hungry. Your poor son over there is dying of starvation. All the way from Princeton on just two bags of chips and a pound of David's Cookies. Shall I try to get news of Jack before we go? I won't bother your mother; I'll call Deena."

"Deena's in class. She was with Daddy all day and said she would stay this evening, but I told her not to overdo like a crazy person."

"Like you," Howard murmured, leaning over to nuzzle into the curve of her neck that always smelled deliciously of her perfume. She reached in back of him and gave his tush a little pinch, very lightly.

"I told her to go to her whatdoyoucallit, her writing class. Working is my therapy; going to school is Deena's. Poor Deena, so much is happening to her all at once, she's got so much on her mind. Which reminds me, Noel, what's Zoe up to?"

"What do you mean, Ma?"

"This last vacation, she was staying out every night after she got back from Stowe . . . and she was letting her mother think she was with you all those times."

"Not me!"

"I know that. You were in California. So come on, out with it. Where was she? Don't give me that innocent look, either. You and Zoe tell each other goddamn near everything."

"Aw, Ma, don't push me. I promised. I can't tell."

"Look, your aunt is terribly upset. It can't be any worse than what she's imagining. *Believe* me!"

He hesitated and he moaned a little and then he said, "Oh, all right. It's no big deal. Just a guy she's seeing. She knows her folks won't approve of him."

"Why? What's wrong with him?"

Noel laughed. "He's the hunchback of Notre Dame, Ma. He's an ax murderer." He made awful faces at her. "No, wait, I haven't said the worst yet. He's—are you ready for this?—over thirty-five!"

"Oh, for God's sake, that's not so terrible. I mean, it's not exactly what a mother dreams of, but it's not *terrible*. So, come on. What's his name?"

"Well . . . actually . . . it's Lawrence. Lawrence McElroy."

Talk about stroke! Howard thought Elaine would have one right then and there. The news took *him* aback, too; but Elaine reacted as if she had been slugged. She sat down, she stood up, she clutched the edge of the desk, she knocked her wineglass over. And then, like a blow, he realized what that meant, what it *really* meant. Oh, Christ, what a mess!

"It's because he's not Jewish, right? That's obnoxious. Nobody thinks that way anymore, for Christ's sake. Nobody cares! Okay, so he's not Jewish, so he's a little too old for her. He's smart, he's handsome, he makes a lot of money, and Papa says he's terrific, so how bad could he be?"

Elaine subsided, sinking back into her desk chair. "Don't ask!" she said, putting her head down onto her arms. Howard moved over to her and put a comforting hand on her shoulder.

"What's the *problem*?" Noel insisted. His voice was tinged with worry. "What the hell is going *on* here, would somebody please tell me?" Howard sucked in a deep breath, casting about for lies, lies that would fool his son, who was nobody's fool. And then Noel gave him that crooked smile and set them free. For now. "I know, I know," he said. "Later, when I'm a grown-up. So come on, let's go. I'm so hungry, I could eat the chair! Never mind old Zoe, give me food, food, food!"

Over their son's head, Howard's eyes met Elaine's. He was sure they were wondering the same thing: how was the family going to stop this romance without giving the whole horrible thing away!

CHAPTER THIRTY-FIVE

Monday, February 3, 1986

Deena sucked in her stomach and stood sideways to look at herself in the full-length mirror. Not bad for a middle-aged broad, not bad at all. Her hair was loose and she'd just brushed it fifty times—hadn't done that in years—and the satin nightshirt, brand new, purchased for the windjammer trip and never worn, looked terrific. It was a vivid turquiose, one of her best colors, and it shimmered beautifully, particularly where her breasts pushed against the fabric. As she contemplated her image, the nipples became hard and she laughed aloud. She looked, she thought, exactly like a woman on the make. And that's exactly what she was. She had just bathed and perfumed herself, preparing to go downstairs to seduce her husband. To try, anyway. When death hovered, it was time to reconfirm life and maybe even save her marriage. It was the least she could do for Daddy; he was so attached to Michael, the son he'd never had and all that stuff.

She studied her reflection. She didn't look her age, whatever *that* meant. Yes, she decided, she'd do for a seduction scene—if the light wasn't too bright and the bit of middle-age spread was concealed. "Yep, the legs are good. Say what you will about me, I have beautiful legs!" Did Michael still think so? Did he care? Did *she* care if he cared? She couldn't say and she didn't care.

She cast herself an encouraging glance and started downstairs. It had been a long time since she'd felt the need to come on to her husband; it had been, in fact, a long time since they'd made love. That was the whole point, really. She was owed an apology. But, even more than that, she was owed a good lay, one blissful hour of forgetting the real world and all its real problems.

That's exactly why, at five-thirty P.M., she was *not* on her way to class . . . on her way to Luke, to be absolutely truthful. Instead, when Michael came home early today, announcing he could be found in the den when needed, she was struck with this idea. They couldn't go on much longer this way, hardly speaking, never touching. Obviously, he wasn't going to make the first move. So she was going to have to.

If he spurned her now, even with her best perfume and a sexy satin nightshirt, she would politely excuse herself, leave, go to class, go out with Luke, and go find a divorce attorney. If, on the other hand, he responded . . . well, that might be the beginning of . . . what? She didn't even know, but after twenty-three years, she couldn't run from the captain's bed into Luke's without at least stopping to give her marriage one last chance.

Now, to see if she could make herself irresistible to him. She trotted silently down the carpeted stairs in her bare feet to the kitchen to get the champagne, popped the cork, grabbed two Waterford glasses, and headed for the den.

He was there. Of course he was there. A Beethoven symphony was playing on the stereo and he was at the desk, head bent over his interminable papers, so engrossed that he had no idea she was there . . . not until she had tiptoed behind him, put her arms around him, and kissed him on the back of his neck.

"What?" He was startled—she should have realized he would be—so it was not exactly the beginning she had planned. He jumped and turned his head, scowling. "You

scared me, coming in so quietly. . . ." But then he reared back
in his chair a little, looking her over. "Well, well . . . and
what's this?"

She slid onto his lap, smiling carefully, and said, "I have
champagne." Under her, she could feel him becoming stiff,
but she pretended not to notice. "Shall I pour?"

"Forget the champagne," Michael muttered. Already his
eyes were taking on that hot glaze. He ran a hand over her
satin-covered breast, lingering there, rubbing the nipple erect
as he put his open mouth over hers. Oh, God, it was so good!
She had forgotten how much she enjoyed his mouth, his scent,
his taste. He had full firm lips and an insistent, probing
tongue. She opened her mouth to him, digging her fingers into
his thick hair, remembering times she had come just from
kissing like this.

His hand dropped to her lap, pushing the satin aside, and
she moaned at his quick intake of breath when he found his
finger on damp, hot, flesh. He thrust his tongue farther into
her mouth, groaning a little, and Deena thought very briefly
hallelujah, it still works, it's still there, we still have this.
And then she found it very difficult to think of anything else
but his hands probing her, his hands caressing her, his hands
impatiently pulling the nightshirt over her head.

Together they slid onto the thick rug. Together they tugged
at his clothes, undressing him. The sight of him, rampantly
erect and empurpled, was delicious. It had been so long, so
long! She reached up to fondle him, but he gently put her hand
down, muttering, "Not yet, not yet." And sat back on his
heels, drawing her legs apart to gaze at her. His tongue came
out to lick his lips and he smiled and Deena began to tremble
with anticipation.

He bent his head, burying it between her thighs, and
lapped at her as if she were an ice cream cone, moaning his
pleasure, holding on to her hips as she pushed herself closer to
his mouth, shrieking, begging him for more. She hardly had
to beg; he was avid for her, growling in his throat and giving
her gentle little love bites. This is what had kept them together. He had always been eagerly hungry for her and it was
his delight as much as the physical feel of his tongue—now
soft and flat, now curled, hard, pointed—that always had

brought her to fever pitch. She was shaken by one orgasm
after another, sudden wrenching ones that came over her
like surf beating on her body, one receding and the next
sweeping over. Her throat was so dry, she was breathing so
hard, her legs were trembling, she couldn't breathe, couldn't
breathe, *she couldn't breathe*! She could hear herself gasping for air, and then Michael lifted his head and pushed
himself up.

He was so hard, he felt so gigantic in her, and her tender
flesh was so engorged with heat that it was a kind of pain as
he thrust himself deep into her. A pleasure pain that made her
cry out, even as her juices poured from her and her buttocks
lifted to meet that lovely, that wonderful, that hard, that hot,
that beautiful cock. He moved even more deliberately, pulling
back, waiting that exquisite little instant while she struggled to
lift her loins into him, and then, pushing into her, filling her,
rubbing her, pleasuring her, bringing her again closer and
closer and closer and closer. For what seemed like an eternity,
she hung on the edge of her orgasm, unwilling to let go of the
pulsating buildup and then it overtook her, it took her over,
shaking her to her toes. She reached for his buttocks, digging
her fingers in, pulling him closer and closer into her, wanting
only to melt into him to become one body as she felt herself
melting from within, flooding, exploding, coming. And then
he began his final course, thrusting harder and faster, crying
out uncontrollably. He came, but kept on pushing into her,
murmuring wordlessly, slick with sweat, clinging to her, kissing her neck, winding his fingers into her long hair, gasping
for air.

It took her a while to catch her breath. She was comfortable, lying beneath him, her legs still wrapped around him,
feeling him relax over her, listening as his breathing eased,
became deeper and more regular. And then . . .

"Hey!" She wriggled under him. Suddenly he was a dead
weight. He was sound asleep. Once, this was the time they
told each other of their love, told each other how lovely had
been the lovemaking, how wonderful the other was, how good
they were together. But he never stirred. He was all but snoring. When her arms and legs began to cramp, then she'd wake

him. Poor Michael, he was *so* tired, he really needed the sleep.

Wait a minute, she said to herself. Why does that sound so disgustingly familiar? Because that's what I always say. That's how I've always excused his coldness, his lack of interest in his family, his priorities that never included me . . . by telling myself how busy he was, how tired he must be, how important his work.

She saw herself, aged eighteen, in the kitchen with her mother, arguing. Sylvia was saying, "Deena, Deena, the least a boy can do is, when he makes a date for eight o'clock, he comes at eight o'clock. Or he calls. Or *something*. This is not good, Deena. If he really cared for you—" Deena couldn't remember whether or not her mother got to finish that sentence. Probably not. Because she didn't want to hear the end of that sentence, she didn't want to think about it, either. What she recalled was her impassioned defense of Michael. "He studies so hard, Syl, come on, be fair. He's going to graduate top of his class. He can't help it if he forgets the time."

She lay very still under Michael's growing weight, her mind racing. She'd always made excuses for him, only she, poor benighted, ignorant female, had been *proud* of all her sacrifices and all her hard work, and her trouble and solitude and loneliness. *Proud* to be doing it alone, strong and independent! Of course, she wasn't the only mommy in the Pierrepont Street playground in that situation. Oh, no. They all were the wives of ambitious young stockbrokers, bankers, academics, attorneys. They were used to doing it by themselves. Back in those days, she had been dumb enough to *love* it when Michael said, "*We* graduated top of the class" to other people, and gave her shoulder a pleased squeeze. She had beamed and bridled. What bullshit! It was hard to fathom, that young women had swallowed it all whole. She should have been doing something herself—just like Sylvia tried to tell her—such as getting her *own* degree.

Now irritated, she pushed at his inert body, struggling to free herself. In his sleep he muttered, grumpy at being disturbed. "Michael! You're too heavy!" A lie, but better than the truth: she didn't want him touching her.

When he awoke, it was sudden and complete. He rolled away from her, yawned, stretched, took in a deep breath, and pushed himself upright, reaching for his clothes. Damn him for turning his back and disappearing her from the scene without even a little kiss, some kind of acknowledgment, a word, a glance in her direction! "*Michael!*"

"Yes?" He might just as well have been talking to his secretary or a stranger.

"Where are you running?"

He stood up and stepped into his trousers. "I'm right in the middle of something."

"You *always* have something you're in the middle of. You always run away from me to get on with your *real* life!"

His lips tightened. "I hate it when you start using emotionally loaded words, Deena. I'm not going to ask you what you mean. I have too much to do right now."

"Exactly."

He sighed openly. "Why are you doing this? We just made love, so why are you picking a fight?" He always did this—how could she have forgotten? There was never, *never*, a right time for her to tell him she was unhappy. He didn't want to hear it. He didn't want to think about it. He always chose to think of it as her way of attacking him. Suddenly, she saw it all clearly. Nothing she could say would make the least bit of difference. Already, as she stood watching him, he was turning his mind elsewhere, finished with her and her strange, rather crazy female notions. Well, she was finished, too. She was finished trying to fix up something that was unfixable. She was finished with him. It was as if a great light had gone off in her head.

She contemplated them for a moment. In the words of the *Ladies' Home Journal*, can this poor excuse for a marriage be saved? "You know something, Michael?" she mused aloud. "This is not a life for a Jewish girl. As Sylvia used to say."

"Grow up, Deena! Say what you mean!"

"This is no good for either of us . . ."

"I don't know what you're talking about. *I'm* happy!"

She took in a very deep breath, and then another. "Well, I'm not."

"Deena, if you're trying to make me angry, you're succeeding; but this is not the time for a discussion. I have a very important meeting and I'm already late."

"Michael, what can I say? Go to your very important meeting." She started walking out.

"Every marriage has its ups and downs, for God's sake. The thing is to ride it out, not run away. We love each other!"

"Speak for yourself, Michael. I'm no longer sure how I feel."

"Deena, I've had enough of this for tonight."

And I, she thought, defiantly, have had enough, period. She was really beginning to believe there was no happy ending to this story. "Okay," she said. "I'm going to class."

As she left the room, carefully not looking at him, he shot after her, "I hope you don't think anyone else's marriage is any better! Because it isn't!"

When Deena walked into class, late of course, it was mayhem. Everyone was shouting at once. One of the guys was even pounding on his desk and Luke was laughing and calling for order, both at the same time. When they quieted a bit, he said, "So I'm a bachelor, Wellburn. So what? I don't believe in the responses you've given the wife in your script. To want to die, just because her husband cheated on her? *Once?*" He shook his head. "Nope. Unbelievable."

Once again, bedlam, as everyone in the room tried to answer him at the same time, at the top of their lungs. Finally, Luke put two fingers in his mouth and gave a shrill whistle. It had the desired effect. Everyone stopped talking. He laughed. "Much better. Now I'll take questions and/or statements—but one at a time, please! Yes, Ms. Berman? And we're happy you finally decided to join us this evening."

She dared not look at him, so she looked at a spot just over his head. "I have a question *and* a statement. First, how do you whistle like that?" A ripple of laughter went through the class, and then she added, "And, why do you consider adultery a minor thing? It can be devastating!"

"I know it *can*. I just doubt that adultery is really all that significant these days."

More babble from the class. "Cheating is cheating!" one woman shouted. "When a man cheats his business associates, it's called cooking the books and he gets hard time!"

"Right! But if a man's only cheating on a mere *woman*," Deena said, looking straight at Luke when she said it, "then people like you say, What's the big deal?"

"Hey!" Luke said, smiling. "Who said I meant just men? When we say adultery, do we mean only a man cheating on a woman? The scene we're discussing had a husband committing adultery, yes. But what about a woman? *Do* we feel differently about that?"

There was a momentary silence from the class, and then one of the men said, "Here's what I think. Since men have stronger sex drives than women—" He got no further, drowned out by hoots and catcalls from the women.

Luke's voice was mild. "Actually, it's been proved, I believe, that women have the stronger drives. Maybe it's more quote natural unquote when a woman commits adultery."

Now it was the men yelling. Deena sat back in her seat. She had a feeling that Luke was sending her a message. More than a feeling. And it felt good. After all, this was why she had taken a shower and changed at breakneck speed in order to get here before the class was over.

Now they were talking about love, love and marriage, spoken like one word, as if they really did go together like a horse and carriage. She remembered believing that. One of the men was saying that the man's adultery in the scene was beside the point. The adultery was only one incident; but his love for his wife was forever.

Deena sprang to her feet. "Nothing is forever!" she blurted out. "Nothing!" And then she sat down again, feeling very silly and wishing she hadn't opened her mouth.

She sat staring down at her feet on the bare dirty floor, surprised at the tears that sprang suddenly into her eyes. She felt hollow inside, small, lost and empty. So many things were coming to an end and she was scared. The mother of four grown children and she was scared to death. How simple for some people to talk so glibly about forever. What did they know? Their Daddy wasn't in a hospital bed, weak and subdued, suddenly an old man. No, no, not him, not Daddy! She wouldn't even think it! She clenched her fists tightly. She had to stop this, stop thinking this way. Life goes on; isn't that what everyone always said? Life goes on.

Luke looked straight at her again. "I agree with you, Ms. Berman. To believe in eternal love is naïve. Even a commitment made in good faith can be bad." And then the bell rang and he laughed and said, "Talk about saved by the bell!" Everyone laughed and they all got up and began putting on their coats and shuffling their papers. Over their heads Luke gave Deena a look that said as plainly as words, Don't go. Deena waited.

Where was she going to go? Home? To Michael? To her failure? Not likely! Or how about the hospital, where machines whispered and beeped as they measured out her Daddy's life? She shivered a little. She was being morbid, she knew; but she couldn't seem to stop her own thoughts.

Luke came up, close behind her, warm and solid. A longing to lean against him, no, more, to blend right into him, swept over her and when he started walking, she just moved right along with him, not looking at him, wondering whether she was really going to go through with this.

Half an hour later she had her answer. Yes. As they reached his door, he turned to her, grabbed her, and kissed her hard. They both gasped a bit as their lips touched; it was electric. Quickly, he pulled away from her, unlocking the door, pulling her in after him. Once inside, they flew into each other's arms, mouths hot and eager, hands clutching.

This was wonderful, this dizzy desire, this heat that blocked out everything else. She gave herself to the sensations that shuddered through her, letting him pull her clothes from her, tearing at his clothes until they were both naked, still right next to the door, exploring each other's bodies, moaning, groaning, straining to get closer.

It all became a delicious blur of feeling and sensation, of slow building, of exhausted haze, of explosive climax and reawakened lust. He took her on her back, he took her on her belly, he took her in the shower with water coursing over them both, she fell to her knees and took his erect penis into her mouth, loving the salt taste of his sweat and of her. He pulled her up on her toes and plunged into her, yelling with each thrust. Dripping, they got out, and he took her on the carpet on their knees. They rolled over to look at themselves in the full-length mirror, and he turned, taking her from behind while he held on to her breasts. There was more, there was much much more, until she could no longer move, no longer think, no longer stay awake. . . .

She opened her eyes, shreds of a dream clinging to her thoughts, and didn't know where she was. Then suddenly she remembered, and at the same moment realized that the window over there was pearly with morning light. Oh, my God, she thought, stricken, her heart palpitating with panic. I've been here all night. Oh, God, Michael! And Daddy in the hospital!

There was an arm flung across her belly and a leg flung across her leg. Luke. She pushed away from him, and he immediately awakened and sleepily pulled her closer.

"You look beautiful," he murmured into her bare shoulder.

"I probably don't have a smidgen of makeup on. Luke, Luke, don't *do* that; it's morning, I've been here all night and, don't, Luke, you don't understand, my father's in the hospital and they've probably been trying to get me."

He let her go immediately. "Oh Jesus. Why didn't you say—"

She smiled at him. "My mind was elsewhere."

The mirror in Luke's bathroom showed a woman with tumbled dark hair and not even a trace of the makeup so carefully applied last evening. Christ, she looked ten years younger, even in her bare face! In fact, she looked happy when she should be looking ashamed. At least a *little* ashamed. She'd done the unthinkable: she'd laid two different men in one day. Nice ladies didn't *do* that! "Well, I guess I'm not a nice lady," she told herself, and giggled. She leaned on the edge of the sink and gazed at herself. Last night had been so good . . . *so* good.

Her marriage was over. There was nothing left worth working on or worth saving. What a relief! She could feel her heart lift. She was no longer obligated to make it work. Her marriage was over. She was scared, but only a little, only a little. Convincing Michael she meant it—that was going to be the hard part. Just thinking about confronting him made her very uneasy. She was going to do it, but not quite yet. Soon, she promised herself. Soon.

CHAPTER THIRTY-SIX

Saturday, February 8, 1986

It had just begun to snow, big fat white flakes that came swirling lazily down out of a white sky. Marilyn stood at the base of Snowcap Ski Resort's novice slope, watching the skiers making their last run of the day. She was looking for Saul— for his bright scarlet knitted ski cap, actually—but no luck. They all looked the same at a distance and, in this pale mistiness, you could hardly tell them apart even when they got close.

It was four-fifteen in the afternoon and already beginning to get dark. She'd told him this morning when he started out that she expected him to meet her at four on the dot. "I really mean it, Saul." Yeah, yeah, stop bugging him, he knew how to tell time. Sure. So now he was late and she was annoyed. She'd been on her feet since six this morning, office hours seven to one on Saturdays. Not only that, but John had come home from Snowcap at two-thirty, as he did whenever he could on Saturdays, and they'd had an hour of the most wonderful, breath-grabbing lovemaking. She had been in no mood

370

to get out of the warm bed and out of the warm house and into the cold Jeep . . . so where was he, the lousy teenager?

Just then, some jerk skidded to a stop right under her nose, spraying her with wet snow. He could have knocked her over! He could have killed her! "Hey!" she protested. "Don't you know better than—" And then she stopped. Saul. Laughing like a loon. "Very funny," she said, brushing herself off. "Three weeks of skiing and you're already Mr. Hot Dog!" Even as she complained, he was getting out of his skis and preparing to leave, grinning and preening. He was very god-damn pleased with himself. "And no wonder I couldn't find you," she added. "I gave you that red hat on purpose, so I could spot you easily. So, of course, you're wearing it in your pocket!"

Saul picked up his skis. "Sorry, Moo, but I looked like a dweeb in that hat."

"Oh, well, then, that explains it! Don't wear it, by all means, don't wear it. I wonder how you'd look in pneumonia?"

Saul gave her a sharp look. "Hey! You're funny, you know that?" He nudged her in the ribs with his elbows, tantamount, Marilyn knew, to a big hug and kiss.

Bumping along the narrow twisting road down into Mt. Hebron, she thought about him. It wasn't that there had been a miracle, that everything was smooth and wonderful and that the sullen, unhappy boy had magically been transformed into a happy-go-lucky teenager. No. But at least now, after three weeks, Saul was more and more doing sixteen-year-old-boy things instead of depressed-little-old-man things.

When they first got here that Sunday night, he'd hardly said a word to either her or John. In fact, for maybe a week or ten days it had been like talking to a wall—as Sylvia always used to say. Grunts. Sidelong sullen looks. Many many slammed doors, oh, *many* slammed doors. Many plates of food pushed away untouched, without explanation. Many mumbled responses that no human ear could understand.

And then, one evening after dinner, Marilyn looked up from the dining room table, where she and John were attacking a pile of bills. She felt a chill, and small wonder: the fire in the big stove was dying rapidly, and the hopper was empty of logs. Saul was curled up in a corner of the sofa with a cat on his lap, reading a comic. "Saul," she called to him, "The stove needs wood. Will you please go out and bring in some?"

He said, without looking up, "I'm busy."

And John said, "Yo. Around here we all carry our own weight. You heard your aunt. On your feet!"

And Saul glared at him and said, "Fuck off!"

Marilyn succeeded in keeping her voice even. "Saul, I think you know we don't talk to each other that way around here."

"Around here!" Saul sneered. "Around here! Well, maybe I don't like it around here!"

And John said, "You don't like it? Why don't you leave?"

And Saul answered: "*You* leave. You can't tell me what to do! You're nothing to me. You and Moo aren't even married!"

Marilyn was all ready to give Saul what-for, but John quickly said, "Wait a minute. First of all, I didn't tell you what to do; I only told you what *we* do. Second, I may be nothing to you, but you're something to me. I happen to like you a lot. And, third, we're not married because Marilyn won't have me. But I haven't tried for a while." And he turned and looked directly at her, very serious. "Marilyn, I'm asking you again. Will you marry me? Saul doesn't like our arrangement."

To her great surprise, she said. "Yes. Probably. I think."

And then they all burst out laughing. Well, it *was* funny. And Saul heaved himself to his feet and went out to the porch and returned with an armload of logs. Victory! There had been ups and downs since then; but after that little blowup, Saul had seemed to feel a part of the household.

When they opened the back door today, the delicious smell of John's beef stew with beer wafted out to them. "Boy, am I hungry!" Saul said. "Boy, am I glad John's cooking."

"And just what does that mean, young man?"

"Well . . . gee, Moo, a guy could get tired of tofu and veg-gies. Oh, they're great, Moo, really terrific. But . . . *beef*!" He said it like a prayer. "Oh, boy! When do we eat, John?"

"Hi, Saul. How about a hello?" But he was grinning, pleased. "Your math teacher called about half an hour ago. Falco. Something about a computer project?"

Saul blushed. "Yeah, yeah, Henry found out I know a little about computers... I didn't tell him I'm a fugitive from justice... so... well... he asked me to help him with a project."

Marilyn said, "But that's great, Saul! Why didn't you tell us?"

"Agh! No big deal."

"Well, I think it's terrific. Can you tell us about this project?"

He paused a moment and then, almost delicately, said, "I'm not sure you'd understand what I'm talking about... it has to do with games theory and, oh, hell, it's not that I'm so smart or anything, it's just..."

Marilyn got up and went to him. He'd grown during the past couple of weeks, she'd swear she had to tip her head back farther to look up at him! "It's just that Henry Falco happened to need a New York guy and you just happened to be there, no big deal, we know, we know!"

"Well, all I know," John put in, "is Falco referred to you as the Genius. Yeah. That's what he said: Could I speak with Saul the Genius."

Saul blushed. "He does that... calls people funny names. He advises the math team and he asked me to be on it...."

"Terrific!"

"Yeah, and it's not just a hick team, either, it's really *good*, they won the state championship last year." He stopped mid-word. "I'm sorry, Moo. That was lousy, calling people up here hicks. But my attitude's been pretty lousy, hasn't it?"

Hallelujah! "You haven't always acted precisely like Prince Charming, but you'll do," Marilyn said. "Probably. I think."

After dinner Saul sort of even helped clear the table. He took three dishes to the sink and then remembered something terribly important in his room and disappeared. "Next step," John remarked, "is to keep his attention long enough to say 'garbage' and 'out.'"

"It's a big improvement. It looks like some of his anger is beginning to dissipate."

"Yours, too."

"What are you talking about? *What* anger of mine?" The

minute the words were out, she realized how angry they sounded and, helplessly, she began to laugh.

"Ever since I met you, you've been pissed as hell a good deal of the time."

"At who, Dr. Freud?"

"Insulting me isn't going to accomplish anything, Marilyn. But if you want my professional opinion, I'd say you're mostly mad at your family."

"That's ridiculous! Although . . . wait . . . maybe it's not completely crazy. To tell the truth, I never really felt I belonged with the rest of them. My sisters always left me out—"

"Hey, your sisters are a lot older than you; of course they'd leave you out! To them, you were the baby."

"It's more than just my sisters, John. That thing with Linda and Daddy . . ."

"You saw them kissing, that's all! Okay, that's not such a wonderful thing for a young girl to see. But, come on, it wasn't a murder! You were thirteen years old, Marilyn. A bit of time has gone by since then . . . don't you think it's time to let it go?"

"It was violent in its own way, whether you want to believe that or not. No, what I started to say was that I tried to tell Sylvia. I *did* tell Sylvia—"

"I know, you told me."

"And she pretended to me. For God's sake, John, she knew damn well what I was talking about, that it wasn't a girlfriend, that it was *me*, that it was Daddy and Linda! And she never offered me comfort, she gave me blah-blah instead. *I* had to carry that burden for years and years and years—! And look at me, here I am, getting mad about it all over again."

"Good. Get angry, get it out, and get rid of it . . . and maybe we can get on with our life together."

She was glaring at him when the phone rang. She was grateful to the instrument because she didn't know what she might have said; but she almost surely would have regretted it later.

It was Sylvia. That was a kind of shock. "What's wrong?" Marilyn said sharply, reverting instantly to doctorhood.

"Nothing . . . no, not nothing, but nothing terrible. But I'm worried, Marilyn. Could you come back down for just a day or two? I know it's a lot to ask. . . . ."

What it amounted to was that Daddy was all right but was not recovering as fast as Kopmar had thought he would. Nothing Sylvia could put her finger on, just a lot of little things. Nothing medical, according to the doctor. But the physical therapist said she thought he wasn't really trying.

Marilyn stifled a sigh. She doubted very much whether she could do much good, at least not for her father. But she couldn't bring herself to say no. And to tell the honest truth, she didn't really want to. It was good, for a change, to be the expert in the family, to be the knowledgeable one, the smart one, the best one, the chosen one. They were on *her* turf, this time, and this time, dammit, they *had* to pay attention to her!

CHAPTER THIRTY-SEVEN

Wednesday, February 12, 1986

The hospital cafeteria was crowded and noisy—too noisy, Sylvia thought, and too crowded, if you asked her. Nobody asked her, of course. Still, every time she had come in here for the past week, she had the same reaction. Surely, in a hospital, there shouldn't be so much tumult, so much laughing, so much horsing around. Marilyn had explained to her that this was a teaching hospital and there were a lot of medical students and nursing students and such. But still...this was a *hospital*. There were sick people here. There were *doctors*.

Today was a Saturday, besides, so what were all these students doing here in their blue jeans and T-shirts with messages. Always with messages—SAVE THE WHALES...THE ONE WHO HAS THE MOST WHEN HE DIES WINS...WELCOME TO N.Y.— NOW GET OUT!—*narrischkeit* like that.

If *she* were running this hospital, it would be very very different. She said so; and they all laughed—Marilyn and Deena and Elaine; and Marilyn said, "But you're *not*, so how about accepting the noise level and the student body and the plastic furniture and the paper cups and let's get down to business here."

Sylvia eyed her baby, sitting there across the aqua plastic table, hands folded neatly in front, hair cut short and curling around her face. She wore no makeup, she almost never did. It hurt Sylvia's heart to see her. Marilyn had all the makings of a beauty and she refused to do anything to bring it out. Such a shame. She ought to be married; she ought to be having babies of her own, should have done it a long time ago. Soon it was going to be too late for her, doctor or no doctor!

"The first order of business," Elaine said, raising her coffee cup, "is a toast to the original Superwoman, our mother, Sylvia Weinreb Strauss." Oh, that Elaine! But it was nice to hear; and it was nice to see them all smile and drink to her, even with terrible hospital coffee in paper cups.

"You've been super, Sylvia," Deena added. "A tower of strength. I don't know where it all comes from, honestly I don't."

Sylvia murmured something and sipped decorously at her already cold and bitter-tasting coffee. That was a mother's job: to always be that tower of unending strength. They should know that by now. But no, you never got over that awe of your mother, no matter how old you were, no matter that you were a mother yourself. It was amazing. As long as your mother was alive, in some part of your mind and you were still a child. And maybe she wanted them to keep thinking she was unsinkable and maybe that's why she kept pushing herself beyond her limits. Because there had been a few moments this past week or so, when she just wanted to break down, put her head on someone's shoulder and say all her fears out loud, maybe cry a little, get it all out. But she never weakened. She never let anyone see how scared she was.

Especially not Jack. Jack needed her strength more than ever. Just this morning, she was sitting there needlepointing, and before he even made a sound, she knew he was awake. Something about the way he was breathing; she didn't know exactly. But she *knew*. She put down her work and was by his bedside before he opened his eyes, and was helping him to sit up and asking him if he wanted a drink before he had to ask. Private nurse or no, it took a wife to know what a man needed

even before he did. "Sylvia," he said this morning, clutching
her hand very hard, "you are a wonderful woman. What
would I do without you? How could I get along? You're an
angel come down to earth," he told her. And she blushed like
a girl and bent to give him a kiss. It had been such a long
time. He used to talk to her all the time like that when they
were first married . . . but not lately, not for years.

He'd been like this since the first time he woke up in the
intensive care unit and saw her there, waiting. He could not
get enough of her; he wanted her with him all the time and he
looked so sad whenever she left, it made her feel terrible. It
made her want them to bring in a cot so she could stay there
with him, but Dr. Kopmar said she needed her rest and what
did she think the nurse was for and made a couple of jokes and
called her darling and before she knew it, she was on her way
home.

Ah, but it felt so good to know again that Jack loved her
the best. He was hers again, hers alone, like in the old days
before that woman had come between them. Not once since
his stroke, not even in his sleep, not even at his sickest, not
once had he asked for that woman or spoken her name. Not
even that time when he called Sylvia over to him—he was
still very weak—and whispered to her, "If I don't make it—"

"*Shah*," she said quickly. "I don't want to hear you talk
that way. You're going to make it, period, *fartig*, finished, the
end." The truth was, she was afraid to hear what he might say,
and she didn't want any confessions from him.

He said, "I love you, Sylvia. I want you to know everything. Will you forgive me?"

And very quickly she said, "Yes, don't talk now." She
didn't want to hear it, not any part of it. Her job was to look to
the future, not to the past! She was going to get rid of those
cigars, that was number one, and then she was going to make
him retire and then they could spend the winters in Palm
Beach, they could afford it, God knows, and they deserved it,
too. She'd ask Marilyn for a diet for a man who's had a
stroke. A *small* stroke, she reminded herself with relief. Only
a small one. If he took care of himself, Dr. Kopmar said, he
should have many years in front of him. The trick with Jack
was to make sure he took care of himself. He was careless,

always had been, always thought he was one of God's favored, that he would always be strong and vigorous, that he
would last forever.

She would make sure. *She* would take care of him. So if he
limped a little, did she care? So if the left side of the body was
a little weak, so she'd walk always on his left, in case he
needed to lean on her. . . .

"Sylvia, are you listening to me?" Marilyn demanded.

"Yes, of course I am," she lied. When Marilyn began to
talk her doctor talk, there was a drone in her voice that almost
put Sylvia to sleep, every time. Marilyn had done it again,
had sent Sylvia's thoughts spinning away. "I heard every
word."

"I'll repeat it anyway," Marilyn said. "Because you didn't
look as if you really understood."

"So then, tell me again . . . this time in plain English."

"Daddy has had a very mild cerebral accident. The CAT
scan shows very little damage. He was lucky . . . considering
his normal diet and the number of cigars he smokes, I would
have expected much more clogging of the arteries. But there it
is. He escaped almost unscathed."

"We already know that, Marilyn. I think it wasn't such a
bad stroke because he was so healthy. It came out of the blue."

"It . . . *what*?"

"Came out of the blue. He said so himself. He told me it
just happened out of nowhere, all of a sudden, like that." She
snapped her fingers. "No warning."

"Wrong," Marilyn said, frowning a little. "He had warnings, several of them."

"Marilyn, what are you talking? The man said himself—"

"Syliva, what about those TIAs?"

"Excuse me, Marilyn . . . in English, please?"

"Sorry. Transient ischemic attacks. Um . . . little strokes,
they're sometimes called. Dizzy spells."

"Dizzy spells?" Sylvia hunted through her memory; but she
couldn't recall any dizzy spells. "He never mentioned any
dizzy spells."

"Well, that happens. They occur so quickly and recovery is
so complete that people often think they imagined it. That's
probably what happened to Daddy . . . and you know how he

is. Even if it worried him at the moment, he'd never mention it, he'd put it firmly into the back of his mind."

"That Jack! How does he think he's helping himself, keeping secrets? Remember how he ignored his appendicitis pains? Nate Levinson said another hour later and he'd have been a dead duck. Oh, bite your tongue!" Sylvia chided herself.

"Sylvia, listen. The TIAs are in the past and, anyway, they're beside the point. There's a reason I asked that we get together this morning. By all rights, according to all the tests and to everything his doctor tells me, he should be even further along than he seems to be. . . ."

"I heard," Sylvia said, "a funny tone on 'seems to be.' What are you trying to say, Marilyn?"

"I'm trying to say he's not as sick as he'd like us to believe."

Deena burst out with "What a horrid thing to say!"

"Excuse me," Marilyn answered, "let me reword that slightly: he's not as sick as he *acts*."

"Make up your mind, Marilyn. One minute he's a man who denies when he's sick. Now, suddenly, he's a man who acts sick when he isn't. So which is it?" Sylvia said.

"He's a fighter, a tough cookie—" Elaine put in.

"Jack would never ask for help if he didn't really need it. He wouldn't *let* me . . . you should know that, Marilyn."

Stubbornly, Marilyn said, "I don't know why, but he's acting more helpless than he has to."

"How do you make such a definite diagnosis after such a short time?" Deena again.

"Excuse me, it's not *my* diagnosis. Dr. Kopmar remarked on it and asked me what I thought. He thinks Daddy may not be really trying."

"That's nonsense!" Sylvia said angrily. The nerve. Kopmar wasn't even their own doctor, what did he know?

"Sylvia. Please. Don't get defensive on me. We all want Daddy to get better; we're all on the same side, okay? Look. Many men, especially men like Daddy, who have been strong and active and in charge of their whole lives, react this way to an illness. They're scared; afraid to get back to their normal way of life. They may walk very slowly and carefully.

Many, you'll excuse me, Sylvia, are afraid to resume their normal sex life again. Do you see what I'm saying? I think Daddy's overreacting to the fact that he's had a stroke. I think the word itself scares him. And . . . well, Sylvia, please don't take this the wrong way, but you're too quick to do for him."

"I'm helping him. Is that so terrible? That a wife should be by her husband's side when he needs her?"

"Of course not." Marilyn's voice was patient, but her mouth looked tight. "He needs you to encourage him. But you ought not to *do* everything for him. What he needs is for you to allow him to try it himself. There's no reason his speech should still be slurred. There's no reason for that limp, no reason at all. I think if he sees you won't do everything for him, he'll start doing for himself."

"Oh, now I'm making Jack an invalid, is that it, a man who had a stroke not even two weeks ago? A man seventy years old! *I'm doing it!*"

Marilyn sighed dramatically and leaned over the table to get closer to her. "Sylvia. Mother. Listen to me. Nobody's saying that. But he's better than he acts, do you hear me? He's better than he thinks. Kopmar agrees."

"Well, when Kopmar tells me to stop helping my husband, when Kopmar tells me I'm doing him a disservice, then I'll stop. But until then—"

Marilyn pushed her chair away from the table. She looked disgusted but she said not another word, just stalked away. For a moment Sylvia wondered. Maybe Marilyn was right? Maybe . . . ?

Deena yelled after her, "Who are *you* to come along and make pronouncements? You never had any feelings for him!" Then, to her mother, she said, "Don't let it bother you, Sylvia. You know she has a problem with Daddy . . . it's not important right now. Right now what's important is for everyone to do what's best for Daddy and stay calm. . . . *Stay calm*! I'm a fine one to talk! I'd better go after Moo Moo. I really should apologize. That was a lousy thing I said."

All the way to Daddy's room, Deena practiced her apology to Marilyn. It had been a childish gesture, screaming at her that way.

She rounded the corner of the hallway and slid into Daddy's room without a pause. And then she stopped dead in her tracks. For a moment she couldn't believe her eyes. But it was true. Linda McElroy and Lawrence, big as life, standing right there in front of her, next to Daddy's bed, watching him as he slept.

She stood there dumbly, wanting to give them hell and push them out of his room, out of the hospital, and out of everyone's lives! But dammit, she was helpless. What could she do? She might awaken him. What if he had another stroke? Oh, God! She almost wished she hadn't asked Michael to stay home this afternoon: she almost wished she had let him come. But she was not feeling kindly toward Michael these days, and anyway, Marilyn had said she wanted a pow-wow and Deena got the feeling that Marilyn meant sisters only, no husbands.

In any case, here she was, all by herself, facing the enemy. And now, as if they were puppets on the same set of strings, they turned together to stare at her. For the first time, Deena saw how very much Lawrence resembled Daddy and it sickened her. How dare he? She didn't even know which one she meant: the son or the father.

Between clenched teeth, she gritted out: "If you had any decency at all, you'd get out of here before my mother arrives."

If she expected them to wilt and slink away at her words, she was naïve. They looked, the two of them, utterly unmoved. "We have a right to be here," Linda said in a quiet, rather tight voice. To Deena, the words sounded well practiced; and she had a sudden vivid image of Linda mouthing those words over and over in front of the mirror until they came out in just the right tone. "We care about Jack!"

Lawrence seemed a little more aware of the delicacy of this situation. "Look, Deena," he said ingratiatingly, "we called before we came. The hospital said he could have visitors. And we waited until nobody was here, you'll notice."

"I don't give a damn *what* the hospital said. I'm his daughter and I say you leave." And then she felt breathless because she had just given him the perfect opportunity to answer her

by saying, "And I'm his son and I say I stay." She felt her
heart-thumping panic just as if he really had said it.

But the voice she heard next was her sister Elaine's, quivering with rage. "Just what do you think you're doing here?
Who invited you?"

They were all there, standing in the doorway: Elaine, Sylvia, and—to Deena's surprise—Marilyn, too. In his bed her
father groaned, moving restlessly. Sylvia, who had blanched
the moment she saw the McElroys standing next to Jack's bed,
made a small movement, as if to go to her husband, and almost immediately checked herself. Deena, watching, became
enraged. That her mother should feel diffident about going to
Daddy's side . . . that she should feel kept away from him by
the presence of those two, who didn't belong here and
shouldn't be here . . . it was too much! But it was all over in a
split-second. Sylvia squared her shoulders and pushed right by
them, without a word, without a glance, bending over him,
murmuring to him in Yiddish, cutting them out.

When Deena had first glanced at him, Jack's eyes had been
wide open and fully alert. As she watched, he took in the
scene for about five seconds. She could almost see his brain
clicking away, making its typical rapid-fire calculations. Now,
as soon as Sylvia came near, he allowed himself to collapse
back against the pillow. His eyes closed and he did something
very subtle with his body, something that made him sag a bit,
cave in a bit. Was Marilyn right, then? Was he faking it? He
couldn't be! It just wasn't Jack Strauss's style. Maybe, instead
of calling it fakery, one could call it cowardice. He didn't
want to face it, and here he was in a hospital bed, so why not
take advantage of the situation?

Holding tightly on to his hand, Sylvia stood straight and
expressionless, looking at Elaine and pointedly ignoring the
mother and son who were now also holding hands. Squared
off against each other, Deena thought, the two pairs.

"Well? Why are you standing there? Get out, I said."

Lawrence gave her a stiff smile. "See here, Elaine, no need
to take that tone with us. We're not exactly strangers, you
know, and Jack is allowed visitors. We checked."

"Did *he* tell you he wanted to see you? I thought not. In
that case, *out*. Out, until you're invited."

Lawrence was determined not to be ruffled. "Elaine, please. Don't get so excited. I understand how you feel, and we had planned to see Unc—to see Jack when nobody else was here, I mean, we're not without sensitivity, you know. But it happened. I'm sorry it happened, but I see no reason for a temper tantrum. This is neither the time nor the place for our private quarrel. . . ."

"You dare! You *dare*! You call this a private quarrel, you son of a bitch!" Elaine was beyond all reason. She shook off Marilyn's warning hand, ignored her mother's violent head-shaking, and without turning, interrupted herself to snap, "Stay out of this, Deena!" Then she turned once more to face the McElroys. "You've done enough damage to us, both of you. Now get out before I have you thrown out!"

All this time Linda had been standing absolutely still, chin raised defiantly, moving not a muscle. Now, suddenly, ugly color flooded into her face and she wrenched herself away from Lawrence, visibly trembling. "So this is how it all ends, is that it?" She spoke in a clogged voice Deena would never have recognized as hers. "So this is the thanks I get for all my years of service and sacrifice! This is the thanks I get for devoting my entire life to the Strauss family business! *This* is the thanks I get for thinking only of Jack's happiness! *This* is the thanks I get for putting aside any hope of having my own life, my own husband . . . !"

With every repetition, Linda's voice rose higher, shriller, louder. Deena began to panic. The woman was working herself up to hysteria. In a minute she was going to say it! She was going to stay it in front of them all . . . in front of Sylvia!

"Linda!" Deena shouted. The thunder of her own voice surprised her. It surprised everyone because suddenly, everyone was staring at her, even Daddy, eyes once again wide open.

"Sylvia!" he moaned in his best, weak voice . . . and now Deena knew for sure that Marilyn was on the mark. The groan he gave now sounded to her so like a performance, she didn't see how anyone could take it seriously.

But Linda turned, ran to his side. It was as if she didn't even see Sylvia standing right there. She threw herself half onto the bed, calling his name, tears streaming down her face.

"My darling, my darling!" she sobbed. "Don't let them send me away! You promised! You promised you'd always take care of me, of us both! Please, Jack, darling—"

In a tone that would have carried, Deena thought, to the last row of Yankee Stadium, her mother said, enunciating every word very carefully: "That will do, Linda. You've made enough trouble. Now, please leave. Jack is being cared for by his *family*."

"*Family*, is it? Family! Well, if Jack is with his *family*, then we certainly belong here, don't we? In fact, we have more right here than you do...I..." And she drew herself up proudly. "*I* gave him a son, his *only* son!"

Deena could not remember running to Linda; she was in one minute across the room, pulling the woman off the bed, her heart pounding and pounding in her ears, propelling Linda out the door, kicking, actually kicking, at the backs of her ankles to make her move, shouting "Out, out, out, out, out!" At the door she shoved Linda as hard as she could. "You stupid bitch!" she screamed.

She turned back to see Lawrence, doubled over, and issuing from his throat was a howl of such pain that chills went racing up her spine. In a moment he straightened himself up, his face chalky, his whole body shaking, his teeth chattering. He clamped his jaws together and then sucked in a long, agonized breath, staring at the man in the bed. "All those years—! All those years—!" He choked out. And then he let out another of those terrible sounds and went racing out of the room. He bumped heavily into Deena as he went by, and she had the feeling he never knew it.

Silence roared in her ears. It was so strange, so strange, the sudden quiet after all the passion. And into that small pool of quiet, Deena heard with horror, her mother comforting her father, saying over and over, "It's all right, it's all right, I already knew . . . it's all right, Jack, I've known for years."

CHAPTER THIRTY-EIGHT

Wednesday, February 12, 1986

The four Strauss girls—Sylvia, Deena, Elaine, and Marilyn —swept into the patients' lounge at the end of the corridor like four ships in full sail, Sylvia leading the way. She was talking very rapidly, a frown between her eyes. "This is crazy, I should be in there with your father, he needs me, he looks so pale—"

An elderly woman in a wheelchair, engrossed in *Mister Rogers' Neighborhood* on the color TV, turned sharply, and said: "Shhh." This gave Sylvia pause for about ten seconds, and then she went right on.

"Why do we have to talk *now*? Now is not a good time, we'll talk later, we'll talk some other time. . . ."

Deena's voice was a little louder than usual, but not particularly excited. "Sylvia. Quit it. You know we have to talk now. Stop stalling."

And, running right on top of Deena's words, Marilyn: "Listen to me, Sylvia. Daddy is okay, he's really okay. Yes, he had a little shock, he got a bit upset. But he's not going to have another stroke, believe me, he's not. Please don't make

386

more out of it than is absolutely necessary. Fussing like this isn't good for either of you."

"I'm not fussing. You're a doctor, but you're not a wife."

"Stop it. You're evading the issue again."

"There is no issue. It's all in the past, all over and done with, long ago."

Elaine, flushed and angry, interrupted. "It's not over and done with for *us*! *We* just found out, Sylvia. We just learned the truth about something . . . something very important, in case you didn't realize it, something pivotal to *all* of our lives!"

"And we didn't find out from our mother." Deena sounded bitter.

Elaine waved her off. "We had the dubious pleasure of hearing it from that bitch, over a month ago—and was she delighted to let us know, because it allowed her to feel superior! Oh, she loved it, Sylvia: loved lording it over Jack's spoiled little girls, giving it to us at last! And since that time, Sylvia dear, do you know what your daughters have been doing? Going crazy, trying to keep it from you. Isn't that a laugh? We were killing ourselves to protect you!"

"Listen. Elaine. I'm sorry it happened this way. I—".

"You knew all the time!" Deena cried. "All the time, all those years, you *knew*!"

Sylvia turned to look directly at her. "Since when is it a crime to protect your children, eh? You thought you were so wonderful, sparing me for two weeks? I spared you for thirty-five years! *Who* do you think I did it for? I did it for *you*, to keep you from being hurt, all of you! I don't understand why you're yelling at me."

"Because it was central to our lives, Sylvia, don't you see that?" Elaine demanded. "Our father disdained us all those years. And you let him!"

Sylvia's shoulders slumped a little. "I let him," she admitted. "I thought I was doing the right thing. I wanted only to be a good wife and mother. And let me tell you something: I think I *was*. It's easy for you now to say I should have done something else. Believe me, I thought it over plenty. I struggled with it. It wasn't easy, making that decision. But you all grew up in a real family, a family with a mother *and* a father, without the disruption of a divorce: that I gave you. So let me hear a little thanks, how about it?"

Into the small silence came the sound of hands clapping slowly and deliberately. It was Marilyn, her lips thinned out with anger, two spots of color high on her cheeks. "There's your thanks, Sylvia," she said. "You're forgetting me in this equation, you know. Oh, yes, surely you remember listening to my little fable about the father of a friend. Oh, you do remember. That's good. And do you mean to tell me you didn't know it was Daddy and Linda I was talking about? Of course you knew. But you refused to acknowledge my pain ... even when I *asked* for the truth, you lied. And all those years I've had to deal with it by myself! Where was my good mother then?"

Sylvia colored but staunchly stood her ground. "In those days," she said without a quaver, "that was the best way. You weren't supposed to discuss such personal adult things with your children. And I'm not liking it now, if you want to know the truth. You want to know how I feel about it right this minute? That it *still* isn't any of your business!"

"But the point remains: you lied to me, you lied to all of us."

"Marilyn, I'm trying to be patient with you. You were twelve years old. I tried to comfort you; in fact, Marilyn, I *did* comfort you. Oh, yes, I remember, maybe better than you. After I spoke to you, you were relieved. Didn't I say your friend's father loved her, that she must know that, she shouldn't worry that he'd leave her? Didn't I?"

Marilyn was silent and Elaine moved to her, putting an arm around her. But Deena, frowning, stamped her foot. "Dammit, of course it's our business! You think that because you keep something a secret, your children's lives aren't affected by it?"

"Deena, Deena, all of you! I don't understand. Why all this fuss over something that happened, what? Yesterday? No, over something that happened thirty-five years ago. All right, it's a shock, I understand it's a shock. But why all the carrying on? You had a wonderful childhood, all of you! You were the happiest, most admired, most loved girls in New York City, don't deny it. You thought you were lucky. And you know what? You were!"

"Yeah, we thought so and we thought so about something that was a mirage, Sylvia! Get it? *That's* the thing that's bothering us now. The childhood we remembered so happily wasn't *real*, don't you see?"

"What are you talking? Of course it was real... you lived it, didn't you? You can't say now that you were miserable because I was there and believe me, miserable you weren't!"

"Maybe not exactly miserable, no. Maybe miserable is the wrong word, Sylvia. But I've been writing about my childhood lately and I've begun to realize how much I had to ingratiate myself with Daddy... use little-girl wiles."

Sylvia laughed. "What's so terrible? You were adorable and you loved your daddy and he loved you and you flirted with him. Everybody thought it was so cute."

"Yeah, so did I. But now I think that doing a song and dance for him all the time was my attempt to keep him home, to keep him interested in *us*."

Sylvia made a little face. "Deena, Deena, stop making up things. You're talking nonsense. You weren't trying to keep him home. I was there, I know what was going on. You did a song and dance for him because you didn't want him paying attention to Elaine." Her voice had taken on an irritated edge. "And in the meantime, you learned to make a man feel warm and loved and wanted. Is that so terrible?"

"It is, yes, Sylvia, if you grow up and relate to *every* single man in the world in that way, no matter how he treats you." Deena took in a deep breath, visibly calming herself, and then added in a more even tone: "And yes, that includes Michael. I lived with my husband for years, thinking that whenever he treated me badly, it was somehow my fault and somehow up to me to behave in a way that would magically make it right. Just like I did with Daddy."

Sylvia got up from her chair, holding her hands up. "Deena, Elaine, Marilyn, all of you. I'm sorry this is upsetting you so much. But you're all grown women; you've all lived long enough to know. These things happen. What else can I tell you? Enough is enough already. Let's forget it and get on with our lives!" She made a move toward the doorway.

Marilyn, who had been standing silently, her head turned away from the others, her arms tightly folded across her chest, almost separate from the rest of them, now suddenly turned and exploded into speech: "The hell of it, the real hell of it, Sylvia, is that we weren't ever good enough for him. Oh, he loved to brag about us, he loved to tell everyone all about his beautiful wonderful brilliant girls. But he never meant it. He really wanted a boy, he wanted only a *son*! And what do you think that makes *us*?" Her eyes filled but no tears fell. It was Deena who began quietly to cry.

Sylvia rounded on her, her fists clenched. "That's right, cry! You think I didn't cry? I cried, believe me, I cried plenty! I cried into my pillow at night and he slept through it." One tear slid slowly from her eye, over her cheekbone, down her face. "I'm sorry. That's all past and done. I knew that tears weren't going to accomplish anything, they weren't going to change what was, they weren't going to make Jack a different person. So I dried my tears and raised my daughters the best way I knew how. And if you blame me for that . . ."

"Aw, Sylvia . . ." Deena and Elaine spoke together and together moved to their mother, embracing her together. After a moment, after Elaine gestured to her, Marilyn joined them, and for a few moments they huddled together without words. Only now did the old woman in the wheelchair turn from the television screen, noticing their presence in an incurious way.

"Let me go to your father," Sylvia said quietly. They released her and she strode briskly away without looking back.

"Jesus, let's sit down for a minute. I can't go back there, not quite yet," Elaine said. She let herself down onto a settee with a gusty sigh and stretched, unkinking her neck. "Christ, what a day. What a week!"

"And it's not over yet . . ." Marilyn said. "Daddy has to be convinced that he's not an invalid. My feeling is, get him back to the office and back to work, even just an hour or two a day, just as soon as you can." She was looking directly at Elaine.

"First, I have to get *them* out."

"I don't quite understand why you haven't done that already."

"Because, Marilyn, the business couldn't function without them. Don't shake your head, you don't know. I couldn't do it alone; my God, it's a miracle I've learned as much as I have. So I've swallowed my pride and let them stay. I figured, let me use them until Daddy is well enough to give them the heave-ho himself."

"I don't think he'll do it," Deena said. "I agree with Marilyn. I was watching him in there before and the minute the situation got tough he played weak and helpless. I think you're going to have the pleasure of firing them all by yourself."

"*If* that bastard has the nerve to show up tomorrow ... which he might very well do. Talk about *chutzpa!*"

Now Deena chuckled. "I'm awfully glad Lawrence is *your* problem, Lainie."

Elaine frowned. "He's *our* problem."

"Oh, no! I don't have any part of it, not me!"

"Oh, really, Deena? Well, you have more of a part in it than you know."

"Just what's that supposed to mean?"

"Never mind. I've said too much."

"Dammit, Elaine, you've been doing that to me since we were kids! Stop making yourself important!"

"All right then, if that's what you think, I'll tell you. Lawrence and Zoe are involved!"

Deena looked as if she might faint. "*What?*" she said in a tiny voice, all the color draining from her face.

Marilyn cast a withering look at Elaine and reached out for Deena's hand. Deena grabbed on to her sister, staring straight in front of her, shaking her head. Finally, she said, "Where did you get that?"

"From Noel."

"Oh, my God! My little girl!"

"Oh, shit, I'm sorry, Deena. Me and my big mouth!"

Deena and Elaine turned to stare into each other's eyes

and, without thinking, Deena let go of Marilyn's hand. "Oh, God, Lainie, what a mess, what a mess! What am I going to *do*?"

"Don't worry, we'll work it out, don't worry, don't worry, he wouldn't dare, don't worry. . ."

They did not notice when Marilyn backed away from them and, with no expression whatsoever on her pale face, left the room.

CHAPTER THIRTY-NINE

Thursday, February 20, 1986

Home Again. It was so good to think it. It was so good to have him back. Sylvia's heart was full to overflowing with happiness and goodwill. She was ready to love the world—including even Janette Berkholtz in the apartment upstairs who, talk about overflow, let her tub overflow at least once a month and had done it again yesterday. The plastering job they were going to need in the second bathroom. Don't ask!

But never mind . . . her Jack was back home again; and almost his old self already, joking with the elevator operator and slipping the doorman a twenty for carrying his bag in, and even *kvetching* a little at her. "Where are my cigars, Sylvia? I left three full boxes and—ah-ah!" And he turned to her.

"Oh, no, Jack Strauss! Don't give me any of your dirty looks. You know what Dr. Kopmar said!"

He smiled. "Kopmar's not *my* doctor."

"Never mind that nonsense. Nate Levinson also told you: no more cigars, not for the rest of your life. Which, God willing, will be many many years."

"Not without a cigar! It won't be worth living! Just kid-

393

ding, just kidding." The "just" was lisped a little from where his tongue had been affected, and he made a face of disgust. His speech was much better; he had a little trouble only when he got excited or tired. It didn't bother her a lot; you could understand him perfectly. But it made him so angry. Well, it was her job to make sure he didn't get overwrought or exhausted. And she would.

He was already so much improved . . . why, he was talking about getting back to the office already. Not that he could go back to work yet, oh, no, but it was a good sign that he wanted to get busy. Dr. Kopmar told her all about how some men became depressed, warned her about the signs, told her to call him the minute she thought Jack might be slipping. And she would. She was going to keep an eagle eye on him. And then, when he was well enough and strong enough to get back into harness, no way was she going to let him work more than a couple of days a week. And not a full day, either.

"Listen here, Jack," she'd say to him, "I need you more than the business does. Your family needs you. We almost lost you," she'd say to him. Of course, she knew that wasn't quite true, but if she had to exaggerate to get his attention, well . . . what else was new?

"No, no," she told him now as he reached for the valise. "Don't you dare, not yet. You have plenty of time to play strong man. Right now it's time for a little lunch. I had Earline make you her pecan pie as a welcome home, and there's Zabar's best in the fridge. So . . . into the den with you."

"You'll join me there?"

"Soon. Soon." She busied herself with the coats, hanging them up, folding his scarf carefully. Ever since they'd gotten into the cab, outside the hospital, he'd been trying to tell her something, trying to get her to sit still and listen to him. She had a horrible feeling she knew what it was. She recognized the look on his face, the wetness in his eyes, the softness. She hated that look; it was a look that asked for forgiveness ahead of time.

Her mistake had been to let him know she knew. After all these years of keeping everything to herself, in one moment of weakness she'd let it all out! Stupid! That's all he needed! It wasn't a secret anymore, so now he could confess his guilt and pour his heart out.

She did not want him to pour his heart out. She didn't want to hear the whole story. *Genug*! Enough!

"I really want to talk to you alone, Sylvia darling."

"I know. Soon."

His eyes became softer even. "I had a lot of time to think in the hospital, lying there in my bed, only half alive . . ."

Oh, God! Worse, even, than she had thought! She laughed at him gently. "Jack, Jack! What half-alive are you talking about? You look rested for the first time in ten years, you look better than before. You look like a man who just had a vacation! All right, maybe *not* like a man who just had a vacation, but almost."

At least that made him smile, and while she was chattering, she was also walking him down the hall and into the den and now she got him to sit down on the couch. She put pillows behind him and she brought the mohair lap robe to put over his knees and handed him the television remote and . . . finished! She stood back, hands on hips, regarding him, and said, "There. Now I'll get you lunch," and exited before he had a chance to argue with her.

In the kitchen, moving around in her familiar surroundings, she found her thoughts returning to what she wanted most to forget. How many times had he tried to bring it up? "Sylvia, there's something I have to tell you . . ." or "Sylvia, about Lawrence . . ." No, no, no more. She'd dealt with it and she'd lived with it and that was enough for one lifetime. To rake it over, to get even more details, would only make her miserable again. So she concentrated very intently on getting his lunch ready.

Just as she set the tray down in front of him on the coffee table, the intercom began to buzz loudly. "I told them downstairs, no visitors," she grumbled.

But Jack said, "Never mind, just find out who it is!"

In a minute she put her head into the doorway and said, "It's Elaine!" And as soon as she saw his grin, she knew. He was so bad!

Dr. Kopmar had said, "Take a few days before you see

people, take it easy, let yourself get back into your life slowly." And did he listen? Of course not.

"You told Elaine to come by, didn't you? To talk business."

"What? It's against the law for a man to see his daughter, his firstborn, to maybe take a look at his mail, maybe ask a couple questions, see if his business is still solvent?"

"Oh, Jack!" But maybe it would do him good and, as long as he was talking with Elaine, he wasn't going to try to confess to her. So let them talk.

Elaine was amused. Her mother let her right in to see her father—after giving her seventeen or eighteen rules for dealing with him, a quick hug, a quick once-over and a satisfied nod at her outfit, and once again warning her, "Don't excite him, don't argue with him, he's supposed to stay calm, Elaine darling."

"Yes, Sylvia," she said with a laugh. "No, Sylvia, I promise I'll be good, Sylvia." Then, more seriously, she said: "So? How is he?"

Sylvia laughed. "How should he be? A real pain in the ass, like all men when they think they're sick." They exchanged a look, the two of them, and Elaine thought, After all she's gone through, for more years than any of us realized, and she never gave up. Talk about strength! Talk about guts!

Then she went on in, already going over the list in her head of things she needed to tell or ask him.

He looked good, damn good for a man who'd just spent nearly three weeks recovering from a stroke. "So this is your new hangout. Well, you look comfortable," she remarked, and sat herself in one of the easy chairs facing him. "No, don't stop. Eat, eat. I already had my lunch."

"You want to know the truth? I'm not so terribly hungry. And I'm not so crazy about this room, either, never have been ever since your mother had it . . . *decorated.*" The way he said "decorated," as if he were saying "polluted," made her laugh. "But you know"—he leaned forward a little, in a conspiratorial manner—"I didn't want to hurt your mother's feelings. I *never* wanted to hurt her."

Elaine gave him a sharp look, and he said, irritated, "Why do you look at me that way? I have heart! And when you've looked death in the face, Elaine, then you know what's im-

portant." Did he really expect her to fall for this? But his face
was full of pain; maybe the scare really had done something to
him. Maybe it had changed him a little; maybe he was ready
to rethink a few things.

He went on. "Listen, Elaine, I almost lost the most wonderful woman in the world . . . by my own stupidity. Yes, I
admit it, your father did some stupid things." Well, well,
Elaine thought, that's a first. "I could have lost your mother,
Elaine. I'm lying there in a hospital bed, wondering am I
going to get out of this thing, thinking about all the years. I
was such a fool, you know? Such a fool . . ."

He looked down, blinking rapidly, and Elaine had a moment of panic. What if he cried in front of her? What in
God's name would she *do*? She could never remember him
being ill, not ever, not in her whole life. She didn't quite
know how to feel about him now. His obviously sincere
repentance moved her. But no tears, please! That she wasn't
prepared to deal with. And besides, she was too damn likely
to cry herself.

So she picked up the bulging shopping bag and announced:
"Your mail!" It was a sure way to change the subject.

But as he reached his hand to take the bag from her, she
caught a sly little glint in his eye. That man! Nothing in the
world was sacred to him, not even his own inner feelings. He
was setting her up; he had a zinger for her; he was just getting
ready to send it her way. He wanted something from her, and
in a minute she was going to find out what it was.

So *that's* what was behind all this emotional display. The
hell of it was, it had worked. Only for a moment, but it *had*
worked. He hadn't changed at all. Well, what did she expect
from a man of seventy? Miracles? And this way, at least, she
knew damn well with whom she was dealing. The same guy
she'd been dealing with her whole life.

Once she heard the names Linda and Lawrence, she only
half-listened to him. He wanted her to be his ax man. Of
course, he was describing it somewhat differently; he was
putting a nice sugar coating on his request. "You've proved
now that you have the stuff of an executive . . ." That kind of
blah-blah. What did he think she'd been doing all those years,

building up Sweet Somethings, if not proving she had the stuff of an executive?

She'd proved long ago that she was a damned good businesswoman! The whole rest of the world knew it; her husband knew it; God knows her accountant knew it. Everyone knew it. Except Daddy. He didn't want to know it, he had never wanted to know anything about any of them that might destroy his particular images. Even now he was telling her how smart she was only because he wanted something from her! Well, maybe he'd get it and maybe he wouldn't. In the meantime, it was too damn bad that they couldn't talk to each other. Because she wished she could tell him what had really happened with her and Lawrence at the office.

She had been in Daddy's office early Thursday morning the thirteenth, the day after the shit hit the fan in the hospital. What with Linda screaming and Sylvia going tight-lipped and confessions spilling out all over the corridors, it was obvious that she was going to have to do something about the McElroys, and pretty damn fast. The last two weeks she'd been willing to let them hang around, biding her time until Daddy was back. It hadn't been wonderful, all of them in the office at the same time. Mostly, they avoided each other; and she just took to coming in later and later in the afternoon while Linda began to leave earlier and earlier. Lawrence, of course, was usually out on the job; and even though she knew he had been stealing—let *Daddy* get rid of them. He'd promised. Let him keep that promise!

But now it was different. Now her mother was involved. Now the guilty secrets were out in the open. She had seen the look on Lawrence's face last night; if ever she saw pure hatred in a man's eyes, it was then. There was no telling *what* he might take it into his head to do. He had keys, he had knowledge, he had access, he had years of experience in this company. And, dammit, he had Daddy's trust. And now he hated them all! She could no longer have him anywhere in the company.

She'd made up her mind all through a long and sleepless night, had rehearsed what she would say to Lawrence, what tone of voice she would use, what threats. The first thing was to leave a note on his desk for him to see the minute he came in.

But when she opened his office door, he was there, sitting behind his desk, calmly reading *The Wall Street Journal*. He must have been there for hours; there were five paper cups lined up on his desk and he was sipping from yet another.

It was a surprise but not enough of a surprise to put her off stride. "I'm glad you're here," she said. Cool and distant, that's the tone she wanted. "I have a couple of things to say to you before you leave."

If she thought she was going to fluster him, she was wrong. He looked up, expressionless, almost bored, and answered, "I've been waiting for you. Come on in . . . but you already have, haven't you?"

"You owe this company four hundred forty-seven thousand three hundred eighty-six dollars. A certified check would be acceptable."

"I don't think I owe this company anything."

"Lawrence, let's skip the bullshit. I know all about it, the phony address, the phony company, the whole thing. You're a thief and I repeat: a certified check will be acceptable. Today would be best."

"And I repeat: I don't owe this company a goddamn thing. I've given my life to this company. I've worked hard and I've gotten very goddamn little in return."

"You were a vice-president. You've held a position of, you should pardon the expression, *trust*. Which, I'll remind you, you have violated."

"Fuck that! Don't give me any of that position-of-trust bullshit. You want to talk about stealing and cheating? I'll talk about stealing and cheating! Let's talk about my stolen birth-right, why don't we? Oh, yeah, give me that look! But it's true. I've been cheated out of a father my whole life!"

"Lawrence, I'm sorry for your situation. But that doesn't condone what you've done. You've been stealing not just from my father—"

"*My* father, too!" he spat.

This took her aback. She stood for a moment, feeling as if he'd kicked her in the stomach. She could not speak, could not find the words to answer that. It struck her for the first time that it was true. She felt turned around somehow, felt her thoughts twisting, and she didn't like it.

"Oh, yeah," Lawrence went on, his voice rising slightly, shaking a little. "That's right, he's my father! I never knew it either. I never knew it, not until last night. You think I can forgive him for cheating me, for ignoring me, for never admitting who I am? Whatever I took from him, it's *nothing* compared to what he owes me, Ms. Strauss, Miss Upper West Side, Jewish American Princess. The boss's daughter! You think I don't know what's going to happen now? He'll give you the business, like it's a toy to hand to one of his darlings!"

Elaine could only stare at him; he was so wrong, so wrong. But discuss it with him? Never! She kept her voice cold.

"He promised me a chance to run it. Years ago. I've waited and waited, Lawrence, and he's put me off and given *you* the opportunities. You think that's been a pleasure for me, watching you get what he promised to *me*? *I* deserve it."

"*You* deserve?" Now Lawrence put aside his playacting; no more cool-as-a-cucumber young executive. Now his face flushed and he gripped the edges of the desk so that his knuckles whitened. "You, who always had everything you wanted just handed to you! While I had to scratch for everything!" He stopped, choking over his own words. "You had a father, dammit! When you came home, he was there for you. He took you places, he gave you presents, he showed you off to the world. And he kept *me* hidden away, like I was something disgusting, something to be ashamed of! So don't talk to me about stealing and cheating! Don't talk to me about owing! You don't know what you're talking about!"

"You can't say that, Lawrence, because in the end, you're the one who got the payoff. You're the one he trusted with the most precious thing in his life—his business. If you had only been decent and honest, you would have ended up with everything. And you know why? Because you're what he wanted more than anything in this world—a son." Now *she* was choking and she stopped. She was damned if she was going to break down in front of him.

"Well, he got what *he* wanted. He got his son. But he cheated *me*! I never got a father!"

They stared at each other. For a split-second, Elaine

thought, This man is my brother. And then it flashed into her head that Daddy had cheated *all* of them! Including himself!

Of course there was no way she could report that conversation to Daddy. And she couldn't tell him how Lawrence had bolted, pushing past her, slamming the door behind him. Couldn't tell him that Lawrence had never appeared on the job, not that day, not any day since. Lawrence had disappeared. Linda swore up and down she didn't know where he was, and from the way she looked—haggard, worn, red-eyed, weary—Elaine had to believe her. The police had been told and the detective she had spoken to had more or less said that men quote disappeared unquote every day, that most of them had disappeared themselves, and the police didn't have the manpower to track down every guy who wanted to get away for a while. "He'll come back when he's ready, believe me, lady."

Now Jack said, "Look, I want you to take care of Linda and Lawrence. It's time they left the company; but they shouldn't go away empty-handed, if you know what I mean."

He gave her a wink, and it was the wink, the conspiratorial, just-us-guys-together wink, that did it. She damn near bawled. Here it was, her acceptance into his world. She remembered that wink; that was the adults-only signal. She recalled being very little, looking *way* up, past his legs, up to his face, so small and far away, and seeing him wink at one of his friends or at Sylvia and wishing, wishing, *wishing* that she were big enough to be part of that special grown-up world up there. She remembered jumping up, jumping *up*, trying to get there; but it was too far away. But if she tried long enough, Daddy might look down and notice her and reach for her and lift her up and she would say, "Blink at me, too."

And now, at last, he was blinking at her. Without being asked. She'd made it at last. He was accepting her at last. She fought the tears that threatened to fall. And now he was putting the frosting on the cake, saying that if she did this job real well, not only would she be given the responsibility of hiring replacements, but that he would put the entire reorganization of the office into her hands. Her *capable* hands, yet.

"Oh, that's wonderful, Daddy. And I'll have to be your

vice-president," she said, winking back. "Since we need a replacement for Lawrence," she added, ignoring the flash of amusement in his eyes. "I'll save you the cost of an ad in the *Times*. Very cost-effective, don't you think?"

"Well, that's an idea. We'll talk about that." He was giving her the business right back, a twinkle in his eye. Just as if they were equals . . . colleagues . . . associates. There was a new balance between them, very tenuous, very fragile. She didn't say anything for fear of disturbing it somehow. And he continued. "But first things first, Elaine. That's a cardinal rule of good business. First, you'll have to fire him."

He didn't have to teach her the rules of business, goddammit. Where did he think she had learned it all? But maybe it was time he learned something from *her*.

"You're right, Daddy," she said sweetly. "So now I'll tell you: there's good news and bad news."

"Oh?"

"The good news is, I don't have to fire Lawrence. He already left. And the bad news . . . he left with almost four hundred and fifty thou of your money in his hot little hands."

"Left! Goddammit! With four hundred fifty thousand? Where the hell *is* he?"

"Nobody knows. He didn't leave an itinerary," Elaine said. "But don't worry, we'll get the police working on it."

"Er . . . Elaine. Listen, darling. No police, okay? We don't want the police."

"Why not? He's a thief!"

"He's also my—I don't want him chased and I don't want him prosecuted. Let him go, let him go. I was planning to give him some money anyway. You can't care that much about him! Elaine?"

She wasn't going to tell Daddy, but she couldn't care *less* about Lawrence McElroy! Let him fall off the edge of the earth! It would be worth losing that money never to have to see him again.

CHAPTER FORTY

Thursday, February 20, 1986

"I'm bored!" Zoe announced. She stood at the window, look-ing down at the beach, wishing she were there. It wasn't such awful weather now, a little overcast but it was warm and there were a lot of people out. There were even some in the water. "I'm bored," she said again, but Lawrence didn't care. He was reading the sports section of yesterday's *Miami Herald* and pretending he didn't hear her. She was going to have to get up and go over to him, put her arms around him and nuzzle his neck, kiss his earlobe and tell him how handsome he was, and press her breasts into him. *Then* he'd pay atten-tion to her!

And he did. He dropped his paper and pulled her down onto his lap, kissing her with a lot of tongue. Phooey, he tasted of booze. She hadn't realized before this week how much he drank; and when she'd said something about it be-cause, come *on*, first thing in the morning? he laughed and said, "Drinking is part of a vacation, don't you know that?" But even with the strong taste of Scotch, she kept on kissing him. She loved him so much and he loved her, too. And the proof was, he'd brought her here with him, hadn't he?

When he called her at school last week—God, was it only a week? It felt much longer—she was knocked out just hearing from him. He hated talking on the phone. And then, when he said, "I'm running away, honey, and I want you to run away with me. How about it?" Well! She just about died, right there on her bed in front of her roomie.

"You're kidding!" she shrieked.

But he said very seriously, "No, I'm not, Zoe. I mean it. I have to get away for a while and I'd like you to be with me." She clutched the phone, hardly able to believe her ears, hardly able to breathe.

"Where are you going?"

"To the sun. One of the islands."

"You mean . . . the *Caribbean*?"

"That's what I mean."

Well, she looked around the dirty, messy room and she contemplated with gloom the pile of books on the floor that had to be cracked because exams were coming up; and then she looked out of the window into the dark, where it was snowing again and the wind was howling around the corners. She could just imagine them, lying together on the beach, on a big fluffy towel, smelling of coconut oil, and he'd be rubbing her back and telling her how beautiful she was and the sun would be warm and the ocean would go gently plop, plop onto the beach and oh . . .

"Oh, yes," she said into the phone.

He wanted her to pack her things right this minute and when she said "But I don't have any summer clothes with me, Lawrence, it's winter," he said for her to just get on a plane and meet him at LaGuardia and he'd buy her a whole new wardrobe when they got there.

It was going to be wonderful, he said, like a honeymoon. And it began just fine. He did meet her and he scooped her up in his arms and hugged her and kissed her over and over again. And they held hands all the way to Freeport.

As soon as they'd registered in the hotel, he took her downstairs to a shop and told her she could have whatever she wanted. And it turned out their room was a suite, with a living room and a balcony. And they had dinner in a fancy French restaurant right downstairs and she wore her new strapless dress and he told her she was the loveliest woman in the room. It was heaven!

She noticed that he drank a lot that night, and in bed later, he was a little rough with her. But it *was* sexy and, well, she had drunk a lot of champagne herself.

The real trouble started the next morning. The sky was bleak and overcast and stormy.

Lawrence took one look outside and said, "Shit! If I'd wanted this kind of weather, I could have stayed in New York."

"But then I wouldn't have been in bed with you," she purred, snuggling into him. They could make love again, sleepily and slowly, and then order up a wonderful breakfast from room service and then . . .

But he pushed himself up and leapt from the bed, stalking naked to the window, cursing. He didn't even look at her, just went to the scotch and poured himself a big shot. She was so hurt by his behavior that she started to cry. He came right over to her then and cuddled her and said he was sorry, he just wanted everything perfect for them and he had a lot on his mind. No, he couldn't tell her what it was, not yet.

A week had gone by and he still hadn't told her anything. Not only that, but he was drinking more and more. And even though the weather was better, they hardly ever went to the beach . . . or even outdoors. He was always in the casino. But now that she had loved him up a little, he was in a pretty good mood. "Let's go out, Lawrence."

"There's no sun."

"We don't have to go to the beach. We could do something else."

"We could, at that." He began to kiss the hollow of her throat and slid his hand under her shirt to finger her nipple. She wiggled, trying to move away, but he held on tighter, pinching.

"Lawrence, that hurts! Come on, you promised!"

"What did I promise?" His voice had become husky. He was getting hot. Well, she liked making love with him, but the past few days it wasn't as good as it used to be. He just rolled over onto her and stuck it in and never asked her what she wanted, just pumped in and out, sometimes he had to work very hard to come and he closed his eyes, concentrating, and then she felt like an *object* or something and, well, it just wasn't as good as it was in the beginning.

She kept asking him, "Do you love me?" and that made him angry.

"Of course I love you! Why do you think I asked you to come with me?" But somehow she didn't feel as if he loved her.

"Lawrence! I don't feel like it. Let's go outside and . . . I know! Let's rent bikes and take a nice long ride. That'll be fun."

"That'll be fun!" he mimicked in a falsetto voice. She hated when he did that. "Let's take a bike ride! Right now, the only fun I want is this . . ." And he reached between her thighs and pushed his fingers into her.

She didn't like it, but she let him. She loved him, didn't she? But she could hardly wait until he was finished, and then she got up from the bed and went into the shower. She felt grubby and she relished the needles of hot water pounding on her back. She did a really good job, shaving her legs, washing and conditioning her hair, massaging her feet, and stayed there for a very long time.

By the time she came out, wrapped in towels, Lawrence was up, tucking a clean shirt into his pants. Her heart sank when she saw him counting the cash in his wallet. She knew what *that* meant. But she asked anyway. "Where are you going?"

"Casino."

"Can't we have lunch together?"

"I'm not hungry. Order up something from room service if you want to eat. Or go downstairs and put it on the bill." There was a pause while he tucked the wallet into his pocket and checked to make sure he had everything he needed. Then he said, sounding very bored, "You wanna come with me?"

"You know I don't know how to play cards."

"You can play the slots."

"That's no fun. I want us to do something together."

"So come with me. We'll be together."

"Lawrence!"

"Look, Zoe, that's what you do in Freeport. You go to the beach or you go to the casino. I'm sorry the weather's been so lousy, but it's not my fault."

"The weather's not lousy at all. It's just your excuse," she flared.

He scowled. "I'm not stopping you from doing anything you want! Go bike riding if that's what you want! Go shopping! You know how to do *that*, all right."

She went to him, wanting to cry but not daring. "Lawrence, I thought this was going to be fun. I thought . . ." And then she stopped because she didn't know how to tell him she was unhappy. How did you tell that to someone? She just couldn't!

He didn't bother to hide his irritation. "Whining all the time! You sound like a goddamn baby! And I'm beginning to wonder what the hell I'm doing here with a baby!"

"Well, and *I'm* beginning to wonder what I'm doing here with a man who won't talk to me and doesn't even want to be with me."

"Zoe, I'm with you. Try to understand. I've got so much on my mind, and you're not helping."

She began to cry out loud, just like a baby. And then she thought of how he called her a baby and that made her cry even harder. She hated it, but she couldn't stop herself, and she only wanted him to put his arms around her tell her he loved her.

But it just made him mad. "Quit that bawling!" he kept saying, and when she couldn't, he grabbed her by the shoulders and walked her backward and sat her in a chair and said, "Look. I'm sorry. Maybe I shouldn't have brought you here. I thought it would be easier. I thought you'd enjoy it, that you'd keep me company. It's just not working out."

She didn't want to hear that! It made her heart just squeeze together. "You told me you'd explain! Maybe if I understood . . ."

Lawrence turned and walked away, his fingers pressed into the bridge of his nose, brows drawn together. Even half hidden, his face looked in pain. Without facing her, he began to speak. "You want me to explain? Okay. Here goes. Your beloved papa, the great and wonderful Jack Strauss, is my father."

She couldn't believe what she was hearing. It was so crazy! Papa! That's who he meant. He was saying that Papa was his father . . . that *Papa* was his *father*! "No!" she burst out. "Your father died in the war! Your father was a soldier."

He laughed and it was not a nice sound. "That's just a story my mother made up to protect herself! But the real truth is, I'm Jack Strauss's bastard. Ain't that a pisser? Oh, for Christ's sake, Zoe, if anyone around here should be crying, it should be *me*. I'm the one who got cheated out of all the good schools and expensive clothes and trips to Europe and all the other stuff you Strausses just take for granted! I'm the one got treated like shit!"

Zoe's head was whirling. All she could do was stare at him. It was a nightmare! It meant that Papa . . . and Linda . . . ! Oh, gross! And oh, my God, it meant that she and Lawrence were *related*! Wasn't that incest? "Why didn't you ever tell me?" she cried.

"Take it easy, will you? I only found out a week ago myself. And do you think anyone told me? Hell, no. I found out by *accident*. Think how *I* feel, instead of sitting there blubbering for yourself. Think how I feel, knowing he's my father, and he's never loved me enough to say so! I worked my ass off for him, for years! And what did I get for it? Nothing. Hell, I took a little money from the company . . . I wish to Christ I'd taken more! I wish I'd taken it all! And even *that* wouldn't be punishment enough to pay back for what he's done to me!"

He slammed out then, without a backward look, leaving her sitting in the chair, stunned and sobbing. She had never felt so alone in her entire life! She was so miserable! Why had she listened to him; why had she come here? She couldn't stand it, she just couldn't stand it! She wanted her mommy!

As soon as she thought of her mother, she cried even harder, hiccuping. Oh, how she wished Lawrence had never called her, that she hadn't been home that night, that she'd been in the library like she should have been, then none of this would have ever happened! She was trapped here, trapped in this awful place, far from home and with no money! What in

the world was she going to do? She sprang up from the chair,
wringing her hands, moaning aloud, pacing wildly. And then
she caught sight of herself in the mirror, wild-eyed, her hair
all in a tangle, and it shocked her into a sudden calm. She
looked crazy! She couldn't crack up, not here. If she were
going to crack up, she'd do it at home where Mom would take
care of her. But maybe she'd never see him again! That
squeeze in her chest, it hurt. But she couldn't let that get in
her way now. She had to get out of here! Everything in her life
was so turned over, so turned around, she couldn't deal with
it. She had to get home, that's all she knew.

And then, as soon as she thought that, she suddenly realized she could leave. She wasn't trapped, not really. She knew
where Lawrence kept the money. She had thought it was
funny, all that cash . . . and she went right over to the closet,
praying he hadn't taken it all with him. But no. There it was,
hidden in the lining of a jacket he never wore. She reached in
and pulled it out, a bill at a time. They were hundred-dollar
bills. Would anyone stop her? Would they look at her and say,
"What's a kid doing with hundred-dollar bills?" Well, she'd
just think of something. She'd put on high heels and put her
hair up and get dressed up and they wouldn't know how
young she was.

She was scared the whole time. What if Lawrence got
bored at the casino and came back? What if he felt sorry and
wanted to apologize to her. What if, at this very moment, he
was downstairs at the desk, arranging to rent two bicycles?
Oh, God! And her hands were shaking so hard, she could
hardly get the eyeliner on straight.

But then it was done and she was in the elevator and out of
the elevator, walking fast across the tiled lobby, her heels
making a racket, and out in front asking the doorman to get
her a cab. And nobody seemed to take note of her at all.
Nobody was interested in who she was or where she was
going or what she was doing. Seated in the back of the cab,
she drew in a deep, shuddering breath. "The airport," she told
the driver, and he never blinked, just put the car in gear and
began to drive.

She began to giggle nervously. It looked like everybody in
Freeport was bored, too bored to think about *her*. As she

watched the palm trees zip by the car window, as she got farther and farther away from the hotel and the casino and Lawrence, she began to feel a little bit easier in her mind. Oh, when he came back and found her gone! When he saw that she'd taken six hundred dollars of his *money*! Oh, God, he'd kill her: *if* she ever saw him again! Well, he'd better just never say anything about it . . . it was Papa's money and he'd stolen it, he said so! Oh, God! Her life was ruined.

At the airport they just took the money and gave her a ticket and told her when her plane would be leaving. And nobody asked her a thing. She had several hours to wait. She went to a phone booth and placed her call. If Mommy wasn't home—!

But her mother *was* there and it was such a relief and then it was so weird because for the first couple of minutes, Mom thought she was calling from Ithaca and they were having a lot of trouble understanding each other. And then she told her and Mom yelled: "You're *where*? In *Freeport*? In the *Bahamas*? What in hell? Never mind, don't tell me, I think I don't want to know. But what in hell are you doing in Freeport?"

"I came here with Lawrence."

She waited for the explosion, but Mom only took a deep breath and said, "I know. About Lawrence." And Zoe began to cry.

"It's over," she wept. "Oh, Mommy!" And Mom said it was going to be all right and that she should try to calm down and she should try to sleep on the plane if she could and she'd be home in a few hours and then they could have a nice long talk whenever she wanted. "When you get off the plane, sweetheart, I'll be there waiting for you." And then they hung up. And Zoe suddenly realized that she was *starving*.

The plane got into Kennedy a little after nine. Walking out into the terminal, she felt a bit displaced but so happy to be back home. She looked down the line of craning faces and there was Mom and oh, shit, him, too. Dad. Why did he have to come to meet her? He never did any other time. Because he wanted to give her hell.

And sure enough, before her mother had a chance to do anything, he was pushing past her and had Zoe by the arm. "And just what do you think you're doing, young woman, leaving school, going halfway around the world, causing your mother grief . . ." She turned him off, just looked right through him the way she'd been doing for years now. Of course it infuriated him; he was such a pain!

And then Mom rescued her. She pushed right by *him* and put her arms around Zoe and said, "That's enough, Michael," and then, more softly, in Zoe's ear, "My baby . . . poor Zoe." And Zoe found herself dissolving in tears, absolutely unable to stop. It was so embarrassing, but there was nothing she could do about it. She allowed herself to be led out of the airport and into the backseat of the car, where she curled herself into a little ball. Mom took off her fur coat and put it over Zoe like a blanket. It was so nice and warm and it smelled like Mom.

For a while Dad drove in silence and Mom didn't even turn on the radio like she usually did. Zoe was very aware of the sound of the tires on the road, of the noise each car made as it passed, of the engine.

She was almost asleep when her father's voice brought her attention. He was furious, she could hear that. "Dammit, Deena, what's the *matter* with you lately? Ever since you decided you're a writer—a *writer*!—you've behaved as if you're no longer a mother. Don't say a word, you can't deny what's true. You've abdicated. You're never home anymore! You're simply not available to your family anymore! And look at the results: one disaster after another. Here's your daughter, weeping in the backseat, having been seduced and then abandoned by a man with a reputation, a man old enough to be her father, a man we now know to be her—"

"Shut up, Michael." Zoe had never heard her mother sound like that. "You don't know what you're talking about and you're only making matters worse. Zoe is nineteen. She fell in love and went off on a romantic adventure with the man she loved. She's hurting, Michael, that's the operative word here, your daughter aged nineteen is in *pain*. Never mind castigating me! That can wait. I know exactly what you're going to say, anyway."

"You think you're so much smarter and wiser than I am! Well, think again, Deena. I'm going to have to take charge once more, as I had to with Saul."

"You have a bloody nerve! If anyone took charge of Saul, it was my sister Marilyn!"

Zoe couldn't stand it one more minute. "Will you two stop it? Please? I'm feeling bad enough without that!"

"When you're an adult and self-supporting, then you can have feelings," he said. "Right now your job is to pull yourself together and get back to school, where you belong."

"Michael! That's crazy! You cannot order other people's feelings, you just can't. Maybe Zoe needs to talk about it."

"Zoe doesn't need to talk about it. She needs to forget about it. It was a mistake. Everyone is entitled to one mistake. What's done is done and there's no way we can undo it. But we can put it behind us and the best way to do that is for Zoe to get on with her life, the way it was."

"You're dumber than I thought," Mom said, "if you believe that bullshit." Zoe was horrified and fascinated. What was going on? She'd never heard her mother speak this way to her father, never. In the backseat she sat up a little so she could see them, and Dad was furious. Mom went right on. "That's right, Michael, in front of the child. Let her hear. You think nothing of talking about her and her life as if she were an object that belongs to you! All you really care about is yourself."

Zoe waited, fearful. He would never let Mom get away with that! She drew in a breath very quietly; she certainly didn't want to have him turn on *her*. But he didn't say anything, not one word. Then they stopped for a red light and he pounded his fists on the steering wheel, over and over and over, in silent fury. She'd never seen her father out of control before and her heart speeded up with fright. But that's all there was. The light changed, he put his hands back on the wheel, and they rode in silence for the rest of the trip home.

CHAPTER FORTY-ONE

Friday, March 7, 1986

"Michael, for God's sake, stop following me around!" Deena's voice tried to sound amused but the irritation showed.

Well, goddamn it, Michael Berman thought, if she thinks she's annoyed, she should know how I feel! There was no pleasing women! He had recently come to the realization that indeed he had been absent from home a good deal. What with the survivor committee meetings and all the work at the office lately, he had ended up neglecting his wife. He hadn't realized how preoccupied he was; dammit, he was too *busy* to think about his personal life. And anyway, after all these years, she should *know* how important the marriage was to him without constant declaration.

But then, there was Jack's stroke. A big, strong, apparently healthy man, struck down without warning! Marilyn said he had warnings—but a moment's dizziness? Who hadn't had *that* happen to him at least once? It made a man stop and think.

And that's precisely what he had done. He had stopped to take stock; and it had occurred to him that he wasn't going to

413

be around forever. He had reminded himself that Deena hadn't moved out of their bedroom, *he* had . . . and that it had been Deena who came to *him* finally. She had done *her* part, he told himself. And what if *he* were to drop dead tomorrow? The thought chilled him, chilled him to the bone. Jews always remembered their dead, saying, "May his name be a blessed memory." He wanted his name to be a blessed memory, not only to his people, but to his wife and children and to their children after them. What kind of memory would *he* be leaving behind? Of a man who came home late, who worked too hard. That's what they would remember . . . a man too busy to be a good husband and father. That's when he realized that he was going to have to put a little extra effort into his marriage, yes, even after all these years. And for the past two or three weeks he'd been doing his damnedest—with very goddamn little response from her!

His first attempt was to leave the office early to surprise her. And surprise her he had; surprised himself as well. He came in, took her into his arms, feeling tender and loving, and found himself suddenly hungry for her, no, wild for her, found his loving feelings turning into passion. They went right upstairs together, undressed each other, and made wonderful love.

It was almost as good as the time she came to him, dressed so provocatively, so obviously wanting him. He had loved the feeling of being wooed by her. Men were forced by culture as well as by nature to be the aggressors . . . and every once in a while, yes, he was willing to admit it, it was a relief to have her make the first move. But that wasn't the main thing; the important thing was that it had been a true emotional communion, man to his woman.

That was the other thing he'd had to face. He hadn't been giving his wife enough sex. Sex was the way in which married couples communicated; he had allowed himself to forget how important it was. No wonder she had gone running off to have dinner with girlfriends or for a night at the theater or to that ridiculous class! A satisfied wife stayed home.

And then this morning he had come up behind her as she was preparing to get into the shower. He had embraced her and fondled her and nuzzled her neck and told her that he wanted to come into the shower with her and scrub her back. And she had refused him! "Not now, Michael. I have a dentist's appointment in twenty minutes." Well, he had decided to overlook her petulance. He'd gotten dressed and waited for her downstairs to give her a hug and kiss good-bye—made himself late for the office, in fact!—and when he came up to her, she just burst out with it: "Not *now*, I said!"

She had no right make everything so difficult when he was trying so hard to make it up to her. But he had patience even if she didn't. So he held his temper and held his tongue and decided that the next surprise he had for her might better wait until tonight, when she would probably be in a better mood. He must remember, he told himself, that Deena was not a morning person.

Tonight he was home good and early. Deena looked startled when he walked into the kitchen. She was on the phone with Elaine—again with Elaine! Did they never tire of going over and over the same gossip? But she smiled at him and held up two fingers to show she'd only be a couple of minutes. He poured himself a drink—she already had one, he noted, very pleased with himself for thinking to check—and puttered around the kitchen, waiting for them to finish.

It was the usual. They were going over and over that business of Jack and his . . . well, rather lurid past. His peccadillos. His lady friend and her child. They couldn't seem to stop talking about it. Six weeks they'd known about it, maybe more, and it was a month since his stroke. Enough already, as his mother-in-law would say. But women never could get enough of gossip. Talk, talk, endless talk. Speculations, suppositions, suspicions . . . God, the hours they spent at it.

Deena was saying ". . . But what Sylvia doesn't understand, Lainie, is when there's one lie, you can't help but wonder where the others are hidden." She laughed a little, but Michael could see that the laugh was false. "To be continued . . . Yes, yes, I know . . . I know . . . this too shall pass, footprints in the sands of time, Ozymandias and all that garbage . . . Yes, okay, I admit it, I'll get over it, yes. At least Zoe didn't get—never mind, Elaine. Michael just got home, and I really must get off and ask him what miracle brings him here to Monroe Place at a reasonable hour."

She had a tongue on her sometimes. Was it really necessary to put that sarcastic edge on her voice? To talk about him at *all*? It was another invasion of his privacy, by God! He refused to rise to the bait. Instead, he went to the cabinet and made himself another drink, his back to her.

"Well, it *is* highly unusual, Michael. Home at five-thirty P.M.? The last time I remember *that* happening, you had the flu. Oh! Are you sick?"

His back still turned, he said: "I'm feeling fine, thank you."

"Oh, Michael, please don't get fussy. It's fine that you're home early. It's just . . . you know, discussing Daddy and all that mess gets me upset."

He turned to her. "I've been meaning to talk to you about that, Deena. I don't understand why you keep torturing yourself this way. This regurgitation of what happened years and years ago is masochistic."

It was useless, trying to talk sense to her; he might have known. Deena—and her sister Elaine, too— had a habit of dramatizing every event in life. Now he sighed a bit, and putting a hand on her shoulder, said kindly, "Take a lesson from your sister, why don't you? Marilyn has the right idea. You find out something unsavory, you look at it, you deal with it, and get on with your life."

"Like you put the Nazi away, Michael, right?"

"There's no comparison between the worst disaster known to human history and one's man infidelity."

"Of course not, Michael. Nothing compares to your Holocaust." And she relented. "I'm sorry, I don't mean to say it's meaningless. Of course it isn't. It's not just your disaster; it's mine, too. But still . . . what Daddy did is not easy to take. I don't think you quite understand how betrayed I feel."

"No, I don't. You're quite right. I can't understand it at all. It seems to me you're objecting to finding out that your beloved Daddy is less than perfect . . . Now wait a minute, I'm not saying I approve of what he did. You know me better than that. But it's done and if your mother has found it in her heart to forgive him, I don't see why *you* can't." A perfectly reasonable statement, but she colored angrily, as if he had just insulted her.

"I'm dealing with everything that's happening the best I can. Not only Daddy. Zoe, too; and yes, Saul. But can't you understand that we all have feelings, Michael? That we exist —"

Her voice broke then and Michael knew just what to do. He put his arms around her and murmured, "There, there," and reached for a tissue to wipe her cheeks. Now was the moment. "I brought a little present home for you," he said; and reaching into his inside pocket, brought out the tickets. "Six concerts," he announced. He had been so proud of remembering how she had loved the Philharmonic series some aunt and uncle gave them as a wedding present. He couldn't wait to see that brilliant smile break over her face.

Instead, though, she gave the tickets a look of disdain. Handing them back to him, she said: "A Monday night series, I see."

"Yes?" *Now* what was her problem?

"Congratulations, Michael. You finally get us concert tickets after twenty-five years and you manage to pick my class night."

He could not believe his ears. Was she trying to tell him that her stupid class was more important than spending time with him? He asked her, and in reply got a hard look and a bitter laugh. "In a word," she said, "Yes."

He was still standing there, like an idiot, staring at her, telling himself there was nothing to gain in his behaving as badly as she, and perhaps escalating things, when she turned on her heel and left. *And left!* Just like that, without a word of explanation. Well, that was just too much!

He went charging after her, bellowing her name. "Goddammit, Deena, I haven't finished talking to you!"

She was already on her way upstairs. She stopped midstep and turned to him, her face utterly without expression, her eyes cold as ice. A shudder went through him; this was a Deena he had never seen.

And that's when she said it, in that emotionless voice. "Michael, for God's sake, stop following me around!"

"What kind of thing is that to say, Deena? It's my house, too, and you're my wife!"

She dragged in a rasping uneven breath. "Not for long."

He blinked at her. "I beg your pardon?"

"I want a divorce, Michael."

There was a buzzing in his ears, a feeling of unreality. She couldn't have said that, it wasn't happening. It couldn't be happening. She couldn't mean it. "If you're trying to upset me, Deena," he said, "You've succeeded."

He hated the little smile on her face. "I'm not trying to upset you, Michael. I'm trying to tell you something."

"You don't mean it."

"Yes, Michael, I do. I mean it. I've seen an attorney. Her name is Melanie Cohen."

Now he was thunderstruck. She'd seen an attorney. Then she did mean it and it was very very real! He didn't care what she might say to him; he followed her up the stairs and into their room. *Their* room, with their big bed, the one they had shared for almost twenty-five years.

He stood at the doorway, mute, not knowing where to begin, watching as she moved about the room, closing the shutters, turning on the lamps, pretending she didn't know he was there. What was he to do? Did she really mean to end their life together just like this? One minute, married; the next, not? Was that what she intended? No! he thought, and heard a harsh sob burst from him. "Deena," he said and, to his horror, heard his voice break, felt his eyes fill and overflow.

She turned to him and said, "Oh, Michael. I'm sorry. But surely you can't be so surprised! It's been years coming, you know that, years of your criticism and dissatisfaction, years of my unhappiness, years of growing apart. Oh, Lord, you *are* surprised. How many times have I told you how unhappy I am! Didn't you hear me?"

"I thought...I thought...it was a momentary thing. Every marriage has its ups and downs and you're an emotional woman."

"You didn't hear me." She peeled off her sweater and dropped her skirt to the floor, totally without self-consciousness, as if he weren't a sexual creature.

"Is there another man?" His voice was harsher than he intended. Pulling a robe from her closet, she wrapped it around her and faced him once more.

"Michael, I'm going to tell you a little story. Remember, on our way to the Whitaker's cocktail party, we took a walk in the snow and you told me how sorry you were that you'd been so—what did you call it? oh, yes, preoccupied—sorry that you had been so preoccupied. And then you said you were going to do better and we were going to be fine. But Michael, it was too late. It was much too late. Even so, I had a horrible moment of panic because I thought if you were going to try, then that meant *I* had to try to make it work even though I knew damn well that, for me, it was over and I had to get out. And then, Michael, I had the most *wonderful* moment of my adult life. Because I suddenly realized that I didn't *have* to do *anything*. I didn't have to be a good girl anymore, not for you, not for Daddy, not for any man.

"I suddenly came to the realization that happiness was a possibility for me, that I could do it for myself. I could make up my own mind what it was *I* wanted . . . that I had, god-damnit, a *right* to do what I wanted to do." She took in an audible breath. "In answer to your question, no. It's not another man. It's nothing like that."

"But . . . we love each other!"

She moved over to him and put a tender hand on his cheek, looking up at him sadly. "Oh, Michael, I'm so sorry. But we don't, you know. We don't love each other. Well, maybe I shouldn't speak for you; but I don't love *you*."

He stared at her, hating her, hating that sad look, that hand laid along his cheek. This is how she dealt with the children when she was trying to comfort them. He found it not comforting at all. He found it infuriating and condescending.

She couldn't condescend to him, not to *him*! He was Michael Berman, Esq., top of his class in law school, editor of the *Law Review*, partner in his own firm, a landowner and a homeowner, the father of four children and, goddammit, *her husband*! She couldn't do this to him!

He wrenched away from her as if her touch were poisonous and was pleased when hurt flashed in her eyes for an instant. Good. Let her know with whom she was dealing. If she thought that he was going to lie down and let her walk all over him, then she was sadly mistaken.

She smiled at him, a tiny little smile, shrugged, and began to walk from the room.

"Wait, Deena! I'm not finished."

She didn't bother to turn, to look at him. "You don't believe it, Michael, but, oh, yes, you are!"

CHAPTER FORTY-TWO

Wednesday, March 19, 1986

When Deena opened the front door to her mother, she found herself looking at the top of Sylvia's pink angora beret as her mother bent to pick up supermarket flyers from the steps. And while she was at it, it shouldn't be a total loss, she uprooted a long-dead geranium from the big concrete planter and wrapped it in the papers.

She looked up and heard Deena laughing. "So I'm neat, so sue me. I can't help it. And I'm an old lady, it's not nice to laugh at me." She paused, her fur coat hanging open in spite of the blustery March weather, giving her daughter the once-over.

"Come in, it's cold out—for those of us not wearing fourteen or fifteen fully let out female minks." Then Deena added, "Well? How am I?"

Sylvia was nonplussed. "How are you? Radiant. You look wonderful, Deena. So much better than you've been looking lately, it's a relief. Today, if you were still so drawn, I was going to say something to you."

"Well, I'm glad I pass. And thank you for the flower." She took the sodden bundle from Sylvia's hand, closed the door behind them, and gestured toward the kitchen. Sylvia threw her coat down onto a chair as she passed it. "How are the children? What smells good? Why are you looking so good?"

"Fine. Spinach soufflé. And how's Daddy?"

"He's as usual, *kvetching* because Dr. Kopmar won't let him go to the office more than two hours at a time. It's only been a month and a half, and he should take it slow, he knows that, but go talk to a wall! He's restless. He says men weren't meant to stay home and then I ask him what makes him think *I* was meant to stay home. So he answers me. He says, 'So don't stay home. Go see Deena! She wants you. Go! Go! You're driving me crazy.' I don't like to leave him; you know your father, Deena, the minute I go, he'll sneak off to the club, he'll smoke a cigar, he'll run to the office. You have to keep your eye on him every minute. But Earline's there today and she said not to worry, she'd take care of him all right. You know Earline!"

They both laughed because they both did know Earline, whose toughness was legend. Just let Jack Strauss try to escape the apartment if she was blocking the door!

The two women sat at the kitchen table, facing each other. Sylvia narrowed her eyes and scrutinized her daughter. "So?" she said after a moment. "Tell me."

"Tell you what, Sylvia?"

"Ah-ha! You can't even look me in the eye! Tell me the reason you invited me here, that's what."

"I already told you: I thought it would be good for you to get out, to get away from Daddy. You do too much for him, Sylvia, the doctor's warned you about that. It's not good for Daddy and it's not good for you."

"We could have gone to a movie, Deena. We could have met at Bloomingdale's. We could have made reservations at Café des Artistes, if getting me out was the big idea. So? What's really going on? You want to tell me, or not?"

Deena smiled and heaved a sigh. "I want to tell you. Of course I want to tell you. And it wasn't just to get you out, of course not. What are you, anyway, some kind of mind reader?" She paused briefly and then quickly said, "Michael and I are legally separated."

"But not divorced!"

"Not yet. But, we've begun the process—" And here she paused deliberately and leaned across the table, putting her hand over Sylvia's. "But, yes, we will be. Divorced. That's what a legal separation is all about."

Sylvia looked a trifle stunned. "But . . . what will you do? Where is he living? What about your poor children?"

"Sylvia, Sylvia, this isn't the Dark Ages! The kids will be fine; we'll all be fine! Lots of people get divorced. Such as your friend Lil Nathan."

"My friend Lil Nathan is not my daughter Deena Berman."

"I don't want to make a great big deal out of this, Sylvia, but it's going to be Deena Strauss again. As soon as we and several lawyers work through all the details."

Sylvia winced and sighed. "I need a cup of coffee." When Deena got up to get it for her, she added, "All the articles in the *Times* say that divorce really hurts the children, it doesn't matter how old they are."

"Do all the articles in the *Times* say that a bad marriage really hurts everybody?"

"What bad marriage? You've been a wonderful wife and mother! What's his problem? Another woman? Well, a separation, legal or not, isn't final, don't worry, he'll come back."

Deena set down a steaming cup, carefully placed the sugar bowl and creamer on the table, and said, "Sylvia, listen to me. It was my idea. There's no other woman and, by the way, no other man, either."

"How *could* you, Deena? How could you do it to Michael —kick him out, throw away all those years? I don't understand it." Her hands balled into fists. "I *hate* it!"

"I'm sorry, Sylvia. What can I tell you, Sylvia? I've been very unhappy for a very long time and *yes*, I told him so and *yes*, I suggested counseling and no, he wouldn't do it. It finally became unbearable and then it occurred to me that there was no policeman with a gun standing there making me put up with it. I don't have to stay married to a man who's been abusive."

"He hit you?"

"No, no, he didn't hit me. You think that's the only way to abuse someone? He carped and criticized, he—oh, hell, Sylvia, in the end I couldn't do *anything* right." She paused and thought and said, "And that's when I knew I had to get out!"

"A woman without a husband," Sylvia said, in the tone of a major pronouncement, "has only half a life."

"Shame on you, Sylvia! What about your daughter Marilyn?"

"The last time she was in, I looked at her and my heart grieved. She's thirty-six, Deena, thirty-six years old; she should be married. Soon it will be too late to have children and what is life for a woman without children? And I had a few words to say to her on the subject, believe me!"

"Sylvia, Sylvia, you didn't!"

"Deena, Deena, I did! What kind of mother would I be if I didn't try to take care of my children? Being a doctor isn't enough, not for a woman. It doesn't take the place of having a family."

"Excuse me, Sylvia, but Marilyn *has* family. Us. And her life is pretty goddamn full of Saul right now. Does he count? Even if you're right, I'd rather have half a life that's happy than a whole one that isn't."

"Are you referring to me, by any chance?"

Deena brought the soufflé to the table. "Of course not. I was referring to my own marriage." As soon as they had begun to eat, she continued. "However, in all honesty I must tell you: I can't understand why you stayed with him! I'm sorry! I'm not saying you were wrong; I'm just wondering. If I'd ever been in your situation, I wouldn't have been able to look at my husband, much less live with him, cook for him, joke with him, do his laundry for all those years, year after year!

"That's the worst of it for me, Sylvia. We're separated in the eyes of God, man, and the State of New York, and he's still here, in this house. He won't budge until his new apartment is finished. And, of course, it's taking forever. And while he's home he still expects his laundry to be done, his bed in the den to be made, his dinner to be on the table. It's horrible, Sylvia. We're separated; and my feeling is, let's be separate for God's sake. Let him move into a hotel! Why do *I* have to see him every day, make conversation, be polite?"

"What, you can't make a little conversation with the man you spent twenty-four years with . . . the man who gave you four children? You can't stand to be polite?"

Deena put her fork down; in any case, she had only been pushing the food around her plate. "You know what I mean. Come on, Sylvia, you must have gone through hell. The past couple of weeks have been so tough for me; I just don't know how you did it."

Sylvia managed a grim smile. "Number one, I didn't do his laundry . . . Earline did. Number two, I didn't have a choice. What was I going to do out in the street with three babies? And in those days, it wasn't so easy to be a divorcee; it was a *shanda*. Everyone considered you a hot ticket; no man would have any respect for you; and your women friends! Of course they dropped you because God knows you'd be after their husbands in a minute. And then—"

"And then?"

"I loved him of course."

"How could you—after what he did to you? That's what I can't understand!"

"Well, maybe I don't understand it, either. But I did love him, I love him now. I never stopped loving him. Have *you* stopped loving him? I mean your daddy. Since you found out?"

"Of course not; but that's so different!"

"My feeling is," Sylvia said, blotting her lips carefully with her napkin, "that love is love, know what I mean? Doesn't really make a difference if it's a mother loving a child or a woman loving a man or a friend loving a friend . . ." Deena, frowning, tried to interrupt; but she wouldn't allow it. "I admit, I was horribly hurt. I thought for a while that I would die." They were both silent for a moment and Deena reached over to give her mother an awkward pat on the arm. Sylvia gave her a wan smile and said, "I felt so betrayed! But don't worry, it was a long time ago. As you can see"—and she gave an amused shrug—"I lived. I had three good reasons for living." She ticked the names off on her fingers: "Elaine . . . Deena . . . Marilyn."

"All my life, I've heard about your three blessings and it's very sweet. But it's never sounded like enough to me. You were married to a wealthy man, Syl. You could've done anything—traveled, gone to college, anything. You could've made a life for yourself!"

Now Sylvia bridled. "What are you talking? I made a wonderful life for myself! My home, my children, later my grandchildren, my family, my friends . . . And don't belittle my Hadassah, my temple group, my volunteer work at Federation! Maybe I don't get paid . . . and maybe I didn't go to school and get a degree. But I learned plenty and I got plenty of *nachas* and I was there for all of you and that's what I thought my job was and in fact, Deena, if you want to know, I still think so and I don't have any regrets! None whatsoever!" She finished, sitting back in her chair, somewhat breathless, her cheeks pink with exertion and emotion.

Deena smiled at her mother and, getting up, came to her and gave her a tender kiss on the top of her head. *"A laban auf deine keppele,"* she intoned, smiling. "As Grandma Weinreb used to say. Long life to your head, Sylvia. I love you."

But if Deena thought that was the end of the discussion, she was very much mistaken. As Sylvia was getting ready to leave, shrugging into her mink, standing in the hallway, she gestured to the wall full of family photographs: the yearly formal family portraits, the more casual groups snapped at picnics or parties, and the posed smiling family faces taken at various anniversaries, weddings, bar mitzvahs, Sweet Sixteens, and graduations. Michael and Deena and their loved ones, with the children seeming to grow and change before your very eyes.

"Look at that," Sylvia said, her voice thick with nostalgia, "what a beautiful bride you were. Everyone said you made such a good-looking couple. I know, I know . . . But look how happy you were that day, how you're looking at each other with such love."

"Not with love. Michael had just said to me, 'Do you think you could manage to take something seriously for just one minute instead of always acting like a clown?' "

"Michael said that to you? At your wedding?"

"That's right, Sylvia. Michael said that to me. At our wed-

ding. I should have taken it for an omen." She laughed and added, "Don't look like that, Sylvia. They call it gallows humor. I'm not ecstatic about getting divorced. But, God, I feel as if a great weight has been lifted from me.

"Back then I was bewildered. If he loved me, how could he talk to me that way? That's not love eternal you see shining in my eyes, it's tears. But I was good. I resolved to try very hard to do better and to be more mature."

"Oh, but look here," Sylvia said, moving quickly on through the years. She pointed to a color picture of the Bermans with thirteen-year-old bar-mitzvah boy Nat as the centerpiece, everyone dressed up and looking proud—except maybe Saul, who was a babe in Deena's arms. "You look so happy. Don't tell me *that* was a bad time."

Deena put an arm around her mother's shoulder, hugging her briefly. "Sylvia, Sylvia, hope springs eternal. Yes, by the time the photographer took that picture, we were all in good spirits, but most of it was from relief. God, the previous six months were a nightmare. I know, I know . . . I never said a word, but now is truth time, I guess.

"Nat hated Hebrew school, he didn't want a bar mitzvah, he only wanted to be left alone. Well, as you can imagine, Michael wasn't about to go for *that*. Never will I forget it: we were all at the dinner table, and I was just cutting the lemon meringue pie. Nat said once again how much he loathed, hated, and despised his Hebrew teacher, his class, the school, the cantor, the rabbi and everything else about his bar mitzvah. 'I don't see why I have to do it if I don't want to,' he said to his father. 'After all, it's *my* bar mitzvah.' "

Deena laughed briefly. "Little did he know! Michael cleared his throat—I'll never forget it—and impaled poor Nat with his best pompous expression and said, 'You're quite wrong, young man. It's important that you have a bar mitzvah not for you but for the Jewish people.' And he went on from there, as only Michael can, about Nat's obligations as a Jew. And finally Nat said, 'If it's that hard to be Jewish, then I don't want to!' Well! Michael's face turned a color I cannot describe. He rose, he glared, he yelled, and he bore Nat off with him to the den.

"What was said in there that evening I don't know, but it

must have been very convincing. Because, there he is, the bar-mitzvah boy, proof that Michael could bully anybody into anything. But in the meantime . . . that was six months I'd rather forget. Nat decided it was all my fault. I didn't stick up for him, did I? He would hardly speak to me, and when he did, it was with a snarl."

"Why didn't you tell me?"

"We didn't tell anybody, remember? Women were supposed to make it all work. And if it didn't always work, you kept it to yourself, you never betrayed the privacy of your marriage, unquote."

"Well, it's a little late, but I'm sorry I never knew you were having problems, never realized how bad it was."

"Hey. Not to worry. But, Sylvia, now do you understand why my marriage is over."

"Oy, I don't like to hear it. I'm old-fashioned. To me, marriage is forever. I know that's naïve. So I'm naïve." She moved toward the front door and then hesitated and stopped next to a framed soft-focus picture of Zoe in cap and gown and heaved a sharp sigh. "Poor baby," she said. "To be so disappointed, so young. At her age, to have had—" She stopped, and gave Deena a pained look. "I almost wish you hadn't told me about it, about Zoe and that bum. Poor Zoe. I wish there was something I could do . . . I wish I didn't know."

"I know you do; but we've had quite *enough* secrets in this family."

"Well, it's still a secret from your daddy, and if I have my way, he'll never know. He couldn't take it."

"Look, Syl, Zoe is not ruined. She's hurt and she's sad, but at least she found out now. Marrying him! *That* would have been ruination!"

They were at the front door and Sylvia's head was bent as she pulled on her glacé leather gloves. When she lifted her head, she looked straight at Deena and said, without preamble, "Once I went to her. To Linda. By then I knew everything. I just had to talk to her. She had to be reasonable. How could she keep on seeing a married man with children. I figured we'd talk, I'd tell her I knew all about it, she'd be ashamed, and that would be the end of it. And Jack would never have to know a thing."

She put her hand on the doorknob. "But it didn't go the way I planned. The woman didn't know the *meaning* of the word shame. She looked me over, bold as brass. 'Well, I have a right to *my* happiness, too!' she says. Her happiness! *Her* happiness! With someone else's husband. And that's what I said to her!

"And she said, 'I spend more time with Jack in one day than you do in a week. I know him inside out, I know how he thinks, I know his little weaknesses—things you have no idea of! I know him better than you do! Better than you ever will!' That's what she said to me. The whore!"

"Oh, Sylvia, how awful for you!" Deena held out a hand, but it was ignored. "The miracle is you let her live." Might as well try for a lighter tone, she thought.

Bu Sylvia was having none of *that*, either. In the same monotone, she went on. "I left her apartment, I got onto the first bus that came along, and I sat there, looking out the window, seeing nothing. I couldn't believe another woman could be so heartless. I only wanted that one day she should suffer like I was suffering then."

"And she is," Deena offered.

Sylvia paid her no heed. "She adored him, without question. After all, he was her boss. To her he was all-powerful, all-knowing, like a god, almost. She didn't hear him snore all night; she didn't see him when he was moody; she didn't hear him bellow if God forbid we were out of seltzer; she didn't get up with babies at night and hear him *kvetching* that his sleep was disturbed. When he was with her, he was on good behavior, he was at his best. She was willing to do anything to keep him in her life, willing to cater to him, to crawl, to . . . well, you know now what she was willing to do. Anything!

"How could I compete with that? I was pregnant, clumsy, tired, worn out, taking care of two little girls also. *She* could be totally dedicated to him. *She* could always look beautiful, act patient, smile, and flirt, and tell him how wonderful he was. It wasn't fair! But there you are . . . I didn't see what else I could do except learn to live with it somehow. And wait for it to end."

"That doesn't sound like the woman who brought *me* up! It's not like you to sit passively and wait for something to happen. Why didn't you confront him? You could have made him choose between you; he would have chosen you, you must know that!"

Sylvia's head came up. She looked at Deena, her eyes filled with remembered sadness. "Easy for you to say, but I knew nothing. The truth of it is, Deena, from the day we met on the Staten Island ferry, never mind the story about the wind and my legs, it was me wanted him, not the other way around. He came calling on all three of us and I never waited to find out which of the sisters he was after. I went after him. I could never be sure he would've picked me if I hadn't thrown myself at him. So, when it came to a choice between me and that other woman, well . . ."

Deena regarded her mother. "It was the same for me. I didn't wait for Michael to call. I called him first! Oh, Sylvia, it was the shame of my life! I swore to myself that I'd never tell a living soul, never admit it! I, a girl considered beautiful, charming, and intelligent, had done the unthinkable thing. I had chased a boy! God, the humiliation! And, you know what? I've never gotten over it. I've never felt secure. Sylvia, it's so awful, living twenty-five years with a man, always at a disadvantage, always in the role of the wooer."

"Tell me about it," Sylvia said dryly. They smiled a little at each other.

CHAPTER FORTY-THREE

Tuesday, April 15, 1986

The silver stretch limo sped silently up the tight curves of the Taconic Parkway. It was almost alone on the road, going north, past thick groves of trees just showing the tender yellow-green of spring.

In the backseat, Elaine turned to her father. "Isn't this a great way to do business? Someone else does the driving, we get to work."

"Too bad someone else doesn't pay for it!" Jack grumbled. "Never mind. You know my feelings on the subject, Elaine. This isn't what I consider a legitimate business expense. This is luxury and in my humble opinion, you're going overboard."

"What a *kvetch*!" Elaine teased. She smiled at him. "The business can well afford it; and if we want to do projects upstate—and we *do*, Daddy, we *do*—then a limo isn't a luxury, it's a necessity."

"With a phone, yet! Ridiculous!"

"You call it ridiculous that I already spoke to Taylor at the bank? That Brenda was able to warn us that the contractor might be a little late? Come on!"

"I'm not sold on this project, Elaine. Condos all the way up in Columbia County?" He shook his head emphatically. "They'll never go for it, not the commuters. Nobody will commute two and a half hours . . . *each way*! No, no. You'll build, you'll invest a fortune, and nobody will buy. They'll stand empty, like a haunted house. And believe me, Elaine, it'll haunt you!" Now he gave a little bark of a laugh.

Elaine frowned, gazing at him. "What are you talking, two-hour commute? Oh! You mean to the *city*!"

"Of course the city. Where else do people work?"

"These days? All over the place, Daddy. Times have changed. Didn't you notice, on the way up? IBM . . . Holt Industries . . . Lion Press . . . Pepsico. They've all moved their offices into Westchester. Or even farther up, to Albany or Troy. Christ, Troy is the hottest spot in the state right now! Our buyers will be commuting to every place *but* New York!"

"That I find hard to believe, Elaine. You'll have to show me numbers."

Triumphantly, she pulled a thick sheaf of papers out of her briefcase. "Funny you should ask. I just happen to have right here, the demographics of the region . . ."

He waved her off. "Not now. I'll look at it later." And he turned his head to stare out of the window.

Elaine was immediately solicitous. "Are you feeling okay, Daddy? Do you want a drink of water?"

"What do I need a drink of water for? Because I don't feel like wading through a lot of stupid statistics? I have other things on my mind. There's nothing wrong with me! You're treating me like some kind of invalid! Well, I'm not dead yet!"

Elaine held her tongue. How was she supposed to answer that, she wondered. But she knew: she was supposed to tell him he was just as young and vigorous as ever. And then she was supposed to say that he was right and that they would do it his way. He didn't know how to work with a partner, that was bottom line. And working with a partner was something she'd had plenty of experience with. She promised herself for the tenth time today that she would be very very patient with him. No, he wasn't dead yet, who the hell said he was? But he wasn't getting any younger, either.

"Look at that!" Jack's voice was irritated. "They can't leave *anything* alone!"

"What?"

"Don't you remember this place? Mohansic Park. We always had the company picnic here. You remember coming up here, like a little princess, with your mother and your sisters? Remember the grove of trees and the stone fireplaces? Remember the way everyone made such a fuss over you and gave you little presents?"

"Of course I remember."

"Did you see the sign? FRANKLIN D. ROOSEVELT PARK. Who asked them to change the name? Franklin D. Roosevelt Park! Doesn't the man have enough things named after him? He was a wonderful president—I voted for him myself—but, enough already! What was wrong with Mohansic, anyway?"

He fussed on and on and Elaine simply turned off her ears and thought about what she'd say to Bruce Byland, the contractor. Obviously, Daddy was trying to pull his old trick of changing the subject whenever he didn't like the way the discussion was going. Well, okay, if he didn't want to talk about the condo project, she'd deal with Byland herself. She had a few other things she wanted to get to right now, anyway.

She waited a minute or two, and then said, "Oh, that reminds me, there's an idea I've been wanting to toss around with you."

"*Another* idea! Don't you ever run out? Never mind, never mind, that was a joke. Toss away!"

"Okay. I toss you these words: Garden Village Mall."

"There's no mall in Garden Village."

"Right, Daddy. There's no shopping mall in Garden Village. But there *should* be! We still own that big piece of land on the interchange. It's ideal." She grinned at him, waiting.

"We do housing, Elaine, not malls. A mall is a whole other thing. You need a major retailer to be the anchor, you have to have a commitment! It ain't easy, *bubeleh*."

She took in a deep breath, telling herself to stay cool, stay cool and don't let him get to you. Later, she'd gently tell him that it wasn't businesslike or seemly for him to call her *bubeleh* like that. He'd done it a couple of times in meetings and she'd let it go, thinking he needed time to learn to think of her

as a colleague. But now she was beginning to think it was a
ploy; it was just another way to keep her in her place.

"Did you hear me say easy, Daddy? Easy is boring. If
you're interested in dealing with facts . . ." She glared at him
until he gave her a little nod and then went on. "I've already
put out feelers and Caldor is definitely interested. So is Jane-
way, but I think I like Caldor better . . ."

"Elaine, you're moving too fast, you know that? You're a
baby in this business, you've been doing it only a couple of
months, and I'm telling you, you're taking on too much, too
fast."

"I don't think so. This one will work, I know it. Your
accountant already crunched the figures, I took a ride out there
and there's no good shopping nearby. And, Daddy, it was your
stroke of genius that put Garden Village out there in the first
place! You had the foresight and the *chutzpah* to build where
nobody thought anything would make it! Now, you can finish
the job, you can make it complete. God, it's a gold mine!"

"No." The tone was stubborn and final.

"No! No? I don't believe what I'm hearing? What: *no?*"

"It doesn't feel right to me. So . . . no. I say no, we don't
do it. No shopping malls, not for Strauss Construction. Period. *Fartig.* Finished."

Elaine sat back deliberately in her seat, pushing her spine
into the soft leather cushion, breathing heavily through her
nose, looking fixedly out the window at the passing rocks and
trees, trees and rocks. She was *not* going to lose her temper.
The business wasn't hers, not yet. He was still in charge . . . at
least on paper. But he wasn't acting like a man in charge,
complaining and *kvetching* and finding difficulties in every
single idea. Maybe he wasn't up to this kind of gamble anymore. Hell, you had to be a gambler and a risk taker to be in
this business. Once you started to shilly-shally, you were finished.

Yesterday he'd had a fit in the office. She'd come in to him
with a plan to buy a piece of waterfront he'd had his eye on
for three years. It was a lot of bucks—more than they could
handle on their own. She noodled around with it with the
accountant and when he suggested a subchapter S corporation,
she knew that was the answer. There was plenty of money

around looking for a good investment. Why not a hot real estate deal? Why not them?

She'd taken her plan into Daddy, all excited, because it was like giving him a gift. He'd been so keen on this property for so long, and now they could do it. She laid it out for him and stood back, waiting for the applause.

No applause. His response was, "I don't let strangers in as partners."

"Daddy! That's neanderthal! Everyone does it! It's legal! You siphon all your losses through it and when it starts to become profitable, you just change it to a regular corporation and—let Stanley explain it, he's the expert!"

"And all of a sudden you wake up one morning and the new corporation has taken over Strauss Construction!"

"Not while I'm around!"

"You come in here with your tricky ideas and expect me to go along just because it's the latest wrinkle! I've been very successful, doing things my way. I'm not going to change just because you heard about something that sounds like a sure thing." He waved an imperious hand at her, shaking his head. He didn't want to hear from her. "You've got a lot to learn, Elaine. What do you know about this business? No, for a while we'll do it my way and you'll see I'm right."

She stood there feeling like a small child, the rejected plan still in her hand. The fool! The idiotic, stubborn fool! Here she stood, offering him a chance to do something he badly wanted and all he could focus on was the threat to his control.

That was the first time she saw it clearly; and today she noticed it more and more. She turned from the window, her anger pushed out of the way, and stared at him. He was slumped a little, his eyes closed, and he looked tired, sagging. My God, she told herself, he's really gotten old all of a sudden. She backed away from the thought. Daddy, old? Impossible. He had always been so alive, so energetic, so dynamic and powerful. But it was true. He was getting old. He was getting tired. Soon he would be too old and too tired to fight her.

At that moment he opened his eyes and looked straight at her. "I've been thinking," he said. "That shopping mall idea, the one in Garden Village. I'm putting you in charge. You set it up and prove to me we can make a profit and we'll do it."

Too old and too tired to fight her? Or the same old Jack Strauss, flattering you as he used you for his own purposes? Oh, to hell with it! Did she care? She leaned over and gave her father a kiss on his cheek, smiling. Let him do his worst, or best. In the end, she'd be the winner.

CHAPTER FORTY-FOUR

Sunday, April 20, 1986

When Deena let herself into the entrance to the Café des Artistes, she had to smile. God, how many thousands of times had she come in this door, into this dim, plush, wonderful-smelling place, to sit with her family beneath the murals of lush nymphs and eat too much? It had always been one of Daddy's favorite neighborhood places and many was the Sunday the five of them had set out from the apartment, already discussing what they were going to order.

"I'm with Mr. Strauss," she told the host, and walked toward his regular table. It was going to be lovely, a nice Sunday morning tête-á-tête with Daddy. She hadn't been alone with him, really alone to talk, for years and years.

There he was, looking a bit thin, she thought, a bit drawn, but with that big broad welcoming smile, standing up, gesturing to her, calling her name. "Over here, Deena. Hello, darling, you look gorgeous."

And then she stopped in her tracks. Because, right beside him, sitting at the table, of all the goddamn people, Michael! If there was one person in the entire universe she did

437

not want to see, it was Michael Berman. Why had Daddy done this to her? It was rude and overbearing and underhanded and insensitive and presumptuous and invasive and demeaning and give her another three minutes and she'd come up with a few more!

Dammit, she thought, Jack Strauss's so-called brush with death hadn't modified him one little bit! He still considered himself head of the family, daddy to the world, sure he knew what was best for everyone and, barging ahead, making everything come out the way he thought was right!

What in hell did he think he was *doing*, bringing her face-to-face with Michael at this particular point in time? She and Michael had just signed the papers last week, after days of stalling on his part. And she'd had such a hard time getting him out of the house! She had called Sylvia every day, in her frustration, telling her every last little nuance, so Daddy *had* to know what was been going on. Maybe someday, she'd be able to sit at a restaurant table with Michael and deal with him: but not on Sunday the twentieth of April 1986. Not today. Not yet.

But there he sat, big as life, maybe bigger, looking a bit uneasy but relaxed. Shit! She turned her cheek, allowing Daddy a brief kiss, and then pulled away and sat herself down, across the table from Michael. She didn't really want to look at him, but her only other choice was to sit next to him, which she wanted even less.

"Well, isn't this nice!" Jack sat himself back down, beaming. "Here we are, together again. We're having Bloody Marys, Deena darling. The same for you?"

Through her clenched teeth, she gritted, "Yes," and sat very straight in her chair, hands folded tightly on the table in front of her. She refused to meet Michael's eyes and she decided she wasn't going to say a word, not one. What their game was, she didn't know. So let them tell her! As she took the first sip of her drink, her father cleared his throat and she thought, Here it comes. The pitch.

"Now, Deena, I know you're upset and I know you think you're sure of what you're doing. All I'm asking is that you listen with an open mind. No, don't get that stubborn look on your face, your welfare is uppermost in my heart. Relax. Come on, do it for Daddy. That's better."

Deena let her gaze rest on him, keeping all emotion off her face. As usual, he was sure he had her, but this time, she had him fooled. She'd let him talk, all right, it looked as if there was nothing she could do about that except walk out. But if he thought he was going to change her mind about the divorce, well he had another think coming. In any case, he'd better talk damn fast because she had a date with Luke at three o'clock and she intended to keep it.

"I've been talking to Michael, here, the last few weeks; and he's ready to go for marriage counseling. Now, that's a fair offer, isn't it? Don't you think you ought to hold off on finalizing this divorce until you've gone together to see if it can't be patched up? After close to twenty-five years, Michael thinks that's not too much to ask . . . and I agree."

It took all of Deena's willpower not to stand up and over-turn the table complete with its drinks and napery and flower arrangement and silverware, right onto Michael Berman's lap. He was a mule! Once he got hold of a notion, nothing short of an atomic blast could shake it free. No matter how many times she told him she no longer loved him, she no longer valued the marriage, she no longer believed there was enough left to make it worth saving: no matter *what* she said to him, he refused to believe that she would reject him, hell, that she *was* rejecting him. He was hopeless!

Why, just last week she'd had a major run-in with him. It was the Goldsmiths' Twenty-fifth, and they were throw-ing a big bash at the River Café. She and Michael had been invited, together of course, weeks before; and she wanted to go. So she called Sue Goldsmith and said, "Look, Sue, I'd love to be at your party, you know that, you and Mel are among our oldest friends. But Michael has moved out and it's all legal . . . well, nearly, the papers are in the mail. Would it bother you to have both of us appear? Because, if so, I'll stay away. I wouldn't want to do anything to spoil your party."

And Sue, bless her, said, "It would bother me if you didn't come."

So Deena went. She loved the River Café, loved the ambience, and they lucked out with a mild clear night so everyone was able to mill around, having their drinks on the deck. A lot of old friends were there, the wine flowed like wine, and the twinkling lights in the breathtaking Manhattan skyline across the river looked like tiny diamonds ... it was really lovely.

That is, it was really lovely until Michael appeared. She was talking with Rita and Allen Schwartz and up he came, put his arm around her, bent to give her a kiss and then, damn him, *stood* there, with his arm *still* around her. Just as if they were still together! It infuriated her. In all their years of marriage he'd never been so affectionate in public.

And it didn't stop with that. He interrupted the conversation over and over again, saying, "Doesn't she look wonderful? Isn't she beautiful?" And he went on running around, bringing her little tidbits from the buffet table, and he kept gazing adoringly into her eyes and, worst of all, he kept putting his hands all over her! She wished she had done the awful thing and come with Luke. She wished she could pick Michael up and throw him into the East River.

"Go away, Michael," she told him at one point, when she tried to escape and he just followed her, like a puppy dog. "*Gurnisch helfen*, Michael. Let me give you a translation. That means, it won't do you any good, Michael. Leave me alone!"

And his answer was to look soulfully into her eyes, and to say, "Deena, Deena, when I think that we'll never share *our* twenty-fifth ..." And his lousy eyes filled with lousy *tears*! She couldn't bear it.

She turned on her heel and marched away from him. He was impossible and she was going to have to leave. She'd find Sue and Mel and wish them a happy again, and apologize for having to go so early. And then, when she did, *Sue's* lousy eyes filled with lousy tears and Sue said, "Aw, Deena, when I saw the two of you everywhere together, and Michael so attentive, I thought maybe ..."

Deena did not say Fat chance! as she dearly wanted to. She just made an attempt at a smile and left.

And now, here he was again, looking lovingly and wist-
fully across the table at her and making her want to throw
up. "Am I going to be forced to run out of the Café des
Artistes like I had to run out of the River Café, in order to
escape you? Is there no safe restaurant for me in all of New
York City?"

Michael looked hurt and then irritated. Ah, that's more
like it! she thought. Get mad, please get mad! And then get
lost!

"This tough act you've been putting on lately doesn't suit
you, Deena."

"Guess again, Michael. It's no act."

Jack, in a shocked voice, said: "Deena! Such a tone! This
is not like you!"

"Would you both quit it? Who do you think you're talking
to?" She knew her voice was too loud and too shrill and she
didn't care. Because she had been behaving herself for forty-
three years and, goddammit, she was sick and tired of always
behaving herself so that some goddamn man would approve of
her!

"The two of you make me sick, sitting there so sure it's
your right to tell me who I am, how I feel, and what I should
do. I am a person, get it? A person!"

As she paused for breath, rather proud of herself, Michael
said, "You see, Jack. I told you. All she does lately is spout
this women's liberation bullshit."

Deena scrambled to her feet. She'd starve before she'd
stay here another minute. "Daddy, you should have asked
me before you arranged this surprise party. I'm leaving."

"Deena, Deena." Now Jack's voice was placating. "Sit
down, relax, I'm sure Michael's sorry for what he said. We
won't talk about it anymore. We'll eat and we'll enjoy."

"Sorry."

"Deena, I don't understand." Daddy shook his head sadly.
"I've never seen you act so aggressive, so hostile, so . . .
Michael had the right word, so tough. You've always been my
reasonable one, always so sweet, so flexible, so accommodat-
ing." He shook his head sadly and gazed at her sadly.

And now she was supposed to give a sigh and give up and

give in and give him a kiss and do as she was told. She knew the rules; she'd played the game often enough!

"In other words," she said tartly, "I've been a wimp all my life. Well, excuse me, but my wimp days are over." And damned if *her* lousy eyes didn't fill up with lousy tears as she made her escape.

CHAPTER FORTY-FIVE

Sunday, April 20, 1986

"Lawrence, Lawrence darling! Where *are* you? It's been two whole months, do you realize that? Two whole...oh, Lawrence, I'm so glad to hear your voice! I've been so worried!"

"Never mind that. And never mind where I am, either. I'm okay. But I'm broke."

"Lawrence! How could you be out of money? You left with—"

"Dammit, I know how goddamn much I left with! Get off my case, would you? I had some bad luck."

"Gambling. Again. Oh, Lawrence, I told you. I told you to go to Gamblers Anonymous before it got you into trouble."

"Would you shut up about it for a minute, for Christ's sake? I'm in a tight spot, why else do you think I'm calling you? I need some money and I need it fast."

"You don't sound like yourself, Lawrence. What have they done to you?"

"What *they*? It's what *you* did! Giving me a fucking fairy tale instead of a real father!"

"Lawrence, listen, stop being so angry and listen to your mother, just for a minute. Please. I don't blame you; I know it all came as a shock. I meant to tell you one day. I meant to prepare you, but then the years went by and I thought . . . I thought why tell you and hurt you like that? It was for your own good. Now isn't the time to be mad at me, darling, especially not long distance. We should stick together and we'll come out all right . . . What was that?"

"I didn't say anything. What you heard was a great big yawn. Are you going to wire me money or not?"

"I'll send you whatever you need, Lawrence. But first, listen. Things have happened since you left, things you don't know. For instance—are you there? Lawrence?"

"Yeah. I'm here.'

"For instance, I'm not working anymore. I've retired . . . you don't have to make rude noises, it's true, I retired. I'm old enough to retire; I'm sixty; I deserve it. And I didn't walk away empty-handed, either, you needn't think that. There's plenty for both of us, to get a fresh start."

"I don't want any fresh starts. I want two thousand dollars, American."

"Wait, Lawrence, just listen. I'm buying a condo in Tucson, two bedrooms—I picked it out, thinking of you—two baths, a pool and a sauna and a health club and a running track and four tennis courts—"

"I'm not interested."

"Lawrence! I specially picked Tucson because there's so much construction there these days! You can get a wonderful job there, better than what you had with . . . better than what you had."

"I don't want a wonderful job. I don't want Tucson. I don't want to live with you."

"I'm your mother! I love you!"

"Oh, yeah? You love me? Is that why you lied to me my whole life? Is that why you ruined my whole life? Is that why you robbed me of a father? Honest to God, every time I think about Sergeant McElroy, my 'father,' 'killed in action,' goddammit, every time I think about that whole fucking fairy tale, I want to puke!"

"Everything I did was for you, darling!"

"Oh, cut it out! While you were busy making up stories about Sergeant McElroy, my own real father was right there. Goddammit, you could've made him marry you! You say you love me? If you loved me, you would've given me the life I deserved as Jack Strauss's son. His *only* son."

"I tried, I really did, I really did, Lawrence. You don't know what it was like . . . She wanted to get rid of me, and I faced her down, plenty of times. And he promised me, he promised! It's not my fault—!"

"Agh! You make me sick. Don't you have something new to say?"

"Lawrence. Please."

"Do I get the money. Yes or no."

"You come home and you can have whatever you need; whatever I have."

"I told you! Where you are isn't home to me, not anymore."

"But I'm your mother!"

"I'm going to do my damnedest to forget that!"

"Lawrence! Oh, please! No wait, don't hang up. Listen. At least tell me where you are. You don't have to come home. But just tell me where you are."

"Don't make me laugh. I'm not telling you anything. I guess that means no bread, huh? Okay. So long."

"Lawrence, you can't, you *can't*! You're all I have left now!"

"Then I've got news for you, lady: you've got *nothin'*. Because I'm finished with you. *Finito*."

"Lawrence, don't, don't hang—oh, Jesus, Mary, and Joseph, he can't! He just can't. It wasn't my fault!"

CHAPTER FORTY-SIX

Wednesday, April 23, 1986

Earline came marching into the dining room from the kitchen, talking as she made the circuit of the big table. "Look here, you, Noel, I put out dishes specially for the nut shells. What are they doing in your grandmother's good Spode teacup? Pass these bowls around, would you, Saul? Don't think you're too grown-up to listen to me, even though you have a mustache now. And never mind laughing, Judy, I notice you still spill your wine all over the tablecloth, it's no different than when you were four, and here, I'm going to have to go mess around with Clorox Two after I thought we were all through with that in this family."

Deena laughed. "Oh, Earline, are we ever going to be able to live up to your standards? I doubt it."

And Jack added, "We're peasants, Earline, nothing better can be expected from us!"

Earline grunted and smiled, still circling the table, deftly brushing away offending crumbs, stacking dessert dishes, and checking the condition of their coffee cups. "Mr. Strauss," she said as she neared the head of the table, "you want some more coffee?"

"No more coffee for Mr. Strauss," said Sylvia firmly. "Now, Jack. You know what the doctor said."

"Well, he didn't say anything about macaroons! Earline, give me two or three of your wonderful macaroons."

Earline smiled with modest pride. "I suppose you'll want the Haggadahs off the table now. I heard you all singing that song, the one that's always at the end of the Seder. 'Dy-ay-noo.'"

"That's the one. All right, take the Haggadahs and the wineglasses, but leave the rest. We'll sit and schmooze for a while."

"I know, I remember. Passover is when you all are allowed to put your elbows on the table." This comment elicited squeals of delight from the younger members of the family.

"Allowed!" Noel protested. "Forget allowed, Earline . . . we're *supposed* to put our elbows on the table!"

"It's the eleventh commandment," Howard put in.

"Oh, no, Mr. Barranger! Not in *my* Bible!" And she chuckled at her own joke. The kids applauded loudly. Earline smiled and surveyed the dining room, nodding with approval. "Yessir, it surely is nice to have the whole family here, especially you, Nat. My, my, and soon you'll be a real doctor! Well, time for me to get to my work. But it surely is nice to see everyone here together." And as she exited, her arms loaded, Deena overheard her muttering, " 'Cept of course, Mr. Berman . . . pity, shame . . . never will understand . . ." and other editorial comments.

Like everyone else in the world, Deena thought, Earline didn't want the Berman marriage to have failed. She wanted all marriages to be happy and fruitful, like it said in her Bible. And to *last*. Most especially, to last. Well, Deena thought, so did she. This wasn't her most favorite experience. She had her bad moments. But neither was her pending divorce the Next Great Tragedy of the Twentieth Century.

God, how many of her *friends*, upon being told, had said, "Oh, how awful." Why? Why did they assume it was awful? Why not assume it was wonderful? Why not assume it was just okay? But no, from everyone the same look of consternation, the same pained tone, the same three words. Well, never mind. She had promised herself that this evening, for the duration, she was not going to think about Michael Berman, her marriage, Melanie Cohen, Esquire, her divorce, her disappointments, or, even, her . . . what was she to call Luke? Her lover? But she didn't think of him as her lover; it wasn't that much of a relationship, it wasn't that intense or emotional. It wasn't *romantic*. They made love and they talked about her work. They made love and they talked about *his* work. They made love and he tried to teach her what he knew, to somehow help her become the playwright she wanted to be and that he thought she could become.

And *clunk*! a weight landed on her arm and shoulder, a weight that felt very familiar to her. As it should. It was Saul, leaning on her. Saul had always been her cuddler. Long after the age when the others disdained running to Mommy's lap, Saul would come to her and snuggle right in. It was very sweet. And then when he got *really* too old to sit on her lap, too old and too big and too heavy, he began to lean on her. It was a "cool" way of showing his affection and she learned to treasure it—at least most of the time. Of course, during the past year, during his hostile-teenager phase, there had been no leaning. There had hardly been talking.

So it gave her a real lift now to feel his warmth and his weight once again pressing on her. That, at least, was familiar. She had been stunned at her first sight of him, when he and Marilyn walked in this afternoon. It had been only a couple of months, but he had stretched and grown, he had thinned down, his shoulders had broadened, and he had a mustache. A bright red mustache! "Saul!" she had said, and stopped. She couldn't speak further. And the change wasn't only in his physical appearance, either. He grinned at her—where was the sulky boy of yesteryear?—and gave her a rib-cracking hug.

When he let her go, she found herself looking *up* at him. She also found herself crying a little and saying, "No, no, I'm all right, I'm fine, I'm terrific. I just can't get over you. My baby!"

And instead of giving her one of those oh-please-would-you-mind looks she remembered so well, he laughed and said, "My Mommy!" echoing her tone.

However, he was now beginning to get heavy, and besides, he was on her right and leaning on her drinking arm so that she couldn't pick up her cup. She was longing for some coffee, but she couldn't, she just couldn't push him away or ask him to move, not yet. She slid a sideways glance at him, very aware, as she had been all through the Seder and all through the eleven-course banquet that followed, that he was twinkling with some kind of mischief or hidden secret. She wished she could ask him what it was; but there was something too grown-up about him. She had a fleeting pang of loss: where was her chubby baby, where was her toddler, where, even, was her sullen smoldering adolescent? And what, now, was left to her except the certainty of her own aging? Something very akin to panic began to clutch at her; and quickly, pushing it off, she called out, "I want to make a toast to Saul because if he hadn't beat the snow down from Vermont, we wouldn't have had him here to ask the Four Questions."

"And then Noel would have had to," said Zoe. "And he's probably forgotten how."

Noel punched her in the arm and then lifted his glass and said, "I'll drink to Saul saying the Four Questions. What would Passover be without it?"

And then, Judy: "Oh, God, do you remember when he was so little, he could only say 'Ma—' and we had to do the rest?" The kids all began to shriek with laughter, shouting out the rest of the Hebrew words.

"And remember the year he got so mad because he said he knew all of it and we wouldn't let him do it?"

"He was *cute*, then," Zoe said, rolling her eyes.

"Yep. And even cuter now," Saul answered her back, smoothing the ends of his mustache ostentatiously; at which Zoe did that disgusting thing Deena hated: finger to open mouth with sounds of gagging.

"That moth-eaten half-grown animal on your upper lip?" Zoe sneered. "You think that's adorable? It just makes your face look dirty. I wish you'd shave it off! I hate it!"

"I hate your whole face. Whyn't you shave that off?"

"Zoe! Saul!"

Jack was leaning back in his chair, grinning broadly. "More like it!" he boomed. "I was beginning to think this had become a family of *nebbishes*! Everybody being so polite to each other!"

Elaine gave him a measured glance. "Could this be the same Jack Strauss who raised me? Who used to say, 'No back talk!'?"

"No, it's the Jack Strauss who used to say, 'Stop picking on your sister *and* no back talk,' " Deena corrected her. She addressed the children: "You see that even-tempered genial person sitting up there in the place of honor, kids? Cheering you on in your worst misbehavior? Well, that's not how it was in the good old days."

Everyone laughed but Zoe. "I still hate mustaches," she muttered.

"So don't grow one!" Saul retorted, and at the same time Noel leaned over and murmured something to her, waggling his eyebrows and grinning in what Deena could describe only as a leer. She couldn't hear what he was saying, but for sure he was teasing her . . . just like when they were little kids and Zoe got into a snit about something. Noel could always make Zoe laugh, no matter how bad a mood she was in.

But not this time. This time she sat very still, not moving, and then suddenly pushed herself away from the table noisily, yelling, "Shut up, Noel, just shut up, okay?"

"I don't have to!"

"Then fuck off!"

"Zoe!!" The cry came from every pair of adult lips; but Zoe might have been on another planet for all the attention she paid. Her eyes, wide and glistening with tears, were fixed on her cousin. She and Noel stared at each other for a moment and then, with an incoherent cry, she ran from the room.

"Zoe!" Deena called. To no avail, of course. She hesitated. Frankly, she didn't mind that Zoe had left the room. She'd been sitting across the table from her this evening—which had given her the dubious pleasure of watching her younger daughter sulk for two and a half hours. She was tired of it, and bored, too. She knew what was bothering Zoe. Lawrence. But tough. Lots of people here tonight had problems and they were all behaving like human beings!

She didn't want to discuss Lawrence anymore with Zoe; she'd had enough of Lawrence to last her a lifetime. So he'd disappeared, so what? Who cared? Thank God he was gone out of their lives, that's what *she* thought. And after all these months, why the hell couldn't Zoe face up to it? He hadn't come after her, he hadn't so much as dropped her a postcard from wherever in hell he was. After all these months, why couldn't she accept it, and just forget him? Why in hell couldn't she be *grateful* that she had gotten out of it before she really got hurt?

If there was one thing in this world Deena did not want to do again, it was listen to Zoe wail about that bastard. But on the other hand, was she expected to act the Ever-Vigilant Mother and race after her suffering child? And on the third hand, did she care *what* the hell was expected of her?

So she stayed where she was. And almost immediately regretted it because her father turned to her, demanding to know, "*Nu*, what's with your daughter?"

"Would you believe me if I said I don't know?"

"Of course you know. It's your . . . um . . ."

Oh, Christ, she thought, the divorce. No, she should really think of it with a capital "D": the Divorce. Every time Sylvia or Daddy mentioned it, they put quotation marks around it, asterisked it, capitalized it, underlined it.

"No, it's not my Um, Daddy. My Um is not the cause of every single personal disaster in the world."

Deena felt eyes on her, a stare. She turned over and met a look from her son Nat of such condescending anger that she longed to reach over and poke him one. Ever since he got home, Nat had been lecturing her on the proper way to handle this thing, this Divorce. Come to think of it, Nat capitalized it, too. He'd had one course in adolescent development and he was ready to teach her exactly how to do it the *right* way. Just like someone else she used to live with. Maybe if Nat would jump up from the table and run out of the room, too! That would be nice. The look on his face—his whole attitude, in fact—made her blood run cold. Either it was carried in the genes or he had learned only too well from Michael how women were to be treated.

Oh, hell. He was just like his father, and always had been.

A bit stiff, a bit pompous, even as a very little boy, and so certain of the rightness of his thinking. She was glad he had made it into medical school; she hoped to God he would be a good doctor. But she was very afraid that medical training had only reinforced in Nat what had always been there: a feeling of moral superiority. He was her firstborn and she supposed she loved him. But like him? No, not really. She couldn't help it.

Jack was still insisting. "You have to admit Zoe isn't herself lately," he said. "And I can't think what else it could be."

Deena opened her mouth, ready to tell him what else it could be. But she never got a chance to say anything, as Sylvia quickly and smoothly said, "*Shah*, Jack, it's a personal thing with our Zoe, and Deena is not at liberty to share it with the entire family."

"I couldn't have said it better myself, Sylvia." Deena looked at her mother with awe and wonder.

"Ay-yuh!" Saul agreed, sounding so like a caricature of an old-time Vermonter that everyone howled.

"Oh, my God!" Marilyn cried. "I've created a monster!"

And one of the kids said in a stunned voice, "That was *funny*, Marilyn."

And she smiled modestly, saying, "I have one recessive comedy gene somewhere in my DNA."

Then Deena cracked, "It's SBD—the Strauss birth defect!" and they all screamed.

Earline poked her head in and yelled, "Say, don't you all want to go watch the TV and tell jokes in Mr. Strauss's den?" And the Seder was officially over.

As they got up from the table, stretching and patting full bellies and telling Sylvia again how good and beautiful it all had been, Nat said to his brother, "Don't forget what you promised."

Deena could see Saul stiffen. "I can call Dad without being reminded by you, thanks Nat."

"Not always."

"Oh, go take a—never mind. Which phone should I use?"

"Go into my room, *bubeleh*," Sylvia said. Deena smiled; Sylvia Strauss heard everything, always, no matter how involved she seemed in her own business. "There, you'll have privacy."

"You shouldn't let Mom know when you want to call Dad," Judy said loudly to Saul. "She might cut the telephone wires."

Deena closed her eyes, willing herself to stay calm, very calm. It was Passover, a family holiday. She was not going to respond in any way; she certainly was not going to let her children ruin this holiday. She knew the divorce was rough on them, but it was rough on her, too. And they were old enough to have some understanding. When she looked up again, her sister Elaine was giving her the high sign. "Deena and I will help Earline clear," Elaine announced, and Deena was amazed at how grateful and relieved she felt.

When they were both in the pantry, Elaine turned to her and without preamble said, "You poor thing! Have they *all* been taking shots at you like this, all the time? How long has this been going on?"

"How long has Michael been out of the house?"

"You must be Jewish, lady, answering a question with a question."

"It's a Jewish holiday. I'm allowed."

"Take a holiday from being amusing, would you? I'm *really* concerned, you know. It's hard enough without those rotten kids ganging up on you. Let me talk to them."

"Does 'kids' include Daddy?"

"If necessary," Elaine said.

"Okay, let me tell you why you shouldn't bother talking to my kids. First, I'm a lousy mother; I'm never home; and when I am home, I'm busy with my own interests. I spent too many years staying at home and then I spent too many years not being at home. And the crux of the matter is, if it weren't for me, there would still be a father in the house."

"Let me guess. *That* sounds like Judy."

"That's exactly who it is. Nat gives me lessons. And Zoe is drowning in her own sorrows, trying to pull me down with her. Saul hasn't been around, he hasn't had his chance yet." She sighed. "It's mostly Judy, blaming me. Well . . . I'm trying to be patient. She always *was* his favorite. In fact, Lainie, when we were getting ready to leave today, she suddenly marched into my room to announce that she, at least, was going to be with her father on Passover, even if nobody else in the family thought enough of his feelings et cetera et cetera et cetera."

"So how in the world did you get her to come?"

"I told her. He's the one who said they should spend Passover with their grandparents. He's not quite set up in his apartment yet, he says, and he doesn't feel ready to do a whole Seder. Hell, I know for a fact that he wanted to be with his friends from the committee and sing freedom songs all night."

"So?"

"What do you mean so? I just told you."

"I mean, so, what's doing with your Um?" They both laughed briefly.

"Oh, *that* old thing. It's certainly different. I mean, I went straight from my father's house to my husband's house. God, I was so young and so dumb about life. Who knew you should wait and discover yourself first?" She shrugged. "Almost before I knew it, I was surrounded by people, the vast majority of them in diapers. And now, suddenly, I'm alone. I mean alone alone. No other human being living in the house. It's weird, Lainie, it really is. I couldn't wait for Michael to get the hell out and now there are nights when I hear strange noises and I feel nervous and I wish . . . I wish I had a man in the house." She gave an embarrassed laugh.

"Do you think . . . excuse me, Deena . . . do you think you want him back?"

"Oh, no! God, no! Oh, I didn't mean . . . no, no. It's my period of adjustment, that's all. I wake up every couple of hours at night with that awful feeling that something is wrong; and then I remember. Michael's not in bed with me. And then I smile to myself and turn over and go back to sleep. Except, of course," she added, reaching out to take her sister's hand, "when I can't get back to sleep."

"What do you do?"

"Would you like to hear my list of the hundred worst movies ever produced in Hollywood?"

"Poor baby," Elaine commiserated. "It must be tough."

She paused. "Or am I being stupid? Are you seeing some-one?"

"No. Yes. Sort of." She wondered how much she could tell Elaine. And then decided: none of it, not yet. Elaine would never understand how she could be involved with such a young man. How she could get so much pleasure from sex with a man she didn't love. She would never understand Deena's wasting precious time with a relationship that had No Future. "He's a...colleague. Writer." She began to speak very rapidly. "He thinks I'm really talented and he's trying to talk me into applying to Sundance or some other writers' workshops."

"I ask about a man in your life and you tell me about your typewriter! Okay, okay, it's none of my business."

"Someday..." Deena said vaguely. "I'll tell you all about it. It keeps me off the street."

She picked up her pile of dishes and hipped open the swinging door into the kitchen. Elaine raised her eyebrows as if to say, Oh, really? but she said nothing, followed her sister, balancing her load precariously in two hands.

At the sink Earline turned and made a little face. "Be a *mensch*, Elaine, use a tray." Then she moved aside. "Never mind, never mind, just put 'em into the sink and I'll clean 'em off."

"I never could understand why, with a dishwasher to wash dishes for you, you wash them first, Earline."

" 'Cause that's the way your mama wants it." She smiled. "I must be getting old," she said, "because tonight I keep remembering when you were just little girls, this high, bring-ing me dishes, a cup at a time..."

"Yeah, Earline, how come we were only allowed to carry in cups?"

"When we let you carry in plates one year, you dropped two of them."

"Grandma Weinreb's good china?"

"Yep. Now, scat, that hasn't changed either since you were small, I always did have to chase you girls out of here so I could get my work done. Shoo!"

They walked back into the dining room. There was nothing else to carry. The blue linen tablecloth was covered with mat-

zoh crumbs, but Earline would take care of that; and the only
other items left were two wine decanters that hadn't been
moved back to the sideboard. They didn't have to say anything to each other. Without a word Deena went to the china
cabinet and took out two glasses, handing them to Elaine, who
poured. They raised their glasses and Elaine said, "Any regrets?"

"None."

"Well, then, let's drink to no regrets." They raised their
glasses and sipped.

Then Deena said, "Actually, it's terrific to be single again.
I can sing very loud and off key whenever I feel like it. And
don't tell Sylvia on me, but I never make my bed anymore."

Elaine lifted her glass again. "I'll drink to *that*," she said,
thinking, dammit, it *is* a family defect, this joking about every
goddamn thing. Whatever happens, no matter how painful,
it's immediately made into entertainment. And then she
thought, I guess we could have worse traits.

"So?" Deena demanded.

"What . . . so?"

"You think you're the only one gets to ask 'so'?" She gave
Elaine a light punch on the arm. "Know what I mean? So,
Lainie, how do you like being a real estate tycoon?"

Elaine made a little face. "I would love it, I *could* love
it . . . if only you-know-who would stop being a male chauvinist pig."

"You knew what he was like when you went into it."

"I didn't know what it was going to *be* like, though. Here I
am, doing what I always dreamed of: I'm a vice-president in
Strauss Construction. I'm bossing people around, I'm having
an idea a minute, and most of them are good ideas, everyone I
work with says I have the knack and I agree. And yet and
yet . . ." She stopped and gave a bitter little laugh. "If only
Daddy wouldn't fight me all the time. No matter what I come
up with, he automatically finds fault. If only he would let me
have real responsibility . . ."

Deena began to laugh. "I'm sorry, but do you know how
many times you just said 'if only'? God, remember the years
we spent, saying our if-onlys?"

"Do I!" Elaine smiled. "If only Peter Schulhof would ask

me out . . . if only I got the lead in the school play . . . if only I had purple eyes like Elizabeth Taylor . . . hell, if only I had *something* like Elizabeth Taylor!"

They clinked glasses and Elaine took a sip and wrinkled her nose. "Phooey, too sweet. Where is it written, I ask you, that on Passover we have to drink Manischewitz concord grape?"

"Where else? In the book of Sylvia. I told her you can get dry white wine from France that's kosher for Passover and she gave me such a look!" She raised an eyebrow and added: "I note that your disgust does not keep you from refilling your glass at regular intervals."

"Any port—or concord grape—in a storm." They both groaned and then grinned at each other. "Oh, hell. He's *not* going to give me real responsibility; I'm going to have to wrest it from him, I know that. Maybe that's what's depressing me. Deena, suddenly Daddy's gotten old, have you noticed? He's a little slower on the uptake, he repeats himself . . . not badly, not often, not too noticeably. But *I* notice. Pretty soon, everyone else will, too. And then it's going to be awful. If only he'd retire; but he'll never retire. Damm it." She sighed loudly. "In actual fact, I'm pretty much running things now. But he can't admit that to himself; he can't let go. So he plays little games—which I have to pretend to go along with. I'm telling you, it's exhausting!"

Deena made a face. After a few beats, she said gently, "Do you think maybe it's not such a wonderful idea for you to work with Daddy? Maybe it would be better to stick with Sweet Somethings?"

"Are you out of your mind? That place is a goddamn gold mine, Deena!" Then she realized her about-face and she laughed a little. "Oh, hell. Don't let me give you the wrong idea. I love it. I think I'm probably happy; it's just I'm so goddamn exhausted. Deena, listen—" She paused. Would her sister understand? "Work is my life, Deena. Oh, I love my husband and I love my son and all my family is important . . . but my work . . ." And then she had to stop because there was no way to explain it to someone who had never worked at something she passionately loved.

"What are you two *doing* in here all alone?" Sylvia suddenly appeared in the archway. "I've been all over looking for you. *You*, Deena."

"Why me? It's all right, you can talk in front of Elaine. She's my sister."

"Very comical. But not such a funny situation. Zoe . . . she's not in such good shape."

"You, too, Sylvia? Do I need somebody else to tell me what to do? Am I her mother, or what? I know what shape Zoe is in . . . don't I have eyes in my head? For God's sake, get off my case!"

Sylvia flushed and widened her eyes without an answer; and, to her amazement, Deena realized her mother was hurt. Hurt! Sylvia always gave as good as she got. Better! It was a bit of a shock to think she had wounded her feisty mother with her unthinking angry words. And anyway, Sylvia was only trying to help . . . doing a mother's job, actually.

Wasn't she a mother herself? Hadn't she been whining not five minutes ago about her children mistreating her? What was her problem? She looked at Sylvia's face, noting for the first time the lines of worry and fatigue grooved into the forehead, the slight downward curve of the mouth, the tiny puckering around the lips Deena remembered as being lush and full. Sylvia was getting old, she realized with shock. She's seventy. *Seventy!* One of these days she wouldn't have her mother anymore. The thought left her with a sudden hollow feeling, and tears sprang, unbidden, into her eyes.

Blinking rapidly to hold them back, she went to Sylvia and gave her a kiss on her soft cheek. "Sorry, Syl. I'm a grouch these days. Tell me about Zoe."

"I found her in your room, lying across your bed, just the way you used to do, crying her heart out. And when I asked her to tell me what's wrong, she said—let me bite my tongue, it shouldn't come true—she only wants to die."

"Oh, Sylvia, don't worry. She always overdramatizes. Believe me, I've been checking, and at school she's fine, she's doing nicely in class, she's been to parties. Really. It's wonderful she can talk to Granny; I'm really grateful you're here for her. And for me." And overcome with emotion, she gave her another kiss.

"Oh, no, here comes the mushy stuff!" Sylvia laughed.

"Remember? When you were little and your relatives grabbed you and kissed you, you and Elaine always said that?" So much for sentiment, Deena thought, so much for open displays of affection with your mother. But for the first time in her memory, it didn't hurt.

At that moment they all turned to the sound of a familiar bellow. "Where are my girls? I'm waiting and waiting!" All the way from the den! The man's voice was incredible. And his power was, too. The three of them turned as one and set off without pause to do the lord and master's bidding.

The den was loaded, as it always was at family dos, with plates and trays of "extra" food sitting around—in case anyone was assailed with a pang of hunger, heaven forfend. The kids still insisted upon lying on the floor, as they had when they were little When they were very little, they took very little room; but they had not the good grace to stay small. Now with the five of them stretched out in all directions, you had to pick your way through a thicket of legs.

And there, in the place of honor—of course—was the patriarch, leaning back in the brand-new burgundy leather Barcalounger, shoes off, talking and laughing and gesticulating. If you had never seen him before, Deena thought, you would never think that he had been sick a day in his life. She could see, because she was very aware of changes these days, that the grooves at the sides of his mouth were a bit deeper, the flesh under his jaw a bit softer, the eyes not quite so lively. But it was all very subtle, and in the meantime, he was totally in charge of the room and the people in it.

When he saw them, he shouted for silence. "They're here at last! Now, quiet everyone." And to the newcomers, he explained: "Marilyn has something to tell us, she says. Marilyn, *bubeleh*, the floor is yours."

"Well . . ." Marilyn began hesitantly. "The thing is—"

"Stand up!" Jack said. "And speak a little louder. My hearing's not so good these days."

"I don't have to stand up, Daddy."

"You don't have to anything. But I thought it would be nice if—"

Marilyn stood up. "Okay. Satisfied? Now, how do I begin . . . ? Last week . . ."

"Never mind last week! Get to the point!"

"Papa!" Saul hoisted himself up on an elbow and pulled on Jack's foot where it rested. "*Listen*, will you? Give Moo a chance!"

"Yes, Jack, let Marilyn speak," Sylvia said in a tone that brooked no argument.

"No, he's right. There's only one way to tell something and that's to say it right out. Okay, I'm telling you: I'm married!" She held up her left hand, and sure enough, there was a gold band on the ring finger. Now, how in the world did I miss that? Deena thought. And then she answered herself by wondering how in the world Sylvia had missed it. She ran to give her sister a hug and a kiss.

"How wonderful!" she said. She was too embarrassed to say, Who did you marry? but she couldn't be sure.

Apparently, it was not too embarrassing for the father of the bride, who said, "Mazel tov and, excuse me for saying so, but it's about time. Now would you like to tell us who's the new member of the Strauss family?"

Marilyn, pink with pleasure, said, "John. Of course."

"The fellow who was here Thanksgiving?"

"Well, yes. How many men do you think I live with at one time?"

That, Deena noticed, shut him up. So, even at this late date, and even when it concerned his one unmarried daughter, Jack Strauss did not want to believe that a woman got married in a nonvirginal state. Honestly!

"No wonder you kept your gloves on so long," Sylvia said, laughing as she hugged Marilyn. "You knew I'd notice!"

"Oh, really, Sylvia? Well, I had my gloves off for the entire Seder and I waved my hand around and I couldn't get *anyone* to notice . . ."

"Well, no wonder, it's not much of a ring . . ."

They all, in unison, yelled, "*Daddy*!" and he shrugged, grinning. Had he ever apologized, Deena thought, for anything, to anyone, ever? Surely he owed Marilyn a casual I'm sorry, even if it had been meant only as a joke. But she could not remember ever having heard those two words from his lips.

Having thrown her little bombshell, Marilyn was now talking a mile a minute. "I wanted it to be a surprise. I thought John would come with us for Passover, but you know Vermont, we had a major snowfall last week and they're going to try to keep the slopes in shape, trying to hold out for as long as possible . . ."

Sylvia was still holding Marilyn's hand tightly. "You couldn't invite at least your mother and father to your wedding?" she said, smiling to show there shouldn't be any hard feelings.

"Oh, Sylvia, I'm sorry. But he asked me twenty times and I just suddenly made up my mind and he said we'd better get the thing done before I lost my nerve."

There was laughter at this, but Sylvia persisted. "What kind of ceremony was it?"

"A judge we know—" Then Marilyn stopped and smiled at her mother. "Oh. I get it. No, he's not Jewish and no, we didn't have a church wedding, don't worry . . ."

"Who me, worry? Don't be ridiculous. It doesn't matter. I'm only happy you're finally married, thirty-five is long enough to wait and you could still have a couple of children . . ."

"Hey! Slow down!"

Unperturbed, Sylvia continued. "And don't look like that, Jack, if the mother's Jewish, the children are automatically Jewish."

Deena was laughing uncontrollably, as were her sisters. Even Marilyn. Her mother was a pisser, that's all there was to it.

Being with her parents, Marilyn thought, was very much like dealing with two freight trains, both on the express run. You kind of had to go along, or get flattened.

It surprised her, how mellow she was feeling. She looked at her parents today and she saw two elderly people, doing their best, meaning well, and stuck in a particular outlook from a particular generation. Finally, she had stopped expecting something they couldn't be and couldn't give. After all those years of coming home with expectations that were only fantasy, doomed to be disappointed over and over again, she was free. This wasn't home. Mt. Hebron was home. Home was where John was.

How had it happened? She didn't know, really, but had a sneaking suspicion that it had started with Saul. She had offered to take him, thinking the healthy environment would be good for him . . . thinking it would be good for him to get away from his uptight, demanding father. And from his overly emotional mother, too. She used to watch Deena with her children and think that her sister was too attached, too centered on them. Now she knew better. She had thought she was going to change Saul; it had never occurred to her, ignorant woman that she was, that Saul was going to change her.

She had to laugh at herself now. When he first came up with her, she had thought—and, to her shame, had *said*—that the best thing for a boy his age was a little benign neglect. Well. She soon found out that when you live with someone, there's no such thing. You become involved. Day by day she found herself more and more interested in what he was doing and then in what he was thinking and then in what he was feeling.

After that came the feeling of being connected. The first night he was out late and she kept waking up, listening for his footsteps, she couldn't believe it. She had never worried about any other person in this way. It was very uncomfortable. She didn't like it. But there it was. She had to deal with it. She thought about it a lot and she came to realize that the caring she did as a doctor—which she had thought was as deep as you could get—was like *nothing* compared to the heart-stopping fear that gripped her when the clock said two A.M. and it was snowing heavily and he wasn't back yet.

All of this was happening, not in a neat package, but a little bit at a time. What really really brought it home to her was that business at school last week. Saul had become very attached to his math teacher, and Marilyn was pleased. She felt he *needed* someone very different from his father to look up to, and Henry Falco seemed to fit the bill. Henry was an aging hippie with an aging hippie wife, six kids, seven dogs, and an easygoing attitude toward life. To Saul, he was a combination of John Lennon and Einstein.

Marilyn thought privately that he was idealizing the man but she didn't say anything. She didn't want to spoil it for Saul. And then, one evening, Saul came home from Math

Club, glum and silent instead of being full of stories. She asked him what happened and he only mumbled, "Nothin'." But she knew better.

So, after he refused a piece of apple pie, she picked herself up and went over to him, putting an arm around his shoulder. "Come on, Saul. Spit it out. Don't try to tell me it's nothing. I've never before known you to turn down dessert. Something's wrong."

He could hardly keep his voice steady as he told her. He'd finished that special project for Henry Falco and after he'd brought it to him, Henry had said, in front of the whole club, "What do you think of this, Saul?"

And Saul, unnerved by the unexpected question, said, "Well, I think it's pretty good."

And then Henry said, "Well, that makes *one* of us."

As he repeated the words, Saul's eyes filled. She didn't blame him. Hers did, too. What a lousy thing to say to the kid—and in front of everyone? It was so unfair! It was cruel, that's what it was. And she was mad as hell!

She couldn't concentrate on writing out her reports that evening. She was so bothered, so angry. And finally, she just picked up the phone and called Henry and gave him hell. She began being real careful and subtle but finally she couldn't hide the anger. "This kid trusted you, Henry. He trusted you and you repaid his trust by humiliating him." That's what she told him. And give the man credit, he apologized—first to her and the next day to Saul.

After she hung up, she found herself still feeling emotional. Why? She'd done this sort of thing, stood up to all kinds of people for all kinds of reasons plenty of times. She'd done it for herself, for her patients, for friends. But, dammit, she was *crying* this time. And a few minutes later she was in John's arms, holding on to him for dear life, tears streaming from her eyes, telling him she was definitely ready to marry him. If he still wanted her.

What had happened to her that night, that she suddenly was so open to her own feelings? She might never know and maybe it didn't matter. Now she knew she loved Saul, she loved John, she loved herself, she even loved her family— with no conditions attached. What she had always thought she wanted was an impossibility anyway. You couldn't change what was; you had to accept it. It was a good feeling, a *fine* feeling, at last to be with her family and feel a part of them.

That's why today she could laugh when Sylvia talked about her future children, to worry about them. She wiped tears of laughter from her eyes and said, "Hey, Syl, give me a break! I've only been married a week!"

"And I was the maid of honor," Saul said proudly, making them all laugh again.

"Not quite your usual Strauss wedding production," Marilyn went on. "I've never forgotten Elaine's: the candles, the banks of roses, the spiral staircase they wheeled in for the occasion . . . and *Elaine*. Oh, Elaine, I remember you most of all, in your long white lace dress. But you could have worn anything and you would have been beautiful. You looked like a movie star to me! I always wished I could look like you—"

"Me!" Elaine laughed. "The fat sister?"

Sylvia protested. "Elaine, you dieted down for your wedding!"

"That didn't count. That was pretend."

Deena looked flabbergasted. "Lainie, I don't believe it! You still think of yourself as *fat*?"

"And ugly."

Now everybody yelled at her and Elaine held up a hand.

"You asked? You want to know? I'm telling you."

"But you've always been so self-confident!" Deena said.

"Listen and learn: a fat girl in this culture can *never* really be self-confident. Everything around her tells her she's not acceptable: books, magazines, advertising, television, the movies. What part does the fat girl get, even a beautiful fat girl? The clown, that's who, the butt of all the jokes. And for sure, she's the one who never gets the man.

"It's a good thing I know my husband likes the way I look, because nowadays I'm rarely at Sweet Somethings and there he is, alone with all those beautiful women running around in their underwear."

She laughed, and Howard quickly said, "None so beautiful as you, my darling."

"He's right!" Sylvia said. "You were a beautiful baby and a beautiful girl and you're a beautiful woman!"

Elaine just kept right on. "It's okay, I've been a big girl for a very long time, I'm used to it. All of us overweight women are made to feel different, inferior, and unacceptable. That's why I got such a kick out of Sweet Somethings . . . it was my opportunity to give big women everywhere the chance to be sexy and gorgeous, too."

She sat back, breathless. Into this silence, Noel exclaimed, "Give it to 'em, Ma! Yesterday, brassieres; today, shopping malls; tomorrow, the world!" And every one applauded. And then the phone rang and Jack reached over to get it, telling everyone to please shut up.

Deena noticed almost at once that her father's voice had taken on a false hearty tone and she wondered. She made a bet with herself: she knew who it was. And of course she was right because, in a few minutes, Daddy said, "Sure, Michael, she's right here," while she wildly shook her head no.

He looked right at her, her darling stubborn Daddy, and said, "She's going into the other room right this minute, Michael, to pick up where you can talk in private."

Carefully avoiding looking at any of her children, Deena picked herself up. She did, however, manage to give Jack a hard look before she exited. He just stared her down. Men! Oh, what the hell. It would be easier to give Michael the heave-ho if she didn't have an audience.

In the pantry she picked up the extension. His constant calls were becoming a pain in the arse. Didn't he understand the whole point of separation and divorce? Stifling a sigh of exasperation, she managed a fairly pleasant and neutral "Yes?"

"Goddammit, Deena, the least you could do is tell him what he ought to do . . . if he's too self-centered to know it himself."

Oh, swell. A lecture and she didn't even know what the hell about. "Michael! Would you like to start at the beginning? Who is 'he'? What are you carrying on about *this* time?"

"Your attitude is not a help in this situation, Deena. You know what it's about. Saul was to have called me when he got in. And he hasn't. You could have reminded him."

Sweetly, she said, "I didn't have to remind him, Michael. He's tried to get you. Several times."

"Oh. Well . . . that's different, then."

"Excuse me, Michael, but why didn't you call *him*? He was right next to me in the den; why didn't you ask for him, for God's sake?"

Stiffly, Michael said, "I'm the father and he's the son and he should be calling me. I deserve at least that much respect."

Why was it, lately, that talking with him always made her need more oxygen? Elaine appeared at the doorway just then, and Deena eagerly motioned for her to come in, grinning. "Michael, here's my advice," she continued. "You want to talk to Saul? Call him!" She banged the receiver down and said, "Goddammit, that felt good! I ought to do that more often. In fact, I'm *gonna* do it more often."

"Way to go!" said Elaine.

"Maybe if I'd told him what I was really thinking, a long time ago . . . oh, shit. You can't go home again: didn't somebody say that once?" She was half-laughing. "Tell me, why does life get so dopey sometimes?"

"Because," Elaine said, "Mother Nature wants to keep us on our toes. But, speaking of husbands and problems . . ."

"Oh, God, no! Not you and Howard, too!"

"Deena! No, no, Howard and I are not in trouble. I am. Singular."

"What's the matter?"

"I'm jealous. Remember my saying he's alone all day with beautiful slender women ha-ha? Well, all of it's true except the ha-ha part. It's not funny. I'm worried."

"Elaine, your husband is crazy about you."

"I know, I know. But . . . well, you don't know what it's been like these past couple of months. Daddy. I'm worn out. And I have very little to give him."

"He understands all that. Of course he does. And you're not going to feel this way forever. Come on, Lainie, you spent all those years working side by side with him; and suddenly, it's all changed. You don't really think he's fooling around, do you?"

"No, of course not. Not yet. But the fact remains: he's up there with all those sweet young things—all of whom, by the way, think he's the best thing since white sneakers—and in the meantime, I'm running all over the place like a lunatic in high heels! And by the end of the day, I'm too damn tired for sex. And do you think he's going to put up with this forever, before he's tempted?"

"In a word: yes."

They were both laughing when Marilyn poked her head around the pantry door. "Private party?"

"Yeah, for sisters only. You a sister to anyone here?"

"To every last one."

Deena widened her eyes dramatically. "Hey, Moo, that was almost funny!"

"Wadda ya mean, almost?"

And they were all laughing when they heard voices, low but urgent, from the kitchen. Jack and Sylvia. As one, they all stifled their giggles and crowded up to the door, squeezing together to peek through the small window.

"Why are you following me, Jack? You wanted to say good-bye to Earline, fine. You said good-bye to Earline. All I'm doing is seeing if the dishwasher got turned on. Go sit and enjoy."

"Sylvia I have to talk to you—"

"I know what you're saying and I already told you, I'm not interested."

"That was months ago, when I first got home from the hospital. I figured you were sparing me. But now it's time already."

"No. Absolutely not."

"It's been unsaid too long. Let me get it off my chest."

"Oh, sure. Off *your* chest and onto mine. No thanks."

"How can you talk to me like that after all these years? I don't want to hurt you, I've never wanted to hurt you, sweetheart. Come on, let's have a little talk. I feel like such a hypocrite with the girls all here and the children . . ."

"You feel like a hypocrite? That's your problem. Maybe that's God's way of shaping you up, I don't know. All I know is I don't want to hear about it, not one word, not even half a word!"

She had been fussing a little, putting away salt shakers and straightening already-soldier-straight canisters. Now she stopped and faced him, looking straight at him, chin held high. "No, Jack. Don't even begin. I forbid it."

"Sylvia, you've been such an angel." He spread his arms wide in a gesture familiar to both Deena and Elaine, who quickly exchanged knowing glances. "You deserve—"

"Genug! You hear me? Enough!" Color flooded Sylvia's cheeks and she dragged in a deep breath. When he reached out to her, putting a hand on her shoulder, she wrenched away from him and moved to the other side of the table, glaring at him. As she became pinker, he became paler.

"Okay, you want to talk? We'll talk. Here's what I have to say. I lived with it all those years and I never said a word. When you began to come home every night, I thought I was finally free of her. I thought that part of it was over between you.

"And then you had to lie to me again—at your age—telling me you were going to the club every Saturday. And all the time you were with her—again, with her! All of our friends want to know how come Jack had a stroke, he's so healthy, he's so strong, how come he had a stroke out of nowhere like that?

"Should I tell them, how should I know, he was with another woman, his girlfriend, his whore. Is that what I should say?"

Jack made a strangled sound in his throat and then said, "That's not how it was—if you'd just listen for one minute!"

"You want to talk? Go to Nate Levinson . . . go to the rabbi . . . go to a shrink! But not me. I don't care how it *was*. All I know is how it's going to *be*. If you want to stay married to me, then you'll never mention her—or him, either! Never again, not ever! And if you do, I'm telling you now, I won't stop to explain, I'll leave. And not just to a movie, either!"

Jack Strauss's face was a picture of bewilderment. "Sylvia darling. I don't understand. What's happening? None of my girls are the same anymore! *You* talk to me like I'm some kind of a criminal! Elaine's taking over—*my* company—acting like she owns the place! Deena's dumping her perfectly good husband of, what? Twenty-five years! And Marilyn marries a *shaygitz* with a ponytail who skis for a living! Skis for a living! What's *happening* to all of you?"

Sylvia put her hands on her hips and regarded him for a moment, shaking her head. "What's happening? We're all getting another chance at life, Jack, and we're grabbing it! And that includes you, too, my darling! Now you can retire and we can do all that traveling you always talked about but were too busy to do! Why are you fussing about your girls? They're wonderful! Marilyn is finally married, and who knows, she may yet give you more grandchildren and I've never seen her look so happy, not in her whole life! Deena has done a very brave thing; she wants to be her own person and I think she'll do it! And Elaine is finally getting what she always wanted: your approval and respect! Stop trying to hang on to everything the way it was! The way it was wasn't good enough!"

In their secret hiding place the three sisters hugged each other, giggling. What a woman, Deena thought. What a woman! Sylvia, in the kitchen, laughed and said, "Don't feel bad, Jack. Your girls have grown up, that's all. Daddy's girls have grown up. *All* of us."

About the Author

Marcia Rose is not a real person. She is *two* real persons—two women who met as young mothers and began to write books together (much to their surprise) eleven years ago.

Marcia of *Marcia Rose*, a divorcée, has two daughters, and lives in a co-op apartment in Brooklyn Heights, NY. She enjoys good music, theater, and the company of people with the initials HC.

Rose of *Marcia Rose* is married, has two daughters, and lives in a hundred-year-old house in Brooklyn Heights. She enjoys travel, skiing, and theater.

They both love a good laugh, a good cry, and a good book.

Marcia and Rose have written every word of their novels together. After so many years as a team, it no longer comes as a surprise when they think of the same thing at the same time, in the same words. What *is* a surprise is that something that is so much fun has turned out to be a full-time career.

MARCIA ROSE